Pocahontas sat do [...]
fought a losing batt [...]
falling, the growing [...]
atmosphere, and he [...]
her beauty. No man could resist such an opportunity,
regardless of the problems that might result, and he
shifted his position slightly so that they now sat side by
side.

Pocahontas, aware of his nearness, hid her elation.
She smiled and held out her right hand. "Smith has
given me so much that I must give him something in
return," she said softly.

He nodded and moistened his lips, which were suddenly dry. Then he realized that she was holding an
object in her hand, and he took it from her. It was a
hollow reed, four inches long and roughly the thickness
of his little finger. One end had been carved into the
shape of a mouthpiece, and in the center had been
burned the symbol of the sun god.

He stared at it blankly, and Pocahontas reached out,
caught hold of his wrist, and shook the reed gently. The
tip of a tiny arrow appeared at the open end, and she
pointed at it with a slender forefinger. "Women," she
said, "are not permitted to use the weapons of mighty
warriors. So I must protect myself with this blow arrow,
which has been dipped in the poison of the snake-that-
rattles. I give it to Smith, so he will remember Pocahontas." Seeing him hesitate, she added more firmly, "Take
it. I have others."

They looked at each other intently.

Smith, who had been about to slide his free arm
around her waist, let his hand fall limply to his side.
Some of the girls due to arrive soon from England might
interest him, he thought; if not, he had seen a few
Indian women on the seacoast who were mildly attractive. "I will remember Pocahontas," he said, and told
himself he was guilty of understatement.

Other titles in the Hall of Fame series:

THE HIGHWAYMAN
THE SCIMITAR

A HALL OF FAME *Historical Novel*™

Daughter of Eve

NOEL B. GERSON

ace books
A Division of Charter Communications Inc.
A GROSSET & DUNLAP COMPANY
360 Park Avenue South
New York, New York 10010

DAUGHTER OF EVE

Copyright © 1958 by Noel B. Gerson

Virtually all of the characters in this book really existed in the early seventeenth century. As Captain John Smith took numerous liberties in telling their stories, the author has assumed the same right, and to that extent the people who appear in these pages are creatures of fiction and the product of his own imagination.

An ACE Book

Published by arrangement with
Hall of Fame Romantic-Historical Novels Inc.,
produced by Lyle Engel

First Ace printing: March 1979

Printed in U.S.A.

To TIMOTHY SELDES

O brave new world,
That has such people in't!

> *The Tempest,* WILLIAM SHAKESPEARE

Who ever loved that loved not at first sight?

> *Hero and Leander,* CHRISTOPHER MARLOWE

She is a woman, therefore may be woo'd;
She is a woman, therefore may be won.

> *Titus Andronicus,* WILLIAM SHAKESPEARE

Familiarity breeds contempt.
> *Maxims,* PUBLILIUS SYRUS

June, 1606

In the opinion of the late Queen Elizabeth, Captain John Smith was the most accomplished and versatile liar in England. Nostalgic partisans of the old regime had created the myth that her judgments of men had been infallible, and her appraisal of Smith was still widely accepted three years after her death in 1603. Sir Walter Raleigh, the most distinguished prisoner currently being held in the Tower of London, had more time and better reason than most to recall the reign of Gloriana, and he certainly remembered her estimate of the young man.

Looking at the self-confident visitor who approached him with a jaunty step across the great hall of the Tower suite, Sir Walter reflected that Smith's career would have prospered had the Queen lived a little longer, for he was precisely the type she had always favored. Not yet thirty years old, he was tall, he made a virtue of quick-witted audacity, and his masculine strength, although obvious, was unobtrusive and

1

inoffensive. Essex had been that sort of man, as had Drake and Lord Robert Dudley. Stirring in his chair, Sir Walter thought regretfully that Smith was actually a heartier version of what he himself had once been.

It was comforting to realize, however, that neither Smith nor any other member of the younger generation could possibly possess his own dazzling array of talents. Like himself, Smith might be a soldier, a sailor, and an explorer, but there the similarity ended. It was true that there had been a mild stir in literary circles when Smith had published an account of his adventures in Africa, but his wild tales were at least in part responsible for his dubious reputation. And his prose, when judged by the standards of a critic of taste who was himself an author, was ordinary.

But there was no lack of polish in the captain's dress, Sir Walter was pleased to see. In fact, Smith was attired in a way that made him appear dashing, even though he could not afford expensive clothes, and Sir Walter, who had faced an identical problem a quarter of a century previously, had to admire his visitor's ingenuity. Only the experienced would know that Smith's steel military corselet, which he could wear daily and which would never wear out, had cost far less than a doublet made by a moderately exorbitant tailor. His dark green woolen breeches gave the illusion that they were costly, because they were close-fitting and Smith's limbs were long and firm. Current fashions favored full breeches, but a man whose appearance was soldierly could pretend to ignore the latest modes.

His black calf-high boots were shined and in good repair and spared him any need for the long silk stockings imported from France at prices that drained the purses of all but the wealthiest nobles. Imagination rather than money was what gave a man an air, and in the little touches Smith's taste was superb. The thick, starched ruff above the steel gorget or collar of his corselet was nine inches deep and was bright yellow, a color Sir Walter had always favored, too, because conservative, timid people had shunned it since a notorious murderess had gone to the gallows in yellow. The long feather in the captain's steel helmet or burgonet was sprightly, the scarlet gauntlets on his otherwise plain gloves were eye-catching, and the bright, multicolored silk scarf tied to the hilt of his rapier was a brilliant stroke. Only a man who had resorted to the same subterfuge could possibly know that the silk oblong, which hinted at a lady's favor, was being used to conceal the absence of jewels on the hilt.

"Your servant, Sir Walter." Smith's voice was resonant and clear, and even if he came from a family of mere merchants, as was generally believed, he had completely mastered the clipped drawl of the aristocracy.

"Welcome to my castle." Sir Walter had formed the habit of greeting everyone with the same wry words and took a guest's answering smile for granted. "You had the usual difficulties in arranging an interview with me, I presume?"

"I had no trouble at all," Smith replied honestly, accepting the armchair of heavy carved oak that was offered to him.

"Really?" Sir Walter stared up at the high narrow window through which he could see only the sky. It was possible that Smith was an agent sent by the King in the hope of trapping him into admitting the absurd charge that he had secretly conspired with the Spanish ambassador against England. Occasionally James, who lacked the intelligence to alter his tactics, sent such spies to him, and Sir Walter was instantly on his guard.

Smith, sensitive to the older man's mood, was quick to offer an explanation. "This is my first visit to the Tower, so I have no idea how much trouble it takes when someone wants to see a prisoner here." He flushed slightly, obviously annoyed with himself for his crude reference to his host's condition.

Sir Walter laughed without bitterness. "We're usually called guests of the Crown. Like the animals James keeps in his menagerie downstairs in the west wing. You must see his collection before you leave. It's highly educational. And if you'd care to slip your blade into the lion that keeps me awake every night of the week, I'd be much obliged to you."

Captain Smith grinned broadly. "I'm not sure His Majesty would appreciate the gesture."

"No more than he prizes visits to me, I can assure you," Sir Walter said bluntly. "If you don't already know it, a full list of my callers is sent to him each month."

"It so happens I didn't know it, but that wouldn't have deterred me." Smith shrugged and slid his helmet back on his forehead.

"Very interesting." Raleigh couldn't decide whether the young man was being clever, whether he was a fool, or whether he was actually as brave as he sounded.

"The King has no cause to doubt my loyalty," Smith said, his deep blue eyes growing dark.

"He has no valid reason to doubt mine, either, yet here I am. And you can take my word that it's far easier to get into the Tower than it is to walk out again."

The captain seemed puzzled by Raleigh's open antagonism; he had been banking on the hope that a man who entertained few visitors would welcome him. There was only one way to handle the problem. "Does my presence here offend you, Sir Walter?"

"Possibly." Only a seasoned courtier could answer a direct challenge so blandly, preparing the ground so he could either terminate the conversation or retreat gracefully, depending on what he learned. "You haven't yet satisfied my curiosity. Who granted you permission to see me?"

Smith took a square of parchment from his belt and handed it to his host.

Sir Walter recognized the seal and signature of the Earl of Suffolk at once. Suffolk, the Lord Chamberlain, was one of the most powerful men in the kingdom and was one of the few supporters of James I whose personal integrity was, in Raleigh's opinion, indisputable. No matter what the provocation, Suffolk would never demean himself by sending a royal agent to the Tower in disguise. "Well. Why didn't you tell me this in the first place?" Sir Walter clapped his hands together twice, and a uniformed guard appeared at the far end of the hall. "Bring us two cups of sack. Or would you prefer ale, Captain?"

"I'd enjoy a drop of sack very much." Smith made no effort to conceal his admiration for a man who treated his jailers as though they were his servants. The tales he had heard of Raleigh's magnificent insolence were obviously true, and in spite of the difference in their ages Smith knew they were kindred spirits. He watched the soldier bow low before hurrying off, and he laughed. "I envy your ability to command such prompt obedience."

"Either my guards do as I tell them or I have them replaced," Sir Walter said carelessly, surprised that the visitor should find anything strange in his attitude toward his inferiors. But the subject bored him, so he dropped it. "Is Suffolk your patron?" He examined the younger man's clothes again, and for a moment he wondered if they were more expensive than he had at first thought.

The captain instantly understood the meaning of his host's searching glance. "If I were fortunate enough to be a protégé of the Lord Chamberlain," he said with disarming honesty, "I'd be wearing a doublet as rich as yours."

"You're certainly frank."

"Why not? I see nothing to gain by dissembling. Milord Earl has invested heavily in the London Company, which employs me. There's the beginning—and unfortunately the end—of his interest in me."

"The London Company." Sir Walter frowned and looked out at the sky again. "I try to keep up with the affairs of the world, but there are times when I lose touch. I'm afraid I've never heard of the London Company."

"Very few people know of us yet. We hope to change all that in the next few years."

The guard re-entered, carrying a silver tray, and Smith fell silent. The soldier placed the tray on a table, handed each man a silver cup bearing the Raleigh crest, and then turned back to the tray, where he carefully stuffed a pipe with tobacco. His familiarity with the unusual objects he was handling indicated that he had performed the function many times, and he lighted a straw deftly with a tinderbox and flint after giving the pipe to the prisoner.

"I hear regularly from Suffolk myself," Sir Walter said, making conversation. "He's one of my clients."

Smith was unable to hide his astonishment.

"He sends his secretary to me on the first day of each month for a jar of my Elixir of Life." Raleigh paused to light his pipe and then dismissed the guard with a nod. "I think," he added in a confidential tone, "that he finds the senna in the mixture helpful."

"Senna?"

"A mild cathartic. And that reminds me: I've got to concoct a new batch of Elixir by tomorrow. The French ambassador will be here promptly at noon for Her Majesty's regular supply." He smiled when he saw his guest looking at him in some bewilderment. "The Queen of France is a devoted client. The ambassador tells me she takes a little Elixir in her wine morning and night. Like all the French, she's very greedy, and if I didn't limit her, she'd buy my entire supply."

"Forgive my ignorance, Sir Walter, but I didn't know you had developed the selling of this Elixir into a profitable business enterprise."

For the first time an expression of frustration crossed Sir Walter's handsome face. "I have no choice. James, in his infinite wisdom, confiscated all of my estates, and I must either support my family or depend on the charity of old friends, which would be intolerable." Reminding himself sternly that he was a philosopher who had learned to live with that which could not be changed, he softened. "It works out rather well, you know. There hasn't yet been a Thursday when I've been unable to hand my wife a fat purse. She and the children are living comfortably, thanks to my Elixir. Would you care to try some of it?"

"No, thanks," the captain said hastily, and thought he should atone for his lack of manners. "Lady Raleigh is allowed to visit you regularly, then?"

"She arrives in time for supper every Thursday and she leaves by sundown the following day." Sir Walter lifted his sack to his lips and then set the cup on the table with a crash. "James, damn him, knows my weakness and has robbed me of my strength."

Smith deemed it wiser not to comment.

Sir Walter stood and, seeming to forget his visitor, he started to pace up and down the hall, occasionally kicking at the rushes that covered the stone floor. "If you live until you're fifty-four, Smith, you'll find that your energies are depleted too."

"The whole country believes in your innocence, Sir Walter."

"Of course it does! Why else do you suppose little James suspended the sentence of death his court conveniently imposed on me? Come with me and I'll show you something."

Smith placed his cup on the table and followed his host into an adjoining chamber, a small room dominated by a desk littered with thick piles of papers. The walls were covered with embroidered plaques, the seals of the great offices Raleigh had held when he had been Elizabeth's favorite. Of even greater interest to Smith were a number of framed, yellowing documents which had been placed directly opposite the desk, so Sir Walter could see them whenever he sat in the room. It would be best, Smith thought, not to study them too closely, for he had not yet explained the purpose of his visit to the Tower. But he could not resist glancing at them with pretended politeness, his face wooden.

The first in the orderly row was the patent which Raleigh had inherited from his half brother, Sir Humphrey Gilbert, under whom he had once served, granting him the right to claim for England "any remote barbarous and heathen lands not possessed by any Christian prince or people." Next to it were three other orders authorizing him to conduct explorations on behalf of the Crown. And, separate from the rest, was a patent that caused Smith's blood to pound in his temples. Bearing the signature "Elizabeth Regina" and dated March 11, 1584, it was an irrevocable grant to Raleigh, and after him his heirs, giving him full ownership of a vast, hazily defined portion of the New World which he had named Virginia in the Queen's honor. In return for this extraordinary gift, Elizabeth had stipulated that Sir Walter was to pay to the Crown one fifth of all precious stones and minerals found in his domain.

Affixed to the document was another paper at which Smith scarcely bothered to glance; he knew every word of it by heart, and his whole future depended on it. Rarely had a binding contract been less complicated: in it Sir Walter had assigned his rights in Virginia to a company of merchants, in return for a stipulated rent to be paid him in the event that colonies should be established in Virginia. The company also promised to pay the Crown its one-fifth share in all precious metals and granted an additional fifth to Sir Walter and his heirs as well.

"It's hard to believe James could be so stupid, isn't it?" Raleigh's voice cut into the captain's thoughts. "If he was endowed with a little common sense, he'd have the trinkets removed. I bring every visitor who ever comes to see me in here. People look at these symbols of my former power and naturally they sympathize with me. Let's go back into the hall, shall we?"

They returned to the larger chamber, took their seats, and drank a little more sack. Sir Walter, playing the role of the ever-gracious host, smiled and held out his pipe. "Would you care to try a bowl?"

"No, thank you. I haven't acquired the habit."

"You will." The smile faded slowly. "More and more

people are adopting it every day. I planted tobacco on my Irish estates, you know, and I never stop mourning their loss. But you haven't come here to hear about my woes. If what I've been told is correct, every ballad singer in England will fill your ears with an account of my sorrows for a farthing."

Smith leaned forward, his face earnest. "It so happens that I'm here to discuss your problems, Sir Walter."

"You'll pardon my skepticism, I trust. Are you implying you've come here without hope of personal gain of any sort?"

"Hardly," the captain replied in the same dry tone.

"Ah, that's better." Raleigh decided he liked this brash young man. "Now then, just what is it you propose to do for me that will give me solace and make you wealthy?"

"Sir Walter, I represent the London Company."

"So I gathered a little earlier in our conversation. Please be a little more explicit."

"It's an association of noble patrons and wealthy merchants, each of whom has bought shares in it. The Company exists for the sole and express purpose of establishing colonies in the New World."

Sir Walter felt a surge of an old excitement that he had believed dead, and he controlled his emotion with difficulty; the mere mention of America stimulated him.

Smith opened a purse at his belt, removed a sheet of paper, and unfolded it. "You'll want to see a list of the shareholders. I don't have the funds to become a member myself."

Raleigh studied the document for what seemed like a long time.

"The area in which we hope to settle is Virginia," Smith said at last, breaking the silence.

"I see." In the Queen's day Sir Walter had been known as a dangerous card player who never lost a wager. His opponents at primero or ruff had often sworn, after losing several hundred guineas to him, that only an advocate of the devil himself was capable of exercising such superb self-restraint that he could freeze his facial muscles at will.

Smith, watching him closely, was filled with admiration.

He had cultivated the art of hiding his emotions but he would need many more long hours of practice before he would become Sir Walter's equal. "We intend to establish a colony there late this year. The Company has purchased three barks for the initial voyage, and we're planning on sending some two hundred or more colonists. Naturally we'll continue to conduct intensive recruiting here at home after the first group has gone, and we'll increase the size of the colony as fast as it can absorb newcomers."

"How often will you infuse new blood into the community?"

"Twice each year at the very least. Three times, if conditions are sufficiently stable." Smith did not realize that he had raised his voice or that he was sitting tensely in his chair, his fists clenched and his back rigid.

"That seems sound." Sir Walter knew the London Company was not seeking his advice, but it was impossible not to offer an opinion.

"I think so. I believe that by sending ships to the colony several times a year, we can not only keep in close touch but we can furnish the settlers with all sorts of supplies they'll need."

"You appear to be something of an expert on the subject of colonization, young man," Sir Walter observed tartly.

"I don't think I'll qualify as an expert until I've spent a year or two in the New World," was the sober reply. "But I have made a thorough study of all previous attempts to establish colonies in America, including yours, Sir Walter. And if you don't mind my saying so, I hope to avoid the mistakes of the past."

Raleigh would have been quick to detect and resent any note of criticism, but Smith seemed sincere. "There's room for improvement."

"I dare say we'll make enough mistakes of our own." The captain remembered in time that a modest approach would achieve more than an overly confident air. However, he could not refrain from adding, "I needn't tell you what happens when too many voices clamor to be heard in a council."

"I've always maintained that living conditions in the New World are too hazardous to permit government by a council. There should be one man in command, and one man only." Sir Walter's own experiences were ever-present in his memory, and he could not help but feel a bond with a man who felt as he did. So many would-be colonizers were impractical dreamers that it was refreshing to meet someone who seemed to reflect his own views. But he was not yet ready to accept Smith; there was a great deal he needed to learn first. "We digress, Captain."

The visitor, who had been about to enlarge on the topic of a need for a strong command, said nothing and looked politely at the most renowned of living explorers, waiting to learn his pleasure.

"You say you're not an investor in the London Company. A score of your shareholders have known me for years. Why wasn't one of them sent to me?"

"We thought you'd prefer to talk with someone who is actually going to take part in the expedition. Most of the shareholders," the captain continued with an irony that was not lost on Sir Walter, "neither know nor care about the detailed plans. All they worry about is the size of the return on their investment."

"You're going to command one of the barks, then? Or perhaps the whole fleet?"

"Neither," Smith replied, then added hastily, "I'm fully qualified to act as the master of ships far larger than barks, of course. And in case of necessity I could take over direction of the fleet, as everyone concerned with the enterprise realizes. But I believe I'll serve my most useful function as an administrator, and as a soldier, should trouble develop with the natives."

There had been a time, Raleigh thought, when scores of

young Englishmen had been quietly confident of their
abilities to discharge any duties they might be called upon to
perform. Scholars had become soldiers, men of noble birth
had written plays and poetry, and when the Spaniards had
sent the greatest fleet ever assembled to conquer England,
young firebrands who had never before gone to sea had
become sailors and had helped defeat the Armada. Few
members of the generation that had come of age in recent
years possessed either that assurance or the skill to make good
their boasts, but Smith certainly seemed to belong in that
dwindling group. He might be vain, he was blatantly boast-
ful, and there was a distinct possibility that his reputation as a
liar was deserved. But his faith in himself was absolute, and
Raleigh, feeling a wave of nostalgia for his own lost youth,
reflected that Smith would have prospered in Elizabeth's
time as no man could in this more cautious era, when form
outweighed accomplishment.

"You've been appointed as leader of the colony, then. Is
that correct, Captain?"

"There has been no official appointment," Smith replied
carefully. "Several gentlemen will be in the party, and I have
no doubt there will be a rivalry for posts of varying importance. All the same, I feel quite sure it will be my task to act as
the colony's leader." He finished his sack and smiled blandly.

Only a man of exceptional strength and cunning would be
able to wrest the post from him, Sir Walter had to concede;
Smith reminded him of Sir John Hawkins, who had assumed
the right to command as his natural obligation but had never
been able to accept orders from others and had been reluctant
to bow his head to anyone, even the Queen. "You have no
fear that others may dispute your claim?"

"They may dispute it. But if I may quote a motto that I
wrote some time ago, a motto by which I try to live, their
ambition will need to be made of sterner stuff than mine."

Sir Walter managed to keep a straight face. "You wrote
that, you say?"

"I did, sir."

Elizabeth had been right when she had called the man a liar, but even she had not realized how magnificently he performed. "It seems to me, Smith, that I heard an identical sentiment spoken from the stage of the Globe Theatre in a play called *Julius Caesar*."

"Really?" Smith casually adjusted and smoothed his ruff. "A remarkable coincidence."

Sir Walter was enjoying himself thoroughly, and although the subject of founding a colony was not a laughing matter, he could not resist prolonging his baiting. "I'm sure you'll overcome every obstacle. By the way, where did you acquire your military title?"

"That's quite a long story, Sir Walter. I related it in some detail in a book telling of my experiences in Moslem lands."

"You haven't held a command in England's armies, then?" Raleigh persisted.

"I have, but only in a manner of speaking." If Smith was disturbed, he didn't show it.

Sir Walter smiled, sobered, and returned to the business at hand. "Neither you nor your investors need my approval for your venture, as you surely know. At the moment I'm the King's prisoner, I've been discredited with the people of England, and I'm in no position either to give my blessing to a proposed colony or to withhold it. I assume that the London Company has purchased the patents of the old Merchants Company, with which I dealt."

"That's right. We——"

"In that case, should the colony prosper, I'll be entitled to a payment of rents according to a table that was drawn up long ago. And should any metals be mined, I'm to receive a one-fifth share. That you also know. So why have you come to see a man who can neither help nor hinder you? I want none of your blandishments, Captain Smith. Tell me the truth."

Smith met his gaze steadily. "You shall have the truth, Sir Walter, and I hope it pleases you, but if you don't find it flattering, that will make it no less the truth. Someday you'll be set free and restored to the King's favor."

"I devoutly pray that you're right," Raleigh said.

"When that time comes, you could do great harm to the Virginia colony. I'm not sure whether you could have our right to settle in your portion of the New World taken from us, but it's possible the courts would uphold you. In any event, we'd have no end of trouble. I believe in looking ahead and I'm here in the hope of avoiding that trouble."

Sir Walter absently tapped the ashes from his pipe onto the floor. "I commend you for your perception. But I trust that you haven't hoped to charm me into approving your plans."

"I doubt if you're susceptible to charm," Smith said, softening his irony with a smile. "A number of ideas were discussed, and mine prevailed naturally. That's why I've come here myself. On behalf of the Company, I offer you double the rents that are outlined in the agreement."

"Well!" Sir Walter brightened and sat back in his chair. He would accept the offer, of course, but didn't want to appear too eager. "What causes you to be so generous?"

"If the colony is successful, a double fee will be a fair price and no hardship on anyone. If we fail, there's nothing lost."

It was mildly astonishing that a man who could deliberately embroider falsifications in one breath could show such blunt candor in the next. But Sir Walter was thinking first of himself, not of his guest now; Smith was in many ways a recognizable younger version of himself, which amused him, but was important to him only as an instrument through whom the chances of the colony's success would be improved. And Sir Walter wanted the colony to succeed. The double rental fee would be very welcome.

"What of the gold?" he asked, purposely setting a trap. "You no doubt expect to find great quantities of gold?"

"Some members of the expedition dream of gold, but I don't happen to be one of them," Smith said succinctly. "For our sakes as well as for yours, I hope we find some. But I consider the prospects highly unlikely. Too many colonies have failed because the settlers have spent their time searching for gold and precious stones. My studies have convinced me that the future of the New World lies in her timber and furs and crops."

His attitude was so sensible that Sir Walter was startled. "You and I," he said slowly, "are in complete accord." Rising, he held out his hand.

The captain, jumping eagerly to his feet, clasped Raleigh's hand firmly, and they grinned at each other. "I'm sure we won't regret this agreement."

"When you bring me the revised contract increasing my fee, I'll give you whatever advice I can. I'm spending most of my days writing a definitive history of the world, but I'm sure I can make some time to help you."

Smith took the hint but was sincerely grateful too. "I'll return within the week," he promised.

"Meanwhile, let me give you a handbook on the New World that I've written within the past year, chiefly for my own entertainment and the edification of anyone who might find it useful. The natives speak a variety of languages, but certain terms are common to many of the tribes, so my glossary of Indian tongues might be helpful to you. I've also included a section on the habits and customs of the natives that should be interesting. Those who think the Naturals have no standards are badly mistaken. The savages don't believe as we do, but they have codes of their own, very rigid codes."

Smith had always clung to the fundamental belief that men always acted in their own self-interest and that they subsequently rationalized their behavior, paying lip service to principles they happened to find convenient. But Sir Walter did not fit into his preconceived mold, and the captain stared at him. "I'll be very pleased to read your handbook. You wrote it with no hope of gain?"

"Gain?" Raleigh asked contemptuously, suddenly

aroused. "I'll be less of a pauper if your colony succeeds, but my financial state concerns only my family and me. Virginia occupies no more than a small part of America. When you're my age, Smith, you'll begin to think in terms of posterity rather than just of today and tomorrow. I want to be remembered by the generations yet to come, who will know me only if I've contributed something lasting to the New World. I can see the day when the savages will become civilized, when they and our settlers will join together, when they will become one with England. If I've helped bring that day closer, my place in history is secure."

Smith, lacking the older man's vision, remained silent.

"I've been shackled, so others must do my work for me now, and you're one of them. Read what I've written and heed my advice." Sir Walter glanced at the arrogantly handsome young man standing before him and felt a surge of pity for him. "You and I are much alike, Smith, so take special notice of what I've written regarding women."

"Women?"

"Avoid them if you hope to prosper. A woman lifted me to greatness, and when I married my wife, bless her, I fell from grace. I subsequently had to achieve far more than most to achieve favor again, and even now I must pay the penalty for the royal feminine brand that has marked me for all time. Listen to my warning, Smith, and obey it. If you would achieve fortune and lasting fame, shun all women, including those of the New World. They're daughters of Eve, and they're treacherous, every last one of them."

August, 1607

The silent wilderness, lonely and dark, a vast expanse of towering oaks, thick maples and elms, fragrant evergreens and tangled bushes stretched out to the north, the west, and the south. At the mouth of the river, directly to the east, was the sea, and far across the Atlantic was England, which each day became more of a blurred memory to the colonists struggling to establish and maintain a foothold on the shores of a strange continent. In April, when the first settlers had stepped onto the soil of America, the trees had hemmed them in, frightening and overwhelming them. Now they had cleared enough land to build their homes and storehouses, their fort and their church and their school, so the forest was no longer alien to them.

They hunted in it and brought back deer and bear; they caught fish in its deep, swiftly flowing streams; they learned, slowly and painfully, to distinguish the subtle sounds that the untrained ear could not hear. The colonists no longer lived in terror of the ever-present wilderness, but it continued to dominate them, and they came to realize that they could not conquer it, so they either had to change their own habits or perish. No one knew how far the forest extended; some thought it was hundreds of miles deep, and others were sure that a solid sea of birch and hemlock, walnut and yellow poplar and cedar filled the whole of the New World. But regardless of its proportions, every settler recognized its majesty and power.

When the wind rustled through the leaves of the high branches or a small animal scurried through the underbrush, London seemed more remote than ever, and even the dreamers knew that the forest had challenged them. Only the hardy, the practical, the strong could survive. The comforts that an advanced civilization took for granted did not exist in America, and, most important, the sense of personal security that was the heritage of every Englishman was unknown in the wilderness. The last link with the safe, familiar past had been broken when the *Susan Constant*, flagship of the fleet that carried the settlers to Virginia, had sailed for home. When the main topsail of the *Susan Constant* disappeared, the wilderness closed in, the men and women of Virginia knew finally that they were alone.

So much work needed to be done, so many demands were made on the settlers' time and energies, that they forgot to be afraid, and gradually they began to feel at ease in the forests. They named their colony Jamestown, in honor of the King, and the gentlemen who comprised the Council wanted to erect a church as the first permanent building in the community. But Captain John Smith insisted that they must build a stockade before launching any other project, and when it was finished he ordered the settlers to construct a blockhouse at the far end of a curving peninsula that jutted out into the broad river. That blockhouse, he said, would control the approaches by water, the settlement's life line, and although the Council grumbled, the people listened to him and followed his instructions.

He worked with the men, cutting down trees and shaping them into logs, digging holes in the ground for foundations and filling in the walls with clay. As he himself had predicted to Sir Walter Raleigh, his voice quickly became the most influential in Jamestown, and the colonists, amazed and delighted that a gentleman should treat them as equals, obeyed him without question. Some of the other gentry felt he was demeaning himself by soiling his hands and working like a common artisan, and out of spite they deprived him of the official leadership of the community and elected Edward Wingfield, the younger son of a baronet, as president of the Council.

Smith accepted his punishment in silence and redoubled his efforts to complete the blockhouse. When it was done and two of the colony's five small cannon had been mounted inside it, he proposed that the fort be built before work was started on the church. Captain Gabriel Archer, the only other former army officer in the colony, failed to support him, and the Council voted in favor of constructing the church. Two days after the foundations had been dug, however, Smith's logic was substantiated by an unexpected ally, the wilderness itself.

At dusk, when the settlers were finishing their day's work and thinking of the meal the women were cooking for them in community kettles, a party of twenty Indians crept out of the forest, entered Jamestown through an unguarded gate, and murdered a woman and two children who had been sitting in front of their temporary hut. The screams of the third child, who escaped from the savages, aroused the group at the church, and John Smith went into action at once. He dropped the ax with which he had been trimming the branches from a sapling and, not bothering to don his helmet, he rallied the workmen and started at once toward the scene of the commotion.

Drawing his pistol, he raced toward the hut and almost collided with the advancing savages. Without hesitation he fired at the painted warrior who led the party, killing the man instantly, and then demonstrated his valor beyond all question by charging straight into the center of the hostile band, brandishing his rapier. He showed no concern over his own safety, and the settlers, encouraged by his example, dashed after him. A small Indian hatchet struck Smith's chest but bounced harmlessly off his armor, and he continued to attack, slashing at the savages with expert skill. One of the warriors fell, badly wounded, and the colonists joined the fight, heartened by the captain's courage.

The settlers were armed with the tools they had been using to build their church, and their hammers, axes, and spades were no more effective than the bone-handled knives and hatchets the Indians carried. The two groups were approximately equal in numbers, and the colonists might have suffered serious casualties had the participation of John Smith not tipped the scales in their favor. He fought coldly, ignoring the attempts of the warriors to surround him as he thrust his blade at every half-naked, painted body he saw.

His men more than held their own, and the brief battle ended as quickly as it began. In a few minutes the bodies of nine of the attackers littered the ground, and the remaining warriors fled ignominiously, escaping through the gate before other settlers, who were hurrying to the scene, could halt them. Captain Archer, who had stopped to buckle on his steel corselet when he had heard the alarm, appeared too late to be of any help, and a number of the other young men milled around sheepishly.

Smith calmly wiped his rapier on the ground and then stood erect. "Don't follow the Naturals into the forest," he said crisply, and no one dared question his command.

By this time most of the colonists had gathered, and everyone stared in silence at the dead Indians, the first natives the people of Jamestown had seen since their arrival. The colonists had devoted endless hours to speculation over the physical appearance of the Naturals of the New World, and the more imaginative a description had been, the more

eagerly had it been accepted as authentic. Hence the settlers
were surprised and disappointed to discover that their conjec-
tures had been wrong and that even in death the Indians were
remarkably like other members of the human race. The
fallen warriors were handsome men, tall, sinewy, and lean.
Their skins were not much darker than were those of the
colonists who had been constantly exposed to the sun, and
without exception each of the raiders had one head, two
arms, and two legs.

The clothing of the Naturals was shocking, however, and
it was satisfying to realize that no one could have mistaken
them for Englishmen: the warriors wore nothing but short
loincloths of supple, natural leather, and on their feet were
soft leather slippers decorated with multicolored beads and
shells. Worst of all, their bodies and faces were decorated
with broad smears of shining green and yellow paint. These
streaks were conclusive evidence that Indians were savages of
the most primitive sort, so the observant were somewhat
disconcerted when their study indicated that the paint had
been applied in intricate designs and therefore was mean-
ingful rather than haphazard.

The heads of the warriors had been shaved, except for an
area an inch wide that ran back from the brow to the nape of
the neck, and a heavy grease had been applied to the remaining long hair, making it stiff and thick. The appearance of
one of the Naturals was unique, for he wore a bracelet of
beaten silver on his left wrist, and around his forehead was
twisted a broad band of leather decorated with long rows of
tiny red, green, and blue beads. No one could object when
John Smith stepped up to his body and removed the Indian's
jewelry. As the victor he had the right to such spoils as he
wished, and it was only natural that he should want a
souvenir or two of the engagement.

He weighed the bracelet thoughtfully before dropping it
into his pocket; then he looped the headpiece over the hilt of
his sword and gazed calmly at his compatriots. "We will hold

a funeral at once for the victims of our own carelessness," he said. "When the service is concluded, these savages will be buried. We can't blame them for their attack on us, so a prayer will be said for them too."

Several of the gentlemen in the crowd muttered to each other, and Edward Wingfield grew scarlet, but only Captain Archer had the courage to challenge Smith's command. "Why can't we blame them for their attack?" he demanded. "We've been living here in peace, and we've done them no harm."

Smith smiled benignly at the outraged young officer. Archer, he thought, was a natural troublemaker who always envied his superiors. Some men were born to command, while others necessarily followed them, and Archer had to be put in his place. There was no time more opportune than the present. "The Naturals may feel that we've stolen land that belongs to them."

"Virginia belongs to the London Company!"

"So it does, but I'm inclined to believe the Indians didn't know it. In my considered opinion, none of them was capable of reading our patent, which is written in English." Smith paused until the crowd's laughter subsided, and when he spoke again his voice was firm. "We can blame ourselves, no one else, for the tragedy. We built a stout wall, but the Council assigned no guards to stand watch at the gates. We should have raised a fort that would look out on the countryside, but those who were afraid God would be angry with us stupidly insisted that we build a church first."

"Are you a preacher, Smith?" Archer asked. "Are you trying to instruct us in what God thinks is right or wrong?"

"I'm a man of common sense who knows that God will love us no less if we do everything in our power to protect ourselves. I'm sure He knows, even if the Council doesn't, that we aren't dishonoring Him by putting up a strong fort before we make a house of worship." He looked hard at Archer, then at Wingfield, Matthew Scrivener, John Kendall, and the other members of the Council. "Immediately after the funeral," he said flatly, "construction will begin on the fort. And starting right now, a guard of ten men will be maintained at the stockade at all times."

The settlers muttered their approval, and no member of the Council dared to object. The gentlemen knew that Smith had publicly pointed out their error and his own good judgment merely to increase his popularity with the settlers; the Council surely would have reversed its earlier decision and ordered the fort built, but the whole matter could have been handled privately. That, however, was not Smith's way, and the members of the Council, watching him, realized that he would lose no chance to dramatize every mistake they would ever make until he, and he alone, ruled Jamestown.

Smith saw the hatred in Archer's eyes, the uncertainty on the faces of Wingfield and Scrivener, Kendall and Christopher Newport, and he smiled quietly. An expert duelist always struck hardest when his opponent was confused. "Never fear," he said in a voice calculated to soothe the crowd. "I've been afraid of just such an emergency as this and I've already prepared complete plans for the fort."

Again the crowd cheered, which did not surprise him in the least.

"I'll expect to see the building completed by the time I return," he said. "Now, I want three volunteers who will accompany me into the interior. If possible, I'd like men who have had military service and know how to handle a musket."

By order of the Council, no member of the community was allowed to leave the settlement without written permission. So far the decree had been strictly enforced, but Smith was coolly setting himself above the law, and every colonist knew it. Archer, frustrated and outraged, turned angrily to Edward Wingfield. "It's your place to forbid this!"

The president of the Council stroked the beard he had grown in an effort to hide his receding chin. He had accepted authority unwillingly, and he wanted no dispute now, but the settlers were all looking at him, and he knew he had to say something. "What sort of journey do you have in mind, Captain?" he asked mildly.

John Smith took the dead Indian's decorative headpiece from his sword hilt and twirled it absently around his forefinger. "It seems to me," he said, "that the Naturals who attacked us today aren't the only Indians in America. Obviously we have neighbors. If we don't take steps to become friendly with them, there will be more raids. I don't like seeing innocent people killed, just as I know you don't, Master Wingfield. So I intend to seek out our neighbors and become friendly with them."

"That seems very reasonable to me," Wingfield replied.

"And to you, Master Scrivener? Master Newport?" No one could ever complain that Smith's tone was lacking in respect. He waited until the other members of the Council nodded, and then he turned back to the settlers, apparently forgetting that he had not bothered to seek Gabriel Archer's opinion.

A number of the younger and more adventurous members of the colony began to clamor for the right to accompany him on his trip and, after making a show of trying to select only three of them, he announced that the problem was insoluble and that all nine would accompany him. Their loyalty assured, he assigned a onetime militia sergeant from Devon to command the stockade guard, told the man to draw up his own schedules, and then, before the Council could protest, announced that he would himself take charge of digging the graves for the victims of the raid. Having settled matters to his own satisfaction, he walked away quietly and was pleased to see that virtually the entire throng followed him. The Council could elect anyone it pleased as president, but the people of Jamestown needed no vote to identify their natural leader.

That night Gabriel Archer visited the temporary huts of each of his colleagues and tried to persuade them to take disciplinary action against the man who had dared to use his feat of heroism to his own advantage. Smith guessed that the

Council might be plotting to curb him, but he made no attempt to defend himself. While others talked, he worked, and long after the rest of the colony had gone to bed he remained awake, reading Sir Walter Raleigh's handbook on the Indians by the light of a flickering taper.

The following morning he and his volunteers started off through the forests on foot, armed with muskets, a considerable supply of glass beads, cheap plaster statues, and other trinkets. They made no attempt to conceal themselves and within twenty-four hours they were accosted by two young Indian warriors, who appeared suddenly before them and made signs of peace. The natives were astonished, as were the volunteers, when Smith addressed them, haltingly but effectively, in a tongue they understood and told them that he had no desire to fight with them.

The Naturals conducted the party to a native settlement deep in the wilderness, and there Smith remained for ten days, talking with the elders of the mud town, meeting the warriors, and handing out his supply of beads and statues. When the trinkets were gone he ordered his volunteers to open their personal supply packs for his inspection, and when they complied he gleefully seized three decks of playing cards and doled out the colored pasteboards to the Indians.

During his sojourn Smith made constant notes on the language of the Naturals, and he jotted down every item of interest that he learned from his hosts. He found that the town was that of a small tribe which was part of a great confederation ruled by a mighty chief named Powhatan, whose capital was four days' journey farther into the wilderness. At his request two of the young warriors promptly set out to Powhatan's town with a silver-handled knife which Smith sent to the chief with his compliments, together with a message saying that he himself would visit the capital of the confederation in the near future.

Smith seemed completely at home with the savages, but

the young colonists were thoroughly uncomfortable during their brief stay in the Indian community, and at no time could they shake off a feeling of uneasiness in the presence of bare-chested, paint-daubed warriors. The party that had attacked Jamestown had come from this village, but the elders told Smith the raid had been unauthorized, and he accepted their glib lie as though he believed it. He kept the information to himself, as he was afraid his men would become belligerent if they learned they were living with the families of men whom they had fought. In all probability, he knew, the warriors who had escaped were among those who were now extending hospitality to the visitors, but he was cheerful and polite to every Indian he encountered.

Life in the Indian village was pleasant, and Smith found he was enjoying himself thoroughly. He knew his companions were tense, suspicious, and on guard at all times, and he sympathized with them even though he did not share their feelings. His extensive travels in his youth, his years of service in Islam as a slave, as a soldier of the Sultan, and as an officer in the household of the great Caliph had made him adaptable, willing, and sometimes eager to sample new ways. This little tribe, which called itself the Pamaunke, fascinated him, and he spent several hours each day jotting down extensive notes on its customs and habits.

The three or four hundred men, women, and children of the Pamaunke lived a communal life; the men hunted and fished, the younger women grew a variety of crops in nearby fields, and the old women cooked for everyone. Families lived together in crude mud huts, and the English colonists were crowded into two such houses, but Smith was given a dwelling of his own and quickly made himself comfortable. He slept on the hard-packed earth floor, and the only inconvenience he suffered was caused by a lack of light, for his hut had no windows. He therefore spent as little time in it as possible, and when he wanted to write he sat out in the open, where he was invariably surrounded by a swarm of curious, naked children.

Pamaunke food was edible, which was the most he could say for it. The dishes were strange to him, but he ate heartily, not wanting to display discourtesy to his hosts, who considered it an insult to refuse the offerings. They ate two meals a day, breakfast consisting of small grilled fish, which they ate whole, and several soggy vegetables, which were unidentifiable after long hours over a fire. The evening meal, which the men of the community ate together, was the high point of the day, and Smith learned that each warrior dipped into the pots with his bare hands and snatched what he could. A favorite dish was boiled dog, and Smith had to shut his mind to what he was eating. The young settlers who had accompanied him enjoyed the concoction more than anything else they were served, so he carefully refrained from telling them its contents. The venison which the Naturals prepared was invariably undercooked and tough and left an unpleasant aftertaste, and bear stew, which the natives considered a delicacy, was too greasy for a cultivated palate.

The Indians made constant use of a grain unlike anything Smith had ever eaten, and he knew it was something the Jamestown colony could utilize to good advantage. It was called corn and was eaten in a remarkable variety of ways. Sometimes it was boiled, sometimes it was roasted, and when hunters went off into the forests for several days at a time, they took little bags of it with them, parched, and it sustained them. Perhaps it was most valuable in a bread called pulse, of which it was the base, and Smith did not rest until he learned the recipe for making it, much to the amusement of the men of the tribe. Loaves of the heavy bread were baked slowly over heated bricks after being mixed with dried plums, which had been pounded until they disintegrated into a fine powder. Pulse, Smith thought, could become a much-needed staple in the diet of Jamestown.

The women of the Pamaunke were treated as inferiors,

remaining in the background at all times, and the visitors saw little of them. Some of the younger women were mildly attractive, in spite of their voluminous robes of buffalo skin, which extended from their necks to their ankles, but Smith kept his distance from them and warned his men to do the same. The Naturals were being friendly, and he did not want a needless, stupid incident to mar the relationship. Remembering Sir Walter Raleigh's warning, he felt rather proud of himself, for it had been a long time since he had last taken a woman.

Intertribal wars were forbidden by Powhatan, the chief of the confederation of many Indian nations, so the young warriors either hunted or engaged in trials of strength and other games. The attack on Jamestown, Smith learned, had been caused by the boredom of the young braves, and it was a source of considerable satisfaction to him to know that as a result of the nightly ceremonies in which he joined the elders, smoking innumerable pipes of burning tobacco, there would be peace hereafter between the Pamaunke and the English settlers. However, it was clear to him that only a treaty with Powhatan would prevent other tribes from attacking the colony, and a decision solidified in his mind: It was urgently necessary for him to pay a visit of state to the man who, according to the Pamaunke elders, ruled many thousands of New World natives with an iron hand.

The Naturals learned something about the ways of the settlers, too, and were fascinated by the pistols and muskets which Smith and his men carried. Smith gave three or four exhibitions of his prowess with firearms, and the warriors, after conquering their initial fear, spent many hours handing a weapon around a circle, examining it, fondling it, and exclaiming over it. Smith wisely refused to give any of the natives an opportunity to fire one of the guns, and each night he slept with his pistol jammed into his belt and his musket securely tied to his leg, so they would not be stolen.

He took considerable pleasure in the knowledge that he

slept soundly every night, without fear of any kind. His companions, he knew, were apprehensive, and maintained watches through the night, but he was certain in his own mind that no harm would come to him. Now that the Pamaunke had been impressed by the muskets and pistols, they surely realized that if they murdered him he would be avenged by scores of colonists armed with similar miraculous weapons.

The difference between his attitude and that of his volunteers emphasized something he had always believed: he possessed qualities that set him apart from others, that made him unique. Even renowned men of the older generation, like Sir Walter, did not impress him, for he knew he was their equal if not their superior. In the years to come, he had no doubt, he would achieve lasting fame, and his one inflexible desire was to achieve a reputation that would remain untarnished for generations.

It seemed to him that as an explorer and chronicler he could best utilize his extraordinary talents. Much of the New World remained hidden behind the great sea of trees, and he knew he had the stamina and intelligence to ferret out the secrets of the wilderness. Even those small portions of America that had already been discovered and explored were still uncharted, and here his unusual ability as a map maker would certainly serve him in good stead. What was more important, he possessed the gift of being able to express himself coherently, so he would be able to write full accounts of his exploits. Men like Sebastian Cabot and Humphrey Gilbert would be forgotten in time because they had been unable to leave the world the full and detailed story of their exploits, but John Smith would not suffer the same fate. Even the notes he had already made on the life of the Pamaunke, when translated into the prose he could write so fluently, would enthrall all England, and the Pamaunke were an insignificant people who occupied no more than a very tiny portion of America.

As he lay beneath his thin blanket in the mud hut of the Pamaunke, he realized more clearly than ever before in his life that the unknown challenged him, for it compelled him to use all of his strength, all of his wit, all of his ingenuity. In a sense, exploration was similar to making love to a woman: the element of the unforeseen was always present, and there were often surprising difficulties to be overcome. Smiling slightly in the darkness, he reflected that the simile was not really appropriate; when John Smith courted a woman, the results were always the same.

It was unfortunate that he had allowed himself to think of women, for he became restless, and it was a long time before he finally fell asleep. When he awoke in the morning he reminded himself sternly that there was no permanent place for any woman in his future. Even a temporary liaison would be inconveniently time-consuming, when there was so much to be accomplished. It was not accidental that females were called the weaker sex, and he despised weakness. Besides, he was a practical man and, at the moment, no desirable woman was conveniently available to him.

With work to be done in the world, the mere idea of loitering in the village of the Pamaunke became intolerable to Smith, and he and his followers left the same day for Jamestown, taking with them the renewed assurances of their hosts that future relations between the tribe and the newcomers to Virginia would be friendly. Two young warriors acted as guides and conducted the settlers back to the seacoast, and less than twenty-four hours later Smith and his volunteers marched triumphantly through the gates of Jamestown.

Their arrival created a sensation, and with good reason. In spite of the hot August sun that shone down from a cloudless sky, Smith wore a buffalo robe, and it had amused him to smear his face with the war paint of the Pamaunke. His men wore the soft slippers, or moccasins, of the Indians, and all of them carried souvenirs of their visit to the interior in the form

of bone-handled knives or bows and arrows, which were
smaller but more accurate than those used by the English.

Friends and relatives of the volunteers crowded around
them, a part holiday was declared, and President Wingfield
called a meeting of the Council to hear John Smith's report.
The gentlemen gathered at the blockhouse partly because the
weather was a trifle cooler at the far end of the Jamestown
peninsula, partly because the fortress was the only permanent building yet constructed in which they could convene.

Smith waited until he was certain that all of the others
were present before making his entrance, and not until then
did he stroll into the central room of the blockhouse. He was
still wearing his buffalo robe, but, as the heat in the chamber
was stifling, he quickly removed it and threw it over two
bundles which his volunteers placed just inside the door.
Edward Wingfield enjoyed conducting Council meetings
with the pomp and ceremony of a session of the House of
Lords, but Smith hated all formality, particularly when he
was not the central figure, so he gave the president no chance
to complicate the meeting and began to speak at once.

As he recounted the details of his visit to the Pamaunke he
looked in turn at each member of the Council and thought,
not for the first time, that only Gabriel Archer was a threat to
the future he had planned for himself. Wingfield was a
pleasant, harmless nonentity, and so were John Kendall and
John Ratcliffe, both of whom had joined the expedition
principally because their wealthy relatives had invested
money in the venture. Christopher Newport was conscientious but wily and could be depended on to lend his support to
that faction which seemed the most influential at any given
moment. Smith knew he had an admirer in Matthew
Scrivener, and he himself felt a strong bond of kinship with
Bartholomew Gosnold, who had taken part in two previous
voyages of exploration to the New World and who, like
himself, was insatiably curious about America.

He therefore addressed his remarks to Scrivener and Gos-

nold and took pains not to embroider his account of the peace
pact he had made with the Pamaunke. He mentioned Chief
Powhatan of the sprawling Chickahominy Confederation
only lightly and in passing, as he felt this was not the right
moment to comment on the need to make a treaty with the
great Indian ruler. It would be better to wait until he was
ready to leave for the interior again before announcing his
plans, for if he revealed them prematurely, the Council
might decide to send someone else as their spokesman or,
equally unwelcome, might burden him with a colleague. He
had no intention of sharing the glory with anyone.

He did not bother to tell the Council about the tribal
customs and living habits of the Naturals, either, although
he could have dwelt on the subject at length. Archer was a
literate man, and Gosnold had once printed a pamphlet on a
voyage he had made to a region in the north, which he had
named Cape Cod, so Smith reasoned that it was best to be
cautious and give no one a chance to steal material he would
include in the definitive history of Virginia that he would one
day write.

Hence his report was a model of brevity and, at its conclusion, he threw aside the buffalo robe, revealing two lumpy
sacks. He pointed at them, enjoying the suspense as the
gentlemen of the Council leaned forward. "In return for the
trinkets which I gave to the Naturals," he said, pausing
occasionally like an actor to heighten the effect of his words,
"I have received a gift so valuable that I cannot describe it to
you."

Gabriel Archer stood and tugged at his mustache, his
small dark eyes shining avariciously. "Gold?" he demanded
hoarsely.

Smith laughed condescendingly. "The contents of these
sacks are worth far more than gold, Captain." He slit the neck
of the nearer bag with a bone-handled knife that the savages
had given him, reached inside, and drew out a handful of
small yellow pellets. "This, gentlemen, is corn, the natural

grain of the New World! I've brought back enough for us to plant six or seven acres. In time corn will provide us with enough bread and cereal to make us self-sufficient. In another year we'll have no need to depend on the supplies that come to us in the holds of the London Company's ships."

Gosnold understood the significance of the two little sacks and so, rather surprisingly, did Edward Wingfield, but the others were disappointed. Captain Archer made himself the spokesman for the group. "Are you trying to tell us that grain is more valuable than gold, Smith? What kind of fools do you think we are?"

"I have some rather emphatic ideas on that subject," Smith retorted, then deliberately calmed himself, reached into the pocket of his breeches, and drew out a small clay pipe, which was already filled with tobacco. He held it up for the council's inspection as though it were a rare jewel, then clamped the stem between his teeth. "Jamestown can become wealthy beyond all our dreams, gentlemen, if we'll display patience and wisdom by growing two crops. Corn will feed us, together with the meat we kill in the forests and the fish we catch in the sea. And tobacco will bring fabulous prices in the markets of London. I've seen the leaf growing wild in the interior, and the soil here is even better suited to tobacco than were the regions Sir Walter Raleigh explored."

Archer stood, his face flushed. "If we had wanted to become farmers, we would have stayed in Devon and Sussex. We've come to the New World in search of gold."

Smith's many virtues failed to include a balanced sense of discretion. "Gold be damned!" he declared.

There was a shocked silence, and Archer clenched his fists. "Really? There's something you'd better learn, my dear Smith. While you were enjoying your little holiday with the natives, the Council made some important decisions. We're leaving the women and children with a few guards here at Jamestown, and every other able-bodied man in the colony is going on a journey up the James River." His voice became heavy with self-importance. "My investigations have convinced me that the river will lead us to the South Sea Passage. And once we reach the South Seas we won't know what to do with all the gold we find!"

Smith looked in utter consternation at the avid, beaming faces of the gentlemen of the Council. Archer's proposal was mad, and unless it was squelched at once, the colony was doomed. The brief history of America was studded with the dismal stories of settlements, Portuguese, Spanish, and Dutch, as well as English, that had failed because men had devoted their time and energies to wild searches for gold instead of facing the harsh realities of life in a primitive land. "There's work to be done right here in Jamestown," Smith said evenly. "There's corn and tobacco to be planted. The forest must be finished, and permanent homes must be raised for the colonists before winter comes. We've got to erect the church you were all so worried about recently. And the children need a schoolhouse. Yes, and the fleet will be returning to us soon, so we've got to make ready for some hundreds of new recruits."

Archer stepped forward and looked him up and down slowly, insolently. "You may stay here and act the part of a carpenter, if that pleases you. Or you can play the role of a farmer. We're going to find the South Sea Passage."

"This was your idea, I presume?" Smith's voice was dangerously quiet, and only a faint huskiness betrayed a trace of his emotion.

"Naturally." Gabriel Archer turned and smiled triumphantly at his colleagues.

"I forbid it!" Smith said flatly. "We're staying right here, all of us, and we're doing the work I've just outlined."

"Forbid, Smith? That's strong language."

"So it is." John Smith grinned and created the illusion that he was the only man in the room who was relaxed.

"Are you defying the Council?" Archer was almost unable to control himself.

"It seems to me," Smith drawled, "that you've led the Council to abandon common sense, Captain Archer." He knew now what needed to be done and he congratulated himself on his acumen. "These gentlemen have often proved themselves to be discerning, sensible, and practical. You, however, are mad." His smile broadened and he raised his voice. "I appeal to the Council to treat you as you deserve and chain you in a pit."

The insult was effective, and color drained from Archer's pinched face. He was about to throw himself at his antagonist, but thought better of it, and as he stood indecisively, trying to decide what to do next, Smith could almost read his mind. Dueling was forbidden in the colony under a joint ruling of the Council and the London Company, and Smith heartily approved of the law. Any gentleman who provoked a duel would lose his place on the Council and would be shipped back to England, but one who merely exercised his traditional and unquestioned right to defend his honor would be considered virtually blameless and would receive only a meaningless reprimand as a punishment. Obviously Archer thought Smith was trying to incite him and maneuver him into a position so untenable that he would be forced to issue a challenge. It was equally plain that Archer, lacking any really independent initiative, was deciding that two could play the same game, which was precisely what John Smith wanted.

"You think you're very clever, Smith, but you don't fool any of us. You certainly don't fool me."

"So?" Smith planted his feet wide apart, hooked his thumbs in his belt, and waited.

"You're trying to discourage our search for gold because you've already found a cache somewhere in the interior." Archer spoke very slowly, building up his case; when Smith could tolerate no more and demanded satisfaction, it would be clear to the whole Council that Archer was the innocent party.

"Are you implying that I'm trying to cheat these gentlemen out of a fair share of spoils that I've allegedly found?"

Smith scowled but was secretly elated that his scheme was succeeding.

"Imply, sir? I make the flat statement that you're cheating us. Don't deny it, for even if you did, none of us would believe the most notorious liar in England."

It was difficult for Smith to control his temper, but he realized he would be courting certain disgrace if he reached for his sword. "Be good enough to accompany me outside," he said. "I suggest the far side of the blockhouse, facing the water, where we won't be seen from the town."

The argument had gone too far, and the other members of the Council rose hurriedly. Matthew Scrivener joined Smith and put a restraining hand on his shoulder. "Retract your challenge, John. Have you forgotten the injunction against dueling?"

Smith wanted to wink at his friend, but that might spoil everything, so instead he shrugged, and Scrivener dropped his hand. "Well, Archer? I've demanded compensation for your slurs. Are you going to give it to me?"

Captain Archer raised his arms and looked self-righteously at the others. "Gentlemen," he said virtuously, "as you can see, I have no choice."

The Council agreed with him, and when he lifted the 'atch on the door and stepped out into the open, the rest followed him. Smith lagged behind, and Scrivener, deeply worried, hesitated for an instant, but a single glance at his friend's unyielding face was enough to convince him that an appeal to reason would be a waste of breath. The group assembled on a flat stretch of ground in the shadow of the blockhouse, and there Smith eventually made his appearance. He sauntered toward his grave colleagues, and when Edward Wingfield took a step toward him, he halted and bowed ceremoniously.

"I must remind you, Captain, that the law demands a penalty for inciting a duel," the president said in a high, nervous voice.

Smith raised his eyebrows. "Bless me, so it does." He

removed his pistol and handed it to Scrivener. "Be good enough to keep this for me, Matthew."

Archer flushed indignantly. "What's this?" he shouted. "As the challenged party, I have the choice of weapons."

Ignoring him, Smith slowly unbuckled his sword belt and gave his rapier to Gosnold. "I'll ask you to be custodian of this, Bartholomew." Then he drew his knife, gazed at it reflectively for a moment, and tossed it onto the ground behind him. Finally he removed his armor with great deliberation and dropped the breastplate and helmet onto the grass. The others were watching him in silent bewilderment, and he smiled faintly as he walked forward, the fine-spun lawn of his full shirt sleeves rippling slightly in the warm August breeze.

"Under the Code of Fencing, revised by Sir Francis Walsingham early in the reign of Her late Majesty," he said distinctly, "a fight between two gentlemen who do not use lethal weapons is not classified as a duel. Nor are any consequences of such a fight punishable as a dueling offense. That code has not been repealed or altered since Sir Francis drew it up. Let me further remind you that last year, when Prince Henry administered a beating to that French puppy with his fists, the Privy Council declared by a unanimous vote that he had not engaged in a duel. And a ruling made in the case of the Prince of Wales applies to all of us."

Gosnold and Scrivener were relieved and smiled at his adroit handling of a delicate situation. Christopher Newport, sensing a change in sentiment, expressed the feelings of the Council. "By God, he's right!"

Smith knew his strategy had been successful, but he hid the satisfaction he felt by averting his face as he bowed to Newport. Then he straightened and faced his opponent, who was gaping at him. "Now, then, Captain Archer—or whatever you call yourself. Will you remove your weapons and your steel plate?" When the confused man still did not move, he added a final goad: "Or are you too afraid of me?"

Stung, Archer feverishly unbuckled his armor, cursing

under his breath. Had he been challenged to a fist fight, he would have refused, on the grounds that it was beneath the dignity of a man of standing to soil his hands. But he had been tricked and he no longer had a choice; if he turned his back on the contest now, he would be branded a coward.

Smith, watching him closely, told himself the fate of Jamestown would be decided in the next few minutes. If he expected the Council to regain its reason and give up its plans to hunt for gold, he would first have to beat Archer into insensibility, and that would be no easy task. They were approximately the same age, but Archer was an inch or two taller and was at least ten pounds heavier. He was in excellent physical condition, too, but Smith felt tired after the rapid pace of the march to the coast from the village of the Pamaunke. However, his duty to the colony and to himself was clear.

Archer threw his gear to the ground and advanced quickly, his chin close to his chest and his hands raised. Smith immediately realized that his opponent knew what he was doing; he was experienced in hand-to-hand fighting, and Smith, who had himself fought in more London street brawls as an adolescent than he could possibly recall, was aware that Archer's origins, like his own, had been plebeian. It was even possible that they had fought in the same riots in Southwark, across the Thames from London, where a youth needed stamina and courage as well as brute strength if he hoped to survive.

Certainly Archer's technique was that of the Southwark bullies. He feinted with his right, jabbed hard at his foe's face with his left, and then, lowering his head, tried to butt Smith in the midriff. But he found himself pawing the air, for Smith side-stepped neatly and, lunging forward, knocked him off balance with a punch on the right temple. Archer staggered and slipped to one knee, but he was on his feet again in an instant, before Smith could strike him again. They grappled, and Archer's unusually large hands caught hold of his opponent's arms, momentarily immobilizing Smith and ripping the fabric of his shirt.

The sound of the tearing cloth enraged Smith; he had worked hard for everything of value that he owned, and his possessions of quality were precious to him. And Archer, whose finances were in more or less the same shape, certainly knew that the loss of an expensive shirt was a serious matter. Shoving the taller man away and thus breaking his grip, Smith smashed a hard right into his mouth, drawing blood, and then struck again with his left in the same place.

Both punches hurt, and before Archer could recover, Smith pummeled him mercilessly, raining a shower of blows on his head, face, and chest. Archer fought back grimly, but he had lost the initiative and could not regain it. In desperation he stopped trying to defend himself and attacked wildly, both arms flailing. His right eye was badly swollen, and he could not see his tormentor clearly, but a lucky punch finally caught Smith in the face, halting him for a moment.

Archer followed up his brief advantage at once and, leaping forward, threw his full weight at Smith. They crashed to the ground together, with Archer on top; they rolled over several times, and Archer's right knee repeatedly struck Smith in the groin. The pain was excruciating, and Smith could no longer think lucidly. He realized, however, that if he resorted to the same gutter tactics that his opponent was using he would lose stature in the eyes of the Council, and that, regardless of how the fight ended, he would not be able to persuade the others to abandon their gold-seeking expedition. No matter how much he suffered, he had to keep the respect of the Council.

Drawing on his last reserves of strength, he broke away from Archer, rolled to the far side of the grassy plot near a clump of bushes, and there pulled himself to his feet. He was determined to end the fight quickly, and he stood sucking in air for a moment before moving forward again. Archer was on his feet, too, and rushed at him with the obvious intention

of repeating the tactics he had just used. But Smith, instead
of grappling with him, lashed out savagely with a left that
caught the bigger man on the side of the head.

Both seemed exhausted, and for an instant neither moved.
Then Smith, smiling grimly, put all of his weight behind a
vicious right to the face. Archer's knees buckled, and he
collapsed slowly, pitching forward and sprawling grotesquely
on the ground. His face was hidden in the tall grass and he
did not move, but it was plain to everyone present that he had
lost consciousness. Smith stood erect, elegantly flicked a
smear of blood from his cheek, and turned to the silent
members of the Council.

"As I remarked a short time ago," he said calmly, "the
future of Jamestown is not going to be jeopardized by an
insane hunt for gold. We'll all be kept busy right here,
planting corn and tobacco, and building houses. It's good to
know that we're in unanimous agreement on what needs to
be done. The directors of the Company in London will be
pleased too."

Stepping over Archer's prostrate body, he picked up his
armor, retrieved his weapons, and walked off without a
backward glance. The issue was settled, and he wasted no
further thought on it; instead, as he made his way down the
narrow peninsula to the town, he wondered if there was a
woman in the colony clever enough with needle and thread
to mend his shirt so the rips would not show.

December, 1607

In October, the people of the colony agitated for a change in their official leadership and demanded the election of Captain Smith as president. He, and he alone, had supervised the building of their snug homes and sturdy warehouses, which were filled with grain and root vegetables he had obtained from the Indians. There was peace with the natives, who trusted him as a man of his word and respected him as a shrewd but fair trader, and the Naturals of several nearby tribes now visited the settlement regularly. At Smith's instigation, corn and sweet, or Spanish, potatoes had been planted in fields that had been cleared outside the town walls, and even the poorest colonist could look forward to a share of the profits when produce would be sent to England in the spring.

Smith's modesty was also commendable. It so happened that the subject of the presidency of the Council arose frequently in his discussions with individual settlers, particularly after he had helped them build their homes or had provided them with enough food to see them through the long winter. Naturally the people were grateful and, when he mentioned the presidency to them, casually and in passing, they wondered why he did not occupy the post. He always replied to their questions with a quiet shrug that seemed to indicate an unassuming belief that he was not worthy of the post. The colonists knew better and they clamored so loudly for his selection that at last Edward Wingfield stepped down; Smith's election was virtually unanimous, and only the vote of Gabriel Archer was registered against him. In a memorable speech of acceptance, Smith expressed his complete surprise and said that although he was unprepared, he would try to be deserving of the honor that had been thrust upon him.

His first act as president was to send a knife of the finest Spanish steel to Chief Powhatan of the Chickahominy, and the Pamaunke warrior who had acted as his messenger returned with an invitation to visit the capital of the Confederation. Smith began to prepare for the trip immediately: he purchased three boats of bark from the nearby Chesapeake Indians, he appropriated a variety of items from the town's supplies to take with him as gifts, and he announced the names of eleven men whom he had chosen to accompany him. All of his companions were former soldiers and they required only a few days of training together as pikemen to enable them to parade almost as smartly as King James' own household troops.

Gabriel Archer was heard to comment that Smith was putting on airs by trying to create the impression that he was a great noble whose rank entitled him to employ a guard of honor. But the colonists, remembering Smith's diffidence on the day he had become their leader, ignored the jealous tirade. As Smith himself pointed out, Powhatan was an enormously powerful man, so it was important to convince him that he was dealing with representatives of an even stronger and more influential nation.

The party left Jamestown on the last day of November, riding four in each boat, and naturally Smith took his place at the head of the procession. The travelers moved slowly up the James River, covering no more than twenty miles in a single day, as Smith insisted on halting frequently so he could make careful sketches and notations that would be of great help to him when he eventually drew his maps of the area. On the morning of the third day, two long boats filled with warriors of the Chickahominy met them, and the braves escorted them to their destination, where they arrived late the following afternoon.

About an hour before they reached the town Smith insisted on stopping and, to the amazement of the natives, he and his followers changed their clothes. The men donned armor and steel helmets, and they carefully polished their pikes until the steel heads and light copper shafts of the weapons gleamed. Smith, however, put aside his military gear, for the mission was one of peace, as he explained to his companions, and they were too dazzled by his finery to remember it had been his suggestion that they wear their old army uniforms.

Few nobles who waited on the King at Whitehall were more handsomely attired than the captain, who looked dashing in a wide-shouldered, padded doublet of green wool trimmed with bands of plum-colored silk embroidered in gold thread. Strips of the same velvet could be seen under the slashes in his padded sleeves and short breeches, and he wore a double ruff around his neck, the under one of white linen, the over one of lace, matching smaller ruffs at his wrists. His boots of shining black leather, which ended above his knees, were lace-cuffed, too, and his hat of black velvet, narrow-brimmed, with a soft crown and two white ostrich plumes on the left side, rode jauntily on his head. His short cloak of green wool, lined in black velvet, was thrown back over his right shoulder, prominently displaying his rapier, the one weapon he carried.

The warriors stared at him as he stepped back in his boat, and he knew from their expressions that he had been wise to dress in his best clothes, which he had accumulated painfully over a period of years and had worn only twice before. Successful negotiations with Powhatan could bring prosperity to Jamestown on a scale that would make the directors of the London Company rejoice, and they would reward the president of the Council accordingly. Smith stared at the trees on the banks of the James River, and his men wondered what he was thinking, for they had never seen such exalted determination in his face. They could not know, of course, that he was reflecting on the inadequacy of his hat; it needed a final touch, perhaps a band of expensive pearls at the base of the crown, to make it complete.

There were numerous bends in the river, and when the boats swept around the last of them, revealing the capital of the Chickahominy Confederation directly ahead, it was Smith's turn to gape. He was unprepared for the sight of a large city and he quickly estimated that Powhatan was surrounded by at least six or seven thousand of his subjects. The community was built on seven hills, and its buildings were laid out carefully in concentric circles on each, with large houses at the crests.

The variety of dwellings was remarkable, and Smith saw not only the crude huts that reminded him of the village of the Pamaunke but numerous sturdy buildings made of skins which were stretched over poles and supported by a latticework of reeds. There were round and oblong houses of clay, many substantial homes of wood that were similar to the dwellings of the Jamestown settlers, and Smith counted a score of extraordinarily long buildings which he guessed were either dormitories or meeting halls. Obviously the civilization of the Chickahominy was considerably more advanced than was that of a subject tribe like the Pamaunke.

A large crowd had gathered to watch the arrival of the
strangers, and as the colonists were led through the city,
Smith observed everything of interest. The people, he saw,
were much taller than the Pamaunke, and many of the men
towered above the visitors. The warriors, all armed with
tomahawks and knives or bows and arrows, wore leather
shirts, leggings, and moccasins trimmed with what appeared
to be seeds of various colors. Not one of the inhabitants had
smeared paint on his face, Smith was pleased to note, but
many sported headbands in which one or more feathers were
stuck, and he realized that his ostrich plumes were causing a
great deal of comment. The women were dressed in simple,
calf-length garments of leather, and Smith was surprised to
see that they wore their hair in a variety of distinctive styles,
each of which apparently had some special meaning. The
children of both sexes were naked, and there seemed to be
hundreds of dogs underfoot.

It would be inaccurate to call the Chickahominy "red-
skins," Smith thought, for they were no darker than the
tanned members of the English community, and it occurred
to him that they were approximately the same shade as a
number of Welshmen he had known. What impressed him
most about these natives was their striking vitality; all of them
seemed to be in glowing health, and he had never seen such
handsome people. Several of the women, who showed no
shyness whatsoever, had delicate, chiseled features, and he
discovered that they piqued his curiosity.

Most of the houses, he noted as he was taken past them,
seemed to be family dwellings, but some were reserved for
old men or elderly squaws, who sat in the open, cross-legged,
their deeply lined faces and unblinking eyes turned toward
the strangers. There were stone-lined pits outside some of the
houses, but several of the more substantial homes whose
door flaps of animal skins were open revealed indoor cooking
places, with holes cut in the ceilings to let out the smoke.

In a depression between two of the hills, thirty or more
high platforms of wood, each supported by poles at least

fifteen feet long, were laid out in three concentric circles, and at the bases of several were pots and jars of food, items of clothing, beads, and weapons. The natives, who had been laughing and talking animatedly as they accompanied the Englishmen, suddenly fell silent, and when Smith caught a glimpse of a still-blanket-wrapped figure on one of the platforms, he realized that the raised tables were the final resting places of those who had died.

The mystery of the unusually long buildings was unraveled when the party moved past two of them, and Smith was pleased to find that his guess had been right; both were dormitories and seemed to be the homes of younger men. Evidently these warriors were unmarried, and Smith saw that only a few of them wore feathers in their headbands. Unlike the other members of the tribe, who were displaying friendly curiosity toward the colonists, the braves who lived in the long houses showed signs of open hostility. Some of them scowled, others shook their fists, and two or three fingered the knives at their waists. Smith, after briefly pondering the best way to reply, smiled blandly at the youths, but placed his hand on the hilt of his rapier with sufficient emphasis to make certain that they saw and appreciated the gesture.

The native escorts and their guests came at last to the highest of the hills, and after walking a part of the distance toward the top, past concentric rows of houses, they halted before several small buildings of clay, which were offered to the captain's men. Smith himself, it appeared, was to be given quarters higher on the slope. Before he left his followers he inspected their huts and, seeing that the little rooms were clean, although devoid of furniture, he was satisfied. Before leaving his companions he could not resist putting on a brief exhibition for the crowd, which numbered in the hundreds, and he ordered his men to fall into line in front of the huts. There they marched and drilled in unison with their pikes; their maneuvers caused the throng to cheer loudly, and several warriors, not to be outdone, promptly demonstrated their own talents by dancing wildly.

Again the crowd shouted, and when the braves who were accompanying Smith urged him to go up the hill with them, he was able to leave his men with an easy conscience, knowing that in spite of the language barriers they and their hosts were in rapport. Near the summit, directly below an imposing house with a sloping thatched roof that stood alone, was a circle of smaller buildings made of skins stretched on poles, and a young man with four pure-white feathers in his headband waited before one of them, his arms folded across his chest.

When he saw the visitor approaching, he stepped forward and raised his right hand in greeting. Smith, realizing that a bow might be misinterpreted as a sign of subservience, drew his rapier, saluted with a flourish, and then slid the blade back into its sheath. The Indians who had accompanied him had halted some feet below the level on which he stood, and he saw that they were careful not to move closer to the circle of houses. This, apparently, was forbidden ground.

The young warrior, still extending his arm with the palm of his hand raised, began to speak in a clear deep voice. "Welcome to the land of the Chickahominy," he said slowly, and Smith understood every word. "The mighty braves whose numbers are as great as the drops of rain that fall from the skies welcome the chief of the tribe-from-across-the-water. The great Powhatan, Chief of Chiefs, welcomes his brother. All-powerful Ek, the most potent of the gods, who rises each morning in the east and vanishes each night in the west, welcomes the warrior-who-comes-in-peace. And Dalan, youngest of the sons of Powhatan, welcomes the stranger."

Dalan finished his formal greeting and smiled. At that instant the visitor saw someone looking at him from the entrance to a house on the far side of the circle. He had the quick impression that an extremely attractive young woman had been watching him, but before he could catch another glimpse of her she disappeared. Dalan saw her, too, and frowned.

"The only sister of Dalan," he said, "forgets her place as a woman, and there is no one who can correct her, for the great Powhatan lets her do as she pleases." He dismissed her with a gesture. "Come," he said. "The chief of the tribe-from-across-the-water is hungry. He will eat, and then the Chief of Chiefs will greet him."

He led the captain inside the nearest house, and Smith was surprised to see a bed of soft boughs in one corner, between two low tables. On the nearest of these was a steaming bowl of food that had obviously been placed there only a few minutes previously. A robe that seemed to be made of rabbit skins sewn together was spread out in front of the table, and when Dalan waved toward it, the guest sat down. Apparently he was expected to eat alone and, although he was not hungry, he could not offend his hosts, so he picked up the bowl.

In the meantime a trio of young warriors appeared with the packs containing Smith's belongings, and when they placed the bundles on the far side of the room he jumped to his feet, hurried to the smallest of the sacks, and removed his double-edged dagger from it. Savages might eat with their fingers, but he was a civilized man, and he returned to the rug with his knife, which he used to spear the food. From its texture he saw that the meat was buffalo steak, which he detested; its taste was too pungent for his palate and always gave him indigestion. To his surprise, however, the flavor was pleasant, the meat was tender, and the corn and other vegetables that had been mixed into the stew were delicious. Several herbs had been used in the preparation of the dish, and he had to admit to himself that, although the Chickahominy were barbarians, their cooking was superb.

Dalan, who was watching him closely, looked unhappy. "The chief of the tribe-from-across-the-sea enjoys his meal?"

"Very much." Smith had more appetite than he had thought.

"The only sister of Dalan prepared it herself for the guest of her father. She forced Dalan to promise that he would reveal what she had done, but only if the guest liked the meal. Now," he added gloomily, "she will be even worse than before and will listen to no one."

Smith, who was thinking of his meeting with Powhatan, scarcely heard the remark as he speared the last chunk of meat in the bowl, wiped his dagger on the ground, and stood. His larger packs contained his gifts for the chief, and when he hinted at their contents, Dalan immediately summoned two husky warriors, who lifted the bundles onto their shoulders and fell in behind the visitor as they started toward the house on the crest.

As they drew nearer to it Smith saw that it was made of several layers of skins, drawn over poles, and plaited reeds. It was circular in shape and, directly in front of the entrance flap, which was open, a small replica of it stood on a narrow platform. The Englishman caught a glimpse of a carved wooden doll, painted yellow, standing inside the toy house, and he was faintly startled when Dalan solemnly prostrated himself before it. Then he realized that the puppet was undoubtedly an idol, the symbol of the sun god, Ek, so he hastily bowed to it, too, feeling slightly foolish.

Light entered the house through a smoke hole in the ceiling and through a rear flap, which was also open, and when Smith stepped inside the building he saw that it was completely bare except for a mound of furs on the far side of the large room. Before he could recover from his surprise he realized that a tall bulky man was entering from the opposite direction. They looked at each other, and Smith knew at once that he was in the presence of the chief of the Chickahominy Confederation, for no other native carried himself with such haughty pride.

Powhatan appeared to be about fifty years old, and his black hair was liberally sprinkled with gray. He was heavier than the younger, more athletic men, but he carried his weight gracefully, and his paunch in no way detracted from his natural dignity. In spite of his bulk, his skin seemed to be

drawn tightly across his high cheekbones, his prominent
nose, and his sharp chin, but his eyes were his most arresting
feature. Dark and piercing, they took in every detail of the
guest's appearance, and Smith felt uncomfortable. Never
before had he been subjected to such a frank scrutiny, but he
decided at once to employ the same rude manners, and he
stared at the chief in return.

The clothes Powhatan wore were certainly the most elaborate Indian attire Smith had ever seen, and he was doubly
relieved that he had taken the trouble to change into his own
finery. The shoulder seams of the native's short deerskin
jerkin were decorated with red and yellow braid made from
dyed and plaited porcupine quills, and elk's teeth fringed the
jerkin's sleeves and hem. A broad band of buckskin encircled
Powhatan's thick waist, holding together the open sides of the
garment, and the deep neck opening was laced with intricately braided leather thongs. His moccasins were like those
of his subjects, but the side seams of his high, close-fitting
leggings were covered with more red and yellow porcupine
quills, and hanging from his right shoulder was a spectacular
cape. It was a buffalo robe, with the fur turned to the inside.
The outer skin was brightly painted in geometric designs with
an insistently recurring motif of yellow concentric circles,
which, Smith realized at once, identified the chief with the
sun god.

His headgear was unique, too. The band around his
forehead was thickly studded with upright feathers, and the
Englishman, who was making a study of birds in his spare
time, recognized the red, white, and brown plumes as the
feathers of the red-tailed hawk, which the colonists at Jamestown had noted one day in the early fall, flying south.

Powhatan seemed to be satisfied with his own inspection of
the stranger, and he grunted at his son, who immediately
withdrew, as did the warriors who had carried Smith's gifts.
Seating himself on the pile of furs, he raised his hand briefly
in a weary token gesture, then lowered it again. "Powhatan,

chief of the Chickahominy, chief of the Confederation, son of Ek and father of his people, greets his friend," he said rapidly, his tone indicating a desire to dispense with ceremony.

Smith, who had prepared a long address, instantly discarded it. "John Smith, president of the Council of Jamestown, deputy of James, King of England and Scotland, captain of the armies of the New World, greets his friend," he replied, hoping the titles he had hastily bestowed on himself sounded impressive.

There was silence for a moment as their eyes met and held. Each was testing the strength of the other and each realized that the man opposite him was no ordinary person. Either as allies or enemies, each was worthy of the other's respect.

Suddenly Powhatan turned and pointed to the bundles. "You have brought gifts. I will accept them now. Then we will talk. You have strange weapons that make a loud noise and kill animals or men at a great distance. I want many such weapons. You have many mouths to feed in the town you are building on the shores of Chesapeake. In my storehouses there is much grain and jerked meat. So we will bargain, you and I."

Smith grinned and relaxed as he cut the ropes that held the two packs. Powhatan was a man with whom he could deal, and he knew of no complications that would prevent them from enjoying a mutually profitable association.

Ru-Sa toyed nervously with the thick single braid of hair hanging over her left shoulder that showed she was a grandmother, and she wished, not for the first time, that she had never accepted her position as custodian of the Chief of Chiefs' only daughter. Originally she had thought her duties would be light, as the girl was mature now and consequently did not require either a nurse or a serving maid. But there were times when Pocahontas would try the patience of the gods, and this was one of them.

It would have been better for the girl, Ru-Sa reflected, if she had not been the one female in a family of many boys. It was unfortunate, too, that she was so attractive, and even worse that she knew it. She stood now, half hidden behind the entrance flap, peering up at her father's lodge, and Ru-Sa, sighing, had to admit that it was terribly difficult to chastise anyone so lovely. Pocahontas's features were delicately feminine, but Ru-Sa knew from experience that her gentle mouth could become hard when her will was crossed, and that her soft brown eyes, which the young warriors praised so lavishly on the feast nights when they composed songs in her honor, could blaze when she was vexed. It was sometimes hard to realize that a girl who looked so demure could be so headstrong.

At the moment she looked particularly shy and modest, almost like a child. Her hair, so black it showed blue highlights when the sun shone on it, fell loosely down her back and was held in place smoothly at the crown of her head by a narrow band of calfskin decorated with tiny white seeds that identified her as a maiden. Her calf-length tunic, like those of all Chickahominy women, was made of two pieces of soft deerskin, but Pocahontas's garment was joined at the shoulders by clusters of multicolored thongs knotted to form tassels. Even the daughter of the great Powhatan had no real right to display such symbols of rank, but the Chief of Chiefs himself sometimes encouraged her to flout traditions. Obviously she enjoyed defying custom in every way she could, for the unsewn, overlapping sides of her tunic were belted with a wide buckskin sash which was secured by another large tassel of brightly colored thongs.

Other girls were always aware of their proper place in the community and took care to keep in the background at all times, but Pocahontas actually seemed to take pride in her unusual beauty. Ru-Sa thought bitterly that it was no wonder the young braves always stared at her when she walked down to the river. Her clothes certainly were not responsible, for they were very much like those of the other maidens, even though she insisted on flaunting the tassels, and Ru-Sa concluded that it was the way she carried herself that made the difference. She seemed to be conscious of her broad shoulders, high breasts, and slender waist, her long thighs and perfectly formed legs, and her appreciation of herself made the young warriors aware of her too. Yet Ru-Sa had to concede, as she often did to her friends, that the girl's conduct was decorous; at no time had she behaved in a manner that would cause her to be sent to the lodge where the Women Without Virtue were kept. Although nearly every brave in the Confederation who had won the three feathers of valor entitling him to take a wife had courted her, she was still chaste.

But she certainly could be mischievous enough to drive others to distraction. Right now she was laughing softly to herself as she concealed herself behind the flap. She had kicked off her moccasins, and the way her bare toes curled and wriggled was positively indecent. Ru-Sa lost what remained of her patience and could keep silent no longer. "Pocahontas," she said irritably, "come away from the entrance at once!"

The girl giggled more loudly but did not move. "Did you see him, Ru-Sa?"

"I did not!" the older woman declared emphatically.

"Then you missed a sight as wonderful as the flowering of the buds when the snows melt." Her feet were still, but her toes seemed to be dancing. "He saw me too. I know he did. He looked straight at me."

Ru-Sa was shocked. "You are the daughter of the Chief of Chiefs."

"So I am," Pocahontas replied comfortably. "Every maiden of the Chickahominy will want to meet him, but I shall meet him first."

"I forbid you to talk like one of those women who live in the lodge-by-the-water. I forbid it, do you hear?"

The girl turned, her eyes round and innocent. "Is it wrong to greet one who has come from afar, Ru-Sa?"

"Your father has two wives who will welcome the stranger if the great Powhatan wishes our women to make him comfortable."

"It was I who prepared the dish of buffalo and young corn for him, not my father's wives. Besides, they are old and I am young."

"What does that mean?" Ru-Sa asked indignantly.

"He, too, is young and very beautiful. The eyes of the old are dim, and only the young may see each other clearly."

The old woman was genuinely distressed. "Pocahontas, you are wicked, and if you think such thoughts the great god Ris will come down from the moon to punish you. Perhaps even the all-seeing, all-knowing Ek will——"

"Do you suppose that Ek and Ris do not know of this man?" the girl retorted. "Do you suppose they do not shine down on him and watch over him in whatever strange place he makes his home? I want to know more of such places, Ru-Sa. I want to learn all there is to know about all people!"

"You will become the squaw of a chief, as is fitting for the daughter of the great Powhatan, and you will give many fine, strong sons to your husband and his tribe," Ru-Sa said virtuously, trying to sound convincing.

Pocahontas stamped her foot, and a dangerous gleam appeared in her eyes. "You would not talk that way if you had seen him! Everything about him was different. I see the braves of many nations when they come here to pay homage to my father, but not one of them looks like him. His clothes, his hair, his moccasins—even the long knife that he carried at his side—were strange and wonderful."

"It may be," the elderly custodian said fearfully, "that he is one of the devil-gods who live beneath the earth."

The idea was so absurd that Pocahontas laughed merrily. "He is a man," she replied emphatically.

"All the more reason——"

"Besides, I do not hold to the old beliefs. How do you know there are devil-gods below the earth? Have you ever seen them? Has anyone ever seen them?"

Ru-Sa covered her ears with her hands, averted her face, and fled to the far end of the room.

Pocahontas was satisfied; the foe was routed, and there was no need for further conversation on the subject. She walked lightly to her own side of the room and sat down on her bough bed. For a moment or two she stared thoughtfully into space. Then she jumped to her feet again and feverishly began to rearrange her hair in front of a small square of burnished metal that rested on one of the horizontal poles holding up the wall. She swept the long locks to one side, braided them, coiled them over her right ear, and secured them with a comb made of white bone.

Behind her, in the corner, was a shelf of woven reeds, and after rummaging around on it hastily, she found what she was seeking and removed her dress. Then, no longer in a hurry, she smiled dreamily as she put on a handsome costume of two pieces in its place. The top was a deep, capelike collar of kidskin, completely covered with rows of blue-black shells and vivid orange-colored seeds sewn close together. It fitted snugly over her shoulders and stopped a few inches below her breasts, leaving her diaphragm bare, and below it she wore a narrow skirt of cream kidskin, slit at the bottom on each side, which hung from a seeded hip band decorated in the same fashion as her collar.

Sitting again, she slid her feet into flat thick buckskin soles and began to lace their orange-dyed thongs to her ankles. Ru-Sa, aware for the first time of what she was doing, stared across the hut at her in horror. "What are you doing?"

"I changed my clothes," Pocahontas said quietly.

"That is the ceremonial dress of Ris and is only to be worn at the feasts each month when Ris shows us his full face."

"Ris has seen me in this dress before." The girl stood, straightened her skirt, and started toward the entrance.

"You will offend the moon god," the old woman wailed.

"Something pretty can offend no one, not even a god,"
was the logical reply. "And this dress is very pretty. I know the
stranger will agree. You will see."

For a moment Ru-Sa was too startled to react; then she
hurried after her charge. "You must not interrupt the great
Powhatan when he is in council with a warrior from a distant
land."

Pocahontas evaded her custodian's grasp and ran out into
the open, laughing. Two or three braves and several members of the stranger's party were gathered in a clearing below
her house, demonstrating their skill with long metal spears
that belonged to the foreigners. She inspected the visitors
briefly, and immediately lost interest in them. As she had
suspected, their skins were pale, like that of their leader, but
they lacked his beauty and virility. She knew that all of the
men had stopped throwing spears and were watching her, so
in spite of her exuberance she forced herself to walk at a slow,
dignified pace, her hips swaying a little as she climbed to the
crest and entered the lodge of her father.

Powhatan and the stranger were deeply engrossed in conversation and did not see her, so she crept closer to them,
hoping they would look up. Women were not allowed to
speak when in the presence of men until they were granted
permission, and her father would be very angry if she failed to
remember her proper place. Within certain limits she knew
she could do as she pleased and that he would approve, but
the least sign of disrespect always made him violently angry.
Her best tactic, she thought, would be to halt near
them and wait until they happened to glance in her direction. In the meantime, she told herself, there was nothing to
prevent her from staring at the stranger as much as she
pleased, and her heart pounded furiously.

Smith was the first to realize that someone else had come
into the building, and he looked up casually, then promptly
forgot what he was saying. He was always sensitive to a pretty

face and a well-turned figure, and the girl standing no more than six feet from him was the most ravishing creature he had seen since his last night in London. He warned himself to be careful, however, for Powhatan became aware of her presence, too, and the fond, proprietary look in his eye indicated that she might be one of his wives.

"Why are you here?" the Chief of Chiefs asked brusquely, trying to hide the pleasure he always felt when he saw her.

Pocahontas crossed her hands over her breasts and looked down at the ground. "The mothers and grandmothers of the women of the Chickahominy, and their mothers and grandmothers before them," she said meekly, "were charged by the gods to give food and drink to all who come as friends. I, too, bear that charge."

Her mock humility did not fool Powhatan. He knew precisely why she had come to the lodge, and he frowned for a moment, then reconsidered. He studied the girl and his guest in turn, and Pocahontas, who knew him so well that she could always divine his thoughts, was elated. He would make no objections if the pale warrior chose to pay court to her. What she did not know was that Powhatan's thoughts were more complex than she imagined; he was reflecting that her appearance might soften this shrewd visitor, for he was discovering that Smith drove a hard bargain and was demanding considerable quantities of the best furs as well as food in return for his powerful noise-making weapons.

"Smith, King of James," the Chief of Chiefs said, "Pocahontas is the daughter of Powhatan."

John Smith, jumping to his feet as he acknowledged the introduction, told himself sternly to watch his step. He had philandered successfully and discreetly with others' wives on occasion and had escaped detection, but a man's daughter was untouchable, particularly when the man was as powerful as Powhatan. Yet even the cautious Smith could not help but respond to the charming and radiant girl who stood before him and, removing his hat, he swept the ground with it in a gallant bow. To his astonishment she gasped, and when he straightened he saw she was looking in dismay at his hat. He was annoyed, for the plumes had been expensive; if he remembered correctly, they had each cost three gold angels, far more than he could afford.

Powhatan looked at the headgear, too, and his face became grim. "No young brave," he said sternly, "becomes a full warrior until he slays three enemies. He may not enjoy the rights of a man until he has been awarded three feathers."

Smith understood and grinned broadly. "We have different customs," he said, addressing the chief but speaking for the benefit of Pocahontas. "I have killed so many enemies in battle that I have lost count of the number." That wasn't the strict truth, of course, but details were unimportant when he was trying to impress a girl.

Powhatan accepted the statement without bothering to demand proof. No man, obviously, could become a chief until he had demonstrated his valor, and the way of the strangers-from-across-the-sea seemed to be very much like those of the Indians. What bothered the chief was the unmistakable reaction of his daughter; she made no attempt to hide her relief, and he decided to tell her later, in private, that she would need to learn the art of dissembling. A man often became frightened and rejected a woman when she showed him her feelings too clearly. But even as Powhatan looked at her, he changed his mind, for he suddenly realized there was little he could teach Pocahontas that she did not already know.

A sudden transformation seemed to take place in her, and she looked shyly at the ground. "Does Smith wish food to ease his hunger or drink to still his thirst?" she asked, both her manner and voice indicating that she was the most fragile of creatures.

"Smith," the captain replied heartily, "has already eaten a delicious meal. He was told by the brother of Pocahontas that she prepared it with her own hands, and Smith is grateful to her." There were a number of items left in one of his packs of gifts; he had been saving them until the end of the meeting, but he walked quickly to the bundle and, reaching inside, brought out two rolls of cloth. One was a thick, unbleached wool, of the sort the colonists used to make blankets and children's clothes, and the other was a bright blue satin that most of the settlers considered too garish. "Smith is grateful to the daughter of Powhatan for the favor she has shown him," he said, handing her the bolts with a flourish.

Pocahontas's dainty fingers caressed the materials, the first she had ever felt. The wool was even softer than the finest leather, and the silk was so sleek and glossy that it excited her. It would be undignified, she knew, to burst into tears, and she made a desperate effort to control her emotions. "Never has Pocahontas been given such wonderful gifts," she said, her voice trembling.

Smith looked so pleased that Powhatan decided to adjourn the trade discussion until the following day; obviously his strategy was working. Pulling himself to his feet, he walked to the entrance at the rear of the lodge that he alone used. "When Ris, the moon god, appears," he said, "Powhatan will share a feast with Smith, and Pocahontas will prepare it. When Ek shines again, there will be more talk of weapons and furs and grain. We have spoken much of furs and grains. Tomorrow," he added, "we will speak of weapons."

He was gone, and Smith was alone with the girl. She stood smiling at him and hugging the rolls of cloth, and she looked so attractive that he had to remind himself forcibly that she was his host's daughter. He felt more comfortable when she broke the spell by offering to show him the community and the surrounding countryside, and he accepted quickly. Pocahontas left her gifts in her own house as they started down the hill and then guided him around the village. Smith was interested in everything he saw and wanted to know more about the barter shops, where the natives traded goods with each other, and the communal farms, where some of the

squaws grew corn and vegetables for all, but the girl gave him
no chance to speak of these things.

She bombarded him with questions about his own world,
which he could only describe to her with difficulty, and no
sooner did he satisfy her curiosity on one subject than she
launched into another. She gave him no opportunity to
enjoy the stir he created wherever they walked, and when he
discovered that the natives whom they passed stared as hard at
Pocahontas as they did at him, he felt faintly nettled.
Nevertheless, her eagerness to learn, her readiness to accept
whatever he told her gave him an increased sense of self-
importance. He could not recall the time when a woman had
made him feel so wise, and when they returned to the high
hill he realized that her company stimulated him enormously.

It was pleasant to bask in the adulation of a young pretty
girl, but at the same time he did not permit himself to lose
sight of the reasons he had come to the interior. It occurred to
him that he might be able to turn the impression he was
making on Pocahontas to his advantage; he had observed that
her father doted on her, so it was possible that through her he
might be able to obtain better terms in his negotiations with
Powhatan, who was the most realistically astute bargainer he
had ever encountered.

Pocahontas had appreciated his gift of the bolts of cloth so
much that he wondered what else he might give her to bind
her even more firmly to him, and after pondering the matter
for several minutes he halted abruptly, told her he had an
errand to perform, and promised to rejoin her shortly. The
huts in which his men had been quartered were nearby, and
he was momentarily disappointed when he saw they had all
gone off somewhere, but that did not stop him from searching their belongings.

He hoped that some of them had brought books with them
on the journey, for Pocahontas seemed to be a girl with an
insatiable thirst for knowledge. He had once or twice

encountered that kind of woman and he was sure nothing would flatter her more than to pander to her belief that she possessed an intellect. After hastily looking through the packs of some of his men, he found a thick copy of the Bible and quickly leafed through it. It was the so-called "Bishops' Bible," containing both the Old and New Testaments, and although Smith had not read it in many years, he had been nevertheless familiar with it from his childhood, as it was used in all English churches. He wished he could give Pocahontas something livelier, but when he saw that the Bible was illustrated throughout with crude but effective pictures of characters dressed in clothing reminiscent of the reign of Henry VIII, he decided it would suffice.

Taking it with him, he climbed to his own quarters and there picked up the handbook of Indian words and phrases that Sir Walter Raleigh had given him. The glossary was much larger now than it had been when he had first received it, for he had himself been adding to it constantly ever since his visit to the Pamaunke, and he thought that perhaps Pocahontas, by using it in reverse, might with patience glean a smattering of English.

She was waiting for him at the entrance to her house, and she stood aside like a well-bred squaw so he could precede her into the room. An old woman was squatting in a far corner, and he was somewhat surprised to see that she was glaring at him. It annoyed him to be encumbered by the presence of a chaperone, but as Pocahontas ignored the old woman, he did the same.

They sat together on the ground in the center of the room, and he showed her the glossary, carefully explained how to use it, and told her he was lending it to her until his next visit to the land of the Chickahominy. He intended to publish a complete handbook of the native tongues when he returned to England, so he had no intention of allowing her to keep it permanently. He was pleased to see that the glossary fascinated her, and he was astonished at how rapidly she seemed to absorb the principles of the alphabet. Then he gave her the Bible as a gift, and he knew when he saw her ecstatic face that his impulse had been brilliant. Powhatan's trade terms would unquestionably be more generous when he learned of his daughter's joy.

Pocahontas did not thank him but instead turned to the old woman in the corner. "Ru-Sa will go," she said firmly.

The custodian sighed deeply, stood, and walked slowly out of the room, shaking her head. And Smith, who was startled, could only conclude that Pocahontas was expressing her gratitude in the only way she knew by openly inviting him to make love to her. Dalliance with the daughter of the Chief of Chiefs could lead to countless troublesome complications, and he struggled briefly with himself as she walked to a shelf on the far side of the room, took something from it, and then rejoined him.

She sat down again close to him, and Smith fought a losing battle against temptation. Night was falling, the growing darkness emphasized the intimate atmosphere, and he became increasingly conscious of her beauty. No man could resist such an opportunity, regardless of the problems that might result, and he shifted his position slightly so that they now sat side by side.

Pocahontas, aware of his nearness, hid her elation. Ru-Sa and the squaws of her brothers loved to tell her that she was ignorant of the ways of men, but she had long felt that she had a special gift, that she possessed a sure, instinctive knowledge that would enable her to handle any warrior. Even though Smith's eyes were guarded and his movements controlled, she knew he was as interested in her as the young braves who watched her so avidly whenever they saw her. Smith, as befitted a mature warrior, concealed his admiration, but she wasn't deceived. She wished her brothers' wives could see her at this moment, then perhaps they would stop their ceaseless prattling. But in the next breath she decided their presence would spoil everything, for she certainly didn't want to share this exciting stranger with anyone.

Last year she had sometimes joined the very young braves when they tested their strength and skill in games, and she had occasionally allowed one or another of them to kiss her, until her father had learned of the practice and had abruptly put an end to it. She hadn't cared, as none of the youths had meant anything to her, and she hadn't particularly enjoyed the experience with them. But there was no comparison between those callow warriors and Smith, and she felt an almost overwhelming desire to be kissed by him.

No sooner did she recognize her own feelings, however, than a sense of panic swept over her. Perhaps Ru-Sa was right, perhaps she would someday be sent to the lodge of the Women Without Virtue. Smith's desire for her, which was so obvious to her, was very flattering, but she was the daughter of the Chief of Chiefs and she had to act accordingly. She would encourage him but she would remind him that she was no ordinary woman and she could best accomplish this dual purpose by bestowing a gift on him. Then he would understand perfectly. She smiled and held out her right hand, pleased that the impulse that had led her to get something for him a few moments ago had been right. "Smith has given me so much that I must give him something in return," she said softly.

He nodded and moistened his lips, which were suddenly dry. Then he realized that she was holding an object in her hand, and he took it from her. As nearly as he could make out in the twilight, it was a hollow reed, approximately four inches long and roughly the thickness of his little finger. One end had been carved into the shape of a mouthpiece, and in the center had been burned several concentric circles, the symbol of the sun god.

He stared at it blankly, and Pocahontas reached out, caught hold of his wrist, and shook the reed gently. The tip of a tiny arrow appeared at the open end, and she pointed at it with a slender forefinger. "Women," she said, "are not permitted to use the weapons of mighty warriors. So I must protect myself with this blow arrow, which has been dipped in the poison of the snake-that-rattles. I give it to Smith, so he will remember Pocahontas." Seeing him hesitate, she added more firmly, "Take it. I have others."

They looked at each other intently.

Smith, who had been about to slide his free arm around her waist, let his hand fall limply to his side. Some of the girls due to arrive soon from England might interest him, he thought; if not, he had seen a few Indian women on the seacoast who were mildly attractive. "I will remember Pocahontas," he said, and told himself he was guilty of understatement.

June, 1608

Thanks to John Smith's foresight and planning, one hundred and twenty new colonists who arrived at Jamestown, some in the winter and some in early spring, were spared most of the inconveniences and discomforts that the agents of the London Company had warned them to expect in Virginia. They came ashore from the *Susan Constant* and her new sister ship, the *Phoenix*, with feelings of mixed anticipation and dread, ready to return home at once if life in America proved to be too primitive. To their astonishment they were quartered in sturdy, simple houses that had already been built for them, each family was given ample provisions of corn and dried meat from the community's bulging storehouses, and each received a fair share of the fresh supplies the barks had carried in their holds.

Other equally pleasant surprises awaited the recruits too. Friends of several Council members in England had been spreading the rumor that Captain Smith was a despot who had to be replaced as president if the colony was to survive, but the new arrivals quickly discovered that he was no tyrant. He visited every house, and his interviews, which would have been stiff and formal had he possessed less tact, were pleasant social occasions. He assigned men with military experience to guard duty, farmers went to work growing corn and tobacco, and those who had been artisans happily resumed the practice of their old trades. The men were delighted that he was so reasonable, and the women, captivated by his charm, eagerly accepted the menial tasks he allotted to them.

He wisely made no overt attempt to impress the captains of the barks, who would carry word of the colony's progress back to the directors of the London Company, and he was undisturbed by the secret complaints of his enemies, as he knew his accomplishments spoke for themselves. Jamestown showed great promise of becoming the first permanent English settlement in the New World, and Smith was certain he would rightfully receive the credit for achieving what no one, not even Sir Walter Raleigh, had been able to do before him. He took care, however, to speak modestly of his success at the farewell dinner he gave for the masters of the shops shortly before they sailed back to England in May, and he carefully emphasized the view that the future of the colony was still precarious. His unassuming air made it impossible for his jealous Council colleagues to belittle him, and his cleverness in warding off their attacks encouraged him to end his speech on an even more somber note. A single error in judgment, he said, could ruin the whole enterprise, but he assured the ship captains that he had no intention of making that mistake.

The *Susan Constant* and the *Phoenix* sailed the following morning, but Smith wasted no time congratulating himself on the brilliance of his maneuvers. His fame in England seemed to be assured, yet there had been a measure of truth in what he had told the captains: Jamestown was not yet self-sufficient, and there was much work still to be done. He was anxious to consolidate his gains, and the new settlers added to his problems; there were more mouths to feed, more lives to protect. The best means of insuring their well-being and safety was through increased trade and friendship with the natives, and so, even before the barks disappeared over the horizon, he sent a Chesapeake messenger to the interior with a flattering invitation to Powhattan of the Chickahominy. Smith, King of James, he said, requested the honor of a return visit from the mighty Chief of Chiefs.

Powhatan accepted promptly, sending word back to the colony that he would arrive in a moon's time, and Smith made careful preparations for the event. The Council was horrified by his disclosure that he intended to trade a cannon for a year's supply of grain, but no one could refute his logical arguments. It would be many months, he pointed out, before the colony would grow all of the food the present residents needed, and by that time still another company of settlers would arrive from England. Common sense dictated the necessity of keeping the storehouses filled, for there was no guarantee that the weather would continue to favor the settlers' crops. It was already very warm, the summer might be hot and dry, and a single poor season could mean ultimate starvation for all.

He was not going to give the Indians either of the new guns that the barks had just brought from England, he told the Council, but he said he could see no loss in trading away one or even two old outmoded culverins. These little cannon, which threw small iron balls weighing seventeen pounds, were no longer used by civilized artillery corps because their fire was notoriously inaccurate, and Smith further emphasized that they would be virtually useless in the event of war with the Naturals. Battles would inevitably take place in the forests rather than on open plains, which seemed to be nonexistent in America, hence a culverin's small shot would be ineffective against a foe protected by tall trees.

Captain Archer led the opposition to the plan, as usual, but he became confused when Smith sardonically explained that the ammunition of the new cannon, which weighed sixty pounds, would crash through trees and kill an enemy where a culverin's shot would not. And the discussion ended abruptly when Smith, in exasperation, declared that even a semieducated Christian required the better part of a year's instruction before he became a trained gunner; how then, he asked, could illiterate savages inflict damage on anyone, even if they gained possession of every artillery piece in the town's arsenal? The Council, shamed, voted him the right to deal with the Chickahominy as he saw fit.

One of the larger houses was vacated for Powhatan, and two smaller dwellings were made ready for the rest of his party. Hunters shot deer, bear, and buffalo, and Smith privately assigned two younger men to kill some wild dogs for the guests too. The day before the Indians were due to arrive, a former fisherman from Dover went out into Chesapeake Bay at dawn and came back at sunset, his boat filled with oysters, clams, and the crabs of the New World, which had curiously soft shells. The president himself brought down a brace of quail which he proposed to serve to the Chief of Chiefs and himself as a dish of special distinction, and the housewives used their precious wheat flour lavishly to bake bread and pastries for visitors who had never tasted such delicacies.

The entire town was ready to welcome the guests shortly after breakfast, but it was noon before the first of a long string of birchbark canoes floated down the James River and heralded the arrival of the Naturals. Smith had guessed that Powhatan might be accompanied by twenty or thirty warriors and had made plans accordingly, but even he was astonished at the size of the chief's entourage. There were sixty braves in the guard of honor, and the settlers in the watchtower at the main gate counted seventeen elders in the party too. The June heat was intense, but all of the natives wore heavy cloaks, and that of Powhatan, which was made entirely of feathers sewn close together on buffalo skin, looked particularly stifling.

Bringing up the rear was a canoe carrying three women, and the colonists, who had been prepared to entertain only men and had consequently made no preparations for female guests, were dismayed.

But Smith was unperturbed when the news was reported to him at the parade ground, where he and the others of the Council, backed by three files of pikemen, waited to receive the Indians. He met the emergency by asking Edward Wingfield to vacate his house for the women, and the request was such a fair one that it could not be refused; Wingfield had continued to live in the large and comfortable home he had first occupied by virtue of the position he had then held as the principal executive officer of the colony, and as Smith had never tried to dispossess him, he felt that the least he could do now was to comply. He hurried off to remove his belongings from the two-story building, while his colleagues, perspiring in their close-fitting doublets and thick multiple "cabbage" ruffs, watched the main gate through which the guests would come.

The first to appear were four brawny warriors in loincloths, and Smith noted at once that their faces and bodies were daubed with concentric circles of yellow paint, which signified that they had come on a mission of peace. Behind them marched two of Powhatan's sons, bearing gifts; then came the rest of the braves, who jostled each other and made no attempt to maintain even a semblance of a military formation as they returned the stares of the citizens of Jamestown. Powhatan walked alone, his carriage erect and his features expressionless, as his feathered headgear waved gently in the warm breeze.

The elders, who helped him administer the affairs of the many tribes he governed, were close at his heels, and some distance behind them came several slaves, young men who

had been captured in battle. They wore neither headpieces
nor robes, the crisscrossed marks of beatings they had received were plainly visible on their backs, and apparently
they had been included in the party merely to act as custodi-
ans for a number of goats, whom they led by ropes made of
plaited vines. Some distance behind the animals were two
middle-aged women in calf-length dresses of deerskin; they
looked vaguely familiar to Smith, who finally identified
them as the wives of the Chief of Chiefs. For a moment he
thought the initial reports on the number of women in the
entourage had been wrong, but then he saw the settlers
murmur in shocked excitement as they stared at the very tail
end of the procession. Peering past the two squaws, he felt a
surge of unexpected emotion as he caught a glimpse of
Pocahontas.

If she knew she was the center of attention, she gave no
sign of it, and Smith, who realized that she was inordinately
curious, marveled at her aplomb. She looked straight ahead,
not bothering to glance at the men and women about whom
she had asked him so many questions, and she seemed to be
unaware that she, of all the strangely attired savages, was
creating the greatest sensation. The furor she caused was
certainly justified, Smith thought, and by any standards she
looked appealing.

Her hair was held smoothly on the crown of her head by a
maiden's band of deerskin sewn with white seeds, and two
thick braids were looped to form large rings behind her ears.
But her clothing, judged by the conservative standards of the
settlers, was considerably less than decent. She wore a
breastband of sand-colored kidskin, and below her bare diaphragm was a tightly wrapped skirt of pale kidskin which fell
to her knees and was fastened on one hip by a carved sliver of
bone which pierced the leather. Even the sophisticated gentlemen of the Council gaped at her, and Smith found it
difficult to control a grin as he stepped forward to exchange
ceremonial greetings with Powhatan.

The addresses of welcome were interminable, and each member of the Council felt impelled to add something to the occasion. The Naturals, not to be outdone in courtesy, replied in kind, and the elders took turns echoing the flowery words of their chief. Smith was kept busy translating for both groups, but he was as bored as the spectators, as restless as the Indian warriors, and in spite of his desire to maintain the dignity befitting his position, he kept shifting his weight from one foot to the other on the bare, heat-dried earth of the parade ground.

During the first half hour or more of the ceremonies he could not see Pocahontas, as she was hidden somewhere at the rear of the huddle of visitors, but he became aware of her again during an especially dull speech that Matthew Scrivener had laboriously written and now insisted on making. She had edged to one side, past the slaves and their goats, and was looking intently at Smith. Feeling her eyes on him, he looked up and realized at once that she had changed her position so she could obtain an unobstructed view of him. He nodded to her rather stiffly, annoyed with himself because he felt his blood racing, and she responded instantly by smiling at him. He could not recall ever having seen such pure pleasure on the face of another person, and for no good reason he remembered his words of farewell to the captains of the barks. A single mistake could mean the end of Jamestown, and he told himself firmly that he must not forget it, no matter how great the provocation.

Not even the hardiest, most determined speakers could talk indefinitely in the enervating heat, and at last the ceremonies drew to a close. The Indians were shown to the quarters that had been made ready for them and they promptly reshuffled the arrangements to their own satisfaction and the amazement of their hosts. Powhatan kept the largest house for himself but immediately ordered animal skins placed over the windows, for he had never before slept in a place built with such strange openings, and they made him uneasy. His sons took one of the smaller homes, the elders crowded into Edward Wingfield's house, and the remaining dwelling was given to Pocahontas. Smith offered to make other buildings available, but his guests cheerfully refused and erected a number of tents on a portion of the parade ground for those who had no other shelter. This group included the young braves, the slaves, and Powhatan's wives, who shared a small tent near the pen that was put up for the goats.

A banquet was served in midafternoon, and most of the visitors ate heartily and indiscriminately. Smith noticed, however, that Powhatan only nibbled at the dishes placed before him, and when the meal ended he left so hurriedly that some of the Englishmen thought he was offended. To their infinite amusement he went out to the parade ground; there the slaves had slaughtered a goat, his wives had stewed it over an open fire, and he sat down to his meal in full view of the whole community. Plainly the goats were intended for his private fare, and he did not care who watched him eat.

His unusual personal habits did not interfere with his ability to drive a sharp bargain, however, as Smith discovered the following morning, after an evening of fruitless discussion in which both the Chickahominy elders and the members of the Jamestown Council took part. That meeting was a repetition of the earlier exchange of addresses; every man present was anxious to express his own views, and nothing tangible was accomplished.

Smith and Powhatan therefore met privately after breakfast, and in an atmosphere devoid of rhetoric they spent the day maneuvering cautiously. By the time they parted shortly before sundown, each had received a little less than he wanted and had been forced to part with a little more than he had intended to give. The Chickahominy agreed to supply Jamestown with eight hundred sacks of grain and two hundred baskets of dried meat; the settlers contracted to give the Indians two culverins, fifty muskets, and a suitable amount of gunpowder and ammunition. In addition, Powhatan himself was to receive a steel helmet and a pearl-handled pistol belonging to Gabriel Archer that he had admired.

As Smith walked across the town his most pressing problem was to persuade Archer to part with his pistol, and he was so deep in thought that he almost bumped into a group of adolescents engaged in some sort of athletic contest on the open square before the parade ground. Mentally tired after the long day of negotiation, he paused for a moment to watch them and was surprised to see that Pocahontas was one of the participants. Three English boys were turning cartwheels, and when they finished they challenged her to better their record. Her grace and physical co-ordination impressed the boys, but Smith could have predicted that she would beat them. What disturbed him was that she was completely absorbed in what she was doing and, unaware of his presence, was behaving with a youthful naturalness he had never before seen in her.

He had heretofore thought of her as an adult, and all through yesterday's banquet he had been conscious of her as a man could only be aware of the nearness of an attractive woman. At this moment, however, she looked no older than the adolescents, and for the first time in his life he thought seriously of the gray hairs that were beginning to appear at his temples. Pocahontas, he realized, was at least ten years his junior and she was far more at ease with these boys than she had ever been with him.

"I win!" she shouted jubilantly in English, and Smith was about to walk away, but at that instant she saw him.

She straightened her skirt, smoothed her hair, and through some form of necromancy she became a woman again as she came straight to him. "I have hoped to see John Smith," she said in halting English. "I came to Jamestown only to see you."

Her boldness startled him, but as he gazed at her he saw

she was not being unduly forward; he had consorted with so
many hussies in his day that he prided himself on his ability
to discern even the most subtly flirtatious attitude. But
Pocahontas was neither being coy nor thrusting herself at
him. She was telling him the simple truth, and she so
disconcerted him that he did not know what to reply.

"Are you happy to see me too?" she persisted.

The boys were watching them, and a film of perspiration
appeared on Smith's forehead. "It is good," he replied heavily in her own tongue, "to see the daughter of the great
Powhatan."

He bowed and started off, but to his consternation she
waved good-by to the youths and fell in beside him. "When
Smith came to the land of the Chickahominy," she said,
speaking her own language too, "Pocahontas showed him all
there was to see in the town of her father."

Smith knew that unless he took her hint and returned the
courtesy he would be guilty of a lack of civility that could, if
she complained to Powhatan, spoil the trade agreement he
had just hammered out. On the other hand he had no desire
to wander around Jamestown with a half-naked girl as attractive as Pocahontas. There would certainly be gossip, and
most of the things said about him would be right.

"Tonight," he said evasively, "there will be a feast for the
people of the Chickahominy who have come to Jamestown.
The young warriors will march and will make a fire with the
noise-sticks that kill our enemies." He wondered whether to
elaborate on the details of the artillery exhibition he intended
to stage, but the language barrier was too great for him to
translate his plans into her tongue. "It is the desire of Smith
that Pocahontas will be there. I will make a special fire for
her," he added recklessly, hoping the promise would satisfy
her.

"I will be there," she said and smiled brightly. "But it is not
yet night. Ek still shines on us."

"So he does." Smith sighed and thought he had rarely

encountered a more stubborn wench. "Have you seen the school?" he asked desperately. "I remember how eager you were to learn, and there you will find much that will interest you."

"I sat in the room where the young braves and the young squaws learn," she assured him gravely. "And he who is their chief gave Pocahontas many books in the tongue of the English as a gift."

Smith made a mental note to congratulate the schoolmaster, who had shown unusual perspicacity in presenting her with some textbooks. "There's the church too," he said, pointing to it.

"I saw it yesterday and spent much time there," she informed him. "I have read many pages of the Bible Smith gave to me, and it was my wish to see the church first, before I looked at any other building."

She had made up her mind to cling to him, he realized, and the stares of passing townspeople embarrassed him. So, as he could not be rid of her, he decided to make the best of an extraordinarily delicate situation. The blockhouse at the far end of the peninsula jutting out into the river was secluded, and the guard normally maintained there had been withdrawn during the visit of the Indians as a gesture of trust in Powhatan, so it was deserted too. He could show her the new cannon there and the view, which was the best the town had to offer; he could also suggest that she look out at the river flowing into the sea, which would be something of a novelty for someone who lived far inland. Perhaps, he thought, that would content her; however, even if it did not, they would be far less conspicuous out there than they were here in the center of town. He suggested they visit the place, and Pocahontas accepted the invitation with such alacrity that his heart pounded, and he wondered if he was being honest with himself. Surely no one who saw them and guessed their destination would possibly believe his motives were pure in taking such a captivating girl to the most isolated and private spot in Jamestown, and he wasn't certain he believed them himself.

They walked silently down the long neck of the peninsula through high grass, and Smith reached for Pocahontas's hand. She laughed and darted away from him, and he thought for a moment that his initial judgment had been wrong. He had credited her with too little feminine wisdom, but she was being coy and was playing a game with him, just as an English girl would have done. He quickly discovered he was mistaken, however, for she ran to a wild strawberry bush, plucked two of the large berries, and as she rejoined him she popped one into his mouth without displaying even a trace of self-consciousness. She ate the other and then unhesitatingly slid her hand into his.

As they approached the blockhouse several gulls rose into the air, screaming, and circled the building several times before flying away. Pocahontas watched them with grave pleasure and when Smith lifted the latch and stood aside for her, she paused at the threshold. It was wrong, according to her canons, for a woman to take precedence over a man, but the customs of the pale-skinned people-from-across-the-water were strange, and Smith refused to budge. He bowed with exaggerated deference, and when he grinned at her she walked into the blockhouse, her head high. As she had thought from the first time she had seen him look at her and had read his desire in his eyes, he wanted her as much as she wanted him.

Ru-Sa often accused her of being headstrong, of trying to force others to behave as she wished them to act, but there were some things Ru-Sa could not understand. It was not the old woman's fault, of course, and Pocahontas generously forgave her. After all, many years had passed since Ru-Sa had first been married, and it was unlikely that even then she had felt anything other than a sense of duty to her husband. Like most young squaws, she had probably been given by her father to a warrior she had never known, and it was difficult for any woman to love a stranger.

But the daughter of Powhatan was fortunate, for she was not bound by the restrictions that hampered others. The marriage of her own parents had been one of real love, and although her mother had died when she was very small, Pocahontas could remember listening to the songs her mother had sung, extolling her wonderful marital relationship. Powhatan was always reluctant to discuss the matter when Pocahontas asked him about it, but that was natural in a man. Nevertheless, she knew how he felt, for twice each year, at the beginning of summer and of winter, he sacrificed a wild boar in memory of the woman who remained first among all the wives he had ever taken.

Just as her mother had known from the first moment she had seen Powhatan that she wished to devote the rest of her life to him, so she herself had realized that she loved John Smith. It was fitting that the daughter of a mighty chief should marry no one but a chief, and Pocahontas's last doubts had vanished when she saw the way the people of Jamestown looked up to Smith. One of her stepmothers had told her he was the leader of the pale-skinned tribe only because the people had chosen him for the post and that he would eventually be replaced by another, but the girl dismissed such nonsense as the idle gossip of a stupid old woman. Anyone with eyes could see that Smith commanded the instinctive respect and obedience of every man and woman in his town, and even the boys with whom she had beeen cavorting this afternoon had bowed to him as deeply as a young brave made his obeisance to a great chief.

Of even greater importance, Smith's tribe felt very strongly on the subject of love, as Pocahontas knew from what she had been able to decipher in the Book he had given her. Ru-Sa, who obviously enjoyed worrying, chattered endlessly about the differences in the customs of nations and spoke with relish of the Short Men Beyond the Mountains, who called themselves the Sioux. They married only the squaws of their own tribe, and when one of them took an alien woman she was treated as though she were nothing but a slave.

That was not true of Smith's people, as the God whom they worshiped instructed them to love each other as devoutly as they loved Him. So it was plain that they understood the true meaning of love, and Smith, as their leader, naturally had the greatest knowledge of all, as it was his duty to set an example for the others.

It would be strange to live in Jamestown, Pocahontas reflected, and the thought that someday she might be required to sail across the water in one of the huge ships whose pictures she had seen frightened her. She was sure she would never learn to like the drab ugly clothes the pale women wore, and the food they cooked was certainly tasteless and flat. But she would feel more at home here when she acquired greater skill in speaking English, and the books she had been given this morning would be a great help to her. What mattered most, however, was that she would be with Smith, and not even Ru-Sa could deny that a wife's place was near her husband, ever ready to serve him.

Smith was saying something to her now as he stood beside a large tube of thick metal, and she forced herself to listen to him. The weird object was obviously a weapon, and she saw that his eyes shone as he described it to her. It would be rude to tell him she was indifferent to weapons, but it pleased her that he was so happy. All men were the same, she thought, and remembered the ecstasy the son of one of her brothers had felt when he was no more than seven summers old and she had given him a little stone ax. It was right and good that Smith took such joy in his weapons, and she impulsively put her hand on his arm.

He broke off suddenly and stared at her. "You weren't listening to me," he said, his tone faintly accusing.

"I heard every word," Pocahontas protested.

He knew she was lying and led her away from the cannon to the window that opened onto the river. "You'll like this better," he told her, making room for her beside him.

They gazed out at the placid blue-green water in silence, and suddenly Pocahontas sighed. Someday he would want to visit the home of his fathers, and she would have no choice but to accompany him. "Is England a large land?" she asked.

"The New World is larger." He couldn't understand the reason for her depression and he felt irritated. He had gone to considerable effort to entertain her, but the visit to the block-house was turning out to be a dismal failure. The cannon had bored her, and now the sight of the broad river made her disconsolate. She stirred, and he realized they were standing close together; their shoulders touched, and her proximity aroused him. "The view," he said abruptly, "is best from the watchtower platform."

He started off toward a flight of steps, and Pocahontas, following him, knew she had displeased him. She had no idea what she had done wrong, but felt instinctively that she should react more strongly to whatever he showed her. He led her through a room in which there were four beds of the kind the pale-faced people used, and when he explained to her that the guards slept here when they were not on sentry duty, she smiled at him steadily. He responded at once, and when she saw desire flare up in his eyes again, she realized that her conduct was now more appropriate.

Smith opened a narrow wooden door and took her onto what appeared to be a narrow shelf of logs built out past the edge of the building. The platform reminded her of the Chickahominy burial tables, and she giggled nervously; Ek was low in the sky, but he could still see her, and he would certainly be angered by the presence of a living person on a platform of the dead. However, she was no longer sure that Ek had any real power over her. The Book Smith had given her said much about his God that made sense to her, and her thinking these days was somewhat confused. Perhaps, after she and Smith were married, he would consent to discuss the subject with her. She hoped he would, for his position as chief of his people obviously made him their leading medicine man as well, so she could go to no higher authority for an explanation of the problems that perplexed her.

"You can see two or three miles in every direction from

here," he told her. "From the first moment I saw this little hill I knew it was the most logical spot for a blockhouse."

Pocahontas could see only trees and water, neither of which had any particular significance to her. Had she wanted to look at trees, she could have stayed at home and gazed at them all day from the door of her own house on the hill of the Chief of Chiefs. What did intrigue her, however, was the notion of looking down from the platform to the ground; the idea had not occurred to her for a long time, but as a child she had often wondered whether the dead saw things differently from their burial tables. Smiling apprehensively, she inched closer to the end of the platform and glanced down.

A wave of dizziness swept over her, and she was afraid she was going to fall. The thought flashed through her mind that Ek was indeed angry and was punishing her. Gasping, she tried to draw back but could not, and she tried to grasp something on which to steady herself, but her fingers clutched only air. Then suddenly John Smith came up behind her, his strong hands encircled her waist, and he drew her back to safety.

The girl turned to thank him, and his hold on her tightened. Then, before she quite realized what was happening, he kissed her. Never had Pocahontas known such rapture, never had her blood raced so violently, and she clung to him, reveling in his masculine solidity. After what seemed like an eternity he released her, and they stood for a long moment, speechless and out of breath, their eyes meeting. There was no need for words now, and Pocahontas knew what to do.

She moved past Smith and walked with simple, demure dignity back into the bedroom. He followed her, and as he looked at her she slowly removed her breastband and skirt. Seeing the indescribable exultation in his face, she knew that she was right. They loved each other and they belonged together.

But in spite of her certainty that what she was doing was both right and natural, she had to curb a desire to run away as he approached her, his arms outstretched. At the very least she wanted to snatch up her clothes again and cover her body, and it astonished her that she who had never in her life been ashamed to let others see her body was almost overcome by a sense of shyness. She was being weak, she told herself sternly; Ru-Sa had taught her everything there was to know about the intimacies of men and women, and if she failed to meet her test with courage, she would be disgraced, just as the warrior who flinched when he was tortured deserved to be condemned.

Then, as Smith caught her in his arms again, her diffidence vanished miraculously, and a feeling unlike any she had ever before known suffused her. Until this moment she had been proud and independent, reliant only on herself, needing and wanting no one else to make her whole. Yet her instinct told her that by the act of surrender to Smith that she was performing voluntarily she would give up her independence for all time, that from this day forward she would need his love to be fulfilled.

Scarcely conscious of what she was doing, she struggled against him, beating her fists ineffectually against his chest as he embraced her. She wanted him to release her, but at the same time she was demanding that he conquer her, and she rejoiced when he kissed her, ignoring her protests. He caressed her, and she trembled when she realized that alien hands were stroking her, that a will stronger than her own was dominating her.

Suddenly she no longer cared; the man to whom she was giving herself was no ordinary warrior but the one person whom she loved above all others and who loved her in return. Her ecstasy matched his ardor, and as her passion soared, her last articulate thought was that she was learning the final lesson, one that neither Ru-Sa nor anyone else could have taught her: by surrendering herself to Smith, without reservation, she was binding him to her for the rest of their lives. He would always be a part of her, just as she would always belong to him, and nothing could ever break the bonds that were being forged in this instant of complete harmony and satisfaction.

Night was falling, and the clouds that raced toward the east cast deep purple shadows across a lavender sky when Pocahontas and Smith left the blockhouse. He turned to close the door, and in the brief moment that his attention was diverted she left his side and ran down to the water's edge. Something in her attitude, perhaps the set of her shoulders or the way she held her head, told him she wanted to be alone, and he made no attempt to follow her. Satiated and at peace, he waited for her patiently and let the cool breeze from the west play on him as he glanced idly at the dim silhouettes of the Jamestown houses, now almost invisible in the thickening twilight.

Pocahontas stared with unseeing eyes at the swiftly flowing water and tried to think coherently. This was the most important day in her life, yet to her surprise she was essentially the same person she had been an hour ago. Nevertheless, she knew she was not what she had been and she realized that her future was that of a woman, not a girl. Smith was all that she had imagined, and she was convinced that their love was indestructible. She was able to smile at herself, too, and felt a twinge of nostalgia for the naïve ignorance that had characterized her views of the relationship between a man and a woman. Yet at the same time she gloried in her new-found knowledge; her heart was full because reality far exceeded her wildest dreams.

A tiny doubt ruffled the surface of her serenity, and although she tried to dismiss it, she could not. It bothered her that Smith had not yet followed the inviolable Chickahominy custom of tapping her three times on the left shoulder and informing her that she would now become his wife. But, she told herself, it was probable that his people followed a different practice, and she knew that it was her place as a woman to say nothing and to wait meekly until he

chose to announce their forthcoming marriage. As Ru-Sa
was so fond of saying, every nation followed its own habits.

A slight tremor shook Pocahontas. Then she straightened,
reached up, and removed her maiden's headband. It had
been a part of her as far back as she could remember, but she
felt no regrets as she gazed for a moment at the smooth white
seeds. Then she threw the strip of leather into the river and
stood motionless, watching it until it became waterlogged
and sank.

Later that night the blockhouse was the scene of considerable activity when the citizens of Jamestown and their guests
trooped out to the peninsula for a demonstration of artillery
fire. The Indians were duly impressed by the show, as Smith
had been certain they would be; he had chosen the time for
the display with great care, for he had reasoned that the
accuracy of his gunners' marksmanship would mean less to
the Naturals than the sight of the flames leaping from the
muzzles of the cannon and the roar of thunder that accompanied each shot.

Afterward the entire party repaired to the meeting hall in
the center of the town for a banquet which became a celebration when Powhatan and Smith revealed the terms of the
agreement they had made. Over a meal consisting of succes-
sive courses of barbecued venison, buffalo steak, bear stew,
and roasted wild boar, the Englishmen and the natives forgot
their reserve, and by midnight they were drinking toasts to
each other in ale, sack, and an inferior grade of Spanish
brandy.

As a number of the ladies of Jamestown were present at the
supper, Powhatan's wives and daughter were permitted to
attend, too, but they carefully remembered their station and
sat in unobtrusive silence at a table in a far corner. The Chief
of Chiefs, who had been more deeply affected by the artillery
demonstration than he was willing to admit, paid no attention to his women during the earlier hours of the meal. He
believed he had struck an excellent bargain and he was

relaxing for the first time since he had arrived in the town of the foreigners. But as the night wore on he became increasingly aware of Pocahontas; the first thing he noticed was that she was radiant, and not even her natural feminine modesty could hide her buoyancy. Then he realized that she never took her eyes from John Smith, and even someone who was unfamiliar with her moods could see that she was gazing at him with frank adoration.

Something was unusual about her appearance, too, and Powhatan was puzzled until, with a sense of shock, it dawned on him that she was no longer wearing her headband. For a moment he was numb, then he turned abruptly to Smith, who sat beside him. But the captain, who had seen him staring at Pocahontas, apparently knew what was in his mind and, shifting in his seat, began to engage in a busy conversation with someone farther down the table.

Powhatan's fingers closed over the silver fork his hosts had given him as a token of esteem, and he bent the strip of metal until it snapped. He had been wrong to listen to Pocahontas's pleas and bring her on this journey, but what was done, was done. He knew without being told what was in Smith's mind and he realized this was not the occasion to make a scene. There were some hundreds of the pale-skinned warriors in the town, and his own braves were badly outnumbered. Besides, he had no desire to wage an immediate war against men who owned such potent fire-sticks. On the other hand, under no circumstances would he permit his only daughter to be sent to the lodge of the Women Without Virtue, and he decided to bide his time.

He waited until the meal ended, and then he turned to Smith with a friendly, guileless smile. "When the food of the Chickahominy has been exchanged for the weapons of the men-from-across-the-water, we will be brothers," Powhatan said.

"We will be brothers," Smith agreed warily. He had taken a calculated risk when he had made love to Pocahontas, and her father unquestionably realized what had happened, but the captain was counting on his quick wits to save him from any embarrassing consequences.

"When we are brothers," the Chief of Chiefs continued, "the land of the Chickahominy will become the land of Smith, King of James." He spread out his hands and addressed his own followers: "Hear the words of Powhatan, my children. From this time forth, until Ek shines no more, it is the right of Smith to go where he pleases in the lands of the Chickahominy, the Potomac, the Chesapeake and the Manahoac, the Monacan and the Chawon."

A sensation of relief flooded over Smith; he had been certain that Powhatan was going to be troublesome on the subject of his daughter, but even a clever student of human nature occasionally made a wrong estimate. Luckily the Chief of Chiefs' attitude was that of a truly civilized sophisticate rather than a savage: it was evident he did not blame a man for forming a temporary liaison with a girl who was as handsome a baggage as Pocahontas.

Dismissing her from his mind with little effort, Smith looked forward with eager anticipation to his future travels. His explorations would bring him even greater renown than his administration of the affairs of Jamestown, he believed, and Powhatan, by granting him the right to go where he pleased in the Chickahominy domain, was virtually guaranteeing him a high permanent place in the annals of the new century's great men. The visit of the Indians to Jamestown certainly had been an unqualified success from every possible point of view.

The visitors departed early the following morning, and the whole colony gathered to see them off. The atmosphere was relaxed and congenial, the Chickahominy elders and the gentlemen of the Council renewed their protestations of undying friendship, and an impromptu farewell party was held on the banks of the James River. Several kegs of ale were tapped, and everyone enjoyed a final drink. The settlers serenaded their guests with a song that had been popular in England shortly before they had left for the New World, and the Indians responded with a merry, rhythmic chant.

Only one person in the assemblage seemed to be subdued, but she concealed her true feelings so successfully that no one but her father even guessed that she was unhappy. Pocahontas stood quietly on the grassy slope near the canoe in which she was to ride, her arms folded beneath an ankle-length buffalo cloak. She made herself so inconspicuous that few of the revelers were aware of her presence, and Captain Smith, who had been making it his business to say a few pleasant words to each of the Indians, was startled when he came face to face with her. He had been so busy he had almost forgotten her.

"I wish you a safe journey," he said, lifting his mug of ale to her and drinking a token sip.

"Thank you." Pocahontas's voice was steady, but her hands, hidden beneath her cloak, were not, and her finger-nails cut deep into the flesh of her arms. It would be so easy to fool herself, to pretend that the smile he bestowed on her had a special, intimate significance, but she realized she would gain nothing by self-deception. However, there were limits to her courage; although she could not deny that he was preoccupied at the moment, she would not let herself believe that his love-making had been casual and that she had meant nothing to him.

"We will meet again," he said, and bowed politely.

"We will, John Smith." Watching him move off, she told herself that her fears had been groundless. He would come to her when he could, and then they would be married. It was good that the wedding would take place in her own land, for all the people of the Chickahominy would gather for the ceremony and would see how much they loved each other.

Powhatan, who had been watching the brief exchange, smiled faintly, and his wives glanced at each other in alarm.

They knew that smile, and they hoped desperately that they had done nothing to anger him. Shivering beneath their long cloaks, they knew there was grave trouble ahead for some-one.

August, 1608

Supplies of Chickahominy foodstuffs began to arrive at Jamestown within two weeks of Powhatan's return home, and Captain Smith loaded culverins and muskets and gunpowder onto the Indian barges that had carried the grain and meat. The colony's immediate prosperity and security were thus assured, and Smith, bored by the petty details of routine administration, left the settlement at the first possible opportunity. Accompanied by ten adventurous companions, whom he had selected carefully from the ranks of many volunteers, he started to explore the territory around Chesapeake Bay. The Council was disturbed by his absence, and Gabriel Archer expressed the view of the majority when he said it was the duty of the president to govern Jamestown in person. But Smith, enthusiastically mapping areas that had never before been charted, was deaf to the complaints that came to him through the messengers who occasionally brought him news.

He spent the better part of the summer probing into every far corner of the bay, and when he returned to Jamestown he had accumulated so much data that for the first time he was in a position to think seriously about the book he had long wanted to write. He prepared two letters to London printers, explaining the project he had in mind, and then, as August was unusually dry and cool, he decided to take advantage of the weather and investigate the country in the vicinity of the Potomac River. The Council protested, which did not surprise him, but he continued to command the loyal support of the people and he felt no concern when Captain Archer threatened to have him removed from office unless he devoted himself solely to his duties.

The new expedition ran into difficulties at the outset, and two of the men who had planned to accompany Smith were left behind when they fell ill shortly before the party was scheduled to depart. Twenty-four hours later a third member of the group was severely stung by hornets and had to be sent home, and later that same day still another tripped over an exposed oak root and sprained his ankle. He could not walk without assistance, and it was necessary for two of his companions to take him back to the colony. The party was thus reduced to five, and the men began to mutter to each other about bad luck, but Smith's buoyancy was unaffected by the misfortunes, and he remained confident and energetic.

On the third day of the journey through the wilderness, when it was too late for any one person to turn back alone, the youngest of the explorers, a seventeen-year-old Londoner named Curtis Watkins, thoroughly frightened himself and the others by claiming they were being followed. Smith tried to calm him, but Watkins stubbornly continued to insist that someone was watching them from behind the omnipresent trees. The others soon succumbed to the same hysteria in spite of their leader's insistence that they were the victims of their own imaginations, and they swore there were other human beings nearby in the forests, keeping them under observation.

By the next morning Smith was forced to agree that they were right; he had tried to tell himself that he had allowed the fears of the men to influence him, yet he began to suffer the same uncanny feeling that someone was spying on them. He tried to reassure his companions by saying that any natives who might mean them harm would attack them rather than let them continue to wander where they pleased, but his logic failed to allay their uneasiness, and he himself found it increasingly difficult to concentrate on his sketches of the terrain. The tension became so great by midafternoon that he finally called a halt beside a small brook, and rather than push on any farther he proposed that they remain in this pleasant spot for the night and spend the rest of the afternoon hunting. They had caught occasional glimpses of deer and smaller animals throughout the day, and as the region seemed to abound in game, Smith felt that a few hours of relaxation would relieve the strain.

The men eagerly accepted his suggestion and went off in pairs, agreeing to return to the brook before sundown. Smith, who had no interest in hunting other than as a means of acquiring food, sat down beside the stream and began to work on his notes. Any savages who might be watching the party were obviously curious rather than hostile, he told himself firmly, and it was far more important to make the usual full entries in his journal than to worry about them. Indians, he reminded himself, were primitive people and hence were virtually without guile; they saw others either as enemies or friends, and were totally unfamiliar with the subtleties that shaded the judgments more civilized men formed in their relations with each other.

He soon became absorbed in his writing and he smiled absently when a crash of musket fire broke the silence of the forest. One of his companions was enjoying good fortune. But the smile froze on his lips when a scream of terror seemed to make the leaves on the trees tremble and, jumping to his feet, he instinctively drew his pistol and started off in the direction from which the sound had come. The wilderness was quiet again, and after running through the thick under-brush for several minutes he was uncertain whether he was on the right track. Twice he paused and shouted, but there was no answer, and he had no choice but to plunge on.

After racing aimlessly for a quarter of an hour, he heard voices in the distance off to the left; as nearly as he could judge by the angry tones, an argument of some sort seemed to be in progress, and he increased his pace.

The voices became louder, and at last he came into the open at the base of a small, rocky hill that was almost bare of vegetation. Halting abruptly and trying to catch his breath, he could only stare at the sight that confronted him. At least twenty Indian warriors were gathered in the clearing, and with them were his four companions. Each of the settlers was surrounded by several braves, and Curtis Watkins in particu-lar seemed to be in trouble. His musket had been taken from him, two warriors held his arms, and a third was angrily waving a long bone-handled knife in front of his face.

Smith overcame his feeling of shock, and as he stepped forward, his pistol pointed at the knife-wielding savage, it occurred to him that these Indians were tall, light-skinned, and wore the feathered headdresses of the Chickahominy. Something strange was taking place, for this was the land of the Potomac, who were a shorter, darker tribe, and it was unusual for so large a group of braves to journey into the territory of another nation even when they enjoyed friendly relations. However, this was not the time to dwell on such matters, and he cocked his pistol.

"Smith, King of James, greets his brothers," he said quickly in the tongue of the Chickahominy. "Why have you made captives of my men?"

Several of the warriors began to edge around behind him, but he hastily pointed his pistol at each of them in turn, and they halted. There was a tense silence for a moment, then the brave with the knife answered him. "This land is a hunting

ground of the Chickahominy," he said gravely. "The Chickahominy warriors, like their fathers before them, hunt for
food in these forests. But no others may hunt here."

The man was lying; this was unquestionably the territory
of the Potomac, and if it was indeed a hunting preserve, it
belonged to them rather than to their neighboring overlords.
It occurred to Smith that this was no ordinary misunderstanding, and in all probability it was the Chickahominy
who had been following his party for the past day and half. If
his surmise was correct, then the Indians had merely been
waiting for some flimsy excuse to capture him and his
friends. Yet, even though he felt that he had uncovered the
truth, he could imagine no reason why Powhatan should
want to harm him. The trade pact they had made was
mutually satisfactory as well as eminently fair, and it was
obvious that both sides would benefit.

In the present situation, Smith thought, anything less than
a bold course of action might prove disastrous, and he
planted his feet wide apart. Although puzzled, he could not
afford the luxury of analyzing the matter when his companions were in danger. "I demand that you release my men," he
said loudly.

The Chickahominy warriors did not move.

"Smith is the brother of Powhatan, the Chief of Chiefs,
and in his name I order you to release my men!"

Several of the braves glanced at each other a trifle uncertainly, but their leader was unimpressed. "This young warrior," he said, "killed a doe in the hunting ground of my
people. He who steals food from the Chickahominy must
die." Again he raised his blade to the face of the terrified
Watkins.

"You wear seven feathers, so you should be wise, but you
have offended Ek, and he has taken your wits from you."
Smith contrived to laugh deprecatingly, and no actor at the
Globe or Blackfriars had ever sounded more convincing.
"When Powhatan came to the town of Smith, he granted to

Smith the right to travel where he pleases. I call on all who heard the words of the Chief of Chiefs to say whether I speak the truth."

His eyes, hard and angry, searched the faces of the warriors, and two or three of them, men who had apparently been members of the group that had visited Jamestown, nodded. He was about to press his advantage, but the leader of the Chickahominy cut him off. "Only the sons of Ek may use this hunting ground," he repeated stubbornly, and before anyone could intervene he plunged his knife deep into the throat of Curtis Watkins.

The young Londoner died instantly, and Smith reacted promptly. Taking careful aim, he put a bullet into the killer, and the warrior slumped to the ground. It was some small satisfaction to know that a murder had been avenged, but Smith had no chance to dwell on the matter. Before he could draw his sword, four husky braves pounced on him, and he found himself involved in a desperate hand-to-hand fight. His three surviving companions, themselves surrounded, were unable to come to his aid, so he had to battle against his assailants alone.

He fought ferociously, with a savage abandon even deadlier than that of his Indian foes, and he more than held his own against them. They threw him to the ground, and while one of them grappled with him the others tried to pin down his arms and legs, but he was so strong and quick that they could not hold him. He saw a shaved head only a few inches from his own and, grasping his pistol by the barrel like a club, he brought the butt down on the Chickahominy's head. He laughed harshly when his victim screamed and fell away from him, but at that instant one of the others wrenched the pistol from him, and he was forced to fight with his bare hands.

Again and again he smashed his fists into the painted faces and bodies of his attackers, and with each blow he delivered his sense of frenzy increased. Only once in his life, when he

had been set upon by bandits near Damascus, had he engaged in a contest with so many opponents at one time, and
he realized vaguely that although his life was in jeopardy he
was enjoying himself. The warriors pummeled him in return, but fist fighting was apparently unknown to Indians,
and the damage they inflicted on him was negligible.

They preferred to wrestle with him when they could, and
at one point a tall, wiry brave wrapped his legs around
Smith's middle and systematically began to squeeze the
breath out of him. The pain was excruciating, and only by
calling on his last reserves of vitality was the Englishman able
to break his foe's hold. From that moment forward he tried to
hold the savages at bay and not let them come close enough
to tackle or clutch him again. Obviously they knew far more
than he about wrestling, and at odds of three to one he would
soon be overwhelmed if their technique prevailed.

He knew that he could not hold out against them indefinitely and that unless he changed his tactics they would
gradually wear him down, but whenever he regained his feet
they rushed him, and he had no choice but to remain on the
defensive as he attempted to ward them off. Occasionally he
caught glimpses of his companions, whose hands had been
securely tied with long strips of rawhide and who were being
guarded by the other members of the party. These braves,
peculiarly, made no effort to join the fight but stood watching
the fray calmly and unconcernedly; in their minds, at least,
there seemed to be no doubt as to the outcome of the
struggle.

Smith realized that if he could draw his sword he would be
in a far better position not only to defend himself but to
launch a real counter-attack. However, his assailants gave
him no opportunity to free his right hand for even an instant,
and they crowded him so doggedly that he had to keep
punching at them while retreating constantly. Two or three
times he thought he would break into the clear, but before he
could draw his blade from its sheath, which had twisted

around behind him, one or another of the warriors would come at him again.

It was odd, he thought dimly, that none of them had drawn knives, and although all carried tomahawks in the belted middles of their loincloths, they too continued to fight without drawing their weapons. He wondered if they were merely playing with him, after the manner of animals teasing a weaker prey, but it finally dawned on him that they were not. Curtis Watkins was dead, but he had been unimportant to them, and from the way the braves launched each fresh attack Smith could only conclude that they were under orders to capture him rather than kill him.

Mystified, but more determined than ever, he managed at last to wrench free of his antagonists; withdrawing a few steps, he jerked at his sword belt and brought it back into proper position. He shouted in hoarse triumph as his fingers closed over the solid iron hilt of his blade, and when the warriors rushed toward him he withdrew it with a flourish. At the sight of the steel they hesitated and, cursing them fluently in English and Arabic, he started toward them. The lust of battle was in his eyes now and, looking at him, they knew they would be lucky to survive. They backed away from him, slowly at first, and then one of them took to his heels.

Smith, certain now that he would win, wanted to taunt the Chickahominy for cowardice but decided it was wiser to save his breath. Balancing on the balls of his feet, he narrowed the gap between him and the tallest of his opponents, ready to lunge as soon as he was within striking distance. In his new-found exultation, however, he momentarily forgot the Indian spectators, whose attitude changed from one of complacency to active concern when they saw that he was armed and prepared to shed the blood of their brothers. He was aware that they were stirring, and in his present reckless mood he was ready to take on all of them, but they gave him no chance.

A slender brave, older than most of the others, approached

him from the rear so silently that Smith did not hear him. The warrior carried a small tomahawk in his hand, and when he was no more than ten feet from his victim he threw it with consummate skill. The blunt end of the weapon's head rather than the sharp edge crashed against the base of Smith's head, thus stunning him rather than killing him. He knew he was losing consciousness, but even as he fell he continued to fight, stabbing blindly into space with his sword as he pitched headlong onto the rocky ground.

The warriors, afraid he might be conscious, approached him gingerly, and only when they were certain he was harmless did they roll him over and remove the blade from his tightly closed fingers. They showed no elation over their victory, and with no display of emotion they tied his hands and feet firmly with strips of rawhide. Then they buried their dead companion without ceremony and, after quickly scalping Curtis Watkins, left his body for the wolves. A sapling was felled, and after the branches had been cut off, the pole was quickly strung through the loops made by Smith's bound hands and feet.

The sapling was hoisted onto the shoulders of four braves, and Captain John Smith, gentleman, president of the James-town Council and Honorable Envoy of the London Company, author, cartographer, and explorer, dangled from the crude sling like the carcass of a deer. A new leader, the warrior who had ended the fight with his tomahawk, gave a signal, and the Chickahominy, driving their other captives before them, started off toward the southwest through the still, calm forest.

When Smith regained consciousness his agony was so intense that for a moment he thought he was in his own bed, experiencing a nightmare. His arms felt as though they were being torn from their sockets, a deep ache penetrated to the marrow of his thigh bones, and he thought his wrists and ankles were on fire. He cried out, but no one seemed to hear him; then he opened his eyes, and when he saw the way the

Indians were carrying him, his anger and humiliation made him forget his pain for an instant. Calling to them in their own language, he demanded that they put him down, but they ignored his protests and continued their silent march through the wilderness, impervious to his objections and callous to his suffering.

They did not halt until long after night had fallen, and only then, when they halted for a few hours' rest, did they cut Smith down and give him a little pulse and raw fish to eat. When they resumed their journey shortly before dawn they started to truss him again, but he objected with such bitter vehemence that they held a brief consultation and thereafter permitted him to walk on his own feet. But they took no chances that he might escape, and their elaborate precautions were an ironic testimony to the respect they felt for him. Two warriors hovered close behind him, others kept watch on either side of him, his hands were kept tied behind his back, and a noose of thin, waxed rawhide was placed around his neck and was used to keep him in check, as though he were a mastiff on a leash.

The savages were tireless and maintained a pace throughout the day that exhausted their prisoners. Smith had always been proud of his stamina, but by dusk he thought each step would be his last, and he envied the ability of his captors to continue without pausing for either food or relaxation. The countryside began to look vaguely familiar to him now, and although it was not easy to distinguish one section of the wilderness from another in the dark, he became convinced that this was an area he had once sketched.

A three-quarter moon rose slowly in the sky, and by its light Smith caught a glimpse of a broad ribbon of silver through the trees to his left. He recognized it as the James River and he forgot his fatigue as he quickly oriented himself. They were no more than a mile or two from the Chickahominy capital now, and he shouted an encouraging word to his stumbling, weary companions. The noose that encircled his neck was promptly tightened as a warning, so he made no attempt to speak again.

The present ordeal would end soon, and although he had no idea of what might be ahead, he was filled with a determination to survive no matter what the cost. He was completely at a loss to understand why natives who were presumably his friends had turned on him, but in spite of the fact that the long march had numbed his mind, he knew himself to be more intelligent, more cunning, and more astute than his captors. In one way or another he would overcome his difficulties, which would make absorbing reading for thousands of his fellow countrymen when he eventually reduced the record of his experiences to writing. The thought that his present dilemma would increase his future stature at home was comforting, and he held his head high as the warriors led him onto a waiting raft, ferried him and his men across the river to their town, and then, separating him from the others, conducted him to a small clay hut near the water.

The building was surrounded by braves armed with knives, and standing in front of the entrance was a tall man holding one of the muskets that Smith had sent to the tribe earlier in the summer. The feathered headdress of the warrior was ornate, and when Smith came closer to the hut he saw that the man was Powhatan's eldest son, Opachisco, with whom he had shared several meals on his first visit there. But the eyes of the future ruler of the Chickahominy Confederation were cold and brooding now, and he stared through the captive without seeing him. It seemed that Opachisco was going to extraordinary lengths to indicate that he did not recognize the prisoner, and this simple incident was far more alarming than the abusive treatment Smith had received at the hands of the braves who had brought him here. Opachisco, unlike his inferiors, knew better, and his deliberate hostility was menacing.

Smith's bonds were cut, he was shoved into the hut, and two guards immediately appeared in the entrance, where they stood impassively, watching him. Indifferent to their stares, he sprawled on the hard earth, grateful for the chance to rest. He tried to maintain his courage, but the tiny room was bare, and the walls were as bleak as his expectations for the immediate future. The braves stepped aside to allow an elderly squaw to enter, and she glared venomously at Smith as she gave him a handful of parched corn and a small wooden bowl of sinewy dried beef. He had no appetite, and the food was tasteless, but he forced himself to eat, for he reminded himself that he would be even more at the mercy of the savages if he lost his strength. Then a sense of lethargy came over him, and when he finished the cheerless meal he stretched out on the ground and dropped off to sleep.

In the morning he was given more corn and tough meat and he made several fruitless attempts to learn more of his situation by conversing casually with the guards. He joked with them, he cajoled and he spoke firmly, but they pretended not to hear him, and at last he fell silent too. Obviously they were under orders not to talk to him, regardless of the provocation. He tried to reassure himself that his plight was the result of a misunderstanding, but as the morning wore on he became increasingly tense, and by noon he was so upset that he could keep a grip on himself only with an effort. Twice Opachisco came to look at him but said nothing; no words were necessary, unfortunately, and in the bright daylight Smith could see the frank contempt in the other's eyes.

Shortly after noon there was a stir outside the hut, and a long shadow appeared in the open entrance. Smith glanced up, then jumped to his feet when he saw Powhatan, his arms folded beneath his robe, the feathers on his headband brushing the low ceiling. "Powhatan greets his brother," the Chickahominy said urbanely.

Smith hooked his thumbs in his belt, and for a moment his rage made him inarticulate. "Brother, did you say? In my land brothers treat each other with respect and decency, not like criminals!"

There was no change in the Chief of Chiefs' expression. "Powhatan bids his brother welcome to the land of the Chickahominy," he declared imperturbably.

After all that had happened, even the most composed of men would have been angry, and patience had never been one of Smith's virtues. "Why am I being held here? What has happened to my men, and why have we been treated as though we had committed some terrible wrong?"

Powhatan's eyes became cloudy, and a muscle twitched in his left cheek. "A great wrong has been done," he said, sounding so pontifical that Smith was reminded of Sir Edward Coke, England's pompous Lord Chief Justice.

"Tell me what we've done!" It would probably be wiser to show humility, the prisoner realized, but he could not help hurling a challenge at this complacent savage.

"First," the Chief of Chiefs replied slowly, "those who are not permitted to use the hunting ground of the Chickahominy killed a doe there."

The charge was so outrageously absurd that Smith stared at him. "You gave me the right to go where I please in all of your lands! Many of your people and many of mine heard you grant me that right!"

"The right was given to Smith, it is true. But it was not given to others. Yet four others were with Smith." Powhatan spoke reasonably, as though his logic could not be refuted.

"Yes, and one of my followers was murdered in cold blood." Smith had recovered his equilibrium, and his accent was clipped.

Powhatan shrugged, indicating clearly that he was not concerned over so trivial a matter as the death of one of the pale-skinned foreigners. "It was he who killed an animal in the hunting ground of the Chickahominy. It was he who first broke the law of my Confederation which forbids any to use hunting grounds that belong to others. So it was right that he should die."

The savage's reasoning was senseless, and Smith was anxious to get to the core of the matter. "That isn't why he was murdered, and you know it. We weren't trespassing on Chickahominy hunting preserves, and I'm not even certain the area was actually a hunting ground. We weren't on your territory at all. It so happens we were in the land of the Potomac, and I can prove it."

The Chief of Chiefs ignored the interruption. "One of the mightiest of Chickahominy warriors was killed after he punished the stranger who broke the law. Matatulawan was a good man. The gods loved him, for he never failed in his duty to them."

Apparently the life of a bloodthirsty Indian was more important than that of a young Englishman whose whole life had been before him, and Smith struggled to stifle a furious retort. Powhatan, as he well knew, was neither stupid nor ingenuous and surely realized that the position he was taking was inconsistent. "My follower loved his God," Smith declared softly, "and was a good man too. His God loved him." He smiled sardonically and peered at the Natural to see how he would react to this bald refutation of his argument.

Powhatan chose to be momentarily deaf; he had been leading up to a point and he refused to be diverted. Removing his hands from beneath his buffalo robe, he pointed a thick forefinger at his prisoner. "He who kills a warrior of the Chickahominy without cause must die."

"Without cause?" Smith asked incredulously. He recognized the fact that his reply was feeble, but the whole discussion was so warped and demented that he did not know what else to say.

"Smith has killed a warrior of the Chickahominy, so Smith must die." The older man's voice was stern, and his face was set in uncompromising lines.

There was a silence, and then Smith smiled. He could not and would not believe he had truly been condemned to death because he had avenged a follower who had been murdered without just cause. Any real leader who felt responsibility for

his men would have done the same, and he felt certain there
was something vitally significant that Powhatan had left
unsaid. Smith could not let himself forget that his position at
the moment was vulnerable, but he remembered that in their
trade negotiations the Indian had always approached the
heart of his demands by indirect means. Negotiations of
some sort were plainly in progress now, and although Smith
did not yet know what the Chickahominy wanted of him, he
was afraid he would be required to pay a severe penalty if he
refused to play the game.

"Have me put to death if it will give you any satisfaction,"
he said lightly. "But you know as well as I do that if you kill
me there will be war between my people and your people.
And my people have noise sticks far more powerful than
those I gave to you."

Powhatan's forefinger did not waver. "The gods weep for
Matatulawan. They will not be happy again until the mur-
derer loses his blood and his life. Powhatan, in whom live the
spirits of the gods, has spoken."

Smith saw that the Indian was serious. "You seem to give
me no choice," he said simply.

"There is a choice."

The Englishman averted his eyes and spoke very softly,
very casually. "Oh?"

"The spirits of the gods live not only in Powhatan, but in
his children. Like him, they have the right to kill those who
break the law. They sit in judgment on the people of the
Chickahominy, for the gods dwell in them and give them the
power to separate the guilty from the innocent. When one of
my family puts the guilty to death, he acts for the gods. Ek
will not punish one who acts in his place and who had the
right to speak for him. Ris will not punish one in whom he
dwells, nor will any of the other gods who live in the skies or
in the earth or in the flowing waters."

Smith nodded almost imperceptibly. Stripped of its superstitions, the judicial system of the savages was remarkably like
that of England. King James believed he ruled by divine

right, and anyone he or his relatives disliked was beheaded.
Of course it was necessary to observe certain legal formalities
before an Englishman could be executed, and in a sense the
technique of the American natives was better, for they eliminated all hypocritical and time-consuming ceremony. But
the principle was the same.

Powhatan took a single step closer, and his voice became a
trifle milder. "Smith," he said, "may become a member of
the family of Powhatan. That is his choice."

The inference was staggering.

"The daughter of Powhatan," the Chief of Chiefs continued, "is the squaw of no man. But she will become the
wife of Smith if he holds out his hand to her. Then he will be
the son of Powhatan. The gods will then know that the death
of Matatulawan was right and just."

All that had happened since the moment Smith had
known he and his companions were being followed in the
forests became clear now, and Powhatan's carefully planned,
sly trickery was breath-taking. Smith was outraged but he
discovered that his resentment was directed at Pocahontas
rather than at her father. She had thrown herself at him
repeatedly, until in a moment of weakness he had taken her,
and now she was demanding that he pay an impossible price.
He damned her silently and recalled Sir Walter Raleigh's
comment about women. Pocahontas, in spite of her air of
innocence, was a true daughter of Eve.

"She who would become the squaw of Smith is not a
maiden," the Chief of Chiefs said quietly. "She wears the
white headband of a maiden, for I have forbidden her to
appear without it. The daughter of Powhatan must not be
shamed before the people of the Chickahominy. But if Smith
does not hold out his hand to her, then she must go to the
lodge of the Women Without Virtue." For the first time he
lost his composure, and his voice trembled. "It would be
better for her to die than to live a lie. And if Smith does not
marry her he will surely die this day."

Smith wanted to shout that under no circumstances could

he be induced to take a savage wife back to England with
him. If he appeared there with Pocahontas at his side he
would become the laughingstock of London, and one of the
most brilliant careers of the century would be irrevocably
ruined. Pocahontas had tricked him with a cunning that left
him almost no room in which to maneuver, but he could not
believe that she or her father would make good their preposterous bluff and, setting his jaw stubbornly, he shook his
head.

Powhatan, who had been watching him closely, sighed
and then straightened. The muscle in his face twitched again
as he once more folded his arms beneath his robe. "Smith
will not give his answer now," he said. "He will speak later in
the presence of Ek and of all the people of the Chickahominy." Turning with slow dignity, he walked out of the hut.

In midafternoon the throbbing of a drum summoned
every member of the community to a large clearing beyond
the last of the city's seven hills. Here, according to legend, a
flaming rock had fallen and had buried the greater part of
itself in the earth in the days of the father of Powhatan's
grandfather. Since that time the Chickahominy had been
successful in all their endeavors, and as everyone from the
wisest elders to the youngest children knew, the rock was a
gift from the gods and a symbol of their favor. No trees or
shrubs or grass would grow in the sacred clearing, and twelve
warriors, men especially selected for their courage and honesty, alternated in standing guard at the base of that portion of
the rock which jutted above the ground. Only the most
important ceremonies were held here, and no one but the
ruler of the whole Confederation was ever permitted to
mount to the flat top of the rock itself.

The drum continued to beat after the tribe had been
assembled, and even the children were quiet as Powhatan,
followed by his sons and his daughter, marched slowly down
from his own lodge and took his place at the crest of the stone.
Pocahontas, who was following her brothers, had no idea

why the call had been issued and she did not care. She realized vaguely that, when she had been bidden to join the rest of the family, Opachisco and Dalan had both stared at her meaningfully, but she preferred not to speculate on the reason they had looked at her.

It was probable, she thought dully, that they knew she had no real right to wear the headband of white seeds that sat so heavily on her brow, but she no longer cared. Soon all the people of the Chickahominy would know, and then her disgrace would be complete. But what mattered most to her was that she herself was constantly aware of her mortification, and she often told herself that the god of the Christians, like the gods of her ancestors, knew she was living a falsehood.

The warriors looked at her with shining eyes as she passed them, and the squaws tried to conceal their envy, but she no longer took pride in her apperance. Ever since the day she had faced reality and had forced herself to acknowledge the fact that John Smith would never come to claim her as his wife she had been indifferent to the opinions of others. She had remained in her house for long hours at a time, either reading the books the English schoolmaster in Jamestown had given her or else grieving for a love that would never again be given to her. She no longer played at games with the other young people, and she ate so little food that Ru-Sa, genuinely worried about her, no longer scolded her. She had lost weight, her step was listless, and the bright smile that had once made her the favorite of the nation was missing. She would have been surprised to learn that the people thought her as attractive as ever, but even if she had known, she would have been indifferent to their opinion.

She was barefooted, and the earth was hard and unyielding near the rock, but she no longer minded minor discomforts, and when her father had seated himself on the top of the rock she moved unthinkingly to her usual position beside Dalan at the base of the stone. She was startled when Powhatan beckoned to her, and she climbed the rock to him, her heart pounding. It occurred to her that he was going to make a public announcement of her shame here and now, and she called herself a coward because she was relieved when she saw that he was smiling at her and that his eyes were compassionate. He motioned her to a seat on the slope at his feet, and his hand on her shoulder was so gentle that she knew she would not be exposed today.

She saw that everyone was watching her and she roused herself sufficiently to smooth her hair, which hung loose down her back, and to tighten the buckskin thongs of orange, blue, and green that were tied around her waist. Then she modestly tugged at the hem of her kneelength tunic of cream-colored deerskin and wished she weren't wearing a dress that covered only one shoulder. Such clothes were worn only by young girls, not by women, and with the whole tribe looking at her and wondering why her father was paying her such a high honor, her feeling of self-debasement became more intense. Had Powhatan's hand not remained on her shoulder she would have wept, but she reminded herself that until such time as she was sent to join the other Women Without Virtue it was her duty to behave in public with the dignity befitting the daughter of a mighty chief.

Opachisco seemed to be in charge of the event, and when he gave a signal a number of slaves appeared and drove four stakes into the ground at the four corners of the sacred clearing. The pole which was closest to the rock on which Pocahontas sat with her father was thicker and taller than the others, and she glanced up at Powhatan inquiringly. He patted her bare shoulder soothingly, but the remote smile that appeared on his lips was grim and self-satisfied, and she felt a sudden, inexplicable tremor of fear.

The drum sounded again briefly, and Opachisco took two steps out into the clearing from his place at the foot of the rock. Strangers, he told the people, had violated the law that prohibited outsiders from using the hunting grounds of the

Chickahominy. The nation would starve, he said, unless transgressors were punished, and he reminded his listeners that, although they were always just and merciful, there were times when self-preservation required them to harden their hearts. His oratory stirred the people, they agreed heartily with all that he said, and they rejoiced that the eldest son of the Chief of Chiefs was so wise. When the time came for Powhatan to join his ancestors, Opachisco would deserve to succeed him.

Four prisoners were led onto the open field as the drum throbbed slowly and ominously, and the people jostled each other and craned their necks for a better view of the culprits. Pocahontas saw at once that the captives were Englishmen, and when she recognized John Smith she was so appalled that her mind would not function. She began to tremble violently, and when Smith was brought to the large stake near the rock and was lashed to it, her eyes filled with tears. His carriage was proud, and in spite of her anguish she gloried in the nobility he displayed; she felt with him and for him and she wanted everyone present to know that she loved him. He was looking straight at her and, blinking away the tears, she met his gaze. She was shocked by the violent, undisguised hatred that blazed in his eyes and she shuddered as though he had struck her across the face.

Surely there had been some terrible mistake or misunderstanding, and she turned to her father in appeal, but he seemed to be unaware of her and was looking stonily at Smith over the top of her head. But he was more conscious of her than she realized, for when she would have risen and gone to Smith, Powhatan's grip on her shoulder tightened and he compelled her to remain seated. After a fierce inner struggle she subsided, for she had never disobeyed him, and she could not break the deeply ingrained habit of a lifetime.

Opachisco spoke again and said that three of the transgressors had been guilty of comparatively minor offenses, hence their punishment would be light, and when they had paid for their crime they would be sent to their homes so they could warn their brothers that the vengeance of the Chickahominy was swift and dire. At his direction Smith's companions were stripped, and then the squaws were invited to scourge them. The women surged forward and began to beat them enthusiastically with sticks and strips of rawhide, and so many wanted to participate in the sport that they crowded and shoved each other in their eagerness to administer the whipping.

Suddenly John Smith's voice rose loud and clear above the tumult. "Courage, lads!" he shouted, knowing his followers had not understood a word of what Opachisco had said. "They aren't going to kill you and they'll soon set you free. Accept your ordeal now, so you can fight later. Be strong, for God and King James!" One of his guards struck him hard across the mouth, but he did not seem to notice the blow.

Pocahontas's command of English was sufficient for her to understand all he had told his men, and she felt a thrill of admiration for him. Only a leader of great, selfless valor could forget his own danger and try to help his retainers at a time like this, and she thought that even though he had rejected her for some reason she could not fathom, she had not given her love to one who was unworthy of it.

When the battered Englishmen began to droop, Opachisco called a halt to the proceedings and ordered them cut down. Their clothes were flung at them, and they were ordered to leave the land of the Chickahominy at once. They stood groggily, uncomprehending, and they turned to Smith for guidance. He, indifferent to the blow he knew he would receive, did not fail them. "Follow the river downstream to Jamestown!" he called. "Go at once, before they change their minds," he added when they hesitated. "Leave me here—but remember me!"

Obeying him, they picked up their clothes and staggered off, followed by some of the Indian children, who threw stones after them. When they disappeared from sight all attention centered on Smith, and a pleasurable anticipatory murmur ran through the crowd. Pocahontas was quivering, and although she was completely ignorant of what was to be done to him, she knew she would not be able to watch if he was subjected to torture. She felt ill and wanted to flee from the sacred clearing, but she was powerless to move. Her place was here, not as a loyal member of the Chickahominy, but as a woman who loved Smith, whose sole desire was to help him.

Shifting slightly, she caught hold of her father's hand, which still pressed against her shoulder. "Will Powhatan show pity to his daughter and hear her plea?" she whispered.

He gave no sign that he had heard her but gestured abruptly with his right hand, the first active move he had made since the punishment of the foreigners had begun. Opachisco walked to Smith and, drawing a knife, cut the thongs that held the prisoner to the stake. "Smith, King of James," he said, "will bow his head to the Chief of Chiefs."

Smith walked slowly to the base of the rock and looked up at Powhatan. He held himself erect and, not deigning to bow before the savage, he smiled insolently. In the hours since the insane offer to marry Pocahontas had been made to him he had thought of nothing else, and he found it impossible to believe that he would be deprived of his life because he refused. Powhatan was a splendid actor and was putting on a magnificent show in an attempt to frighten him, but the Indian had demonstrated his real intentions when he had released the other Englishmen without inflicting permanent injury on them, and Smith refused to be deceived.

"I am here," he said confidently.

Powhatan's face was as stiff as the masks his people wore at their festivals celebrating the changes of season. "Smith has heard the word of Powhatan," he declared solemnly, "and he knows the choice that is before him."

"There is no choice," the captain replied impudently. "Powhatan has already heard my answer."

"Then Smith must die," the Chief of Chiefs said flatly, and the silence that followed was broken only by the sound of Pocahontas's choking gasp.

The execution of chiefs could be performed only by their equals, not their inferiors, and heavy clubs were handed to Opachisco and Dalan; as the eldest and youngest sons of Powhatan they were privileged to beat Smith to death. Two other sons of the Chief of Chiefs caught hold of his arms and forced him to his knees at the base of the sacred rock, and the people moved forward to obtain a better view. Opachisco caught hold of his head and placed it against the steep incline, and Smith, glancing up at him, grinned. They were certainly going to extraordinary lengths to convince him they were in earnest.

Pocahontas felt as cold as death itself as she looked down at him, and she marveled at his courage. How he could smile now was beyond her comprehension, and she wondered if he realized that in a few moments the heavy clubs her brothers held would crash down on his head and smash it like an eggshell. She wanted to scream at the top of her voice, to leap from the rock and snatch the clubs from Opachisco and Dalan, but her torment was so great that she was like one in a trance and could not move.

Smith glanced up at her, intending to show her that he knew she and her family were merely deceiving him, but when he saw her face his sardonic smile froze on his lips. Never had he seen such horror and anguish in the expression of another person, and at that instant he realized that Powhatan was not tricking him but was literally intending to have him put to death. As a civilized man he had erred in interpreting the mind of a lusty, vengeful savage, and now he was actually going to pay for that error with his life.

A chill came over him, and then beads of perspiration dripped from his brow and almost blinded him. But his ability to think quickly and calmly was unimpaired, and he knew precisely what had to be done. In his years of experi-

ences with women he had become expert in the art of flirting
with them, and he needed to utilize all of that knowledge
here and now, at once. With a great effort he forced himself
to smile up at Pocahontas, and in his expression there were
passion and longing, eager desire and deep yearning. Most of
all his eyes seemed to tell her that together they could enjoy a
future that would be rich and full and dazzling.

With a wild, fierce cry, inarticulate yet clearly indicating
her feminine strength and resolve to all who heard it, she felt
suddenly liberated from her stupor. Her father's hand was no
longer on her shoulder, and with nothing to halt her she
threw herself down the side of the rock, and as her brothers
raised the ugly clubs high in the air, she caught hold of
Smith's head and shielded him with her own body.

She cradled his head against her breast, and they clung to
each other. Smith, who had always thought of himself
as self-sufficient, was grateful for the soft warmth of the
slender body that protected him, and having been badly
frightened for the first time in his life, he looked up at her
with an ardor that was more real than simulated. Pocahontas, realizing dimly that Opachisco and Dalan had lowered
their clubs, returned Smith's gaze with adoration, and the
emotions they both felt were an irresistible magnet drawing
them even closer together.

His arms tightened around her, she hugged him to her
with a possessiveness that was tender yet fierce, maternal yet
filled with desire, and, conscious only of each other, they
kissed.

The crowd was astonished, and Pocahontas's brothers
looked at each other in bewilderment before tossing aside the
clubs they would now have no opportunity to use. But
Powhatan showed no surprise, and when he rose to his feet
there was a trace of a satisfied smile on his lips. He had judged
Pocahontas correctly, which was not difficult, of course, as
he knew her so well, but he was pleased because he had
known how Smith would react too. So far all had happened

precisely as he wished, and that was good. But the incident was not yet ended: Smith had to be taught a lesson in humility before he would become a devoted husband and a loyal son-in-law.

August–September, 1608

Pocahontas and Smith were still locked in each other's arms as Powhatan stood and raised his right hand in a stiff, formal gesture. The people of the Chickahominy, who had been muttering to each other in wonder, immediately fell silent. "The gods have spoken," their ruler declared sonorously, "and the daughter of the Chief of Chiefs will become the squaw of Smith."

He paused to allow his auditors time to absorb the full meaning of his words and, as he had expected, he saw that the crowd was accepting his pronouncement quietly. His subjects had obeyed him without question for so many years that he had been certain they would cause no trouble now, even though the proposed marriage of a member of the ruler's family to a foreigner was without precedent. Pocahontas, who was too dazed to think coherently, leaned back in

Smith's arms and sighed gently, her face radiant. Her future husband, relieved that his life was no longer in jeopardy, was already developing one or two schemes that might enable him to avoid the commitment and told himself that Powhatan had jumped to a convenient conclusion. He himself had never agreed in so many words to marry the girl and he felt under no obligation to her simply because she had chosen to save him. However, he kept his thoughts to himself and tactfully returned her luminous smile.

Powhatan continued to hold his hand high, indicating that he had not concluded his remarks. "Smith will become a son of the Chief of Chiefs," he declared, "so he did no wrong when he killed Matatulawan, the warrior. The gods have forgiven him for this deed." It was possible that a few members of his audience doubted his ability to interpret the reactions of their deities to the affair with such facility, but apparently no one was inclined to enter into a dispute with a man who had the power of life and death over all.

The sovereign looked up at his people and knew instinctively that they were restless. The reason for their vague dissatisfaction was immediately apparent to him: they had been looking forward to witnessing a deed of violence and they felt cheated because Smith's life had been spared. In part, Powhatan's success lay in his ability to gratify his subjects' whims, particularly when a gesture cost him nothing. And their present desire was one he could fulfill with ease; their mood and his plans coincided perfectly.

"When a youth becomes a warrior and sits at the councils of his elders," he said, "he must first prove he has courage. He must be tried by fire and by water, by hunger and thirst and pain. Smith is a leader of his own people, not a youth, so the Chickahominy will not mock him by asking him to accept these trials." Powhatan privately considered the tests of manhood far too simple for one who already had endured far worse without flinching. "But he must prove his right to take the daughter of the Chief of Chiefs as his squaw. So he will show that he is a true warrior by running the Race of the Damned. The gods have spoken, and Powhatan has spoken."

He resumed his seat, and the people cheered loudly. Smith, who had no idea what was expected of him, realized only that Powhatan had found a way to punish him for his intransigence after all. He glanced at Pocahontas and saw that she was troubled, but she answered his unspoken question with a reassuring smile. "Only the weak and the faint-hearted die when they run the Race of the Damned," she said, her attitude indicating that she intended her words to be soothing. "But Smith, who has the heart of the great black bear, will not die."

Before he could reply, Opachisco tapped him impatiently on the shoulder, and he released the girl, then stood. More than two hundred senior warriors, he saw, were forming a double line, facing each other, leaving a space approximately four feet wide between the rows. Some were armed with knives, others held sticks, and quite a few flourished the short rawhide whips their squaws had used to scourge his companions from Jamestown. He knew what was expected of him without being told: he would be required to run the gauntlet between the two rows, and if he reached the far end intact, the Indians would judge that he had passed the trial. However, should he stumble and fall somewhere along the line, they would consider it their right to beat him mercilessly.

By no stretch of the imagination was the prospect of the ordeal pleasant, but he consoled himself with the thought that at least he would not be killed without being given a chance to defend himself. If agility and stamina and bravery had any meaning, he would survive. He looked at Pocahontas, who smiled at him tremulously, and he knew she was powerless to intervene again. She had already done all she could for him, and he would need to depend on himself alone in the trial. Then he saw Powhatan look down at him from the crest of the rock, and their eyes met in a mutual challenge. Smith stared boldly at the Chief of Chiefs and then turned to Opachisco, who was waiting to conduct him to the head of the line.

"Is one who runs the Race of the Damned allowed to wear what he pleases for the test?"

The eldest son of Powhatan pondered the question briefly. "Those who have run the race have worn garments of many kinds," he replied slowly.

"Then," Smith said crisply, "I will wear a loincloth such as the braves of the Chickahominy wear when they hunt in the forests." It would be too difficult for him to attain any speed in his cumbersome doublet and breeches, and there was a chance, too, that a brave might impede his progress by catching hold of his sleeve or his thick ruff. An idea occurred to him, and he added, "Let him who brings the loincloth also bring some of the venison fat that the squaws use when they cook."

Some of those who heard his request were puzzled, but Opachisco looked at him admiringly, and even Powhatan was impressed. The items Smith wanted were quickly provided and he accepted them eagerly. This was no time for false modesty, and even though there were many hundreds of women in the crowd, he stripped to the skin and energetically rubbed himself with chunks of the animal fat. When he thought his body had become as slippery and difficult to grasp as he could make it, he wound the loincloth around him, twisted it into shape, and made it secure.

Then, his shoulders and back glistening in the late afternoon sun, he saluted Pocahontas smartly, half in jest and half in earnest, and walked with Opachisco toward the line of warriors. "Where do I start to run?" he asked, halting about ten yards from the first two braves, both of whom were holding thick, gnarled sticks.

To the best of Opachisco's knowledge this was the first time the question had ever been raised, and he shrugged.

"Good. I'll begin right here." Smith dug his toes into the

hard earth and started to sprint toward the lane between the two lines. It was obvious to him that the greater his speed as he reached his tormentors, the less time and opportunity they would have to injure him seriously.

As Smith ran he deliberately put all thoughts of future complications out of his mind and concentrated on his immediate problem. He needed more than luck to stay alive or, at least, to avoid permanent injury, and if he succeeded now there would be ample opportunity later to deal with Pocahontas. The warriors who were waiting to maul him were primitive men, he reminded himself, and they would employ elementary techniques in their efforts to knock him from his feet. Those who held sticks were dangerous, because they would try to trip him, and he would need to evade those who carried clubs, too, for their blows might stun him. If he could maintain sufficient speed, knives would scarcely touch him, and the rawhide whips would do the least harm of all; they might sting him and cut into his flesh but they could not halt him.

He lifted his knees high, pumping his legs in rhythmic thrusts as he reached the first two braves, and, lowering his head, he plunged down the narrow path between the two rows. The men who formed the gauntlet were shouting at him derisively in an attempt to confuse and frighten him, and the spectators were screaming for blood, but he shut out the sounds of their voices. Springing nimbly down the lane, he danced and weaved from one side to the other, avoiding the sticks aimed at his ankles and legs. Whenever he saw a heavy bludgeon he headed straight for the brave who held it, and in the moment that the surprised native hesitated, he darted away again.

But it was impossible to escape the less severe blows that rained on his head, his shoulders, and his back, and he made no attempt to sidestep them. Occasionally a sharp, shooting sensation in his side or neck told him that a knife point or a stick had dug into him, but these inconveniences did not slow his pace. The lashes raised ugly welts on his arms and thighs, and one whip cut deep into his forehead, but he considered himself fortunate because the blood that was drawn from the wound trickled down the side of his face rather than into his eyes. His head throbbed, but he still knew precisely what he was doing, and he retained his ability to think coolly.

When he reached a point about halfway down the line, he realized that the blows were becoming more frequent and intense, and it suddenly occurred to him that he had allowed himself to fall into a pattern by running three steps forward, then leaping to the left, racing three more steps and darting to the right. Thus the savages were able to predict his movements, and as a consequence he had become an easier target for them to hit. Altering his tactics abruptly, he squandered precious breath by weaving crazily from side to side, but even though he appeared to be unsure of himself now, his goal was unchanged, he continued to drive forward, and each step he took carried him closer to the end of the long line.

A thick club, heavy enough to kill him had it landed on his head, crashed into his left shoulder, and his whole body seemed to be enveloped in a sheet of flame. The pain was so intense that it numbed him for a moment, and he reeled dizzily into the center of the path. The warriors redoubled their efforts to send him sprawling, and a stick that nicked his right instep sent him plunging into a husky brave, almost knocking the man down. They clung to each other for an instant, and the spectators began to chant triumphantly.

The sound of their voices penetrated Smith's consciousness and, breaking the hold of the warrior who was grappling with him, he lurched back into the clear. He forced himself forward again grimly; his tired legs responded to his will at last, and gradually he managed to pick up speed, to the astonishment of his tormentors, who had expected him to collapse. But he was too exhausted to move once more at his initial pace, and the braves who still waited for him were able

to strike him without difficulty, for he lacked the energy now
to confuse them with agile footwork. Nevertheless, he continued to inch his way toward the last two men who lined the
path, and his ability to absorb punishment that would have
halted a lesser man seemed to be limitless.

He had always been strong, and the life he had led since he
had gone to sea at the age of fifteen had given him a physique
and a stamina that few could equal, but more than
his robust constitution and his reservoir of muscular energy
kept him in motion. He was filled with a determination to
show the savages they could not conquer him; no man had
ever been his master, and he did not propose to be vanquished by ignorant heathens whose sole measurement of an
individual's worth was brute strength. Smith told himself
groggily that he who had conversed with the most learned
men of England and Europe and Islam was not going to end
his days as the victim of stupid Naturals who were totally
lacking in intelligence. He was meeting them on their own
level, allowing them to test him by their standards, and
neither their clubs nor their whips could deprive him of
ultimate victory over them.

Even the warriors who beat at him felt reluctant admiration for him as he pushed relentlessly toward the end of the
line, and a number of the spectators, sympathizing with him
in spite of their antipathy to foreigners, groaned aloud when
he dropped to his hands and knees just before he reached the
last two braves. For a moment it appeared that he was
helpless and that these warriors would beat him into uncon-
sciousness. But he drew on reserves hitherto unknown to him
and crawled past them on all fours, dodging their blows with
a skill that was remarkable in one who could no longer think
clearly.

He was free now, and the gauntlet was behind him; the
knives and sticks of the warriors no longer tormented him,
but the blanket of pain that covered him, the agony that
penetrated into every part of his body was still shattering. He

knew he had won, but one final gesture remained before he would be satisfied and, after sucking in air and resting for a moment, he pulled himself to his feet. He wanted to say something, but knew he lacked the strength to speak, and the ground was rising and falling so rapidly beneath his feet that he was afraid he would fall. Raising his head proudly, he looked back at the double line of warriors and saw they were watching him. A twisted smile appeared on his bloody, swollen face, and he laughed at them, hoarsely and triumphantly, before he collapsed.

Warriors and spectators alike crowded around him and stared down at him with respect. They told each other that he was indeed a fitting husband for the daughter of Powhatan, and when Pocahontas ran to him from the rock at the far side of the sacred clearing, they quickly moved aside for her. She saw that he was still conscious and she stood very still as she offered a silent prayer of thanks, first to the God of the Christians, then to the gods of her ancestors, for having preserved him. Suddenly she turned, and the people noted her resemblance to her father in the way she held herself.

"Let a bed of soft boughs be brought at once," she said, and a number of braves who had never in their lives obeyed an order given by a woman responded to the ring of command in her voice.

A litter of the kind normally used to carry corn from the fields to the storehouses was quickly provided, and Pocahontas, taking complete charge, directed several squaws to arrange buffalo robes on it to make it softer. She herself helped to lift Smith gently onto the bedding, and two of her brothers found themselves among those who lifted the litter to their shoulders. "Let Smith be taken now to the house of the daughter of the Chief of Chiefs," she told them, and as they carried him off toward the hill she took her place directly behind him like a dutiful squaw.

Powhatan, following them at a short distance, frowned and waved away those who wanted to speak to him. He wanted time to think and he was disturbed because Pocahontas had already taken matters into her own hands. It was unprecedented for Smith to be lodged in her house; by rights he should be given a hut of his own in which to recuperate, and under no circumstances was it proper for him to live under his squaw's roof until they were married. But it was obvious that she intended to nurse him back to health, and Powhatan, knowing how she felt, lacked the heart to refuse her the privilege. Besides, he had no wish to countermand a public order she had given and he was afraid that in her present mood she might disobey him if he tried.

Sons, he reflected, were far easier to raise than daughters, and he was relieved that Pocahontas would soon be married. He toyed with the idea of having the ceremony performed at once, but regretfully abandoned the thought. It would be far safer to hold the rites now, of course, and that would save him the bother of posting guards outside Pocahontas's house later, to prevent Smith's possible escape when he recovered his strength. But it would be best to preserve tradition, he decided. The marriage ritual would be arduous, the wedding feast would last for hours, and Smith would not be able to play his proper part in the ceremonies until he was sound and hearty again. Powhatan sighed and almost regretted the vengeful impulse that had made Smith an invalid, but there were consolations, and the conviction that the pale-skinned young chief would be far easier to handle in the future was not the least of them. And it was satisfying to reflect that through his ingenuity he had solved his daughter's problems and made her future secure.

During the following days the few people who occasionally caught a glimpse of Pocahontas certainly realized that she had never looked happier, even though she was busier than ever before in her life. She gave her own bed to Smith and uncomplainingly slept on the ground in the far corner, after sending Ru-Sa elsewhere. She waited on the injured Englishman day and night, and although her father offered to send experienced squaws to relieve her, she refused to allow anyone else to come near him. She prepared rich broths and other nourishing foods for him, and at first, when he was too weak to lift a bowl to his lips, she fed him his meals, sometimes coaxing him, now and then urging him firmly when he had no appetite. Whenever she could spare the time, she cooked a fresh batch of the herb and moss poultice that reduced his fever, and each night at sundown, before he drifted off to sleep, she patiently applied the evil-smelling medicine to his cuts and bruises.

Thanks to her ministrations, he began to improve far sooner than any of the Chickahominy had expected, and at the end of a week he was able to converse with Pocahontas for brief periods. She would not permit him to sit up, however, and when she gave him orders she spoke to him with such crisp authority that he obeyed her meekly, much to his own surprise. He watched her in silence for hours at a time as she moved around the room and he often marveled at the change that had come over her.

She was no longer shy or unsure of herself, and although no task seemed too menial or unpleasant for her, she carried herself with a new air of mature dignity. Her girlish buoyancy, which had irritated Smith, was gone, and in its place was an attitude of earnest, sober purpose. She was still young, of course, and now, as previously, he was as much aware of her fresh appeal as he was conscious of her beauty. It was impossible for him to lose sight of the obvious when they lived under the same roof, but he could not rid himself of the feeling that she was very different from the naïve girl to whom he had made love in the Jamestown blockhouse.

After several days of pondering the matter, he realized what had happened to her and he was annoyed with himself for his lack of perceptivity. Pocahontas was a woman whose dearest wish had been granted. She had what she wanted and she was determined to keep it, to let nothing on earth interfere with her happiness. Her single-minded devotion to him was upsetting, and he secretly cursed the day they had met. He had often been told that few women were capable of such dedicated love, and he thought sourly that it had been his ill fortune to become entangled with one of them. Pocahontas would unquestionably be a perfect wife, but he had no desire to be married, particularly to a savage. The very idea of appearing at Whitehall with her and presenting her to King James was so disturbing that his fever rose for a day and a night, and Pocahontas made matters all the worse by daubing him with fresh quantities of her noxious salve.

The second week of his convalescence passed more rapidly, for she permitted him to sit up for longer and longer periods, and each day he felt stronger. He discovered that her command of English had improved greatly, and it was flattering to realize that she had spent the whole of the summer studying his language. Although he had all but forgotten her after her visit to Jamestown, she had been working assiduously with no purpose in mind other than to please him when they next met. It was a novelty to be able to chat with her freely, and as there was nothing else to occupy his time during his enforced confinement in this land of savages, he took a renewed interest in her.

Pocahontas listened so attentively to every word he said that he thoroughly enjoyed showing off his learning to her. She was fascinated by his descriptions of the world he had known before he had come to America and she rarely disputed his word. By tacit mutual consent neither of them mentioned his own personal situation, and Smith was grateful to her for her delicacy, but there were occasions when Pocahontas's lack of intellect and background irritated him. Her infrequent attempts to express her own opinions invariably annoyed him, too, for not only was she a woman and thus completely illogical, but her strange Indian approach to any topic made her views meaningless.

The question of religion seemed to be much on her mind, and she brought it up at every opportunity, but Smith's knowledge of theology was limited and in two or three brief discussions he told her all he knew. However, he was unwilling to admit his ignorance of anything, and one afternoon, when Pocahontas again brought up the subject of God, he began to tell her glibly of the dissensions that had split England since King Henry VIII had broken off relations with the Pope and had established his own church. Pocahontas made no comment until he mentioned the name of Sir Thomas More, and then suddenly she smiled.

"He was a very wise man," she said.

Smith was so surprised that he forgot what he had been saying; controlling an impulse to laugh, he raised an eyebrow and glanced at her quizzically.

She rose from her place at the side of his bed and hurried across the room to a small carved chest in which she kept her most precious possessions, her books. She took one, returned to Smith, and, seating herself cross-legged on the ground, began to flip rapidly through the pages. Her serious absorption amused him, and it occurred to him that she was really one of the most attractive wenches he had ever known. But he warned himself sternly not to let himself think too much about her pretty face and pert figure; they had already caused enough difficulties for him.

Pocahontas found what she was seeking and looked pleased. "It was Sir Thomas More who said, 'Assist me up, and in coming down I will shift for myself.'"

"So he did," Smith murmured.

"That was a very wonderful remark." She repeated it silently, her lips moving and her eyes solemn.

He wondered what had made him think such a stupid girl was attractive, and he raised himself to one elbow. She was an uneducated primitive, and her pretentiousness angered him. "What do you know of Sir Thomas More?" he demanded.

"Nothing," Pocahontas replied simply, "except that he said something very true. His remark reminds me of you and me."

"How can you possibly understand what a man said unless you know who he was and why he said it?" Smith asked crossly. It would be typical of her to quote some absurd legend about one of her pagan gods to justify her argument, he told himself.

"John Smith has helped me and has taught me much. But someday, if I study long and hard, he will not need to assist me any more," she assured him earnestly.

"Sir Thomas," he declared sententiously, "was Lord Chancellor of England." He had no intention of describing the position itself to her, so that would end the subject, and he could return to his previous topic, provided he could remember it.

She did not seem to hear him. "When the day comes that I gain wisdom, I will know as much as John Smith."

The very idea was so ridiculous that he refused to dignify it with a comment. Obviously she was incapable of understanding that she was a benighted savage, and her effrontery in even daring to presume that she would become the equal of a man who would soon be recognized as one of the great savants of the age was childish. "Sir Thomas," he said acidly, "was also a noted astronomer, a distinguished mathematician, and a renowned author. I dare say you've never heard of his great study of civilization, *Utopia*."

"*Utopia*," she replied, memorizing the word. "I hope there is a copy in Jamestown, so I may read it."

She would never again go near Jamestown if he had anything to say about it, but this was not the time to tell her that she had no place in his plans. "Sir Thomas was a theologian, too," he said, and when she looked blank, he added condescendingly, "He was a man who thought much about God and knew a great deal about Him."

Pocahontas was delighted. "Then I will surely read his book. And it proves that what I felt about him was right."

Smith wished he hadn't brought the name of More into the conversation. "How does it prove anything?"

"When one knows much about God, all that he writes and

says must be true," she answered brightly. "So it is as I have spoken. John Smith assists me. He teaches me all that he knows, so I will also become very wise." Evidently the young and inexperienced of every land were alike and were confidently certain they could mold the shape of the future to fit their preconceived patterns. "No one person in the world can ever learn all there is to know, and when I am wise, then I will help John Smith."

No woman, not even one who had been educated by private tutors, had ever dared to think that her intellectual attainments could be useful to him, and he was outraged. But he forcibly reminded himself that he was still Powhatan's prisoner and consequently worded his rejection of her offer obliquely. "Do you know when Sir Thomas made the comment you admire so much? On the execution block, a few moments before he lost his head defying his King."

Pocahontas's expression was smug. "Sir Thomas More knew many things about God and man that his King did not."

"I suppose he did," Smith said uncertainly.

"Then he was much like John Smith, whose knowledge is greater than that of the Chief of Chiefs." Obviously the analogy that existed in her mind strengthened her conviction. "The father of Pocahontas wanted to kill John Smith." The memory of the incident depressed her, but after a moment of reflection she became brighter. "All that is in the past, and we waste our tears when we remember sorrow. It is better to think of the day when we will help each other."

She could dream as much as she pleased, he told himself bitterly, but her fancies would never be realized. She did not know it, but she had done him a favor, for by letting him see that she envisioned a permanent future for herself at his side, she had strengthened his determination to be rid of her as soon as he recovered his health. Her presence during his convalescence was convenient, of course, and he would enjoy living with her for a short time when he was strong again, provided there were no lasting complications. It was unfortunate that she thought of herself as a real wife, but he had only himself to blame. Had he not taught her English and given her a Bible, she would have remained unspoiled. Under the circumstances there was only one way to terminate the present fruitless and dangerous conversation and, pretending to grow drowsy, he turned his back to her and closed his eyes.

In spite of Pocahontas's interference with his peace of mind, Smith continued to improve each day and he devoted himself with increasing energy to the problem of working out a sensible escape plan. A score of ideas occurred to him, but he was forced to reject all of them; some were too involved, some were not practical, and some were far too simple. He had gained a grudging respect for Powhatan's cunning, and realizing that the Chief of Chiefs had successfully trapped him into making a marriage contract even though he had not agreed in so many words to wed Pocahontas, it was logical to assume that he would be watched closely until she became his wife.

When he was strong enough to stand and walk from one end of the hut to the other, he discovered that he had made a correct estimate of the situation. Four warriors, all armed with English muskets, stood guard outside the house day and night, and when he went outdoors for short strolls with Pocahontas, two others always followed them at a short distance. He asked her to explain the reason for their presence, and she replied that her father had assigned the braves to protect him. Apparently she herself accepted this explanation without question and, as nearly as Smith could judge, the possibility that he might try to escape had never crossed her mind.

He immediately thought there must be some way to utilize her innocence to his advantage, but the attitude of the warriors indicated clearly that they were acting under direct orders from Powhatan and would refuse to obey the girl if she tried to send them away. One afternoon, when he and Pocahontas took a walk past Powhatan's lodge, he tested the scheme by suggesting that she dismiss the braves. She thought he wanted to be alone with her and promptly followed his advice, for she could see no reason why he needed protection even from the most vengeful members of the tribe, when they were so close to her father's own house, where not even the most rashly courageous would dare to attack the Chief of Chiefs' guest and future son-in-law. But the warriors blithely ignored Pocahontas's request, and Smith abandoned the notion of using her as his unwitting ally.

He frequently toyed with the idea of stealing some weapons, overpowering the guards late at night, and making a break for freedom, but he gave up that plan, too, when he realized that the Chickahominy, with their superior knowledge of the wilderness, would catch him in the forests or on the river and bring him back. One other factor also deterred him from taking bold action: he knew that even if he should manage to escape and return to Jamestown, Powhatan would not drop the affair but would probably wage war against the whole colony if the settlers gave him shelter. As his own future would be ruined if Jamestown should be destroyed, he consequently would gain nothing even if he found some way to escape and return there.

Smith spent long hours brooding over the situation, and Pocahontas, aware that he was morose, concluded that he was homesick for his own people. She was afraid that his state of mind would retard his recovery and tried to think of something that would help him. She still had the two bolts of cloth he had given her on his first visit to the land of the Chickahominy, and one day the idea of making herself a dress like that worn by the women of Jamestown crossed her mind. If she could duplicate such a garment, she told herself, he would be pleased and would certainly recover his health more rapidly.

She often recognized his rejection of her in his expression or his tone of voice, but she was certain he loved her and, after spending a great deal of time pondering the subject, she became convinced that if she made herself the English gown he would not only demonstrate his affection for her more openly but would be able to visualize her place in their joint life more clearly. Ru-Sa had often told her that men lacked imagination, and for once Ru-Sa was right; Smith's attitude made it plain that he felt uncomfortable at the prospect of spending the rest of his days with a woman who looked like a Chickahominy squaw, but when she appeared before him in the attire of his own people, he would rejoice and with nothing to worry him would quickly regain the weight he had lost.

He usually slept for an hour or two after each of his meals, and she took advantage of this time by quietly leaving the house and going to the nearby hut of Opachisco, whose senior wife was very clever with a bone needle and knife and made most of the family's ceremonial robes. They worked together for two weeks, and at last the gown was ready. One afternoon, after Smith had finished a stew of goat meat and had dropped off, Pocahontas hurried up to put on the dress and surprise him when he awoke. She was so excited that her hand trembled as she donned the dress, and the admiration of Opachisco's wife gave her increased confidence; her plan, she reflected as she struggled into the unfamiliar garments, was certain to succeed.

The sleeves of her close-fitting bodice, or doublet, of the natural cream wool were padded with soft, dried moss and had strips of the bright blue satin set in under long slashes. As she had no lace or cambric, she wore broad bracelets of dyed and plaited porcupine quills sewn onto bans of deerskin at her wrists. Her long blue satin skirt was held out stiffly by an improvised farthingale, or stiffened petticoat, made of woven reeds. Her ruff was unlike any she had seen in Jamestown and was made of multicolored feathers.

It had been impossible for her to duplicate the shoes worn by the pale-skinned Englishwomen, and after several futile attempts to re-create them, she and Opachisco's wife had given up their efforts. Neither Pocahontas's best moccasins nor her newest sandals looked appropriate with the dress, so she compromised by wearing no shoes at all, and when she was dressed she walked barefooted back to her own house. As the people of the town were not permitted to approach the crest of Powhatan's hill, only a few of her relatives and the guards assigned to watch John Smith saw her, but she was so occupied with her own thoughts that she did not realize that the women were looking at her enviously and that the warriors stared at her.

As she approached her hut she heard Smith stirring inside and knew he was awake and, pausing at the entrance, she peered into the room. He was pacing up and down restlessly, as he did so often these days, and her heart began to pound furiously. Pocahontas did not speak, and Smith, although he obviously knew she had returned, said nothing either and greeted her with an absent nod. She was so anxious to attract his attention that she wanted to shout, but instead she stood just inside the door flap and waited for him to notice her. She was so still that eventually he realized something out of the ordinary was taking place, and he glanced idly at her without pausing or breaking the rhythm of his stride. Then suddenly he halted abruptly and gaped at her.

Pocahontas proudly submitted herself to his inspection and stood erect, with her arms at her sides after the manner of the women she had seen in Jamestown. She had imagined this scene so often that she could have closed her eyes and felt she was still dreaming, had an unexpected, acute sense of self-consciousness not made her uncomfortable. In spite of her embarrassment, however, she was sure in her own mind that he would approve, that his sense of inner disturbance would vanish, and that he would understand precisely why she had gone to such pains to please him.

To her astonishment and dismay he began to chuckle, and when she dared to raise her eyes she saw he was looking at her feet and laughing. She wanted to draw her toes under the protective cover of the long skirt, but pride forced her to remain still. It had never once crossed her mind that he might ridicule her, and she did not know how to cope with his amusement. The fear that she had failed flooded over her, and she wished that the evil gods who lived beneath the earth would swallow her, but they ignored her silent entreaties and left her to stand miserably, watching Smith's broad grin.

"No shoes?" he asked.

Unable to reply, she shook her head. If he thought about the matter at all, he would surely realize she knew nothing of bootmaking.

Smith looked her up and down slowly, and gradually the expression in his eyes changed. The smile faded from his lips, and he was amazed to find that she was as desirable in her outlandish imitation of an English gown as she was in her native Chickahominy dress. It was plain to him that she had gone to a great deal of trouble to make herself attractive to him, and after a brief, fierce struggle with himself, he decided to accept the inevitable. For the present, at least, escape from the Indian town was impossible, and he told himself he was being stupid not to seize whatever compensations were offered to him.

Pocahontas, sensitive to every change in his moods, felt his amusement vanish, and a single glance at his face was enough for her to know that he wanted her. Her grief evaporated and she eagerly jumped to the conclusion that she had been mistaken: he had laughed because he was happy, and he had certainly not been jeering at her or mocking her. His blatantly obvious craving for her convinced her that what she wanted to believe was true, and she felt such a great surge of love for him that he responded at once and moved toward her.

She had told herself repeatedly during the weeks of his

convalescence that she would not give herself to him again until she became his wife, and although she was starved for his love, she put a hand against his chest and held him off. According to the standards of her own nation, she was right, and she knew, from all she had read in the Bible, that the English and other foreign tribes were even more strict in their attitude on the subject than were her own people. She could not blame Smith, to be sure; he wanted her so much that he was impetuously discarding rules, but she had sworn not to break the law again. Smith had reappeared in her life after she had prayed to his God, she had promised Him to obey His commands and now, tempted for the first time since she had made her vow, she would prove she could be strong.

Smith was annoyed when Pocahontas gently pushed him away, but she continued to look radiant. "John Smith has been sick for many days," she said. "Ris disappeared from the night sky and has come back again, yet it has taken all this time for John Smith to become strong. Each day I have seen him grow in health and now I know he is well. When a man wants a woman he is no longer sick." Emotion overcame her, and she unconsciously reverted to her own tongue. "Pocahontas will tell her father what has happened, and the Chief of Chiefs will order the wedding to take place at once."

Once again, Smith thought, a snare had been set for him, and he had stepped into it with his eyes open.

October, 1608

Drums carried the glad tidings through the wilderness from village to village, and within a few days representatives of every nation in the Chickahominy Confederation began to arrive at Powhatan's capital for the wedding of his only daughter to the foreigner from across the sea. Many chiefs came in person, attended by their wives, their elders, and their principal war lords, and the few rulers who were either too ill or too busy to make the journey sent their sons in their stead. Gifts from tribes as far distant as the Mohawk in the north and the Cherokee in the south were sent to Smith and his squaw, and Opachisco, who kept careful count to make certain that no nation slighted Powhatan's majesty and power, told the bride-to-be that the belts of wampum and the foodstuffs she and Smith were receiving would make them wealthy.

There were bullocks and cows from the northern tribes, huge baskets of dried fish from those who lived near the

seacoast, and some of the lesser chiefs who lived in the
interior brought whole carcasses of buffalo and bear with
them. The Chesapeake created a minor crisis when they sent
the bridegroom a young and pretty concubine, but Powhatan
disposed of the problem quickly and firmly by saying nothing
to Smith about the gift and taking the girl into his own
household. Opachisco, jealous of his father, thereafter made
certain that all present-bearing messengers reported first to
him when they arrived.

Housing facilities were strained, as each of the visiting
dignitaries required a number of homes for himself and his
entourage, and failure to provide a chief with the accommo-
dations to which his rank entitled him would have caused
serious repercussions. Dalan, who was in charge of these
arrangements, was taxed beyond his experience and was
forced to appeal to his father for help. Powhatan promptly
ordered some new huts built near the sacred clearing, where
the ceremony would be held, and the dilemma was solved.

The Chickahominy warriors engaged in daily games and
trials of strength with the visiting braves, and each night
groups gathered around scores of fires to vie with each other
in telling tales of their prowess at hunting and their skill in
war. The squaws worked incessantly, cooking special dishes
for the wedding feast and preparing meals in the meantime
for their families and the hordes of guests. The elders practiced the orations they would deliver at the wedding, and the
artistically inclined composed songs, created dances, and
made the masks that a select group would be required to wear
at the ceremony. The maidens spent long hours sewing, as it
was customary for every unmarried girl to appear at a wedding only in something she herself had made.

Powhatan took advantage of the visit of so many of his
subsidiary chieftains by holding a series of individual confer-
ences with them, impressing them with his might and
strengthening his hold over them. The powerful Seneca,
who were as strong in the north as the Chief of Chiefs was in

his own territory, sent the son and the brother of the ruling sachem to represent them, and Powhatan, recognizing them as equals, concluded a treaty with them in which each promised to respect the boundaries and the rights of the other.

Ru-Sa, enjoying her day of greatest glory, was in charge of the arrangements for the feast by virtue of her position as the bride's custodian, and she made life miserable for the cooks and mask makers alike. Nothing less than perfection satisfied her, and she forced the unfortunates who were under her supervision to repeat their efforts whenever their work failed to meet her standards. Ru-Sa was determined to provide the wedding guests with a feast so bountiful that songs would be sung about it for years to come, and under her direction huge pots of meats simmered continually, special parties of hunters scoured the countryside for wild dogs to be made into stew, and fish, caught by the hundreds in the rivers and lakes, were smoked slowly over hickory logs. The first hint of autumn was in the air, and this was the season when every tribe laid aside stores for the months ahead, but Ru-Sa dipped into the supplies without thought for the future. Several of the elders became alarmed, but she would listen to no one, and finally Powhatan himself had to restrain her prodigal enthusiasm.

Pocahontas took no part in the festivities preceding the wedding, and none of the visitors were permitted to see her. According to the inviolable traditions of her ancestors, a bride was required to spend half a moon's time in complete isolation prior to the wedding, and as Powhatan was considered the deputy of the gods, great care was taken to insure that his daughter observed custom. A tent of skins was erected for her in the center of the sacred clearing, and the squaws of eight of the most prominent elders were assigned to watch over her. They prepared her meals, they slept with her in the tent, and each day they performed private, mystic rites over her to prepare her for her future life.

In times past a bride not only made the clothes she would wear at her wedding but first treated the raw skins as well; however, the daughter of a mighty chief needed to dress in robes suitable to her rank, so Pocahontas was given specially selected leather that had already been cured. But she made her own dyes, sewed the clothes herself, and glazed the white feathers that would stud her headband by painting them with the boiled gum of the little tree known as the prickly ash. This extraordinarily delicate task was one which girls of lesser families were not called upon to perform, as they wore less ornate headdresses when they were married, but Pocahontas worked so diligently and cheerfully that the old squaws who attended her were impressed by both her skill and her disposition. They predicted that her marriage would be a happy one, and their views coincided with the opinions of three elderly warriors who had been appointed to read the omens for the future in the stars.

Usually a bridegroom was surrounded by his relatives and friends during the two weeks preceding the wedding, but no invitations were extended to the colonists at Jamestown, and when Smith was moved from Pocahontas's house to a lodge farther down the hill, the braves who lived there with him were under strict orders from Powhatan to keep him under observation at all times. Under no circumstances was he allowed to leave the town, and when several of the visiting chiefs politely asked him to accompany them on hunting trips, Powhatan himself hastily explained to the guests that the bridegroom could not accept as he was recuperating from an illness.

Smith did participate in some of the younger men's games, which were held each day inside the ring of hills, and although he was woefully inept in hitting a target with a tomahawk or knife, his prowess with a bow and arrow surprised the Naturals. At his request a contest was held in the firing of muskets, and Powhatan, after pondering the matter, decided that it would be safe enough to let Smith use a firestick, as there were too many warriors present for him to intimidate them and escape. Some of the Chickahominy had been practicing with the muskets they had received early in the summer, but they quickly discovered they were not in a class with Smith, and the competition was abandoned. Instead, Smith gave several exhibitions in target shooting, and the visitors from other tribes were awed by his skill. This suited Powhatan, who reasoned that his satellites and allies alike would be loath to wage war against a nation armed with fifty such powerful weapons.

Somewhat to the surprise of the Chief of Chiefs, who kept an eye that was considerably more than paternal on his future son-in-law, Smith was relaxed, lighthearted, and seemed to have accepted his lot. He joked readily with the warriors who guarded him, he ate heartily at the nightly pre-nuptial feasts, and his curiosity was as insatiable as it had been in the past. He sought out the visitors, particularly those who came from distant tribes, and he questioned them eagerly regarding the country in which they lived, their customs, and their language. They, of course, were flattered by his attention and they told Powhatan he was fortunate; not many young chiefs were as wise as the pale-skinned foreigner.

Two nights prior to the wedding all the guests had gathered, and after eating a rich stew of rabbit, boiled dog, and goat, the visitors and their hosts gathered around a fire. According to tradition, this was the night set aside to pay honor to the warrior who was going to be married, and the leaders of every tribe rose, one after another, to entertain Smith by regaling him with accounts of their exploits and their valor. He realized he was expected to reply in kind, and when he stood at last, he decided to tell them about some of his adventures in Islam. They could not picture the civilization he described and they were completely ignorant of the location of the countries of northern Africa and the Near East, but such minor details were unimportant.

What mattered was that his tales were exciting, and he told

his stories with deceptively simple artistry. The savages were a perfect audience and they responded to every word he uttered with such complete and absorbed attention that he soon found he was enjoying himself. Carried away by the fervor of the Indians, he began to embroider his accounts, and when he discovered they accepted everything he told them, he threw off all restraint. Romanticizing and fabricating, he mixed fact and fiction wildly, but the more preposterous his recital became, the more avidly they listened to him. Encouraged by their reaction, he made a mental note to include several of the stories in his future chronicles of his life in America. He would exercise greater care in maintaining an aura of credibility when he reduced the tales to paper, but he would certainly tell the same stories, for he was pleased to find that he frequently struck something basic in human nature, so English readers would be sure to devour this same blend of truth and fancy.

When he sat down the Naturals cheered him, and he relished their applause. He had been right, he thought, to give in gracefully to the unavoidable. Neither Powhatan nor any other Chickahominy, not even Pocahontas herself, had realized that the ceremony in which he was to participate was not really binding on him. The ceremony that would make Pocahontas his wife was a pagan ritual, and no English court would consider the marriage legal. He would be obliged to act the role of Pocahontas's husband only for the brief time they would be together, and when he left her, which he would do at the first possible moment, he would be relieved of all responsibility for her and to her.

The realization that any pledges he might be called upon to make in the savage rites would be meaningless had occurred to him when he was forced to face the fact that he could not escape, and he was annoyed with himself for not having seen the matter clearly when he had first been brought here as a prisoner. Had he been more alert, and consequently more amenable, he could have saved himself the crippling pain that had been inflicted on him when he ran the Race of the Damned. He had not suffered in vain, however; he knew better now and was conducting himself accordingly. He would say and do whatever was required of him at the wedding, and when he deserted Pocahontas, his conscience would be clear. The natives could think of him as her husband all they pleased, but under English law and in his own eyes he would still be a bachelor.

His one concern was the attitude of the girl herself, and he was afraid she might stumble on the truth. She spent at least an hour each day reading the Bible he had so foolishly given her, and conceivably it might dawn on her that she would not really become his wife unless a Christian ceremony were performed. If she should be sufficiently intelligent to make such a request of him—and he no longer underestimated her shrewdness—he would have to use all of his powers of persuasion to convince her that it was unnecessary to be married a second time.

Smith's spirits remained high, and when the day of the wedding arrived he knew that he was using the right tactics, for Powhatan, impressed by his willingness to co-operate, returned his steel helmet and corselet to him, together with his sword. His boots were shabby, and his shirt, which Pocahontas had carefully mended for him with strands of wool from her precious bolt of cloth, was threadbare, but he had no other. He had not acquired the knack of shaving with a sharp Indian knife in cold water and he cut his face several times while scraping off his beard, but he was buoyant as he dressed. He was hungry, but when Opachisco, who came to escort him to the sacred clearing, told him he was forbidden by tradition to eat prior to the ceremony, he made no complaint. Soon he would be his own master again, and in the meantime petty disturbances could not upset him.

A huge throng had gathered in the clearing to witness the ceremony, and people stared at Pocahontas's tent, hoping in vain to detect some sign of movement inside. Two of the old

squaws blocked the entrance, however, and successfully hid
the bride, who would make her appearance at the appropriate moment in the ceremony. The visiting chiefs were
gathered at the base of the flat-topped rock at one end of the
field, and all had daubed themselves liberally with paint.
Perched on the side of the rock were the representatives of the
sachem of the Seneca, who had been granted this special
honor as a sign of their host's esteem.

All of Pocahontas's brothers except Opachisco stood in a
circle around her tent, knives in their right hands, symbolizing the belief that a bride was inviolate and that anyone who
wanted to carry her off would first be forced to fight her
relatives, under whose protection she remained until she
became a squaw at the end of the ceremony. The women of
Powhatan's family, who usually stayed in the background,
enjoyed unique privileges at weddings, and they sat on the
ground between the tent and the rock so they could see
everything that happened. Opachisco's two small sons, wearing unaccustomed loincloths, sat with their mothers and
were forcibly restrained when they tried to dart off and play
with their friends at the edge of the crowd. Weddings meant
nothing to them, but as members of the Chief of Chiefs'
family they were not free to do as they pleased. This was
particularly true of the older of the boys, who was five; he
would someday become the ruler of the nation and of the
Confederation, provided he survived the harsh tests that
would begin when he reached the age of seven summers.

Sixteen masked drummers, each of them representing one
of the major gods of the Chickahominy, struck up a rhythmic
beat when Opachisco and John Smith appeared, walking
side by side, and the people cheered as the bridegroom was
led to the foot of the rock on which he had almost lost his life.
Smith, looking at the smiling faces of the savages, was
gratified at the friendliness they expressed. Most of them
obviously respected him, and those braves who had tried to
beat him into insensibility when he had run the gauntlet

showed warm regard for him. Only a few of the younger unmarried warriors, who had hoped to win Pocahontas themselves, displayed any hostility to him, and he ignored their stony glares. He enjoyed the good will of the majority, which was important, for he would be free to come and go as he pleased when they began to take his continued presence in their community for granted.

The throb of the drums became louder, and Powhatan, followed by the elders of his council, walked solemnly onto the field and mounted the rock. His robe, which he wore only at festivals of religious significance, was unique, and the people fell silent as they gazed at it. When it was draped over his shoulders he was believed to be more than mortal, and even the guests who worshiped their own gods rather than those of the Chickahominy looked at him in awe. The outer side of the skin was painted with yellow circles signifying Ek and silver crescents symbolizing Ris. Jagged red splotches around the neck meant that he was the representative of Ti-Ba, the god of fire, and the bright blue panels at the front of the robe indicated that he was the deputy of Gan, the water god. And most impressive of all, a jagged orange line down the center of his back was the emblem of Rito-fer, the god of lightning, who, in the opinion of some medicine men, had been the original founder of the tribe and was Powhatan's ancestor.

Opachisco, acting as the family's spokesman, approached the rock and asked for permission to begin. Powhatan nodded benignly, and the elders, each of whom carried two dry sticks, laid them in a pile of kindling. A flaming torch was carried into the clearing by the youngest of the Chief of Chiefs' granddaughters, who was four, and when the child faltered, almost burning herself, the drums beat still more loudly to conceal her blunder. Opachisco took the torch from her and plunged it into the pile of wood; in a moment the flames leaped high in the air, and Smith was invited to step forward.

He was dismayed when Opachisco, gesturing broadly, indicated that he was to walk into the fire. There was a chance that he would be burned severely, and at the very least his boots, the only pair he had brought into the wilderness, would be badly scorched. He was relieved when Opachisco whispered to him that he need not actually set foot in the flames, so he paused and merely made a pretense of moving into the fire. A group of squaws began to chant to the accompaniment of the drums, and he judged by the words of their song that by this act the bridegroom was presumed to have cleansed himself of all evil.

Three elders then approached him and requested him to remove his helmet. Scores of women joined in the chant as the old men smeared his forehead and cheeks with streaks of green paint, the symbol of fertility, and the rhythm of the drums became faster, more insistent. Two warriors dragged a captive wild boar into the clearing, and Opachisco, again whispering instructions, told the bridegroom to slit the animal's throat with his own knife. Smith, disgusted by the barbarous ceremony, quickly drew his sword and put the animal out of its misery. But the worst was yet to come, and Opachisco, catching some of the beast's blood in a gourd, handed the cup to Smith. The Englishman lowered his head as he lifted the cup to his lips, so no one could see that he was not actually drinking, and he conquered his feeling of revulsion only by exerting so much self-control that he failed to hear the chant and therefore did not learn the meaning of this portion of the ceremony. When he wrote his authoritative account of Indian weddings, he thought, he would need to fill in the gap with something that sounded authentic.

The crowd stirred, and the squaws who had been keeping watch over Pocahontas filed out of the tent in the center of the clearing; walking quickly and silently to Smith, they surrounded him and led him to the far side of the field, where, he gathered, he was now to play the part of a spectator for a time. All of the Chickahominy, men and women alike,

joined wholeheartedly in a new chant, and Ru-Sa, enjoying
the moment of the greatest grandeur she had ever known,
stood in the entrance and then moved slowly into the clearing. Clusters of small inedible orange berries, which the
Jamestown settlers called *tomate*, after the Spanish fashion,
studded her headband, and although she would no longer
serve as custodian to Powhatan's daughter, she would be
entitled to wear similar wild berries in her hair for the rest of
her days in recognition of her services.

The drums fell silent, abruptly and simultaneously, and in
the hush that followed Pocahontas stepped into the open.
She halted and, looking neither to the left nor the right, stood
still for a long moment. According to tradition, this was the
one hour in her life when the attention of everyone was
centered on her; after she became a squaw, she would be
expected to retire into the background and remain there
unobtrusively. The Chickahominy looked at her in admiration and smiled approvingly; now, as always, she fitted the
role she had been called on to play. Many of the visiting
chiefs, seeing her for the first time, gaped at her openly and
murmured to each other that the lavish songs of praise that
had been sung in her honor these past few nights had failed to
do justice to her. Even John Smith stared at her and for an
instant he forgot that the whole marriage ceremony was a
purposeless farce.

She looked fresh and young, altogether desirable, but
there was strength in her eyes and the way she held her head,
dignity in her bearing. Everyone who saw her was aware of
her fragile, feminine loveliness, but the more discerning
knew there was a hard core of integrity and resolve beneath
her surface beauty. She certainly realized she was attractive,
but she took her charm for granted, neither flaunting it nor
behaving with false modesty, and the dominion she exercised
over the assemblage came from an inner sense of grace, a
conviction that the unprecedented step she was taking in
becoming the squaw of a foreigner-from-across-the-sea was

right. Her certainty conveyed itself to every person present, and the people rejoiced with her. Only Smith felt uneasy.

Pocahontas was wearing moccasins of pale kidskin and a simple, knee-length tunic similar to that of the other women, but at the neck in front a silver crescent was painted on the leather. A symbol of the new moon, it meant that she was embarking on a venture for which all of her previous life had been a preparation. The white feathers were sewn to a buckskin headband that curved down over her head, covered her ears, and fell over the front of her tunic. A yellow-lined robe of white rabbit fur hung from her shoulders, and the early autumn breeze ruffled the face of the robe.

Opachisco, his features plainly reflecting the pride he felt in her, beckoned to her, and Pocahontas walked toward him, her step sedate and her eyes grave. She had imagined that she would hate this moment, for the white headdress on which she had labored so long and hard gave testimony to a lie, but now that she was actually participating in the ceremony, nothing mattered to her except that she and John Smith were being joined in marriage at last.

She halted and, crossing her hands over her breasts, bowed three times, first to Powhatan, then to her brother, and finally to Smith. She was so pleased to see that Smith's face had filled out in the two weeks since they had parted that she could not maintain the air of solemnity that was expected of her. She smiled, and the people, who would have been horrified if another girl had violated custom so flagrantly, laughed and nodded. Several of the guests glanced at Powhatan to see if he was angry, but he, too, was grinning broadly, and the visitors correctly concluded that in his eyes she could do no wrong.

Pocahontas removed her cloak and handed it to Opachisco, who moved off, leaving her alone. The drums began to tap again, very rapidly but softly, and thirty dancers pranced out into the clearing. Some carried spears, other brandished knives, and one tall warrior held aloft a large round stone painted yellow. All wore short, multifeathered aprons or

skirts over their loincloths, and the upper portions of their
bodies had been smeared with a glistening oil. Their faces
were hidden behind large masks, two or three times the size
of real faces, which were made of cornhusks stiffened and
held together with a thick fish paste and then carefully
painted. No two were the same, but there were many
similarities; the eyes of each were exaggerated, and regardless
of whether the images were laughing or scowling, expressing
fear or serenity, all were grotesque.

The drums suggested abandon now, and the dancers
formed in a tight circle around the motionless Pocahontas,
whirling and gesturing as they capered. They moved faster
and faster, and the spectators, intoxicated by the beat of the
drums, began to sway too. Occasionally one or another of the
dancers left the ring, approached Pocahontas, and waved his
arms energetically as he leaped and pirouetted close to her.
Some seemed to threaten her, others demonstrated passion,
and two or three, whose acting ability was limited, merely
leaped around in a frenzy.

The dancers occasionally twirled and spun so near to
Pocahontas that she could feel the heat of their bodies, but
none of them actually touched her, which was a remarkable
tribute to their skill. They were presumably tempting her,
warning her, and frightening her, and the crowd watched her
closely to see if she responded to any of the dancers' movements. A bride who either shrank from one of the masked
figures or involuntarily joined in the dance was believed to be
doomed to spend her days in misery. But Pocahontas remained immobile even when one of the prancing warriors
seemed about to crash into her; the people, themselves
shuffling and bobbing to the insinuating rhythm of the
drums, marveled at her ability to stand as still as the carved
poles they planted upright in the fields to curry the favor of
the harvest gods. They agreed that no bride had ever shown
such superb self-control and they felt certain that every sign
pointed to a long and successful marriage.

The dancers did not stop until they were exhausted, and

even when they were gasping for breath they did not halt, and the drums urged them to expend even greater effort. Finally they limped from the clearing, and although the drummers fell silent, the echo of a throbbing rhythm seemed to reverberate from the hills. The squaws who surrounded Smith moved forward with him, and Pocahontas, turning slowly, walked into the tent. She reappeared in a moment, carrying a small clay bowl which she held before her in both her hands. The squaws stepped aside, and the bride and groom stood face to face for the first time.

"Eat that which she who will now become the squaw of the mighty warrior has prepared," she said in a high-pitched, stilted voice. "Then tell her if he finds it good." Dropping to her knees in the prescribed manner, she extended the bowl to him.

To her consternation, Smith picked a large chunk of meat from the dish, and she realized he did not know he was expected to take only a token bite of the food. A variety of bitter herbs had been cooked with the meat, and a pinch of earth from each of the seven hills of the town had been thrown into the pot, together with a scoop of mud from the river. The dish was inedible, and Pocahontas, who was not allowed to speak any words other than those required in the ceremony, tried desperately to warn Smith with her eyes.

He thought her expression was strained, but he did not understand it and popped the piece of meat into his mouth. Never had he tasted anything so peppery and sour, and when he made an effort to chew the meat, sand gritted against his teeth. He wanted to spit the offending food onto the ground but knew that if he did his act would be misinterpreted by the savages and would cause numerous complications. So he closed his eyes for a moment, shuddered, and swallowed; Pocahontas was looking up at him in sympathy and concern, and when he glared at her he remembered that he had to respond to her formal entreaty.

"It is good," he said hoarsely.

She continued to kneel and held the bowl closer; now it was her turn to taste the dish, symbolically accepting the food he chose to leave. According to the traditions of the ceremony, a squaw helped herself to an amount equal to that her bridegroom had consumed, so Pocahontas bravely selected a large square of meat and placed it in her mouth. Tears came to her eyes, and for a moment the crowd thought she was going to choke. A murmur of alarm swept through the assemblage, for this was the first omen that was other than propitious, and the people were fearful until she caught her breath.

Then she stood again, Ru-Sa came to her and took the bowl from her, and the crowd sighed in relief. The inside of her mouth was burning, and she knew Smith felt the same; glancing up at him, she could not resist smiling impishly, and to her delight he grinned at her in return. She forgot her discomfort and, touching him lightly on the arm to indicate the next step in the proceedings, she walked at his side to the base of the rock.

Powhatan now took a direct part in the ceremony, and moving with deliberate majesty down the slope, he stood before the couple. To Smith's astonishment he began to sing in a deep, croaking voice and apparently he spoke in the archaic tongue of his ancestors, for the Englishman was unable to comprehend more than an odd word here and there in his long, seemingly rambling recital. After a time he lowered his voice, and his final words were a soft mumble that no one could hear.

Then he drew a new knife with a carved bone handle from beneath his gaudy robe, and when Pocahontas extended her right hand to him, Smith did the same. The Chief of Chiefs took hold of his daughter's index finger, and with a touch that was surprisingly gentle, he inflicted a tiny cut in the tip. Then he grasped Smith's hand and jabbed the knife into his finger far more vigorously than was necessary to draw blood. The bride reached up and placed her finger against Smith's lips, so he did the same to her in return. He realized that this was a climactic moment, for her eyes were starry, reminding him of the expressions he had seen in the faces of many women when they had looked at him. Then the crowd cheered, and one phase of the ceremony was at an end.

Pocahontas nodded almost imperceptibly in the direction of the tent, and Smith started toward it; she fell in behind him, her arms folded and her head lowered modestly. He hesitated at the entrance, but she whispered something to him, so he walked inside, and she followed him as the crowd started to chant a new refrain. Pocahontas lowered the flap, and they were alone in the semidark, isolated from the savages outside. The girl sighed, removed her white head-dress, and threw it venomously into a corner.

"Now I will never again wear the band of a maiden," she said, as much to herself as to him. "I have lived a lie for the last time."

He stared at her and then gazed around the tent. A fresh bed of young, soft boughs stood in the center, but all other signs of habitation had been removed, and the ground had been swept until all traces of dust had disappeared. Gradually it dawned on him that he and Pocahontas were now expected to consummate the marriage, and he took a single step toward her. "Are you now my wife?" he asked.

"I am." Her tone was proud, but her voice trembled slightly.

Smith smiled and tried to draw her to him, but she held him off and he frowned. "Why are we here, then?" he asked.

Pocahontas made no reply.

"Tell me why you threw off your headband," he persisted.

She drew a deep breath, lifted her head, and held herself erect. "I can't pretend to you," she said in English. "You've guessed correctly."

Satisfied, he placed his hands around her waist. "This is the first part of the ceremony that makes sense."

"No!" Pocahontas broke away from him and retreated to a far corner of the tent.

Puzzled and angry, he followed her. "Why not?"

"I am the wife of a Christian," she said with unaffected candor. "If I had married a chief of my own people, I would have followed his customs. But I have read much of husbands and wives in the Bible, and you surely feel, as I do, that it is wrong for us to be together in this way. I intend to live like a Christian, so I must begin now, at the very start."

Smith stopped short and lost his desire for her. Her resolve to behave like a Christian reminded him of the possibility that she might request another wedding ceremony in the Jamestown church, so he sat down on the bed and nodded. This was certainly not the time to insist that she honor his conjugal rights. "I agree," he said mildly.

Pocahontas felt ashamed of herself; he was not an unthinking, unfeeling brute like most of the men she had ever known, and she had done him a grave injustice by arbitrarily assuming that he was insensitive. She should have known that he would feel precisely as she did, and she realized that one of the reasons she loved him was because he possessed the uncanny ability to discern her innermost thoughts, which were almost invariably identical with his own. She sat down beside him, slipped her hand into his, and feeling a sense of complete fulfillment, she waited with him, satisfied and at peace, until the raucous, ribald chants of her people stopped and they could reappear in public.

By the time they emerged into the open again, the wedding guests were ravenous, and the men marched in a triumphal procession to the feast that had been prepared for them. Pocahontas dutifully retired to her own house to await her husband, and the other women scattered to their huts. The meal that the Chickahominy warriors and their guests ate was superb, the oratory that followed was less dull and boring than usual, and the dances that ended the evening's entertainment were lively. The braves had rarely enjoyed a merrier evening or pleasanter companionship, and when they finally went off to their own homes they were of one mind: this had been the most delightful wedding feast they had ever attended.

Smith smelled of venison and smoked fish and tobacco, and when he walked into Pocahontas's little house the room seemed to become filled with the odors. But she did not mind, and when she greeted him in the dark, there was no need for words between them. Her husband had come to her at last and he was all she wanted, all she thought she needed. They moved silently into each other's arms, and for the first time they slept together.

The next two weeks passed quickly, and Smith spent one of the most carefree periods he had ever known. He made love to Pocahontas whenever he wished, he slept long hours, and, unburdened by responsibilities of any sort, he allowed her to wait on him, cook for him, and amuse him. But gradually the novelty of their relationship waned, and little by little he felt a return of his restless desire to achieve what lesser men could not accomplish. His place was in Jamestown, and there was no longer any necessity for him to remain in the land of the Chickahominy. The braves who had guarded him so assiduously had been dismissed on his wedding day, and he assumed he was free to come and go as he pleased now, but he took no chances and first went to Powhatan to discuss the future. Having learned something of Indian ways, it did not cross his mind to mention the matter to Pocahontas until everything was settled.

The Chief of Chiefs proved to be surprisingly amenable and readily agreed that Smith's duty required him to return to his own tribe immediately. Actually, Powhatan was relieved to be rid of him and made no secret of his feelings. Smith apprehensively broached his plan to leave Pocahontas behind and launched into a long, involved explanation of his motives, but the bride's father cut him off. It was enough, he said, that Smith intended to send for her later; what was more, a man was privileged to treat his wife as he saw fit. Powhatan was secretly relieved, for he had been quietly grieving at the prospect of losing Pocahontas to the Jamestown settlers, and he was happy to approve any scheme that would keep her near him for a longer time.

He put no obstacles in his son-in-law's way and offered to provide an escort for the journey to the seacoast, but Smith had spent too many weeks being watched by alert Chickahominy braves and refused. Powhatan insisted on showing his generosity and made the Englishman a gift of a birchbark canoe. It would be stocked with provisions for the trip, he said, and would be ready early the following morning.

Pocahontas was surprised when her husband arose at dawn the next day, but she hurried out to prepare a breakfast of broiled fish, pulse, and corn boiled in goat's milk for him. When she returned to the hut she felt a twinge of uneasiness when she saw that he had packed his few belongings into a blanket. She was speechless, and when he glanced at her and through her, her misgivings increased, for his expression was that of a stranger who did not care if he never set eyes on her again.

"I didn't know you were going hunting," she said calmly, concealing her worry.

Smith's tone when he replied was so casual and offhand that her fears became more intense. "I'm returning to Jamestown today," he declared.

Pocahontas felt as though she were stifling. "I'll get ready immediately."

"I'm going alone." He squinted into the barrel of his pistol, which Powhatan had thoughtfully returned to him.

Her legs shook, so she sat and pretended to adjust her new headband studded with the tiny fresh green leaves that only married women were entitled to wear. "Oh? Isn't this a rather sudden decision?"

"Not really. I've discussed it with your father," he said with subtle emphasis, "and we're in complete accord. Surely you can understand that my place is with the colonists. Don't forget that I'm president of the Council and that I have a responsibility to the settlers."

"Of course." She told herself this was not a moment to stand on ceremony and behave like the stiff-backed daughter of a great chief, so she swallowed her pride. "What about me?" She tried to sound self-possessed, but in spite of her best efforts her voice trembled.

He laughed without conviction and, planting himself firmly in front of her, took hold of her hands and pulled her to her feet. Drawing her close, he smiled at her, shaking his head. "I thought you knew me better than that. Do you suppose for one instant that I'm going to forget you?"

"Well, I——No."

"All right, then. You'll have to show a little faith in me, that's all there is to it." He gazed at her whimsically, and she looked so forlorn that for a moment he actually felt a measure of compassion for her. "You do trust me, don't you?"

"I married you, John Smith," Pocahontas said simply, and wanted to cry because she felt so safe and secure when he held her in his arms.

"If you'll stop to consider my situation, you'll realize I'm faced with a very delicate problem."

Pocahontas's mind was spinning, and she was unable to think clearly. "What problem?"

"Suppose I had been an ordinary man. A carpenter or a stonemason or a farmer. Would your father have permitted you to marry me? Certainly not. The daughter of Powhatan could only marry a chief." He released her and shrugged, his attitude indicating that he was demonstrating extraordinary patience. "As president of the Council, I have a position to maintain too. My people expect me to marry an English duchess, I'm sure." He glanced at her obliquely, and when she seemed to accept his statement without question, he decided to embellish it for good measure. "Or, at the very least, a man of my rank is supposed to take a French princess or a Spanish *infanta* as his wife. Not that you're inferior to the greatest ladies in Europe, of course. If I didn't think highly of you, I wouldn't have married you, would I?"

"No, I suppose not," Pocahontas said dubiously. She felt that something in his argument failed to ring true but couldn't put her finger on the error.

"The English are new to America, and in their minds all natives are alike. I've got to educate them and teach them many things about you, just as I've taught you much about my country and our customs there. I've got to tell them about you bit by bit, so that when they learn you and I are married, they'll rejoice with us. You'll remain here until everything is arranged. Then I'll send for you."

The question was settled in his mind, and after kissing her absently, he sat down and began to eat his breakfast rapidly. Pocahontas, watching him, had no appetite and she could not rid herself of the unreasonable but terrible dread that he was leaving her for all time.

November, 1608

The sentries in the palisades tower overlooking the James River blinked in amazement, thought of sounding an alarm, and finally compromised by summoning both the captain and sergeant of the guard. Never in Jamestown's brief history had sober, sane Englishmen seen anyone like the man who was drifting down the river in a low-slung birchbark canoe with a distinctive Chickahominy curved prow. He was deeply tanned, and at first they thought he was an Indian, but he wore a steel corselet, wool breeches, and leather boots; he carried a sword, and a steel helmet was perched on the back of his head. In it he wore a cluster of feathers, however, and the paddle he occasionally dipped into the water was carved with a variety of native figures.

He was singing, too, and what confused the sentries was that he chanted a repetitive, monotonous tune in the language of the Naturals. When he drew closer, the men in the tower saw that he carried a pistol in his belt, and they trained their muskets on him, as it was safer to take no chances. Then he lifted his head, waved genially, and shouted the password that several of the sentries remembered had been used sometime during the summer months. Their suspicions increased, and the atmosphere in the tower became tense until the sergeant laughed exuberantly.

"It's Captain Smith!" he cried.

The gates were thrown open, and a score of settlers hurried to meet Virginia's leading citizen, while others ran into the town with the good news. When he guided his craft to the shore, eager hands pulled the canoe onto dry land, and Smith was lifted out bodily. Everyone present insisted on shaking his hand, and so many voices were raised simultaneously that no one could hear a word he said. But that was unimportant; what mattered was that he was alive and had come home, and the reception he received was even more enthusiastic than he had anticipated. He protested halfheartedly when two of the men hoisted him onto their shoulders, but he graciously consented to permit his escort to parade with him into the town.

Two or three dozen colonists ran toward him from every direction as his bearers marched through the gates, and he replied heartily to their ecstatic greetings. The parade quickly became a triumphal procession, but Smith, even though enjoying the tribute to his popularity, could not help observing the changes that had taken place in the community. The first thing that struck him was that the town walls were in a state of shocking disrepair, a condition that he would not have permitted to exist and that he would need to rectify immediately. Many of the poles in the palisades had been cut from young saplings of green wood which had become warped, and the spaces between them were wide enough for an Indian warrior to wriggle through. At the moment, therefore, the protection that the wall afforded Jamestown was negligible.

There were numerous strange faces in the crowds that appeared, and unlike the people whom Smith knew, these

outsiders did not join in the procession but gaped at him
silently. He realized at once that a new company of settlers
had arrived and he studied the recruits with interest. They
were pale, he thought, their faces were pinched, and if he
was any judge they were unhappy. The reasons for their
discontent became apparent to him shortly, when the parad-
ers turned down a road that had been built since he had left in
August. The lane itself was in a disgraceful condition, he
saw, and the work had obviously been supervised by indifferent and careless leaders. Deep holes and ruts made walking
dangerous, the underbrush had not been cleared away from
the sides of the path, and several tree stumps, which should
have been uprooted, continued to stand and impeded both
carts and pedestrians.

The road, unimportant in itself, was a symbol of Jamestown's degeneration, and Smith became increasingly angry
as he looked around. The huts that had been built to provide
shelter for the new members of the colony could not be
dignified by calling them homes, and he thought that not
even the Chickahominy savages forced their slaves to live in
such miserable dwellings. The huts were made of mud, here
and there haphazardly strengthened by twigs and branches;
they were without windows, no doors blocked their crude
yawning entrance frames, and they had patently been constructed by men who had not bothered to take the comfort or
convenience of the inhabitants into consideration, for most
of them were so low that no adult man could stand erect
inside them. Worst of all, these pitiful little buildings stood
adjacent to a swamp, and even at this season the water stood
only a few feet from half a dozen of the houses.

Before Smith had departed on his unavoidably prolonged
trip of exploration he had given orders to have the bog filled
in and had specifically instructed the Council to permit no
construction in the area until the land was dry. Someone had
deliberately chosen to disobey his orders, and he silently
cursed the stupidity of his colleagues. He would need to take

immediate steps to build new homes for the recently arrived
settlers and to tear down the huts. If people were still living in
them when the spring rains came, half the community
would fall ill, and there was even a possibility that an
epidemic of the Black Death or some other dreadful affliction
might strike the people.

Two or three of the larger warehouses were off to the left,
and Smith made a mental note to inspect them today at his
first opportunity. He dreaded the prospect, as it seemed likely
to him that the supplies he had accumulated in his trades
with the natives had been squandered. Certainly if the other
conditions that prevailed in the town were any criterion, that
would be the situation. And he had no idea where he could
secure any considerable quantities of corn and meat in the
near future; only the Chickahominy owned enough
foodstuffs to take care of Jamestown's needs, and it would be
impossible for him to deal with Powhatan in the months to
come.

He could afford to take no chances that Pocahontas might
attach herself to him again, and he had decided that the best
way to avoid her would be to maintain a safe distance between himself and all members of her tribe. It was sufficiently unpleasant to contemplate the possibility that she might
simply appear at the gates of the colony someday, claiming to
be his wife. However, he was prepared to face that eventual-
ity if and when it arose, and in the meantime he had no
intention of borrowing trouble. Matters of real significance
were on his mind, and he dismissed his vague concern that
Pocahontas might someday make an attempt to embarrass
him.

The marchers seemed to be parading aimlessly, with no
specific destination as their goal, so Smith asked his bearers
to take him to the house he had occupied before he had gone
off to the land of the Potomac. They shouted to him that it
was now the home of a gentleman who had arrived with the
new settlers, so he requested them to carry him instead to the

headquarters of the colonial government, which had been under construction when he left. The two-story structure, painted white with real glass in its windows, stood on the south side of the parade ground, and two sentries, stationed in front of the main entrance, paced up and down with more vigor than guards usually showed, for it was a chilly morning. As the procession crossed the parade ground a number of men hurried out of the building, hastily donning their cloaks, and Smith recognized his Council associates, who looked older and frailer than he had remembered them.

The last to appear was Captain Gabriel Archer, who gave orders to one of the sentries and then stood apart until a platoon of militiamen appeared from somewhere behind the headquarters. With the pikemen at his heels he approached the celebrants, and Smith was startled to see that he was wearing the broad, watered-silk red sash that was the badge of the presidency. Archer was glowering, and Smith's sense of well-being began to fade.

The gentlemen of the Council remained huddled near the door, but Archer, followed by the militiamen, moved out onto the parade ground, and the cheering settlers gradually fell silent. Smith's bearers, still carrying him on their shoulders, edged forward with him until he and his old enemy were only a few feet apart, and it suddenly occurred to Smith that in the pleasure of returning to Jamestown he had all but forgotten Archer's existence.

"You're back." It was remarkable how Archer could insinuate sly and vicious meanings into the simplest words.

"I am," Smith replied calmly. He wanted to shake hands with his other colleagues, but he was surprised to see that all of them, even Matthew Scrivener, were staring at him glumly. Never, he thought, had a man returned from the dead to be greeted with such apathy by his equals.

"What have you to say for yourself? I warn you that every word you speak is being recorded." Archer held himself arrogantly, his left hand on the hilt of his sword.

Smith tapped his bearers on the shoulders, and when they released him, he jumped to the ground. Sauntering forward, he halted directly in front of Archer and then half turned so the whole crowd could hear him. "I don't know what sort of records you've been keeping, my good man," he said clearly and loudly, "but you may write in letters of fire that no one has ever been happier than I am to come home." He grinned and, as he expected, the settlers nodded and smiled approvingly.

"We certainly didn't expect to see you again."

There was something so ugly in Archer's tone that Smith bristled. "It was one of my fondest hopes that you'd gone back to England by now, but not even your continued presence here can ruin my happiness. My friends," he continued, stepping away from his old adversary and including the councilmen and the people in a sweeping gesture, "I can't begin to tell you how glad I am to see you."

"Here now," Archer said, catching hold of his arm, "you'll make no speeches."

The man's effrontery was colossal, but Smith wanted no fight to mar his homecoming. Many in the crowd were newcomers who didn't know him, and they would be less than favorably impressed with him if he allowed himself to become embroiled in an argument. So he smiled jovially, and when he spoke he actually managed to sound convincing. "Apparently you have substituted for me during my absence, Captain Archer, so I suppose I must extend my thanks to you, both for myself and for the people." He paused, and his voice became a shade harder. "As I'm here now, I intend to resume my rightful place at once, so I'll thank you to return my sash of office to me."

Archer's hollow laugh was condescending. "You were impeached and deposed many weeks ago. I now have the honor to have assumed the presidency."

Something in the stillness of the spectators made Smith uneasy, but he could not believe he had really been im-

peached. He glanced at the members of the Council, and his
sense of bewilderment increased. Those who once had been
friendly to him were gazing down at the ground, unable to
meet his eyes, and others, like Christopher Newport, made
no effort to conceal their bitter hostility to him. "May I be
permitted to know on what grounds I have been impeached?"
he asked, keeping his temper for the sake of the people, who
were his real source of power.

"Your impeachment, my dear Smith, is the very least of
your worries." Archer smiled loftily, shrugged, and snapped
his fingers at the sergeant in command of the militiamen. "In
the name of His Majesty, the King, and by virtue of the
authority vested in me by the Grand Council of Jamestown
in the London Company's Colony of Virginia, I order you to
arrest John Smith, who is sometimes pleased to use the title
of Captain."

Before the startled Smith could speak, the pikemen moved
forward, and two of them caught hold of his arms. His right
hand darted to the hilt of his sword but dropped again when
he realized that armed resistance would merely complicate
his situation. He turned an appeal to the steelers but discovered that the rest of the platoon had formed in a semicircle
behind him, effectively cutting him off from the people. The
cause of his arrest, whatever it might be, was necessarily
absurd, and the men and women of Jamestown certainly
knew he was innocent of all wrongdoing. He could see that
the colonists sympathized with him, but they remained silent, and gradually he realized they were not the same people
they had been when he had left in August. Then they had
been energetic and independent, eager to create new lives for
themselves, and although they had always been properly
respectful to their superiors, the common dangers and hardships that all shared alike in the New World had broken down
the formal barriers that usually separated the gentry and
common men.

But now the settlers were obviously cowed, and none of

them dared approach the pikemen, who themselves seemed to be none too happy with the task that had been assigned to them. Several men and women in the crowd, artisans whom Smith had befriended and housewives whom he had helped, muttered to each other and to their neighbors angrily, but when Archer walked to one end of the row of militiamen and stood gazing out at them, his hands on his hips, they stopped speaking, hung their heads, and shuffled their feet. The colony was surely doomed, Smith thought; no venture could succeed when the people were ruled by fear.

Jamestown was the cornerstone of his future fame, and he was outraged by all that had been mishandled in the few months he had been absent. Everything he had labored to build had been destroyed by stupid men to whom high office meant the exercise of power for its own sake rather than an opportunity to create constructively. For a moment his anger blinded him to the urgency of his immediate, personal problem, but the presence of the pikemen on either side of him reminded him that he could do nothing for the colony and thus make his place in history secure until he disposed of the ridiculous matter of his arrest.

Twisting around in the grasp of the militiamen, he faced Captain Archer proudly. "I demand to know the charge against me," he said in a hard, cold voice.

Archer's eyelids drooped, but he could not conceal his elation; this was a moment he had been anticipating with relish for a long time. "You have been judged responsible for the death of Master Curtis Watkins," he said.

Smith, remembering the luckless youth who had been murdered by the Chickahominy in the Potomac hunting preserve, was too stunned to reply, and looked openmouthed at his accuser. Shaking himself, he thought he was dreaming, but the solemn faces of the councilmen, the somber, fearful glances that the settlers exchanged, convinced him that Archer was serious. "That's nonsense," he said at last.

The new president of the Council stood on sure ground

and smiled contemptuously. "Really? It's too bad you weren't here to defend yourself at your trial. Naturally your guilt made you afraid to return here for it."

"My trial?" Smith asked incredulously.

"You were tried during the period of your desertion, naturally." Archer spoke as though his mock serenity would dissolve were he a less patient and judicious man. "And by a unanimous vote of the judges, your peers, you were found guilty." He nodded faintly in the direction of Newport, Edward Wingfield, and John Kendall, and his attitude made it plain that he, too, had acted as a judge.

Smith's temper became frayed. "Then I demand a new trial," he snapped, "and I insist that the other men who accompanied me into the wilderness be heard as witnesses."

Archer sighed. "They have already testified against you, my dear Smith."

"I don't believe it."

"Believe what you please, it won't alter the truth. Oh, they tried to defend you at first." Archer's eyes became narrow, and through some sort of optical illusion his lips looked thin and pale. "You had done your best to confuse them, but a few weeks on a diet of stale bread and a lusty beating or two did wonders for them and straightened them out."

Smith clenched his fists and would have thrown himself at Archer had the pikemen not restrained him. His faithful companions, weakened by their whipping at the hands of the Chickahominy, had been tortured until they had given the evidence that Archer wanted, and everyone present knew it. The cynical gentlemen of the Council, in spite of their fine clothes and lofty airs, their ability to discuss the latest medical theories of Dr. William Harvey and the philosophical essays of Sir Francis Bacon, were savages as primitive as the Naturals. No, they were even more contemptible, for their education and exposure to the most advanced civilization ever created by man should have made them somewhat superior to animals. But it would be useless to reprimand them, and Smith merely glanced at them scornfully.

"Your crude travesty on justice does not amuse me, Archer," he said harshly.

"I'm sure it doesn't. But you'll be even less amused to learn that you've been sentenced to death. Gentlemen are permitted to die by the ax, but common criminals are hung, and as you're a rogue with no background other than that which you've woven out of your own imagination, you'll hang." Turning back to the spectators, Captain Archer raised his voice and spoke more sternly. "Anyone who disturbs the peace by creating a public nuisance or demonstrating in favor of a convicted rogue will be punished severely."

Somewhere in the distance a young mother summoned a child from play, and her voice floated clearly across the silent parade ground. Men stared sullenly at the new president, matching his contempt with open surly hatred. Independent, free Englishmen were being deprived of their precious liberties, and rebellion was in the air. Archer, afraid that a few inflammatory words from Smith would start a riot, obviously realized he would be courting disaster if he allowed his enemy to speak again. There would be time to gloat later, after the crowd had disbanded and its champion had been rendered harmless. "Remove the prisoner," he told the sergeant in charge of the militia.

The pikemen formed a cordon around Smith and quickly marched him off to the prison that he himself had built. To the disappointment of the people he allowed himself to be led away quietly, but he knew, as they did not, that if he incited a revolt, Archer and the other members of the Council would have a legitimate grievance against him and send a report to the London Company that might permanently damage his reputation. He could not take the murder charge seriously and felt confident that eventually Archer would be made to appear ridiculous for having lodged such a flimsy complaint against him. Similarly, he was not afraid that the death sentence would be carried out, as he knew enough of the law to realize that a trial conducted during his absence was illegal. He would therefore prepare an appeal to the Lord

Chief Justice in London, and Archer, whose lack of inner security made him afraid of his superiors in England, would not dare to execute a rival whose ghost could rise up in the courts and cause him to lose his own head.

For the present, then, Smith counseled himself to be patient and not lose either his sense of perspective or his temper. The colony was disintegrating in the hands of men who had already amply illustrated their abysmal ignorance of the art of governing, and when conditions became intolerable, the settlers would demand the release and restoration to office of the one leader who could save Jamestown from self-destruction. In the meantime, Smith thought, he could utilize a peaceful interlude to good advantage; as soon as he prepared his appeal and made certain that the next ship's captain who came here from England received it, he would devote his full time and energy to the writing of his history of Virginia.

In many ways, he reflected, his situation was similar to that of Sir Walter Raleigh, who was sympathetically regarded as something of a martyr by most people and who would be remembered long after the King who had unjustly imprisoned him was forgotten, principally because the surest way to achieve immortality was to perform brave deeds and then record them for posterity in book form. Smith had not read even a small part of Sir Walter's manuscript but was willing to wager that a man as wise in the ways of the world as Raleigh would not neglect to describe his own exploits in detail.

It was pleasant to reflect that he and his distinguished colleague were being subjected to similar, preposterous treatment and therefore would be coupled in the minds of future generations, but in one respect their circumstances were vastly different. Sir Walter was living in luxury in the sumptuous Tower of London suite that had once been occupied by Mary, Queen of Scots, but the hovel to which Smith was being conducted was a miserable habitation whose previous tenants had been the ancestors of the rats who now lived there. The prison was a one-story stone building, its ugly, squat appearance relieved only by a thatched roof.

There were two cells in the jail, the larger of them a square, bleak room that was used to house thieves, robbers, adulterers, and wife beaters, misguided but harmless men who had committed minor infractions of the law but were not considered real criminals. The smaller, with bars of precious iron set in the stone frame of its single tiny window, was reserved for debtors, blasphemers, and others who had perpetrated serious offenses against society. As Smith rightly guessed, he was taken to the less desirable cell, but he accepted his lot so cheerfully that the militiamen felt impelled to apologize profusely to him before locking the door behind him. He felt a trifle sorry for them because they were so shortsighted; they could not know, as he did, that each day he spent here the popular sentiment in his favor would mount higher and that when he was finally returned to power his control over the destiny of the colony would be all the more absolute.

One of Powhatan's wives sat in a far corner of his private sleeping lodge, chopping nuts, which she would later mix with dried plums to make the confection he enjoyed more than any other food. A glowing fire burning in a pit in the center of the room made the hut comfortable, and a thin plume of smoke drifted lazily through a hole in the roof. The Chief of Chiefs' second wife crouched near the entrance, where the light was stronger, patiently rubbing grease into one of her master's new winter robes of buffalo skin to make it pliable. As always, it was very quiet in the lodge, and when Powhatan arrived home the women neither looked up from their work nor addressed him; he would recognize their presence if and when it pleased him to speak, and until such time as he deigned to become aware of them, they would remain silent, after the fashion of docile, obedient squaws.

All women possess the ability to express themselves without words, however, and the moment Powhatan raised the flap and walked in he realized they were disturbed. There had been no quarrel between them, he knew, as neither had been crying; and no fresh fingernail marks marred their faces. He had warned them he would whip both of them if they fought and, knowing he was a man of his word, they had taken his threat seriously, which pleased him. Nevertheless, he could see at a glance that their backs were rigid, their features stiff, and their manner strained as they worked mechanically, not really thinking about their tasks.

The cause of their disapproval sat cross-legged before the fire, warming herself, and Powhatan, who was tired after a long day in council with his elders, felt his weariness disappear. It was no wonder that his wives were upset, for, according to ancient custom, no one was permitted to enter a warrior's home without an express invitation, and the Chief of Chiefs always insisted that traditions be observed to the letter in his own dwelling. Even Opachisco never came here unless he had been summoned, and when he wanted to see his father he went instead to the large hut, a stone's throw away, in which Powhatan conducted his business.

But Pocahontas had always ignored practices which she found inconvenient, yet she never seemed to take advantage of her unique position, for she unquestioningly accepted her father's special favor as her right. Powhatan knew he should have dealt with her more severely when she was younger and should have insisted that Ru-Sa rule her more strictly, but it was too late now to change her lifelong habits. If he reprimanded her for coming here unbidden, she would be hurt, and then he would blame himself; besides, he felt precisely as he had when she was a little girl. He was so pleased to see her that nothing else mattered.

She bowed low before him, so that he could see only the crown of her head, her hair held in place neatly with a band of green leaves, and he addressed her hurriedly so she could raise her face. "Powhatan greets his daughter," he said, and when she looked up he was dismayed to see that her smile was forced and that there were deep circles under her eyes. "I will speak alone with my daughter," he told his wives.

The older women immediately stopped working, wrapped themselves in bearskin robes, and walked out into the cold, where they would remain until he gave them permission to return. They had been afraid he would indulge the girl again but had been unable to resist hoping that just this once he would put her in her place, and as they left one of them could not resist the temptation to express her opinion of his disgustingly indulgent attitude by sniffling audibly. Powhatan stared after them for a moment, trying to decide which of them had dared to criticize him, but he could settle the matter later and mete out punishment accordingly. Right now it was far more important to learn why Pocahontas had come to see him.

The front of her robe was open, and he saw that her neck and shoulders above the top of her tunic looked painfully thin. Picking up a clay bowl of the nut and dried plum confection, he sat down beside her and offered her a sweet-meat. Again she smiled but shook her head. "You have eaten today?" he asked.

"I have eaten," Pocahontas replied dutifully.

"Then you have eaten too little."

"It is winter," she said.

Powhatan was always confused when he tried to understand feminine logic, but his long years of marriage to five wives had taught him patience. "It is winter," he agreed. "There is snow upon the ground."

"Even the thickest pine trees in the forest are thin." Her manner indicated that she had offered him an irrefutable argument and that in her opinion the subject was closed.

Had she been a man, he thought, she would have been the most subtle and cunning of his sons. Knowing her, he realized there was only one way to deal with her and he dropped all pretense. "The daughter of Powhatan is un-happy," he declared bluntly.

Pocahontas had never lied to him. "I am unhappy," she said calmly.

There was a silence, and he picked up one of the sweet-meats, ate it reflectively, and waited for her to continue. In his negotiations with the rulers of other nations he could sit, unmoving and infinitely patient, for long periods and thus force others to speak their minds without revealing his own thoughts. But he always suffered sharp pains in his middle when his daughter used his own tactics in her dealings with him, and he began to tap his fingertips on the edge of the bowl.

She sensed his restlessness, took a deep breath, and shifted her position slightly so she faced him. She had come here seeking his help and she told herself that her reluctance to speak was stupid, yet at the same time she could not rid herself of the feeling that she was being disloyal to her husband. "More than a full moon's time has passed since John Smith returned to his own people," she said at last.

Powhatan stared hard at her. "You are going to bear him a son?"

"No," she replied wistfully. "If that had happened, then it might be that he would welcome me. More than half a moon ago I sent a message to John Smith. It was carried by a warrior of the Chesapeake tribe who was returning from the land of the Chickahominy to his own land. I wrote in John Smith's tongue and I asked him to give me the right to join him. My place is at his side." She straightened, and for the first time there was strength and determination in her voice. "I am his wife."

"But he forbids you to come to him?" Powhatan de-manded, his mind already sorting and weighing a variety of solutions.

"No." Pocahontas had been stripped of her pride, and although she might have dissembled with others, she could not hide her raw emotions from her father. "Today another brave of the Chesapeake came here and brought word to me of what happened. The warrior who took my message to Jamestown waited for a day and a night, but John Smith has sent no message to me. He does not accept me and he does not reject me. He pretends I do not exist, just as a hunter ignores the snow and the rain when he is on the trail."

The bowl struck the ground with such force that bits of clay and chunks of the confection scattered in every direction. "Smith has shamed the daughter of Powhatan. He has also shamed the Chief of Chiefs and the Chickahominy nation. It is good that you have told me of this act of dishonor." He folded his arms, stared into the fire, and after a moment's silence he pronounced judgment in a low, hard voice. "John Smith will die."

Pocahontas clutched his arm and shook her head, unable to speak. She had come to her father hoping he would find some way to reunite her with her husband, but he had completely misunderstood her desire. She wanted Smith, not revenge; what was more, she had learned in the Bible that vengeance belonged to the God of the English, not to mere men.

Powhatan softened and looked at the girl indulgently. "Squaws are weak, and warriors are strong," he reminded her. "That is why men go to war and women stay at home. You have been the squaw of Smith, and so you are sad for him. But your heart will be light again when you hold his scalp in your hand. Powhatan," he assured her, "will not let his daughter suffer."

"If John Smith dies," she said slowly, "then I want to die too."

It was evident that she meant every word, and her father, who otherwise would have insisted that his sentence be carried out, reconsidered. "Then we will bury all of the wampum and other wedding gifts you received where no one can find them," he said, "otherwise the chiefs who gave them to you will want them back. I will go myself into the forests to hide your riches and will take with me only your brothers, whom we can trust. After your wealth has been buried, I will hold a ceremony and will end your marriage to Smith. When it is all done," he added cheerfully, "we will give a special feast."

Pocahontas didn't know whether to laugh or cry. "I am the squaw of John Smith," she said. "I want to be his squaw as long as I live!"

"I see." Powhatan nodded and reflected that she might be right. All women were stubborn, of course, but Pocahontas's insistence that Smith accept her as his wife could prove to be the best solution to an unpleasant problem. It was a husband's right to put aside a wife whenever he wished, and as Powhatan had availed himself of the privilege twice, he was in no position to criticize his son-in-law. It would be difficult to reconcile the murder of Smith with his own conscience, too, even though the Englishman had grossly insulted him by scorning his daughter. It would therefore be very convenient if Smith could be forced to take Pocahontas under his roof until she grew tired of him; such an arrangement would save Powhatan considerable personal embarrassment and make it unnecessary for him to spend many moons propitiating the gods, which he would be required to do if he had the fair-skinned foreigner killed.

Unfortunately, Smith was headstrong and canny and consequently would be impervious to ordinary persuasions. Pocahontas herself would be an unreliable ally in carrying out any scheme that might be developed, too, Powhatan decided as he looked at her strained, anxious face. Women in love, as he knew from personal experience, were undependable and flighty and frequently acted like their own worst enemies. Hence he would need to handle her with care.

"It is the right of every squaw to appear at the lodge of her husband," he said. "If he drives her away, then she knows he has grown tired of her. But John Smith might not beat his squaw or send her from him with curses. He might take her into his house. No one can read the heart of another, so no one can say what Smith might do. So the daughter of Powhatan might show wisdom if she goes to the town of her husband and stands at his door."

Pocahontas had often contemplated making such a journey, but each time the idea had occurred to her she had drawn back from it. "I could not," she said.

Her father gazed at her sternly. "You have too much pride. You forget you are only a woman."

She tossed her head angrily. "Because I am a woman I have only as much pride as my husband feels when he looks at me. When a woman gives herself to a man, he takes more than her body. She makes him a free gift of her pride, and he may do with it as he pleases. If there is love for her in his heart, a new pride is born in her, a pride greater than any she has ever before known. But if he turns her away from his lodge, her pride becomes as nothing, like the pools of water that disappear in the heat of summer. I am not too proud to go to John Smith. I would go to him and throw myself at his feet, I would beg him to take me into his lodge, if I thought he would listen to me. But he has shown he would not. I would not care what others said about me. But I would feel great shame inside myself because John Smith found me unworthy and turned me away from his house. Then I would surely want to die."

It became increasingly clear to Powhatan that he would be required to take action on her behalf. "Pocahontas has spoken in a manner worthy of the daughter of the Chief of Chiefs," he said soothingly. The problem had to be handled realistically, and the less she knew about his plans the less she would be able to interfere. "Go now," he declared abruptly, "and return to your own house. But first go to Opachisco and tell him the father of all the Chickahominy will speak with him."

Pocahontas knew from his tone that he intended to offer

her no explanation, but it was enough that he was going to
help her and that he intended to take his eldest son into his
confidence. She had to curb an impulse to kiss him, as no
woman, not even the Chief of Chiefs' daughter, had the right
to embrace him unless he first indicated that he was willing to
discard his dignity and permit such a familiarity. Happiness,
relief, and gratitude were mirrored in her eyes as she jumped
to her feet and bowed before him. The sense of depression
and futility that had gripped her ever since John Smith had
waved farewell to her from his canoe was gone now, and she
felt like laughing as she ran lightly out into the late afternoon
cold.

Her father's wives stood near the entrance, huddling in
their bearskin robes and stamping their feet to keep warm,
and she felt sorry for them. She would have asked them to
visit her house and wait there until Powhatan finished his
conference, but she knew they hated her and would refuse.
Yet she felt she had to make some gesture to them, as they
were suffering from the cold on her account, so she bowed to
them and was pleased to see their astonishment. She had
paid them the highest of compliments, as it was unusual for
one of royal blood to make a gesture of homage to women
who were merely the squaws of a chief, and she understood
their amazement. But she could not dwell on the matter, and
after smiling fleetingly at them she hurried to the lodge of her
brother and told him breathlessly that Powhatan had summoned him.

Opachisco knew his sister was involved in some way, but
he asked her no questions and, dropping the powder horn he
had been carving, he snatched his heaviest wolfskin robe
from a wall peg and hurried to the top of the hill. He was
vaguely aware of the presence of his stepmothers outside the
house, but he did not bother to acknowledge their respectful
greetings as he entered the lodge. His father was staring into
the fire, absently picking up sweetmeat crumbs that were
scattered on the floor and eating them, and Opachisco sat

down beside him, folded his arms, and awaited Powhatan's
pleasure.

The older man, wasting no time on greetings, began to
speak; he described Pocahontas's situation, and Opachisco,
listening intently, grew angry. He had always been fond of
his sister. He had formed a poor opinion of Smith from the
first, and he hoped he would be given a personal directive to
avenge the family honor. The winter was dull, so he would
enjoy plunging a knife into Smith and bringing home a
foreigner's scalp lock as a souvenir. But he knew better than
to interrupt and he remained silent when his father stopped
speaking and again looked into the fire.

"Smith, King of James," Powhatan said at last, "has a
strong heart. But even the strongest of warriors can be ruled
by fear. Remember that, my son, when I go to join my
ancestors and you sit in my place."

"I hear the words of my father and I will remember them,"
Opachisco replied automatically, and swallowed his disappointment. Obviously Smith would be allowed to live.

"On the day that Smith ran the Race of the Damned, he
showed he had no fear for himself. He is a true warrior, and
this is good. But he is the chief of his people. He is responsible for them. So he must have fears for their safety." Powhatan scratched himself absently and smiled. "An attack will be
made on his town. Many of the fair-skinned men and their
squaws will be killed. Smith has learned to read the sign talk
of our people, so one warrior, who will be named to do only
this one deed, will not join in the fighting, but will give to
Smith a belt of wampum on which the emblem of Pocahontas will appear in beads. I will instruct Pocahontas herself to
make the belt and to put her emblem on it."

His son found a sizable chunk of the nut and plum confection near his left foot and ate it. "I understand," he said.
"Then Smith will know that if he does not take Pocahontas
into his lodge his town will be raided a second time and will
be destroyed, and all of his people will die. Opachisco has

heard the words of his father and finds them good." Suddenly he straightened. "I ask for the right to lead the warriors who will raid the town of Smith, King of James."

Powhatan chuckled and shook his head. "Sometimes I am tired and wish to join my ancestors in the land of the gods. But I must remain here until my son learns he will not become a mighty chief until his heart stops ruling his mind. Ek would become angry with us if the Chickahominy raided the town of Smith. Ek might think we were seeking vengeance. The raid will be made by our cousins, the Rappahannock, who are true braves and will do as they are bidden. Besides," he added, "many warriors will die in the fight. The Rappahannock have grown strong in the past few years, so strong they might someday challenge our rule over them. It will be good for the Chickahominy if some of the finest of Rappahannock warriors are killed."

Opachisco felt unbounded admiration for his father's wisdom, but he saw one fault with the over-all plan. "In battle," he said, "it is not always possible to know what will happen before it happens. We will tell the Rappahannock to spare the life of Smith, King of James. But if a warrior with the heat of war in his blood places his knife in the heart of Smith, what then?"

"Then," Powhatan replied with a satisfied smile, "it is the will of the gods. The all-seeing, who rule us from above, will know it was the Rappahannock who killed Smith and will not punish the Chickahominy. And," he said, "we will know that the all-wise gods have decided to solve the problem of Powhatan's daughter by making her a widow. So either way she will be happy."

January–March, 1609

The *Susan Constant* and her new sister ship, the *Royal Hope*, were anchored near the blockhouse, and each day Smith went to the window of his tiny cell to peer at the two vessels. Both of the captains had been given copies of his appeal to the Lord Chief Justice, and thanks to his strategy, the Council had dropped its threat to have him executed. The ships were his guarantee that one day he would be set free again and restored to his right place in society, but it was hard to be patient and equally difficult to curb his disappointment over his continuing imprisonment. When the barks had first arrived, his hopes had risen, for the captains had protested against his incarceration, and when they had made a point of calling on him, they had told him that several members of the Council were weakening in their resolve to hold him prisoner.

But Gabriel Archer had remained obdurate, apparently

feeling that if he reversed his previous decision he would be admitting he had been mistaken. Therefore, Smith continued to languish in prison, and it was unpleasant to realize that many months would pass before the *Royal Hope*, which was scheduled to sail back to England in two weeks, would return to the New World with the writ from higher authority that would force Archer to release him. In the meantime, although it was true that he had almost completed the first volume of the book he intended to call A *General History of Virginia*, it disturbed him to see the colony decomposing and crumbling.

His many visitors, whom Archer no longer dared forbid him to see, all told him the same dismal story. The newest recruits, more than one hundred and fifty in number, who had arrived on the ships, were receiving treatment even more miserable than that which the last group had been accorded. No preparation of any kind had been made to receive the newcomers, no homes had been built for them, and the older settlers were forced to share their houses with the homeless, which suited no one and created resentment on all sides. Sensible and farseeing administrators would have realized that the present boundaries of Jamestown were inadequate and would have helped themselves to a large slice of America's virtually unlimited territory. But the palisades still stood where Smith had erected them when the population had been only a little more than half of what it was at present.

The walls themselves were in disgraceful shape, Smith was told, and even men with no military experience could see that the colony was almost defenseless. Equally upsetting was the militia's lack of morale, for Archer maintained no regular schedule of drills, capriciously punished anyone who happened to displease him, and promoted his inexperienced favorites over the heads of the veterans whom Smith had placed in positions of authority. Many of the newcomers, who had seen army service in England, were so contemptuous of the militia that they flatly refused to join it.

Worst of all was the food situation, Smith realized from the scraps of information he pieced together. Archer had not bothered to ration the grain and meat that his predecessor had acquired from the Chickahominy, with the result that a serious famine had threatened but had been temporarily averted by the arrival of the ships from England. However, Archer had learned nothing and was repeating his error; the supplies that had been carried in the holds of the vessels were limited but were being consumed at such a carelessly prodigal rate that the storehouses would be empty long before the first harvest of the year could be reaped.

Smith was powerless to intervene, for the members of the Council kept their distance from him, and whenever he made suggestions to some of the honest settlers who came to see him, the ideas were subsequently rejected by Archer, who needed only to suspect that advice came from Smith to do the opposite. Even the ships' captains, who were in a sense the emissaries of the London Company's directors, were able to exert no influence on the new president, and when they warned him they would report his lack of efficiency to their superiors, he defied them. Thereafter he made himself inaccessible for days, and it was rumored that he was preparing long letters to each of the Company's officers, justifying his conduct.

Every evening, after Smith completed his day's labors on his book, he spent several hours working by candlelight, meticulously keeping a record of the data brought to him by his loyal friends. Someday, after he was set free, the full story of the mismanagement of the colony would be valuable information to place before the directors of the Company and would certainly result in the outright dismissal of Gabriel Archer. The work was tedious, but Smith did not object, as he was looking toward the future. There was an immediate benefit too: by staying up later than was his custom each night, he slept later every morning and thus helped to pass his endless days.

Ordinarily he did not rise until two or three hours after sunrise, but one morning he was awakened by the unaccustomed sound of musket fire shortly after dawn. He sat bolt upright in his cot, and when he heard the town's cannon boom, he dressed hastily and began to pace up and down the narrow confines of his cell. He looked out of his window repeatedly, but as it faced the blockhouse and the water he could see only the two ships and had no idea what might be taking place in the town itself. After a little while he made out a number of shadowy figures on the deck of the *Susan Constant* and finally distinguished them as seamen, armed with muskets, cutlasses, and knives; some were manning the merchantman's two demiculverins, while the others grouped themselves around the base of the bark's main topsail. As nearly as he could judge, they were waiting for an attack of some sort, and after a quarter of an hour he guessed that the fight, whatever it might be, was going unfavorably, for all six of the ship's sails were raised. The *Royal Hope* hoisted sail, too, and both vessels appeared to be poised for flight.

The guards who usually were on duty at the prison had disappeared, and Smith alternately shouted and rattled the door of his cell, but no one bothered to come near him. The intensity of musket fire increased; then, during a momentary lull, he heard a long, sharp war whoop and realized that Jamestown was being attacked by natives. He was only mildly surprised, and while he was still digesting the news he heard footsteps in the little corridor outside. Then his door burst open.

A sergeant of militia, followed by a score of other settlers, some in uniform, some in drab shirts and breeches, crowded and jostled each other in an attempt to reach Smith's side. All were shouting, all were waving weapons of various kinds, and in the confusion he could hear nothing they said. Jumping onto his cot, he gestured for silence, and the men responded instantly to his authority; they became quiet, and the sergeant stepped forward.

"Captain Smith," he said, "we been attacked by surprise. There's Naturals all over the town. Inside the walls, everywhere."

"What tribe are they?"

The sergeant looked blank, but someone in the rear of the crowd called out, "Billy Jeffreys killed one, and his war paint was black and green."

"Rappahannock," Smith said, and felt relieved. Had the attackers been Chickahominy, as he had feared, Powhatan would have sent an expedition of sufficient size to wipe out the colony.

"Captain Archer," the sergeant declared, finding his voice again, "he don't know what he's doing out there. He's directing cannon fire into the forest like he was a general on a French battlefield. Meantime them Indians keep sneaking into town through openings in the walls and do terrible damage before we can flush them out. You got to help us, Captain. You're the only one who can."

No second invitation was necessary. Smith jumped to the floor, someone thrust a musket into his hands, and he pushed his way out into the corridor. The men followed him as he stalked out into the open, bareheaded and clad only in his doublet and breeches; but he needed neither armor nor a uniform to identify him as a military leader, and when he paused to survey the situation, the settlers sensed his authority and felt for the first time that a complete disaster might be averted.

The defense, Smith saw, was confused and disorganized. Gabriel Archer was directing the fire of two cannon from positions behind the west wall and was wasting precious manpower and effort while he sent iron ball after iron ball crashing harmlessly into the trees of the wilderness beyond the gates. However, the day was not yet lost, for a few colonists with some concept of fundamentals stubbornly clung to positions on the crude observation platforms located at intervals on the top of the palisades. Ignoring the showers

of arrows that rained on them, these courageous men maintained a steady musket fire, and their efforts seemed to be
solely responsible for holding the majority of the raiders at
bay. Archer, however, was apparently unaware of their value
and sent no reinforcements to help them or take the place of
those who were killed or wounded.

Meanwhile Rappahannock warriors were squeezing
through gaps in the walls, sneaking into the town, and either
knifing or tomahawking the terrorized settlers. Groups of
militiamen and other colonists ran through the streets, hunting for the braves who were at large in the community, but
they were operating without a cohesive plan, and their efforts
were impeded by sword-waving members of the Council,
who seemed to be everywhere, issuing contradictory commands. Two fires were burning on the far side of the town
and both seemed to be spreading, but it was impossible to
determine whether or not any concerted effort was being
made to put them out.

So much needed to be done that Smith scarcely knew
where to begin, but there was no time to lose, and he turned
to the group behind him, which had grown larger as news of
his release had spread. His first act was to send men who
carried muskets to the platforms on the palisades, and they
obeyed him instantly, dashing off in small groups. Next he
sent several boys in their early teens, who were too young to
take part in the actual fighting, to rally the settlers and to send
every able-bodied man to him.   .

Those who remained were dispatched to bring the fires
under control, and Smith ordered them to enlist the aid of
the women, whose help would be needed to bring buckets of
water from the river. Then, as others drifted to the informal
post he established on the crest of a small knoll, from which
he could see much of what was taking place, he sent the
colonists singly and in pairs to take up stations around the
town's perimeter to prevent still more Naturals from entering
the community. One of the fires was quickly extinguished,

but the other continued to burn fiercely, so Smith instructed the sergeants who had previously served under him and had now been drawn to him again, to see that all of Jamestown's adolescents, boys and girls alike, were put to work fighting the blaze so the grown men would be free to take part in the battle.

Gradually some semblance of order was restored, and even though an unknown number of savages still lurked inside the palisades, ready to spring at the unwary, Smith could not concern himself with this relatively minor danger until the impetus of the enemy attack was checked. Occasionally, as he gave orders, made sure they were intelligently obeyed, and listened to the reports of his sergeants, he was vaguely aware of the presence of one or another member of the Council in the immediate vicinity, but he ignored them, and they were either afraid of him or too abashed to come near him.

He concentrated on the most urgent tasks for the better part of a half hour, and only when some semblance of discipline had been established and the colonists appeared to be holding their own did he turn his attention to Gabriel Archer, who was still devoting himself to directing the cannon fire and seemed neither to know nor care about any of the other phases of the battle. With two sergeants and a pike-bearing corporal at his heels, Smith finally descended the little hill from which he had been supervising the defense, and, his mouth set in a thin line, he approached the cannon.

"Cease fire!" he shouted, and the gunners, making no secret of their pleasure at seeing him, obeyed instantly. "Join the rest of the militia at the palisades," he told them, "and don't let any savages through. Men from crew number one go to the west wall. Those from crew number two go to the south wall. Our line there isn't as heavy as it should be."

Abandoning their guns, the men scattered, and Archer, his face powder-blackened, stared at his enemy. "You've been illegally released from prison," he said, and turned to the sergeants. "Take him back to his cell at once! I'll deal later with whoever is responsible for this outrage. Smith, you've destroyed the effectiveness of my cannon! In addition to your other crimes, I hold you responsible for whatever failure we may now suffer."

"There will be no more cannon fire," Smith replied evenly, and looked away for a moment to observe whether the militiamen on the nearest towers were still functioning efficiently or whether they needed fresh reinforcements.

Archer brandished his sword at the sergeants. "Do you dare disobey the order of the president of the Council? I'll have you hung for mutiny unless you take this criminal back to the prison!"

They did not move, and Smith had no time to waste on a futile argument with a pompous dunce. "You're no longer in command, Archer," he said crisply. "I've taken charge of the town's defenses."

This was the last straw, and the enraged Archer raised his sword and slashed wildly at his foe. But Smith side-stepped calmly, and in the same motion knocked the blade from the other's grasp with the butt of his musket. It was absurd to indulge in a private feud when the Rappahannock were attacking the colony, and Smith was determined to end the farce at once. Moving forward on the balls of his feet, he smashed his right fist into Archer's face, then followed the blow with an equally brutal left.

Frustration and righteous anger gave him added strength, and Archer, moaning and covering his battered face with his hands, sank to his knees. Smith, his features expressionless, turned to the pikeman. "Take him off the the prison and lock him up in my old cell until the battle is over," he said. "He'll be out of harm's way there and won't be able to do any more damage. If you can find a couple of people who aren't too busy, get them to help you. But under no circumstances let him go free, or there's no telling what might happen to Jamestown before the day ends."

Beckoning to the sergeants, he hurried off to the palisades and promptly forgot Gabriel Archer. One of the men had picked up Archer's sword and gave it to him, and he felt better when his fingers closed over the hilt. For some reason he could not explain he felt a surge of renewed confidence, and his lurking doubts that he might not be able to drive off the invaders vanished. He inspected the perimeter, encouraging the men who peered out between the logs, occasionally taking a musket and firing it himself, and his buoyant optimism gave new courage to the defenders, even those surly and frightened newcomers who had given up all hope of salvation. He devoted special attention to those near the holes in the walls and showed them how to redistribute themselves on either side of the gaps so they would not be seen by the savages outside yet would be able to move forward quickly to kill any native braves who might try to climb through the openings.

When he was satisfied that the palisades were secure, he raced to the area where the fire was still burning but was delighted to see that the women and adolescents had brought it under control. Three or four houses were gutted, and another was still burning, but considerable quantities of water had been poured on the cabins closest to the flames, and there seemed to be little danger that the fire would continue to spread. Smith lavishly praised everyone in sight and then walked rapidly to the nearest observation platform to gauge the Naturals' strength.

The arrows of the Rappahannock were thickest here, but Smith was impervious to personal danger, and instead of crouching close to the wooden flooring, as the militiamen did, he stood, coolly looked out over the top of a little three-foot-high parapet, and surveyed the surrounding territory. When he had been president of the Council he had insisted that all trees and foliage within two hundred and fifty yards of the walls be cut down, but during the intervening months no one had bothered to maintain such simple precautions, and only those portions of the land that were being used to raise crops were still clear. Elsewhere the underbrush had sprung up again, and here and there he could catch glimpses of the dark bodies of Rappahannock warriors inching closer to the palisades through the tall dry grass.

Luckily the sun had come out and filtered through the bare branches of the trees in the forest, so he was able to make out shadowy outlines in the forest too. But there was no way to judge how many braves the Naturals had sent against Jamestown, and Smith reflected that it would be suicide to send a counterattacking force out through the gates. The idea of confining himself to a defensive battle was repugnant to him, but he had no alternative, he knew, and would have to rely on the marksmanship of the settlers to discourage and disperse the Indians.

The colonists were paying a stiff price for their recent negligence; however, Smith noted, the arrows of the savages wounded many but killed only a few, and a surprisingly large number of those who were struck managed to pull out the shafts, bind up their wounds, and, ignoring their pain and discomfort, continue to do battle. The Naturals' losses were far heavier, Smith was happy to see, for the accurate musket fire of the militiamen took a frightful toll of the enemy. No army, regardless of whether it was composed of trained soldiers or primitive tribesmen, could remain in the field indefinitely when its ranks were being systematically decimated, Smith knew, so he felt certain that the settlers' ultimate victory was now assured. Sooner or later the Rappahannock chiefs who were responsible for the assault would realize they could absorb no more punishment and would withdraw, provided the defenders did not relax.

Smith did not believe in taking risks that could be avoided, and as he was persuaded that troops always fought best when they understood the principles of the battle tactics involved, he made a quick tour of the perimeter again, visiting each observation platform in turn. He explained his conclusions,

he encouraged the men to be vigilant and maintain a steady
fire, and he assured them that if they did not falter the savages
would be forced to admit defeat and would withdraw. He
arranged to send gunpowder and ammunition to the platforms at regular intervals and he instructed the sergeants to
call on every settler who was experienced in the use of
firearms for platform duty.

Then, firmly convinced that the defeat of the Indians was
inevitable, Smith turned his attention to the comparatively
minor but nevertheless hazardous problem of exterminating
the warriors who were hiding inside the walls. First he
rounded up every able-bodied man who was not already
occupied, and as so few colonists were available for the task,
he pressed the members of the Council into service and
requested help from the captains of the *Susan Constant* and
Royal Hope, whose barks were no longer in danger of being
captured and sunk.

Dividing Jamestown into four sectors, he assigned a group
to scour each; every building was to be searched, and he
warned the men that the savages were desperate and cunning
warriors who would use imagination in finding unusual
hiding places. It was far easier to illustrate his thesis than to
explain it, and so, accompanied by six colonists and three
sailors whom he chose at random, he started down the
nearest street while the others watched. He and his companions searched three houses in vain, but when they reached
the fourth their luck improved, and one of the sailors uncovered a painted brave who was waiting in ambush for potential
victims under a pile of cornhusks and trash in a small yard.
Before the warrior could either fight back or escape, the sailor
put a pistol shot through his head, and the onlookers
cheered.

Smith, understandably nervous over the damage that
might be done to the colony's meager supplies, led the way
into a warehouse in which sacks of flour and barrels of salt
fish were stacked. It was dark inside the barnlike structure,

and he and his men fanned out before proceeding cautiously into the building. They had gone no more than a few feet, poking into every crevice, when a tall warrior suddenly materialized out of the shadows, waving something in his hand.

"Smith, King of James," he cried in his own tongue, "hear my voice!"

But Smith had no intention of being tricked and, lunging forward, skewered the savage on his sword. As the Rappahannock brave fell, he flung something at the man who had killed him, and Smith felt a soft strip of leather strike his face. It looked like a wampum belt, although he could not see it clearly, but he had more important matters on his mind and jammed it absently into his pocket. The hunt continued, and the curious incident completely slipped his mind.

The searching parties now knew what was expected of them and departed for their respective sectors, while Smith returned to the walls. During the next hour nine more warriors were found inside the town and all of them were killed, although two of the settlers lost their lives in the process too. Many of the women and smaller children, who had gone to the barks at Smith's orders earlier in the battle, sent word to him that they wanted to return to their homes now that Jamestown was once more safe, but he refused to grant their request, as he was afraid the attackers might resort to throwing lighted firebrands over the walls when they realized that their frontal assault had failed.

But his fears proved to be groundless, and shortly before noon the musket fire slackened and then stopped. Smith, staring out over the parapet of an observation tower, finally realized that the Rappahannock had conceded victory to the colonists and had withdrawn. There was a chance, of course, that the retreat was not genuine and that the war party was lurking in the wilderness nearby, waiting to return as soon as the settlers relaxed. But Smith refused to be fooled and, taking with him a number of the original colonists who had become familiar with the forests, he spent the next hour painstakingly following the tracks of the savages.

Only when he was thoroughly satisfied that they were indeed gone did he return to the town and announce that the victory was absolute. And even then he gave Jamestown no opportunity to rest on its laurels. Burial parties were organized, young men were put to work repairing the holes in the palisades that had almost proved fatal, and guards were posted at the warehouses to prevent looting. Smith had eaten nothing all day, but rather than pause for a meal he dropped a few handfuls of parched corn into his pockets and roamed the town restlessly, overseeing the repairs. Everyone in Jamestown wanted to shake his hand and thank him for saving the colony; he accepted the gratitude and congratulations of Council members and ordinary settlers alike, and as usual he was graciously modest.

The church had been converted into a temporary hospital, and he spent more than an hour cheering the wounded. Then he visited the families of each of the dead and promised them the names of the heroes who had died defending the town would be chiseled on a stone tablet he intended to erect in their memory. Men marveled at his boundless energy when he reappeared at the parade ground, rounded up another group of volunteers, and gave directions to clear the ground where the gutted houses had stood, to extend the west palisades and begin preparing the ground beyond the present boundary for the new houses he intended to construct at once for all who were homeless.

The colonists were tired, physically and emotionally, but his enthusiasm infused them with renewed energy, and everyone who was able to work pitched in. Smith, dipping into his pockets for parched corn as he walked, made a special point of speaking to each of the new arrivals whom he had not met previously, and they responded instantly to his kindness and the strength they sensed in him. At one time or another each of the Council members came to him and offered him an apology; neither they nor he specifically raised the issue that he was still under a technical death sentence, but it was tacitly agreed that the charge against him would be quietly dropped.

By late afternoon only one urgent issue had not yet been settled, and Smith started toward the prison for a final reckoning with Gabriel Archer. He was still hungry, and as he dug in the pocket of his breeches for any stray kernels of corn he might have missed, his fingers touched the wampum belt that the Indian warrior whom he had killed had thrown at him. Taking the beaded strip of leather from his pocket, he glanced at it idly; then he stopped short and stared at it. In the center of the belt was a crude but recognizable figure of an Indian woman, and his heart pounded when he saw she was wearing an ornate, multifeathered white headdress.

Several people who were laboring to clear up wreckage nearby saw his strained, pale face and thought he was ill, but when they hurried to him he silently waved them away and continued to gaze at the wampum. He knew now beyond all doubt that Pocahontas had inspired the attack and that the Rappahannock had carried it out under her father's instructions. Until this moment the raid had been meaningless to him, and he had been at a complete loss to understand why a tribe that was presumably friendly to the English would have launched such a vicious surprise assault. But the figure on the belt explained everything to him, and his amazement gave way to a hard, cold anger.

Powhatan had tricked him once and had forced him to undergo a series of humiliations, culminating in the native wedding ceremony that had made Pocahontas his "wife," but no one, least of all an ignorant savage, could successfully threaten him a second time. He realized that the attack had been a clear warning and that there would be worse to come if he failed to send for Pocahontas, but he told himself that the attempt to frighten him merely strengthened his resolve to have no more to do with her.

The wench and her father had erred in their judgment of

him, and he reflected grimly that no power on earth was great enough to persuade, cajole, or force him to bring Pocahontas to Jamestown. He would be on his guard now, and the next time an Indian attack was launched against the colony he would be ready for it. Powhatan would be cautious, of course, after the defeat his Rappahannock had sustained, but when he eventually gathered his full strength and tried again, he would be repulsed with even greater losses. Pocahontas needed to be taught a lesson, and perhaps, when her father was utterly crushed, she would learn that it was unwise to try to intimidate John Smith.

Self-righteous anger flared up in him, and as he jammed the offending leather strip back into his pocket he damned Pocahontas with all his heart. Never in all his experience had he encountered a woman so insensitive to a man's desires and wishes, and he was sorry he had ever set eyes on her, sorrier still that he had encouraged her to use what little mind she possessed. But he would show her he could match her callousness, and when Powhatan again tried to intervene on her behalf, he would give the Naturals a demonstration of brutal warfare they would never forget.

What irritated him most was Pocahontas's blind, unreasoning insistence that she had a place in his life. Naturally her horizons were too limited for her to understand that a permanent relationship between them would hamper his future, and she could not know that King James would never elevate a man who was married to a stupid American savage to the nobility. What she certainly could realize, but obviously would not, was that there was no legitimate reason for him to remain tied to her. By any civilized standards he owed her absolutely nothing. On the contrary, she was indebted to him for having taught her to speak and read English, and the very least she could do for him in return would be to disappear gracefully and permanently from his life. The next time he indulged in an affair, he promised himself, he would select a married woman and would avoid complications.

Dusk was beginning to fall as he roused himself and went

on to the prison, and the men who had been working to clear up the debris of battle were now drifting toward their homes. When they saw Smith halt outside the prison, they knew that something out of the ordinary was going to take place, and a few moments later, when two militiamen escorted Gabriel Archer into the open, word spread and a large crowd gathered. Smith's resentment and anger at his rival was as great as his rage at Pocahontas, but he knew he would need to exercise a measure of caution before the people of the colony. If he allowed his true feelings to show, he would lose sympathy.

"Archer," he said loudly when the prisoner was brought before him, "I'll relieve you of your sash of office. It rightfully belongs to me, and I'll take it from you."

The last time they had stood in almost this same spot their positions had been reversed, and Archer was well aware of the delicacy of his position. He was unpopular with the settlers, who idolized his enemy, and they would give Smith their wholehearted support. Nevertheless, he was not lacking in courage. "I challenge your right to remove me from office," he shouted. "Only the Council elects and deposes its president."

Smith laughed and managed to sound genuinely amused. "A majority of the Council is here right now," he said. "Ask them if they intend to sustain you. Or better still, ask the people which of us they prefer."

The crowd shouted in favor of its hero, and those members of the Council who entertained private doubts as to the legality of Smith's seizure of power did not dare to express themselves aloud. They knew, too, that Archer's inefficiency and bungling had caused a near catastrophe and that only Smith's energetic intervention had saved the colony from destruction. So they said nothing.

"The sash, if you please." Smith held out his hand.

Archer glared at him but did not move, and one of the veterans of the battle dashed forward out of the crowd, jerked the ribbon from his body, and handed it to Smith. Smiling faintly, Smith draped it across his chest, and again the throng cheered. He had recovered the symbol of office so easily and quickly that he was a little surprised at how simple the move had been. He had anticipated far more difficulty, but now that he was again the president of the Council, he decided to be rid of his nettlesome foe permanently.

"Gabriel Archer," he said slowly in a voice that carried to every corner of the parade ground, "you were derelict in your duty to the King, to the owners of the London Company, and to the citizens of Jamestown. Your failure to provide adequate defenses for the colony has cost us the lives of more than twenty brave men and three innocent women. You are therefore unworthy to be a member of this colony. If I treated you as you deserve, I'd send you out into the wilderness to starve or be killed by the savages. But, just as King James is a merciful ruler, so I, as his chief officer in the New World, am merciful. I therefore sentence you to be returned to England. Is Captain Matteson of the *Royal Hope* present?"

"Right here, Captain Smith!" shouted a man in the crowd.

"Captain, I request you to give Archer passage to Plymouth when you sail in a fortnight's time. Until then be good enough to lock him in irons aboard your bark so he can cause no more harm here."

"Aye, aye, sir," the master of the *Royal Hope* replied.

Archer, goaded beyond endurance, broke away from the militiamen who held him. They tried to recapture him, but they were clumsy, and in the brief scuffle that followed he cleverly caught hold of the pistol one of them carried in his belt. Darting away from the guards, he cursed under his breath and after a brief, frantic effort managed to cock the weapon. Meantime Smith did not remain inactive and, realizing his sword would be ineffective against firearms, he reached out and took a whip from one of the nearest spectators, a man who had been driving a cart pulled by two

Indian work horses acquired some months previously from the Chesapeake.

By the time Archer turned and aimed the pistol at his enemy, Smith was ready for him, and the whip cracked. The long rawhide thong wrapped itself around the pistol, and when Smith jerked the handle the gun was wrenched from Archer's hand and sailed over the heads of the crowd, landing somewhere on the far side of the parade ground. Archer lurched forward, his bare hands extended, his fingers curling, but Smith halted him abruptly by striking him smartly across the chest with the whip.

Again and again the long strip of leather sang through the air, and Archer's desire to commit murder cooled as the lash cut into his flesh. Smith coldly subjected him to the ultimate degradation by methodically whipping him until he could stand no more pain and tried to flee. But the rawhide ribbon curled around his right ankle, halting him, and when he stumbled and fell to the ground, five or six militiamen pounced on him. The crowd would have applauded, but Smith, his face grave, silenced them with a wave of his free hand. Tossing the whip to its owner, he glanced for a moment at the prostrate figure of his adversary, and those who stood near him swore afterward that pity and compassion were plainly written on his face.

Then, adjusting the sash of the presidency and carrying himself as though the burden of the office were unbearably heavy, he walked off slowly into the twilight.

In the next few weeks the colonists worked day and night, rectifying costly mistakes and making up for lost time. Yet no one complained and no one felt abused, for Captain Smith asked nothing of any settler that he was unwilling to do himself, and even the few who disliked him had to admit he set an inspiring example. When the *Royal Hope* sailed for England with the discredited Gabriel Archer on board, the settlers were far too busy to pay any attention to his departure, and the feud that had caused so much turmoil in the short history of Jamestown came to an ignominious and apathetic end.

Under Smith's direction the revitalized colonists built enough homes to house themselves, and at least one hundred more families were expected to arrive during the next year. Food supplies were carefully rationed, and one hundred acres of the wilderness were cleared in preparation for spring planting. Jamestown would never again be reduced to near starvation if Smith had his way, and he was planning to make the colony self-sufficient, so that trades with the natives would be unnecessary. New walls were built, and the president inspected them often to assure himself that they were sturdy and secure. The observation platforms had been proved less than satisfactory in battle, so Smith had new fortifications erected; enclosed towers, each of them a miniature, self-contained blockhouse, studded the palisades at regular intervals, and guards were stationed in them twenty-four hours a day.

From time to time the sentries reported the presence of Indian scouts in the forest, and had they been left to their own devices the settlers would have fired at anything they saw moving behind the screen of trees. But Smith had given strict instructions that Natural spies were not to be molested, and his orders were obeyed willingly, for the militiamen were forced to agree with his logic. Warriors who saw Jamestown's bristling state of preparedness, he said, could only report to their chiefs that the colony was invulnerable. Muskets showed in the chinks between logs, a vast area outside the walls had been cleared of all trees and underbrush, and cannon poked their long barrels above the palisades on every side, so even stupid savages who had no real understanding of modern scientific warfare would hesitate to start a battle they obviously could not win.

Smith secretly hoped that Powhatan would launch a new assault, as he was anxious to put the Chickahominy in their place for all time, but Pocahontas's father apparently recognized the superior power of the settlers and kept his distance. Obviously he was biding his time, waiting for the town to relax its vigilance, but Smith knew better than to be lulled into a sense of false security, and held himself and his men ready for action at all times.

Ten days before the *Susan Constant* was scheduled to leave for England, a fleet of four vessels sailed up the James River, and a new group of recruits arrived, together with more foodstuffs, arms, and ammunition than had ever before been sent to the New World by the directors of the London Company. A knight, Sir Thomas Dale, was in charge of the party, and he carried written orders naming Smith as governor. The shareholders, disturbed by the squabbles that had stunted Jamestown's development, had decided to place full authority in one man, and Smith was their obvious choice.

Quietly elated over his promotion, Smith conducted Sir Thomas, who was to act as his deputy, on a tour of the town. They were accompanied by several gentlemen who had just arrived, and one of them was smoking a pipe. This thoughtless act, which was meaningless in itself, accomplished what neither Powhatan nor Gabriel Archer had been able to achieve.

The party inspected homes, stockades, warehouses, and the church, and as they were examining an arsenal in which muskets and ammunition were stored, a spark from the glowing pipe landed on a bag of gunpowder and set it on fire. The powder flared up, and Smith, who had been engaged in earnest conversation with Sir Thomas, turned just in time to see flames reaching out in every direction. He realized that within a few seconds the fire would spread and that only a miracle would save the precious war matériel. Not believing in miracles other than those he performed himself, he unhesitatingly threw himself onto the flames and extinguished the fire by rolling back and forth across the burning gunpowder.

The incident ended a few moments after it had begun, but

its consequences were far-reaching, for Smith suffered severe burns. His pain was intense, but he bore it stoically, knowing he had once again performed an act of heroism that would add to the luster of his name. However, the community's surgeon, who applied bear grease and sassafras poultices to the burns, declared that Smith would be unable to resume his duties as governor for at least six months. He strongly advised his patient to return to England, and Smith, who was confined to his bed and hence had nothing better to occupy his mind, thought of little else for several days.

Finally, after carefully weighing all of the factors involved, he decided to follow the surgeon's suggestion. The colony was now firmly established, thanks to his efforts, and if he remained here he would be required to spend most of his time and effort on administrative duties in the next few years. Methodical, conscientious men like Sir Thomas were far better suited to such work, which was necessary but dull, and Smith wanted to conquer fresh fields. Thanks to Powhatan's enmity, he did not dare go out on any new trips of exploration anywhere in Virginia, as he was sure he would be captured and returned to Pocahontas if he ventured far from the palisades of Jamestown. Hence it would be wise to return to England now, while his glory was fresh and he could capitalize on it.

Then, at some later date he would sail on a new expedition to some other part of America. The New World, he was convinced, was far larger than even explorers like Sir Walter Raleigh realized, and there was unlimited opportunity for him to win new honors for himself in regions where Pocahontas's influence could not reach out and touch him. And so he made up his mind to leave on the *Susan Constant*, the same ship that had carried him here. He thought only of the future now, of the sensation he would create in London, and of the book that would make him famous throughout Europe.

The settlers mourned when they heard he was leaving, but

he was in high spirits in spite of his burns, and he insisted on packing his belongings himself. He entrusted his maps and manuscripts to no one, and when his other possessions were carried aboard the bark, he kept his papers apart and permitted no one else to touch them. Somewhere inside the bundle was the wampum belt that Pocahontas had sent him, and it amused him to think that he might someday incorporate some carefully edited portions of their story in the second volume of his *General History of Virginia*.

It would be a shame not to use material that would certainly interest romantically inclined readers, and although the experience itself had been insignificant, Englishmen, who loved the unusual and bizarre, would be fascinated by his account of the little savage who had tried without success to transform herself into what she could never become, a Christian, a civilized person, and a lady.

November, 1609

Every room in the Whitehall Palace was drafty, gloomy, and damp, and the King's private conference chamber was no exception. Heavy tapestries covered the walls, and thick rugs were spread on the floors, in imitation of the Spaniards, whom His Majesty professed to hate, but the roaring fire in the hearth at the north end of the room failed to dissipate the chill, and the heat escaped through wide cracks between the stones in the walls near the high ceiling. As usual, the only person present who was reasonably comfortable was King James, whose chair at the head of the Privy Council table was placed conveniently close to the hearth, but as usual he made the only complaint.

"We feel sure that even in the wildest parts of America you suffered no inconveniences worse than the discomforts that make our life here so unpleasant, Captain Smith," he said in his high, shrill voice marked by a thick Scottish burr.

His Lord Chamberlain, the Earl of Suffolk, exchanged a

covert glance with the Duke of Buckingham, who sat opposite him. When the King was in a petulant mood he frequently wasted hours whining about imagined hardships.

John Smith wasn't certain whether he was expected to reply but, seeing the others at the table stiffen, he weighed the matter carefully. He had waited many weeks for this appointment and he intended to miss no opportunity to impress either King James or the other great gentlemen who could, if they wished, make him wealthy and powerful. This was obviously a day when good luck and boldness would pay heavy dividends, provided he was willing to take chances, and he decided that false modesty would avail him nothing. Fortune had first smiled on him while he was waiting to be received by the Privy Council, and the King's two young sons, Henry Frederick, the Prince of Wales, who would someday be Henry IX, and his little brother, Prince Charles, had happened to wander through the anteroom. He had promptly regaled the boys with stories of the New World, and they were so enthralled they had begged their father for the right to attend the meeting. James had given in to his sons' request, so Smith hoped the enthusiasm of the princes would win him the sympathy of their elders.

"The inconveniences of life in Virginia are vastly different from those of Whitehall, Your Majesty," he said, and knew he had been right to speak when the King nodded complacently and both the Duke of Buckingham and the Bishop of Winchester smiled appreciatively at him.

"You wouldn't believe this, Smith," James replied, "but we've been trying for years to have some rooms of the palace rebuilt to incorporate bay windows of the sort that Inigo Jones developed. They make rooms exceptionally light and they hold the heat too. Many of our subjects, including common merchants, have bay windows in their houses, but when we want them here, all we hear is one excuse after another." He glared at each of his councilors in turn, then added absently to his younger son, "Charles, stop biting your fingernails."

Sir Francis Cockburn, Treasurer of the King's Household, sighed wearily. "Your Majesty forgets," he said, "that each of your seven country houses is now equipped with bay windows. But the architects cannot install them here without tearing Whitehall down."

"There are times when we wish it were torn down." James stared moodily out of the window, and there was a long silence.

Smith, staring at him surreptitiously, thought it was astonishing that the King had inherited none of his mother's fabled beauty. He was, in fact, the homeliest, most unprepossessing man in the room and could have taken lessons in regal deportment from his son, Henry, who was no more than fourteen or fifteen. The Duke of Buckingham's doublet was trimmed with sable, the Earl of Suffolk wore a magnificent emerald-and-diamond ring on the index finger of his left hand, and even the ornamental dagger at the waist of the Bishop of Winchester was studded with gems, but James's ruff was food-stained, there was a rip in the lace of his right cuff, and the stubble on his long Stuart jaw was clear evidence that he had not bothered to shave. Smith concluded that if he was any judge of men James was too slovenly to insist, as had the late Elizabeth, that no one address him without first being given the right to speak. In all probability he would become difficult only if he felt he was being shown real or fancied disrespect.

"Your Majesty will be pleased to learn," Smith declared, "that several of the more imposing homes in Jamestown were constructed with bay windows." Nothing could be farther from the truth, to be sure, but that was irrelevant.

The King appeared anything but pleased and tapped the top of the long polished oak table. "We trust that all houses there have been built in the new symmetrical design which we now require here in London," he said, frowning. "We would hate to learn that a town named in our honor was less than symmetrically perfect."

Smith thought of the clay huts with thatched roofs, the log cabins, and the Indian-style lodges of the New World, but his face remained grave. "Naturally, Your Majesty," he said blandly, "the symmetry is magnificent."

Sir Francis had more on his mind than architecture, and so did the others. "His Majesty is very much concerned," the treasurer said, bowing slightly in the direction of the head of the table, "over the lack of specific information from the directors of the London Company regarding the gold being mined in Virginia. I happen to have a very pressing need for gold," he added in a mutter to no one in particular.

"And what about jewels, Captain Smith?" the Duke of Buckingham asked, fingering a ruby amulet that hung from his neck. "According to all I've been told about America, there are diamonds and sapphires lying loose on the ground everywhere, just waiting for someone to come along and pick them up."

"I saw no diamonds and no sapphires in Virginia, Your Grace," Smith replied carefully. "I'm in no position to know whether jewels are to be found in other parts of the New World, but I myself explored many hundreds of miles of Virginia and I found no gems of any sort."

"There you are, George!" King James turned to Buckingham and gazed at his favorite vindictively. "You're always so sure your sources of information are better than anyone else's, but there are times when you're mistaken!"

Sir Francis intervened before the inevitable squabble developed. "What about gold, Captain Smith? Why hasn't the Crown been paid its share of gold from the Virginia mines?"

"To the best of my knowledge and belief, there is no gold in Virginia," Smith declared truthfully. He was sorry to disappoint his distinguished audience, but on this one subject, at least, it would be unwise and even dangerous to lie.

The Earl of Suffolk patted his starched, pale violet ruff. "Then what use is such a colony?"

His question seemed eminently sensible to the King. "Yes,

what value has it, then? In our opinion the natives were hiding their gold resources from you, Smith, and you weren't sufficiently clever to ferret them out."

Ignorance and stupidity always irritated Smith, and he became furious when anyone cast aspersions on his own abilities. But he forcibly reminded himself that he could easily lose his head if he failed to control his temper, so he smiled and tried not to sound condescending. "I spent many months in the interior, Your Majesty, and I visited all of the important native tribes. I actually lived with them for weeks at a time. And during those periods I saw no sign of gold in any form. If they had gold, they would have used it either in their homes or their ornaments. All I saw was a little copper——"

"Copper!" Sir Francis said, his tone indicating extreme disgust.

"—and a few bits of silver." Smith paused and saw the faces of the privy councilors brighten. "I made numerous inquiries, milords, very careful inquiries, and unfortunately the silver was not a product of Virginia. The natives there gained possession of it through trades with other tribes living hundreds of miles farther south."

"Then why didn't you move your colony to the land of the silver mines?" the Bishop asked.

"Because, milord, Spain has already laid claim to that territory, and His Majesty has strictly forbidden all companies of English explorers to trespass on Spanish soil."

James pouted and shifted his position abruptly. "We are tired of hearing about the accomplishments of the Spaniards. Spain grows rich while we become poor." He looked fretfully at his councilors in turn, as though he held each of them to blame.

The first gentlemen of England refrained from comment and looked stonily into space, ignoring each other and pretending they had not heard the King. Smith knew better than to speak, for there was no touchier subject than that of the country's policy toward Spain, and he had no desire to become caught in the crosscurrents of a controversy that had split the Privy Council into two warring factions and had caused considerable unrest throughout the nation. The Duke of Buckingham, who was the outspoken champion of a complete break in diplomatic relations with Spain, contrived to look bored, and an expression of sardonic amusement lighted his handsome face. Sir Francis, who favored the preservation of peace at any price, was flushed and angry, and his gray beard quivered.

The King, whose vacillation was responsible for the ill feeling between his ministers, apparently liked to think of himself as being above petty strife, and he refused to be diverted from the subject most on his mind at the moment. "We are not complimented, Captain Smith, to be the patron of a colony lacking in both precious metals and gems. Of what importance is Virginia to us? What contribution can she make to either our realm or our own purse?"

Smith had anticipated such a question and had prepared his answer in advance. "The wealth of the New World, Your Majesty, lies in her timber and natural produce."

"Timber? Perhaps. But we don't know what you mean by natural produce."

"I'm thinking principally in terms of tobacco, sir."

The adolescent Prince of Wales gasped, and the men stirred uncomfortably. King James shoved back his chair so violently that his short ermine cape, which had been draped over the back, fell to the floor, but he paid no heed to it as he stood and glowered at his visitor. "We have been informed, Captain Smith, that you are something of a man of letters," he said acidly, "but we are inclined to doubt the accuracy of those reports. If you were at all familiar with literature, you would know we are an author and have composed a number of volumes of poems and essays that will be read for hundreds of years. We are, if we may say so, England's first literate monarch since Alfred the Great."

"I've read everything Your Majesty has ever written," Smith said quietly.

"Not quite everything." James rocked back and forth on his high, painted heels. "It's plain that you're unfamiliar with a treatise we published five years ago, which we were pleased to call *Counterblaste*, in which we exposed the evils of tobacco. It is our unalterable belief that smoking is a vile and noxious habit!"

"I quite agree, Your Majesty," Smith replied calmly, relieved that the length of the table separated him from the King and that James therefore could not smell the odor of tobacco on his breath. "Your treatise made a very strong impression on me long before I went to the New World. It had such a great effect on me, in fact, that I refused to light a single pipe the entire time I was in America. However," he added firmly, "not many men have had the wisdom or the strength to follow Your Majesty's advice or example. Whether you and I like it or not, sir, England has become a nation of smokers."

"Yes," the King said querulously, "and when we told the Commons to pass a bill forbidding the filthy habit anywhere in the realm, do you know what they did? They laughed at us. They actually dared to laugh at us."

"The Anglo-Saxon sense of humor is often misplaced, Your Majesty," Smith replied smoothly. "But it seems to me that you're in a position to have the last and loudest laugh. If you can neither persuade them to refrain from smoking nor legislate the habit out of existence, you can at least show a handsome profit from your subjects' stupidity."

At the mention of possible profit the atmosphere brightened. The Earl of Suffolk smiled, Buckingham stroked his beard, and Sir Francis positively beamed. Even the King appeared intrigued, but he had been approached by so many schemers that he was cautious. "How might we do that?" he asked.

"The tobacco of Virginia is vastly superior to that grown in

Ireland and other places," Smith said. "The demand for it will soon become overwhelming, and I know of no reason why the Crown can't impose a tax on every ounce brought into England."

James resumed his seat, rubbed his hands together, and smiled. "Neither do we," he said, then hesitated. "You're sure the tobacco of Virginia is of a superior quality?"

"As positive as a nonsmoker could be, Your Majesty. I've seen men go into ecstasy over the stuff the Naturals smoke."

The young princes were bored by the discussion of their elders, but eleven-year-old Charles grinned at the mention of Naturals and, whispering something to his brother, nudged him twice. The Prince of Wales nodded and cleared his throat, a precaution he always took in these days when his voice was changing. "Be good enough to tell us something of your adventures among the natives, Captain Smith," he commanded.

The King struck the table with the open palm of his right hand and gouged the surface with the inside of a heavy signet ring. "Henry," he said sharply, "you and Charles will withdraw at once."

"But——"

"At once! Captain Smith will entertain you some other time. We're discussing matters of importance to the state!"

Charles looked as though he would burst into tears, but Henry struggled successfully to keep his dignity, and together the brothers bowed to their father and backed toward the door. When they were gone, James turned to Smith, a lascivious gleam in his eyes. "We couldn't speak freely in the presence of children of such tender years," he said, and something in his tone reminded his visitor of long nights at sea when sailors exchanged bawdy jokes.

"Yes, Your Majesty?"

"You may work out the details of a tax on tobacco with Sir Francis. And, Suffolk, it has come to our attention that Smith wants the right to explore other portions of America.

Give him a patent or whatever is necessary." Disposing of these minor matters, the King leaned forward and rested his elbows on the table. "Now, tell us," he said, "about the native women. Certain rumors about your activities in the New World have reached our ears."

The Bishop of Winchester stood abruptly. "Obviously this is no place for me," he said, and walked quickly out of the room.

But the others did not share his sentiments, and their expressions were eager as they stared at Smith, who contrived to look surprised. "Rumors, sir?" he asked.

"We have it on good authority that you had a rather piquant relationship with a girl of one of the Natural tribes. To be frank with you," James continued, giggling slightly, "we agreed to receive you today simply because we've been curious to hear the story from your own lips."

The blow to Smith's pride was crushing; after the many days he had spent petitioning for this interview, he was pleased when he had finally been summoned to court, for he had naturally concluded that his achievements were about to be recognized and rewarded. He had been hoping he would be granted a patent to continue his explorations, but the offhand way in which the King had granted him the privilege made it painfully evident to him that James was indifferent to his accomplishments. At the moment, at least, he could take no real satisfaction in the knowledge that soon he would be in a position to form a new company and could start to lay plans for an expedition to some hitherto unknown part of the New World.

All he could think right now was that the King had consented to see him solely because of his encounter with Pocahontas, and the realization stunned him. The avid faces of the privy councilors annoyed him, too, and had they been lesser men he would have challenged them to duels, one after another. All the work he had done to establish Jamestown and make it secure meant nothing at Whitehall, and

the greatest men in the kingdom seemed to be unconcerned
over his unprecedented, brilliant feat in setting up the first
permanent English colony in America. Idle gossip about a
vapid wench meant more to them than the creation of an
overseas empire. Yet, he thought as he deliberately calmed
himself, he could not truly blame either James or the lords
for their interest in her.

Pocahontas herself was to blame, he reflected bitterly,
remembering that almost everyone whom he had encountered since his return to London had asked him about her.
He had virtually forgotten her during the long voyage home,
but so many of the Jamestown settlers had written to relatives
about his experiences with her that she had been forcibly
recalled to his mind. Questions about her never failed to
nettle him, but King James's inquisitiveness was the last
straw. His vanity hurt, Smith could not help but wonder
dismally whether Pocahontas was going to haunt him for the
rest of his life. And he was alarmed at the possibility that the
affair could do him permanent harm, just as an incident
involving Sir Walter Raleigh, who had once spread his cloak
in the mud for Queen Elizabeth, had caused immeasurable
damage and had made it impossible for many people to take
Sir Walter seriously from that day to this.

"Stories are often exaggerated, Your Majesty," Smith said
lightly, hoping to end the speculation once and for all. "It so
happens that I did a few little favors for a native chief, so he
made me a gift of his daughter. But she was such an ignorant
little creature that I soon tired of her and gave her back to her
father. That's all there was to it."

James and his nobles looked disappointed. "We were
told," the King said, "that an Indian maiden saved your life
under highly dramatic circumstances."

Smith feigned amusement so convincingly that his
chuckle sounded completely genuine. "I'm afraid we live in
a romantic and sentimental age, Your Majesty. I've been
looking after myself for many years—and under a variety of

trying circumstances. Can you imagine a mere female, and a dull-witted savage at that, saving my life?" He laughed more loudly and shook his head. "Impossible, Your Majesty! Absolutely impossible!"

Pocahontas walked slowly from her house to the lodge at the top of the hill, where her father and the elders were assembled. Her wolfskin robe flew open and the bitter November wind cut through her thin tunic, but she was unmindful of the cold. She moved past the familiar image of Ek outside the entrance to the building without bothering to glance at it, as she no longer believed in the gods of her ancestors. She had prayed to them in vain, she had made countless sacrifices before them, but they had not heeded her wishes, and she was convinced that they were mere graven images of the sort the Bible had warned her to avoid. The God of the Hebrews and of the Christians, who was one and the same, seemed far more real to her than Ek and Ris and Gan and Ti-Ba, but she could not be certain she had any real faith in the God of Abraham, either.

Perhaps, as she so often told herself, He was testing her, as He had tested Job. Or it might be that she needed to show more faith in Him, as Daniel had done, before her desires would be granted. On the other hand, she was afraid that if she followed the command of Jesus Christ and asked God to do His will, not her own, she would never be reunited with John Smith. The Bible stated repeatedly that mere humans could not understand the way of God, and she did not want to believe in Him either if it meant giving up all hope of spending the rest of her life with Smith. She realized that she would need to show far more humility than she had yet demonstrated if she was to become a good Christian, but it was difficult to love God, as David had, when she yearned to be at the side of her husband.

Her groping efforts to discover the true state of her thinking had led her nowhere; she knew only that she was utterly miserable and she could not accept the promises of so many of the biblical authors, from Isaiah to Paul, who assured her that through trust in God she would find peace of mind. She wanted John Smith, not solace.

The men inside the lodge were talking, but conversation stopped when Pocahontas raised the flap, entered, and bowed to Powhatan. Opachisco, as was his privilege, sat in the place of honor on their father's left in the semicircle around the fire, and she knew every other brave who was present. On Powhatan's right, puffing a long clay pipe, was Ratulawan, the principal adviser to the Chief of Chiefs, who had been a great warrior in his younger days, and next to him sat Parranha-Boli, who had achieved several notable victories in the war with the Cherokees that had just come to an end. The frail little elder with the nose resembling an eagle's was Udesuekan, who was in charge of storehouses, and at the far end of the semicircle was the warrior Daj-Weenu, long one of her father's closest confidants. She had been summoned to appear before the greatest lords of the entire Chickahominy Confederation, and although she knew they had already been discussing her future, she would not let herself show fear in their presence.

A woman had no choice but to obey orders, yet Pocahontas knew she was not helpless and that she could utilize her natural feminine assets to advantage, for she saw the bold admiration in the eyes of her father's advisers as they gazed at her, and she was aware, too, of the pride that Powhatan and Opachisco felt when they looked at her. She had changed in the long, cruel months since she and Smith had been separated, and although she no longer cared whether others thought her beautiful, she realized that never before had she read such great desire in the eyes of warriors or such frank envy in the expressions of women; these days everyone seemed to stare at her constantly.

On the infrequent occasions when she glanced at her reflection in a pool of water or a little square of burnished copper, she could see that her appearance had improved, but she took no pleasure in the knowledge that she had become increasingly attractive. Sorrow had molded her face into firmer lines, suffering had altered her bland, almost childish features, and there was real dignity in her expression now, a strength of character that had transformed her from a rather insipidly pretty girl into a strikingly lovely young woman. There had been a time when she would have been ashamed to use her beauty to prevent others from shaping her life for her, but that was before John Smith had loved her and then deserted her, and she did not hesitate now to protect herself in the only ways she knew. Lifting her head when her father granted permission, she smiled at Parranha-Boli and Daj-Weenu, who, as the youngest of Powhatan's advisers, were obviously the most susceptible to her charms.

"The daughter of Powhatan," she said to Parranha-Boli, "has rejoiced each time you have beaten the Cherokees who invaded our land. Your name and that of Opachisco will be remembered as long as songs are sung in honor of those who have won great victories." She looked affectionately at her brother, who had shared the glory of winning the war.

All of the men except Powhatan beamed at her, but he, vaguely conscious of her purpose, felt uneasy. "The braves of the Chickahominy have beaten the Cherokee for all time," he said, "but many of our finest warriors have been killed. We are weak now, and many moons will pass before our older boys grow to manhood and take the place of those who died." It would do no harm, he reasoned, to remind his subordinates of the harsh realities they were inclined to forget when they looked dreamily at Pocahontas. The unexpected war that had broken out six months ago had drained the manpower of the Chickahominy and had strained the resources of the nation to the breaking point, and harsh measures were needed now to restore prosperity.

Opachisco, understanding the motives behind his father's comments, decided to come straight to the point. Folding his

arms across his chest, he stared up at Pocahontas, who had
moved to the center of the semicircle, directly in front of the
fire. He had no desire to hurt her, but she had been pam-
pered long enough. "It is time," he said bluntly, "that the
sister of Opachisco learns the truth."

She knew he had challenged her but had no idea what he
meant. "I am sure I will always have much to learn," she said
meekly, refusing to show her hand until the issues were clear.

Powhatan took over the burden himself. "Many moons
ago we believed that Smith, King of James, had left the town
of the foreigners and had gone to the land of his fathers in one
of the great ships which has wings like the white eagle's."

"So my father has told me. Many times." Pocahontas
lowered her head and spoke softly.

"Our warriors have been busy fighting the Cherokee. The
braves of our allies have been busy too. So there has been no
chance until now to make sure that what we have believed is
true." Powhatan paused and looked significantly at his
daughter's headband of green laurel leaves. "This day two
Chesapeake braves have arrived in the land of the Chickahominy from the town of the foreigners."

She knew what was coming, but she refused to accept even
the inevitable without a struggle. "They were admitted to the
town?" she asked, knowing that the settlers had kept their
gates locked since the abortive attack by the Rappahannock.

"The Chesapeake braves were wise beyond their years.
They took with them many shining seeds of oysters, which
the foreigners prize. So they were allowed to enter the town.
And there they learned much. Smith left the land of the
foreigners on a great ship many moons ago. The new King of
James is called Dale."

Although Pocahontas had been almost certain in her own
mind that Smith had sailed to England, the news nevertheless shocked her. But she hid her feelings, knowing the men
were watching her. "The Chesapeake warriors did not say
whether Smith has gone to the land of his fathers never to

return or whether he has gone there only for a visit," she said calmly, and had someone unacquainted with the facts of the situation been present, he would have assumed from her tone that Smith had told her all his plans and that his absence was temporary.

Powhatan, however, knew better. "He will not return," the Chief of Chiefs said flatly.

"That is what you think," his daughter declared stubbornly. "But you do not know it is true."

Ratulawan, in spite of his advanced age, was currently married to three wives and was therefore considered to be something of an authority in handling women. "When the gods made people," he said in the deep, resounding voice of a professional medicine man, "they gave wisdom to warriors, not to squaws. But," he added as a courteous afterthought, "the daughter of Powhatan gives joy to all who look at her."

His condescension to her sex was infuriating, but Pocahontas refused to let herself become involved in an argument with a member of the older generation whose thinking was inflexible and who could not accept new ideas. It would be useless to tell him of the freedom and privileges enjoyed by English women, as he would be sure she was lying. So, as she could not use logic as a weapon, she would have to rely all the more on her femininity. "It does not matter where John Smith may be," she cried, deliberately making no further attempt to curb her emotions. "I don't care if he is in the land of his fathers or in Jamestown. He is my husband, and I am his wife!"

Powhatan sympathized with her, and he knew that he loved her as few men loved their daughters, but there was no question in his mind that his judgment of what was good for her outweighed her own feelings. "Come here," he said sharply.

His peremptory tone frightened her, and she hesitated for a long moment before walking slowly toward him. Her father's attitude toward her had changed since the war with the

Cherokee, and he was so preoccupied, so short-tempered these days that he was almost a stranger. What disturbed her most was his calculating appraisal as he looked up at her; she had seen that expression in his eyes when he had dealt with others, but it had never occurred to her that the time might come when he would callously manipulate her, either for his own benefit or that of the nation, in the impersonal way he manipulated everyone else.

"Powhatan's daughter begs him to tell her his wishes." He was the one man in the lodge whom she could not handle, she reflected.

"Kneel," he said, and averted his face when she looked straight at him.

It was strange that he chose this formal way of dealing with her, rather than calling her to him privately, as he had always done in the past, and she felt increasingly uneasy. However, any Chickahominy ordered to kneel before the Chief of Chiefs had the right to protest if given an unwelcome command, and if her father tried to forbid her to communicate with John Smith again, she would defy him.

She looked at each of the others in turn and was not encouraged by what she saw and felt. Opachisco stared at the ground, which was a bad sign, and Ratulawan, smiling faintly, stroked the feathers of his headband. Parranha-Boli and Daj-Weenu were gazing at her with covetous eyes, and that bothered her even more, as it was immoral for any man to demonstrate his desire for another's squaw. And Udesuekan, whose features were usually as stiff as the faces of his ancestors carved in hard wood on his family's burial pole, was actually licking his thin, bloodless lips and looking pleased with himself.

"Kneel," Powhatan repeated, his grating voice revealing his tension.

Pocahontas, her fists tightly clenched, dropped to the ground and obediently folded her hands over her breasts.

"Ek and Ris have made their wishes known to the Chief of

Chiefs of the Chickahominy," her father intoned rapidly. "Powhatan is their son and he does their bidding. So, in the hearing of the leaders of the Chickahominy nation, the father of Pocahontas ends her marriage to Smith, King of James. She is his squaw no more." Reaching out quickly, he snatched her headband and threw it into the fire.

He spoke and acted so quickly that Pocahontas, taken completely by surprise, was too stunned to protest. It had not crossed her mind that Powhatan would terminate her marriage without first consulting her or at least telling her his plans in advance, and she felt completely lost. She wanted to weep hysterically, but that would be stupid, she knew; for many months she had not really been the wife of John Smith, although she had cushioned her hurt with the rationalization that they were still bound together by a legal tie and that someday he might return to her.

But she had been stripped of her last illusions now and felt defenseless. Powhatan seemed to understand, for he suddenly reached out and put a hand gently on her shoulder. "Powhatan welcomes his daughter back to the people of her ancestors," he said quietly.

Had he been angry with her she could have tolerated her pain, but his solicitude was more than she could bear and, shaking herself free, she jumped to her feet, then felt even worse when she saw how deeply she had offended him. But Powhatan was too proud to reprimand her in the presence of his subordinates and, turning away from her, he spread out his arms. "If any wish to speak, let them now be heard."

Parranha-Boli could not conceal his admiration for the girl who stood with her feet apart, her hands on her hips, and her eyes flashing. She reminded him of the wildcats that roamed the western mountains, and more than anything else in the world he longed for the right to tame her. "Parranha-Boli, who beat the Cherokee four times in battle, speaks before the Chief of Chiefs and the leaders of the Chickahominy," he said, continuing to watch Pocahontas.

"Parranha-Boli, who has won twelve feathers in war, claims the daughter of Powhatan as his squaw."

Pocahontas glared at him and was about to express herself in no uncertain terms, but her father spoke first. "Powhatan must refuse the claim of Parranha-Boli," he said, his voice reflecting genuine regret. "But in these days of hardship, we must think first of all the people of the Chickahominy."

"I will not marry anyone," Pocahontas said in a thick voice. "I love John Smith and I refuse to become the wife of any other man."

Her father looked at her with compassion, but when he addressed her his voice was stern and uncompromising. "It is arranged that in seven moons the daughter of Powhatan will travel to the land of the Potomac for a visit. The Potomac have long been the cousins of the Chickahominy. Today they are strong, for they did not take part in the war against the Cherokee. Tacomo, the chief of the Potomac, still heeds the word of his cousin, Powhatan, but the day might come when his gods might tell him to walk alone. If that time should come, it would be well if his squaw were of the Chickahominy, for she could remind him of his duty to Powhatan, his cousin."

Parranha-Boli swallowed his disappointment, and the others nodded sagely. As always, the Chief of Chiefs spoke sensibly. But Pocahontas was unconcerned over matters of state and she laughed scornfully. "Tacomo!" she said.

"Tacomo of the Potomac has often told Powhatan of his admiration for the daughter of Powhatan."

"He has spoken also to Opachisco," her brother added.

"Tacomo," Pocahontas said distinctly, "has teeth like a chipmunk and ears like a rabbit." Daj-Weenu chuckled, but she ignored the interruption. "I am the daughter of a great chief and I have been the wife of a great chief. So I will not marry some puny man just because he wishes to take me into his lodge. I love John Smith and I will never love another."

Powhatan could have shaken her until her teeth rattled,

but at the same time her fierce sense of independence pleased him, and he told himself that she was truly his daughter. "Powhatan has not ordered his daughter to become the squaw of Tacomo," he said mildly. "In seven moons' time Pocahontas will visit the people of the Potomac and she will live with them as their guest for twelve moons. Then she will decide whether she wishes to marry Tacomo." During the course of a prolonged stay in strange surroundings she would gradually forget John Smith, Powhatan believed, and although Tacomo was admittedly homely, he would be nearby, constantly pressing his suit, so eventually he might wear down the resistance of even the most stubborn and headstrong girl.

The Chief of Chiefs' advisers knew better than to criticize him to his face, but no words were necessary; their expressions made it plain that they thought he was being exceptionally lenient with a mere female. It was true, he knew, that he could command her to marry Tacomo, and that would be the end of the matter, but Pocahontas's happiness still meant much to him. And he realized, as his advisers did not, that her informal visit to the Potomac would be even more useful than an actual marriage in keeping the allied tribe under control; Tacomo, living in hopes of making Pocahontas his wife, would be sure to honor the alliance, and the Chickahominy would thus be granted a breathing spell in which they could regain their strength.

Pocahontas knew full well that her father expected her resistance to disappear during the course of a protracted visit to the Potomac, but she could not refuse a request that seemed on the surface to be so reasonable. This was a time when every Chickahominy had to work for the good of the nation, and the daughter of the ruler would be derelict in her duty if she failed to carry out a mission that, regardless of whether she married Tacomo, would be certain to strengthen the bonds between the two tribes. "The daughter of Powhatan hears his words and will obey them," she said, and refrained from adding that no power on earth was strong enough to force her to remarry.

She appeared calm and at ease, but Powhatan, sensing her unhappiness, felt a new surge of anger at John Smith. Had she never met him, she would today be the squaw of some chief, contentedly raising a family, and he hated the whole race of strangers-from-across-the-sea with all his heart. When the Chickahominy were strong again he would exterminate them, but until then he would make life as miserable as possible for them. One of the foreigners was responsible for Pocahontas's misery, and all of them would be made to suffer accordingly.

June, 1611

"I confess I'm not sorry to be leaving the New World," Sir Thomas Dale said, glancing around the supper table at his guests and smiling wanly at his distinguished successor, Lord Delaware. "Jamestown has changed since I first came out here, and I can't pretend I like this new climate. Your task won't be easy, milord."

Delaware, a heavy-set man in his forties, with a florid complexion and deep-set eyes, removed his silver fork and knife from a pouch at his belt, rubbed them slowly on the linen tablecloth to polish them, and shook his head thoughtfully. "I'm sure I'll have a great deal of work ahead of me. On the other hand, I'm optimistic or I certainly wouldn't have brought Lady Delaware with me. I can imagine no reason why we can't make our peace with the natives."

The three younger men at the table exchanged covert, cynically amused glances. George Percy, the younger brother of the Earl of Northumberland, who had spent a year in the colony, and Captain Samuel Argall, master of the bark, *Swallow*, who was paying his fourth visit to Jamestown, were thoroughly conversant with local affairs, and even John Rolfe, the newcomer to the group, who had arrived in America only a few months ago, realized that his lordship had no idea what he was saying. Rolfe, a lean, serious young gentleman in his late twenties, took it upon himself to explain.

"Perhaps my own situation will help you to understand our difficulties, milord," he said, his hazel eyes grave. "I came here for the purpose of growing tobacco. I had the good fortune to meet Captain John Smith in London on a number of occasions, and he convinced me that the soil and climate here are perfect for the growth of tobacco. My intention and hope, as I explained to the directors of the Company, was to establish a tobacco plantation and to encourage others to follow my example."

Sir Thomas, helping himself to venison steak and roasted yellow potatoes, interrupted. "Master Rolfe," he said, "believes Virginia can become rich through the cultivation of tobacco, and that the colony can absorb unlimited numbers of immigrants to work on the plantations."

Argall and Percy, who found their pleasures in the dangers of wilderness living, were bored and concentrated on their food. But Rolfe, absorbed in the subject, nodded and ran his fingers through his crisp dark brown hair. "I came to Jamestown via the West Indian Islands," he continued, "as I wanted to secure some samples of their best tobacco for purposes of crossbreeding."

"So I've heard," Lord Delaware murmured. Just this evening he had been told that Rolfe's wife had died of a fever on the island of Barbados, leaving her widower with a six-year-old daughter.

"I felt nothing but enthusiasm when I arrived here," Rolfe said, making no mention of his personal tragedy. "But what has happened, milord? My helpers and I must take muskets with us when we go out into the fields to plant tobacco, and the Lord have mercy on anyone who happens to stray from the others, for he disappears. Natives are constantly lurking in the forests, and they're so vindictive that occasionally they even steal into my plantation at night, after I've returned to the stockade, and destroy all I've done."

"That's the very least of it," Sir Thomas declared, spearing a chunk of venison with his knife. "The Naturals refuse to trade with us, and no matter what inducements we offer them, they won't sell us an ounce of corn or a pound of meat."

Rolfe's mind was still on tobacco. "Several tribes in the interior grow a superior quality of tobacco, far better than the variety we're planting here. The Potomac, for example, grow superb tobacco. But when I've had the opportunity to accost one or another of the natives and try to buy some of their product from them, they pretend not to understand me, even though I've gone to the trouble of learning their language. The result, milord, is that I'm at best able to make a few gold angels for myself and for Jamestown, when we could be achieving success beyond all of our dreams."

Lord Delaware, forcing himself to eat the venison, wondered if it were possible to obtain a leg of mutton in this outlandish place. "You give me to understand, gentlemen, that the Indians are responsible for Jamestown's lack of development."

Captain Argall rubbed his bristling red beard scornfully and laughed.

But Sir Thomas saw nothing humorous in the situation. "In my opinion, milord, as I've written the directors of the Company several times, the Naturals are trying to starve us out. And they're succeeding, this meal to the contrary." He glanced at the platters of bear chops, stewed wolf, grouse and fish. "I thought I'd give you something of a banquet to celebrate your arrival, but the reason there are so few guests, to be frank with you, is that the governor's larder is too bare to serve a larger group."

Delaware, who had been selected for his post because the directors of the London Company believed him to be a realist, refused to be diverted by matters irrelevant to the main issue. "Correct me if I'm laboring under a misapprehension, but I've been told that the savages haven't attacked the colony in force since Smith was here."

"They're afraid of our muskets," George Percy replied contemptuously.

"And our culverins," Captain Argall added.

Sir Thomas sighed and thought that, as usual, young warriors of any race could not see beyond the limits of their own valor. "That's only part of the story," he said. "Luckily for us, the Naturals dissipated their strength in a series of wars with each other. But they've been at peace for quite some time now, and it's my deduction that they're waiting until a lack of food weakens us. Then, when they're fairly certain they'll beat us, they'll muster all their strength and attack us."

"Very strange," Lord Delaware muttered, trying not to shudder as he drank Dale's inferior, faintly rancid wine. "We haven't cheated them in our dealing with them, have we?"

"Certainly not!" Sir Thomas replied indignantly. "We're Christians."

Samuel Argall chuckled behind his hand, but no one saw him.

"Then why should they hate us? If we're honorable and decent, why shouldn't they let us live here in peace?"

"That, I'm afraid, is a complex question that can't be answered in a single word." Sir Thomas had been looking forward to the feast for weeks, but he had no appetite now and could only wish he were already back in England.

Percy threw his knife onto the table in disgust and wiped his fingers on his doublet. "I can answer your question in a single word, milord. That word is—Smith."

Lord Delaware looked around at the others in bewilderment: Argall was grinning unpleasantly, Sir Thomas obviously understood the allusion, and even Rolfe, who was a true gentleman in every sense of the word, appeared embarrassed. "Smith?" his lordship repeated blankly.

"John Smith," Captain Argall declared loudly, helping himself to another serving of grilled sea bass garnished with chopped clams. "As I'm the one who pieced the whole thing together, let me tell you about it. I always make it my business to know what's going on, wherever I may happen to be. And the reason the Indians are trying to drive us out is because Chief Powhatan hates the very mention of the name of John Smith."

Delaware was disturbed and unconvinced. "Captain Smith is a credit to England, Argall," he said reprovingly. "At the moment he's working hard to form a new organization which will explore the northern part of this continent. He calls it the Plymouth Company, and I myself believe in him to the extent that I've invested one thousand sovereigns in the venture. And I cannot bring myself to believe that a person to whom the King has given an exploration and discovery patent has treated any man dishonorably!"

Argall had far more courage than tact, and Rolfe, who felt distinctly uncomfortable, thought his sly smile was remarkably like that of the procurers who roamed the waterfront district of Southwark, across the Thames from London. "I have no doubt that Smith's dealings with men have been above reproach," the captain said self-righteously. "But it so happens I'm talking about the way he handles women. One woman in particular, the daughter of Powhatan. The old chief has forbidden every tribe under his jurisdiction to have anything to do with us, but you'd be surprised how eager the braves are to disobey orders when you have a jar of brandy or sack under their noses. That's how I learned the truth about Smith."

Sir Thomas was sorry he had invited such a crude guest to his house. "It's common gossip, milord," he said, "that Captain Smith and the daughter of Powhatan enjoyed a somewhat intimate relationship. Some of the natives claim that he actually allowed a native wedding ceremony to be performed, although I myself can't believe that he'd have gone so far."

"Hardly," Lord Delaware agreed.

Samuel Argall was annoyed by the complacency of men in high places who invariably judged others by their own sanctimonious standards. "Facts are facts," he said bluntly. "The wench was sent off by her father to the Potomac tribe north of here more than a year ago. She was supposed to marry the chief, but she's pining away for Smith and won't even listen to the poor devil's proposals. And there you are, milord. Sooner or later, thanks to John Smith, Powhatan is going to scalp every man and woman in Jamestown."

Delaware rubbed the top of his bald head gingerly. "Is this true?" he demanded.

"Yes, substantially," Sir Thomas admitted.

"I can't believe," John Rolfe said firmly, "that there weren't mitigating circumstances. Probably the woman herself was dishonest."

George Percy finished his meal, smacked his lips, and drew his sleeve across his mouth. "What difference does it make whether she's as pure as Queen Bess is supposed to have been or whether she's a harlot, like the woman of Whitefriars? Either way, you aren't growing much of your precious tobacco."

"That's so," Rolfe said gloomily.

"And there's nothing can be done about it," Sir Thomas declared.

"No, gentlemen. No!" Delaware pushed back his chair, and both his voice and gestures were reminiscent of the attitudes he struck when he addressed his colleagues in the House of Lords. "We'll win the good will and approval of the benighted girl's heathen father in due time."

"How?" Argall asked skeptically.

"Through patience and kindness," his lordship said serenely.

The long, dead silence that followed was finally broken by Sir Thomas, who proposed a toast to the King, and the supper party came to an end. A quarter of an hour later the three young men walked out into the night together, leaving their elders to a private discussion, and Argall linked his arms companionably through those of the others. "Come back to the *Swallow* with me," he said. "Francis is going to meet me there." Francis was Francis West, a kindred spirit, the younger brother of Lord Delaware, who had preceded the new governor to the New World by more than a year.

"Have you any wine on board?" Percy made a wry face. "I can't stomach that vinegar Sir Thomas serves."

"There's all the brandy you can drink," Argall promised.

"Excuse me, if you will, gentlemen," John Rolfe said courteously. His daughter was undoubtedly asleep, and he had virtually nothing in common with the elderly housekeeper he had hired shortly after his arrival in the colony, so the hours that stretched ahead would certainly be lonely. But he had become accustomed to a solitary, dreary existence, and much as he would have enjoyed some convivial conversation, he had no desire to spend the rest of the night drinking.

"This isn't a social invitation," Argall said.

"Oh?"

"There's something I want to discuss. But I can't talk a few feet from the open windows of the room where his lordship and Sir Thomas are sitting. You want to grow tobacco here, don't you? All right, I'm in a position to help you, provided you'll co-operate with me."

Argall started off toward the new docks that lined the river front, with Percy at his side, and John Rolfe followed them reluctantly. They were both an irresponsible type he instinctively distrusted, but Captain Argall was reputedly hardheaded and shrewd, so there was a slim chance that he might indeed have something of value to suggest. And Rolfe was willing to go to almost any lengths to put his plans into operation on a large scale; his alternative was to rot in this town on the edge of the forests, and rather than subject his child to unnecessary hardship and dangers, it would be far preferable to return to England.

The *Swallow* rode high in the water, her hold empty, and five of her six sails were furled. The captain's tiny gig was tied to the wharf, and he rowed his guests out to the bark silently, then preceded them aboard. A seaman armed with a belaying pin stood guard near the tiny quarterdeck, but otherwise the ship seemed deserted, and Argall led the way to his cabin, where a lantern was glowing. Rolfe, following the others, saw that Francis West had already arrived and was making himself at home. West, a recklessly handsome version of his older brother, was perched on the foot of the captain's bed, drinking sack from a pewter tea mug, and he waved cheerily, but Argall, closing the door firmly, gave him no chance to speak.

"The meeting will come to order, gentlemen!" the master of the *Swallow* said.

"Meeting?" Percy was disappointed. "Where's that brandy you were going to give me?"

"Later, George." Argall leaned against the nearest bulkhead and hooked his thumbs in his broad, copper-studded rawhide belt. "A few years ago in the jungles of one of the West Indian Islands I saw a fat snake curl itself around a tiger and squeeze the poor beast to death. Jamestown is like that tiger, gentlemen, and even though we have claws and teeth, we're too frightened to use them. Francis, your brother is as bad as old Dale. He'll sit reciting platitudes while the Naturals tighten their coils around the colony."

"My brother," West replied, staring into the mug of sack, "is a philosopher. He can quote to you by the hour from the latest treatise written by some long-winded friend of his like the Earl of Rutland, but put a sword in his hand, and he's helpless."

"So you've warned me, and I saw for myself tonight that

you're right. I'd been hoping he'd be an improvement over Dale and would actually do something for Jamestown, but I know better now. And that means we'll have to take action ourselves."

John Rolfe, watching him impassively, said nothing and reserved judgment.

But Percy, who had taken the only chair in the cabin, glanced up in alarm. "Just a moment, Sam. There's nothing I enjoy more than a good fight, as you well know, but if you're thinking of trying to depose his lordship, that's going too far. I have no wish to be hung for treason."

Argall tugged at his red beard, and his eyes were mocking. "I'm loyal to the Crown myself," he said solemnly, "and I can assure you, gentlemen, I have no intention of inciting a rebellion. Far from it. I've asked you to join me here because I want your help in a little scheme I've concocted, a plan that will force the Indians to make their peace with us."

Percy and West brightened at once, but there was no change in John Rolfe's expression, and he met Argall's challenging gaze coolly. "I'm listening," he said.

"I should hope so," the captain replied indignantly. "Your plantation would flourish if our relations with the Naturals were pleasant, wouldn't it? And you'd love to get your hands on some of the native tobacco, wouldn't you?"

"So you heard me say at supper tonight." Rolfe was unruffled and continued to speak quietly.

"That's precisely why I'm offering you a chance to become one of us. George and Francis will do anything for a little excitement, and I have my own reasons for wanting peace with the Indians."

"What are those reasons?" Rolfe asked, straightening his doublet of conservative dark gray wool.

"That's a fair enough question to ask, I suppose." Argall shrugged and grinned insolently. "The *Swallow* and I aren't in the employ of the London Company. I own this bark, every timber of her. And every farthing I earn belongs to me, not to some fat directors in England. I want peace because I can become as rich and fat as they are by filling my hold with muskets and baubles and trading them to the natives for furs. Oh, I know what you're going to say. Trade between private individuals and the Naturals is strictly forbidden."

"So it is, but that's a matter between you, your conscience, and Lord Delaware's bailiffs," Rolfe declared, neither shocked nor indignant. He himself tried to live virtuously, but he had long ago learned it was a waste of time to try to reform others.

George Percy laughed and took the mug of sack from West. "It so happens that I'm the chief bailiff here, so you'll have to struggle with your conscience, Sam, not with me. But before you start peddling beads for beaver pelts, you'll have to convince Chief Powhatan that Jamestown is filled with folk who want to be his loving neighbors. And I'm damned if I can see how you're going to persuade him to become friendly."

"Nothing could be simpler." Argall paused dramatically and looked at each of the others in turn. "Through his daughter."

West slapped his thigh, Percy nodded enthusiastically, and Rolfe frowned.

"As we know," Argall continued, "she's with the Potomac up at the other end of Chesapeake Bay. So the four of us will sail up with some of my crew, and then we'll go inland to their town. We'll bring the wench back here with us and we'll hold her as a hostage until her father agrees to make a permanent peace treaty with us. In fact, we'll probably keep her on here even longer than that, just to make sure he doesn't go back on his word. How do you like it?"

Percy sucked reflectively on a slender golden toothpick. "Not bad. But I don't see how we can do it. Granted that you and Francis and I are the best swordsmen in Virginia, I can't see how we can fight off three or four hundred savage warriors while we capture her."

West looked dubious too. "I've never shirked a battle in my life, and you know it, Sam. But the odds against us are too high."

Captain Argall smiled condescendingly. "Have I said one word about fighting the warriors of the Potomac for the girl? Certainly not! Credit me with some sense and imagination. I tell you we'll have no trouble at all bringing her away with us. How we'll do it is my secret, and I won't repeat it, just in case one of you happens to become careless and spoils the whole scheme. You'll have to trust me and take my word that there won't be a battle."

"Fair enough, fair enough," Percy replied. "But how will we get into the land of the Potomac in the first place? They'll kill us before we come within miles of their town."

Argall walked to the bunk, reached under it, and drew out an old musket and an earthenware jug, which he waved like a conjurer entertaining an audience between the acts of a play at the theater. "Brandy and firearms will be our passports. Four or five tribes have greeted me with open arms when I've offered them prizes like these, and the Potomac will be no exception. Don't touch the brandy, Francis," he added hastily. "It's so raw it will burn a hole straight through your middle. Wait until we're finished talking, and then I'll open a cruse of some decent Spanish brandy I picked up at Port Royal."

There was silence for a moment, then Percy held out his hand. "You've answered all my objections, Sam. I'll join you."

"So will I!" West added.

All of them looked at John Rolfe, who had not spoken. "Well, Master Rolfe?" the captain demanded.

"I can't say I like the idea of abducting a woman. To my way of thinking that isn't fair dealing."

"Do you prefer seeing innocent settlers slaughtered?" Argall glowered and shook his fist. "Do you call that fair?"

"No, it isn't," John said unhesitatingly. "But I can't become enthusiastic over lowering ourselves to the primitive level of the natives."

Francis West made a wry face. "That sounds just like what my brother would say."

"Which is exactly why his lordship isn't going to learn about the scheme until we've brought the wench back here with us," Argall declared, and turned to John. "We need four men to carry out the stratagem, Master Rolfe, not three."

"I'm highly sensitive to the honor you've offered me."

The captain stared at him, suspecting irony, but his face was bland. "I heard you telling Lord Delaware about the wonders of Potomac tobacco, Rolfe. Here's your chance to get some. Do you want it or don't you?"

John struggled with himself before replying. "I want it very much," he said at last.

"Then you'll come with us." It was a flat statement, not a question.

"Not so fast." John's surface calm gave no hint of his inner turmoil. "There's something more I need to know. Do I assume correctly that you aren't intending to do Pocahontas any harm? I don't want the blood of an innocent woman on my hands."

"I can see no reason for us to hurt her," Argall replied with a sly grin, "unless she tries to make trouble for us."

"Very well, then. You may include me in your plans." In spite of his misgivings, John felt better now that he had reached a decision.

"Good." The matter was settled, so Argall opened a sea chest and removed a copy of Captain John Smith's map of Chesapeake Bay and the territory around it. He spread it out carefully, then suddenly looked up; something was obviously bothering him, and he wanted to get it off his mind. "Rolfe," he said, "you'll be far more useful to yourself as well as to the rest of us if you'll get one fact straight. The wench we're going to kidnap is no civilized Englishwoman, you know. She's a savage, little better than an animal. She's incapable of thinking or feeling or suffering as we do, so don't worry about her!"

Pointing to the map, he began to trace the route they would follow, and for the next quarter of an hour conversation was confined to practical details. When their work was finished, Argall refolded the map, put it aside, and rubbed his hands together. "Now," he said, rummaging in his sea chest, "we'll drink to our success. We'll sleep on board tonight, so we'll be ready to sail in the morning as soon as my crew returns."

He struck a delicately wrought cruse against the nearest bulkhead, breaking its neck, and drank deeply before passing the jug to Percy, who happened to be nearest to him. Eventually it was John's turn; he took a token sip, wiped his mouth, and started toward the door. "Good night, gentlemen," he said. "I'll see you in the morning."

The others stared at him, and Argall leaped forward, blocking the door. "Where do you think you're going, Rolfe?"

"Home."

"Didn't you hear me say we'll sleep on the *Swallow* tonight?"

"Yes, I heard you. But I don't happen to agree with you and I'm going to my own house."

"Suppose we understand each other." The captain's tone and manner were menacing. "By agreeing to become one of us, you've put yourself under my command. When I give an order, I expect you to obey it."

A smile of mild amusement creased John's lips. "When we leave Jamestown I'll be under your orders, naturally. It's essential that we agree to put one man in charge of the expedition, and I certainly wouldn't challenge you for the leadership. However, we haven't sailed as yet, so I'm still my own master."

"Why do you insist on going to your house?" Argall demanded, his eyes narrowing.

"I have a small child," John replied in a crisp, matter-of-fact voice, displaying no sentiment which an outsider might deride. "I must make provisions for her future in the event that something untoward happens to me on this mission. I realize we're taking considerable risk, and as I'm responsible for my daughter, I've got certain arrangements to make."

"You could do all that from here. You——"

"Equally important," John went on without raising his voice, "I wouldn't think of going off, under any circumstances, until I've said good-by to her. She's only a little girl and she'd be very hurt and confused if I disappeared without telling her I was going away. I wouldn't consider it."

Percy and West exchanged glances and grinned at each other; the captain would teach a lesson to an upstart, and they were prepared to enjoy his performance.

Argall certainly looked as though he meant business: his feet were planted far apart, his right hand rested on the hilt of his sword, and he scowled fiercely at the young planter. "How do I know you aren't going to the governor's house to tell Lord Delaware and Sir Thomas about our scheme? How do I know that a company of militiamen won't march down the docks and put all of us under arrest?"

John shook his head. "You don't know, really, except that you trusted me sufficiently to tell me of your plan, and you have enough confidence in me to expect that I'll do my part on the mission without endangering all of our lives."

Captain Argall continued to glare at him. They were roughly the same height, but Rolfe was slender, and in a fight Rolfe would be no match for a man who had been brawling all of his life. What was more, Argall felt certain, the planter was not his equal as a duelist.

John carried a sword, of course, but made no effort to reach for it. "Stand aside, please," he said in the same quiet, courteous tone.

Much to his own surprise, Argall moved away from the door. He was none too certain why he was complying so meekly, but he realized vaguely that he could not help responding to the other's absolute self-assurance and authority. Watching Rolfe walk quickly down the deck to the stern, where the gig was tied, he was sorry he had not chosen someone else as the fourth member of the raiding party. He had underestimated his man and he was afraid of what might happen in the days immediately ahead. The attempt to abduct Pocahontas would be enormously difficult, and he dreaded the complications that might be created by a forthright man of high principle.

June, 1611

John Rolfe couldn't make up his mind whether he and his companions were being treated as guests or prisoners. Thirty or forty shouting, capering braves surrounded the Englishmen, brandishing knives, crude spears, and the muskets they had just received as gifts, and the visitors could not have broken out of the tight circle had they wished. Women and children, attracted by the noise, hurried out of mud huts on all sides of the clearing in the center of the Potomac village, and a number of older braves appeared and stared at the strangers too. As nearly as John could judge, the Indians were demonstrating neither friendliness nor hostility but were simply excited because some foreigners had appeared in their midst and had brought them unsolicited and unexpected gifts.

The childish, spontaneous nature of the celebration made the situation dangerous, John thought, for the slightest incident could turn the savages into a vengeful, howling mob.

Several of the younger warriors had already sampled the raw brandy they had been given, and their shrill, high-pitched laughter hinted at the possibility that they were no longer responsible for their actions. Under such circumstances only a stupid man would fail to feel apprehensive, but George Percy and Francis West appeared to be enjoying themselves. They were grinning broadly as they watched the braves, whose drinking they encouraged in exaggerated pantomime.

Captain Argall was too intelligent to be blind to the risks, but he showed no fear and stood quietly, his hand resting on the hilt of his sword as he surveyed the crowd coolly. John, sorry he had joined this mad venture, tried desperately to conceal his own nervousness, as he knew that survival depended at least in part on the maintenance of a bold, calm front. He was afraid the Indians would see through his façade and he felt a surge of relief when the warrior halted abruptly and fell silent at the approach of a rather frail young man in a long deerskin cape decorated with beads. Several other braves in shorter capes were clustered behind him, and as he pushed his way to the front of the throng, Samuel Argall chuckled.

"That's Tacomo," he murmured to John, and picked up a large crock of brandy, which had been resting on the ground beside him.

The chief of the Potomac halted, blinked myopically, and looked in turn at each of the Englishmen. "What do the devil-men-from-across-the-sea want here?" he demanded.

"Greetings to the mighty Tacomo," Argall replied heartily. "We bring gifts to the chief of the Potomac."

Before the native could speak again, Argall thrust the brandy into his hand, then gave him a musket that looked superior to the others because both the steel barrel and oak butt had been polished. Tacomo inspected his gifts, handling them uncertainly, and John realized he was going through an inner struggle. It was wrong for him to accept either the liquor or the weapon from the foreigners, but his greed was as strong as his conscience, and for a long moment he could not make up his mind. Even though a rejection of the gifts might mean death for the intruders, John could not help but sympathize with the chief.

As he watched Tacomo he felt someone looking at him and, gazing past the leader of the Potomac, he found himself staring at a young woman. Their eyes met for an instant, then she glanced away again, and he examined her covertly. She was striking in appearance, far handsomer than any of the other women in the village, and although she was dressed in an unadorned tunic of soft leather similar to the clothing of the others, her proud, dignified bearing set her apart. This, John guessed, was Pocahontas.

It was something of a shock to see that she pitied Tacomo, just as he did, that she knew the young chief was having trouble making up his mind, and that she recognized his weakness but did not censure him for it. Her discernment and compassion were as startling to John as her beauty, and he shifted his weight from one foot to the other uncomfortably. Until this moment he had tried not to dwell on the purpose of the mission that had brought him to this native wilderness community, and when he had allowed himself to think of Pocahontas at all, he had conjured up a self-justifying image of her as an ignorant, dull woman. Obviously she was neither and, aside from himself, was the only person present who was sufficiently sensitive to realize that Tacomo was wrestling with a difficult problem and consequently deserved charitable understanding.

At last the chief reached a decision, and his hold on the gifts tightened. But his question still remained unanswered and, squaring his slender shoulders, he did his best to look stern. "It is forbidden for the devil-men to be made welcome in the land of the Potomac or by any other people who call the Chickahominy their brothers."

"Rules are made by men and may be broken by men," Captain Argall declared blandly. "We have many fire-sticks and much that is good to drink. We would trade these things for a few little objects that are of no real value to the Potomac."

Tacomo glanced anxiously over his shoulder at the girl, and John was certain now that she was Pocahontas. The chief of the Potomac was apparently unable to dissemble, and his expression indicated clearly that had Powhatan's daughter not been present, ready to report his defection to her father, he would have been willing and even eager to ignore the inconvenient restriction. Argall, instantly aware of his avarice, smiled confidently, and John secretly applauded Pocahontas, who made no attempt to hide her contempt for the captain. He shared her scorn for the unscrupulous opportunist and was sure he knew precisely how she felt. Her intelligence and her ability to see through surface sham amazed him, and he told himself he could take no part in the attempt to hoodwink her. He could not betray his compatriots, of course, but there was nothing to prevent him from trying to persuade them to abandon their scheme.

Tacomo, it seemed, was going to save him the bother. "Devil-men are not welcome in the land of the Potomac," the chief said loudly, half to Argall and half to the girl. "It is not allowed, so the devil-men will go."

"We can't leave tonight," the captain replied reasonably. "The sun will set in a short time, and we can't find our way back to our ship through the forests in the dark."

His argument seemed both logical and fair to the chief, who nodded thoughtfully. "The Potomac are pleased with the gifts they have received, so they will not turn strangers away at night. The Potomac do not drive out even their enemies to become lost and die." He turned to his people and raised his voice. "Take the devil-men to two houses at the far side of the town. Give them food to eat, and let them sleep there. But when the light comes again after the darkness, let them be gone forever from the land of the Potomac. If they are still here when it is light, they will die over the slow fire that burns for seven days."

His warriors thumped their chests with their right hands,

which was apparently a sign of obedience, and several braves
surrounded the Englishmen and started to move with them
out of the clearing. The mission had failed in every respect,
John thought, and was glad; but he rejoiced prematurely, for
Argall was too cunning to accept defeat meekly. The captain,
too, had recognized Pocahontas, and as he was being led
away he spoke, ostensibly to John, but actually for her benefit. "It looks like we won't be able to deliver Captain
Smith's message," he said distinctly. "When we get back to
Jamestown we'll have to tell him we had no opportunity to
meet the princess and tell her the news that he's been so
anxious for her to hear."

The change that took place in Pocahontas was remarkable,
and John was reminded of his little daughter's reaction on the
rare occasions when he allowed her a special treat. Pocahontas was a young woman, not a child, but her eyes became as
large and luminous as a six-year-old's, her full lower lip
trembled, and her expression, a blend of incredulity and
fierce joy, was heartbreaking. The natives began to leave the
clearing for their own homes, but she remained and stood
motionless, watching the foreigners being taken away.

Argall, who had noted her reaction surreptitiously,
seemed to be unaware of the warriors. "It's fortunate I knew
she speaks English, eh? There are some who say I waste my
time learning every detail I possibly can before I begin a
move. But thoroughness pays, Rolfe, and don't ever let
anyone tell you otherwise. She'll join us an hour after sunset,
you mark my words. I'll wager any sum on it that you'd like."
He nodded complacently and looked smug as the Indian
waved him into a bare mud hut with only a single opening for
a window.

John, who followed him into the hovel, glanced back at
the braves who hovered outside. "They're going to hold us
under guard," he said, trying not to show his satisfaction.
"And they'll keep her away. Your scheme to attract her
attention was very clever, I must admit. You have a real
knack for such things. But you've wasted your efforts. If we're

to leave at dawn and the Naturals keep us under close watch until then, nothing can possibly come of your plan."

The captain stroked his red beard and laughed. "I'm surprised," he said tactlessly, "that any man who was married for a number of years should have so little understanding of women. No matter what the obstacles, the wench will find a way to evade them so she can hear my imaginary message."

For several hours it appeared as though Argall was unduly optimistic; night fell, the guards brought their guests a supper consisting of lumpy goat meat and ground corn pudding, and the village gradually became quiet as the Potomac, their own evening meal finished, retired to their houses. John, exhausted after the long day and convinced that Pocahontas would not appear, stretched out on the hard earth and tried to shut out the arrogant drone of the captain's voice. This unappetizing journey had strengthened John's conviction that Jamestown was the wrong place for a widower trying to raise a small daughter. The future here was uncertain, and the atmosphere of the New World attracted too many adventurers like Samuel Argall.

A quiet but clear feminine voice sounded at the entrance, and John sat up quickly to stare at Pocahontas, who stood just inside the flap. "You have word for me from Captain Smith," she said in excellent English, not bothering with the formalities of a salutation.

Argall, his faith in himself justified, smiled triumphantly.

John struggled to his feet and continued to peer at the girl in the gloom. "How did you manage to pass the sentries on duty outside?" he asked incredulously.

Pocahontas took a single step into the hut. "I told them I wanted to see you," she replied simply, her tone making it plain that the daughter of the ruler of the Chickahominy Confederation had no need to resort to subterfuge.

"I see," John said, and told himself angrily that it would be preferable hereafter to remain quiet rather than make inane remarks.

The captain swaggered forward and favored Pocahontas

with a courtly bow. "All that matters is that you're here, Your Highness," he declared gallantly. "And let me compliment you on your ability to speak our tongue. Not many foreigners show your aptitude."

"Thank you," she said. She smiled faintly, and added, "In this land it is you who are the foreigners."

John chuckled, and the girl's glance indicated that she was aware of his appreciation, but Argall saw nothing humorous in her comment. "It is my hope," he said, bearing down swiftly, "that you will use your influence on the Potomac to persuade them to trade with us."

She studied him for a moment, her face expressionless. "As you called me 'Your Highness,' a title usually used in speaking to royalty, you're aware of my position. Do you suppose the daughter of Powhatan would encourage one of his allies to disobey him? And if that was your purpose in bringing me here, if you pretended to have a message for me so you could persuade me to help you, I'll bid you good night."

Argall reached the flap first. "My apologies, Your Highness," he said with mock humility. "I went too far in thinking of you as a friend of my people. And I do have the word for which you've been waiting."

Pocahontas drew in her breath sharply. "You've had a letter from Captain Smith, then? Perhaps he's sent a letter direct to me?"

"A letter?" Argall simulated surprise and shook his head. "There was certainly no need for him to write to me when we had breakfast together only two days ago." He paused, saw that she reacted precisely as he intended, and then continued casually. "I'll try to remember the exact words of his message if I can. You have an excellent memory, Rolfe. Do you recall them?"

John said nothing, but Pocahontas was too excited to read significance into his silence.

"Our mutual good friend," Argall went on smoothly,

"asked me to tell you he's aware that your life has not been easy since he last saw you. He begs you to accept his apologies and says he'll atone for them in person."

"In person?" she asked faintly.

"Of course, Your Highness. Captain Smith sent us to escort you to him. My ship is waiting for us right now in Chesapeake Bay."

She put out a hand as though to steady herself, then recovered. "He's in Jamestown." The wonder in her voice indicated the fear that she was dreaming.

"Naturally." Not even a great London actor like Richard Burbage could have sounded more impatient, and Argall frowned for good measure. Then he softened and smiled. "I forget that you're as yet unacquainted with his desires. He landed in my own bark, the *Swallow*, a fortnight ago," he said glibly, "and was determined to go into the interior and bring you back with him immediately. However, if you'll pardon the indelicacy, Your Highness, he was persuaded that Powhatan hates him so much that the risk would be too great for him."

"That's true," Pocahontas murmured. "My father would kill him."

"So everyone in the colony told him. Of course that only spurred him all the more. You know Smith."

She nodded and managed to smile. Smith would take a risk that any other man would consider foolhardy, merely to prove his indestructibility; in some ways, she thought, he was still a small boy.

John, able to see her more clearly now in the dark, told himself he had never read such longing in the face of another human being. Smith was incredibly lucky; no man deserved such love, but he was a fool, too, for having discarded it.

"To make a long story short," Argall said succinctly, "we convinced him it was his duty to stay in the town. So he sent us to bring you to him. You'll come with us, of course." It was a flat, bold statement rather than a question.

"Yes," Pocahontas said unhesitatingly.

"We must leave at once, then," Argall declared briskly. "If we wait until dawn, the Potomac sentries will stop you. Have you any suggestions for getting rid of them tonight?"

"I'll tell them you've decided to leave now, rather than wait until the morning," she said.

"They won't try to come with us?" the captain demanded dubiously.

"I'll tell them they aren't to molest you." This was the daughter of Powhatan speaking, and her air of authority left nothing more to be said.

"And you'll walk out of the village with us?"

"No. I'll meet you in the forest. Do you remember the thick grove of trees near the edge of the large swamp you passed about two or three miles from this village?" She searched her vocabulary for a moment. "You call them cottonwood trees, I think."

Argall looked blank, but John nodded. "I know the place," he said, and was instantly sorry he had spoken. He wanted no part of the deception, but it was too late to retract his words.

"I'll meet you there. Soon." The anticipatory lift in Pocahontas's voice made it painful to listen to her. "Give me a little time first to send away the warriors who stand guard over you. They'll watch you as you go and they may follow you until you reach the big bend in the River of the Potomac, but then they'll turn back."

"One moment." John roused himself from the lethargy into which his participation in this shameful enterprise had submerged him.

Argall eyed him narrowly and grasped the hilt of his sword. So far his scheme had succeeded brilliantly, and he had no intention of permitting a squeamish settler's conscience to spoil the whole plan.

"My purpose in coming on this journey," John said, "was to get some Potomac tobacco."

Captain Argall made a disgusted sound in the back of his throat.

Tobacco, John thought, was more important by far to the future of Jamestown than the abduction of a lovely young woman who had harmed no one. "I won't leave without it," he repeated stubbornly.

His sincerity touched Pocahontas, and she smiled at him. "You admire Potomac tobacco and wish to grow some?"

"I do."

"Then I will bring a few of the plants with me. I must walk through the fields where they grow as I come to meet you." She laughed happily as she drifted toward the entrance. "It is a small favor to repay those who are taking me to Smith."

They watched her as she left, then they heard her talking in low tones to the braves outside. When it became quiet again, Argall walked arrogantly into the open, strode to the adjoining hut, and called to George Percy and Francis West. They appeared at once, calmly accepting his seeming mastery of the situation and the absence of the sentries. He announced that they were leaving immediately, promised to give them a full explanation shortly, and without further ado headed for the forest beyond the limits of the village. They followed him, leaving John to bring up the rear.

As Pocahontas had predicted, the warriors trailed after them for a time, but the savages moved so stealthily that only an occasional faint crack of a twig underfoot revealed their presence. Argall told his friends what had happened, and when he finished speaking they trudged in silence for a time. After they had traveled about two miles, the Potomac, satisfied that the strangers were really leaving, turned back to the village, a fact which John discovered and confirmed about ten minutes after the Indians had gone. He announced the news as he and his companions were making their way through a particularly unpleasant bog, but the revelation revived the others' spirits, and they became more boisterous.

Argall, slapping at the mosquitoes that swarmed around him, turned to John and laughed. "Rolfe," he said, making no attempt to hide his dislike of the man who had been no help whatsoever in persuading Pocahontas to join them, "wasn't it you at the governor's house the other evening who predicted that someday there will be large cities all over the New World?"

"I believe I said something of the sort," John replied as he struggled through thick mud that clung to his boots.

"Would you care to risk your reputation as a prophet? Do you suppose there are enough impractical, unrealistic men in the world—like you—to build a town someday in these Potomac marshes?"

His friends enjoyed his wit, but John, refusing to be baited, remained silent, and Argall, feeling better now that he had made the uncooperative member of the party appear stupid, increased his pace. No one spoke again until they reached firmer ground once more, and then Francis West halted suddenly, his handsome, dissolute face dark with suspicion. The others clustered around him, and Argall, anxious to reach the rendezvous, glowered at him. "What's the matter?"

"Suppose," West said slowly, "that the wench knew we were planning to trick her. Suppose she realized what we had in mind and agreed to meet us simply to get rid of us. Our whole idea would collapse like a starched ruff dripped into a tub of boiling water. We can't go back to the village. The Potomac would murder us one by one. There wouldn't be any way to get in touch with her again and convince her of our sincerity. So we'd have to go back to Jamestown without her. Maybe she's sitting in her mud hut back there right now, laughing at us."

"Rubbish," the captain replied briskly. "I know people, women in particular, and I tell you she'll be there. Even Rolfe here, who doesn't understand anything on earth except his precious tobacco, agrees with me. Don't you, Rolfe?"

There was nothing to gain by taking offense at Argall's rudeness, and John nodded slowly. He had often observed that most human beings grasped at any frail thread that would confirm what they wanted to believe, and Pocahontas was no exception. She undoubtedly possessed critical faculties, but she wished so desperately for the return of Smith that she hadn't bothered to evaluate the flimsy story Argall had told her.

"She'll meet us," he said heavily, and the march was resumed.

During the next ten minutes, while the others exchanged ribald jokes, John fought a fierce battle within himself. He alone knew the place where they were to meet Pocahontas and he could spoil the whole elaborate ruse simply by pretending that a spot far from the actual rendezvous was the place. Argall could then spend the rest of the night in a fruitless hunt for the girl in the swamps, and the party would become convinced that she had indeed outsmarted them. Pocahontas herself would never understand why the Englishmen had failed to appear, but her disappointment would be mild compared to what she would suffer if the hoax were played out to its completion.

On the other hand, John told himself, he had accepted certain obligations by becoming a member of this group and he would be disloyal as well as dishonest if he failed to perform them. He had known from the start that his companions were intending to play a cruel joke on the girl, but he had accepted the plan on the grounds that perhaps the ends justified the means and that the disillusionment of one native woman was a small price to pay for lasting peace between the settlers and the Indians. His discovery that Pocahontas was a sensitive, perceptive person who bore no resemblance to the dull savage he had pictured was consequently irrelevant to the issue that confronted him. Peace with the Naturals was still at stake, and the happiness of even the most extraordinary young woman was far less important than the preservation of scores of lives.

"This is the place," he said loudly, and halted beside a thick clump of towering cottonwood trees near the edge of a swamp.

Pocahontas had not yet arrived, and the men talked incessantly to hide their nervousness while waiting for her. Argall, as always, set the tone of the conversation. "I intend to profit in three ways from this little maneuver," he said. "Powhatan will sign a treaty fast enough when he hears we're holding his daughter as a hostage. And the first thing I'm going to do when there's peace is return to the land of the Potomac. Unless I miss my guess, Tacomo will sell us his whole tribe for a few trinkets."

Percy laughed admiringly. "What's the third way you're going to profit?"

The captain eyed him in mock scorn. "Use your imagination, George! You saw the girl herself, didn't you? I'd heard various natives praise her, but I discounted most of what they said. That's where I was mistaken. I should have realized that any doxy of John Smith's would be a real beauty. His taste is almost as good as my own. And I say that if he was able to subdue the baggage, there's no reason Sam Argall can't do the same." He stroked his red beard and looked off into the trees, a speculative smile on his lips.

"Not so fast," Francis West protested. "She's the type of wench I like, and I have a strong feeling I'm going to dispute you for her favors."

"You?" The captain chuckled deprecatingly. "Aside from the fact that you're already married, which is something of a handicap, you can't hope to equal my technique with the ladies."

John tried to shut his ears to the banter and felt slightly ill. His companions were incapable of realizing that Pocahontas was a lady, and he felt sure they intended to make good their vulgar boasts and treat her like a common trollop. He had no right to intervene, yet he was at least in part responsible for the predicament in which she would soon find herself, and he tried to think of some way to help her. While he was still pondering the matter she appeared suddenly between two large cottonwood trees, and the men abruptly fell silent. She held her hands before her, John saw, and realized she was carrying several small tobacco plants, each four to six inches high, wrapped in wet corn husks. She had kept her promise to him but had brought nothing of her own on the journey and was still dressed in the simple tunic and sandals she had worn when she came to the hut where he and Argall had been held.

He took the plants from her, inadequately murmuring his thanks, and the others bowed to her before continuing the journey. They traveled rapidly now, and Pocahontas kept pace with the men; in fact, she was the least tired member of the party when, after a two-hour march, they arrived at the place on the River of the Potomac where they had hidden their gig. West and Percy rowed the boat through the placid water, and shortly before dawn they saw the dim outlines of the *Swallow* lying at anchor in Chesapeake Bay.

Argall, with a surreptitious wink at his friends, gave the girl his own cabin and then became busy ordering the anchor hoisted and the sails raised. West and Percy helped the crew with the bark's main topsail and fore-topsail, but John, who knew nothing of ships, loitered for a moment in the entrance to the cabin and looked at Pocahontas, who stood at the little window, staring out at the water.

"I want to tell you again how grateful I am to you for bringing me the tobacco plants," he said. "Jamestown—and all England—will benefit from your thoughtfulness. And now, ma'am, I wish you a pleasant sleep."

She turned away from the window, and a laugh bubbled up in her. "Sleep? I doubt if I shall sleep a wink. You don't know what it means to love someone, Master Rolfe!"

John thought of his wife's lonely grave in Barbados and swallowed hard. Now was the best moment to break the news of the wicked deception to this ingenuous young woman who revealed her innermost feelings so freely, but he could not bring himself to speak. Instead he drew the knife he carried in his belt and handed it to her, hilt forward. She stared at it for a moment, then instinctively shrank from it.

"You've done me a great service," he assured her somber-

ly, "and this is the least I can do for you in return." He
paused, and they could hear Captain Argall bawling commands from his tiny quarter-deck. "Not all English gentlemen live up to their name, you know," he added.

Pocahontas unhesitatingly took the knife, and the wise,
bitter expression that crossed her face convinced John that
she was not as naïve as he had feared.

June, 1611

No incidents of note marred the voyage to Jamestown, but the trip was certainly less than serene. It was
impossible to achieve privacy on a bark the size of the
Swallow, and in midmorning, shortly after the tired travelers
from the land of the Potomac went to bed, John, who shared
a small room with West and Percy, heard Captain Argall use
a key he had kept and enter his own cabin. The sound of
voices had been muffled by the bulkhead, but Pocahontas's
tone had been calm, although the master of the *Swallow* had
shouted angrily. It was difficult to determine whether she
actually had been forced to threaten him with the knife John
had given her, but regardless of the type of persuasion she had
used, Argall had left within a very few minutes after he had
arrived, slamming the door behind him. He made no mention of the affair later in the day, nor did Pocahontas, but the
girl's quiet smile of appreciation the next time she saw John
was as significant as the foul temper the captain displayed.

The wind failed at sunset; the bark was rowed into a small cove for the night and did not sail again until dawn, so it was noon before the palisades of Jamestown were sighted. Argall anchored offshore in the river and immediately announced that he was ready to break the news to Pocahontas that she was a prisoner. He told his companions that he wanted to go to her alone; West and Percy reluctantly agreed, but John, seeing the maliciousness in the captain's eyes, insisted on accompanying him to the master's cabin. And Argall, who might have tried to enforce his order on the grounds that on board his ship any command he gave had to be obeyed, gave in, as he wanted no dispute at a time when he was anxious to tell the governor about his remarkable exploit.

So he and John went together to the cabin, and when they tapped politely on the door, Pocahontas's voice was gay as she told them to enter. She had found a comb among the captain's belongings, and her hair was coiled smoothly on the top of her head, but her clothes, of course, were the same that she had worn in the village of the Potomac. Nevertheless, there was a subtle, exciting change in her appearance, and John thought he had never seen a more radiant girl. Her skin glowed, her eyes sparkled, and her joyous vitality seemed to fill the cabin. This was the moment John had been dreading, and he wanted to back out into the cramped corridor, but his feet refused to respond to his will. He had no idea what consolation he could offer her, but he felt it was his duty to remain and to do what he could.

"I thought Smith would come out here for me, but he must be waiting at the dock," she cried, and peered at the land. "Is he there? Have you seen him? I would have sworn I'd know him anywhere, but the light on the water makes it hard to see so far."

"I'm sure he's not there," Samuel Argall said dryly.

"Then he must be waiting for me at the governor's house," Pocahontas declared eagerly. "He told me once that when he sent for me that's where he would meet me. I thought he'd forgotten, but he hasn't. Are we ready to go ashore?"

There was a long, heavy silence, then the captain said bluntly, "You aren't going."

She stared at him, her eyes round.

"You're the prisoner of the people of Jamestown," Argall told her. "You'll be held here on board the *Swallow*, under guard, until Chief Powhatan signs a peace treaty on our terms. And then we'll keep you as long as the governor decides it's necessary to insure that the Naturals keep their pledged word."

A lesser woman would have given way to hysterics or at the very least would have wept bitterly. But Pocahontas was a true daughter of the Chickahominy and had been trained to receive harsh blows without showing her feelings. The pupils of her eyes dilated, she blinked once or twice and stood erect as though someone had struck her on the jaw, but otherwise she displayed no emotion, and John was impressed anew by her dignity. Folding her hands over her breasts, she stared straight ahead, looking at neither man, and after a brief silence she bowed her head.

"That which I must do for all the warriors and all the squaws of the Chickahominy, I will do," she said in her own tongue.

In spite of her shock, or perhaps because of it, she had retreated into an impenetrable shell, and Captain Argall looked at her sourly for a moment. Her nobility and seemingly calm acceptance of her fate robbed him of his chance to gloat over her, and he felt cheated. Nothing he might say to her now could touch her, he knew, so he turned abruptly and stalked out. John followed him into the corridor, but the captain did not halt until they reached the open deck.

"All right, Rolfe," he said. "Are you satisfied now that I didn't eat her alive?"

"You didn't tell her," John said sternly, "that Smith isn't in the New World and that you lied to her from the start. Don't you realize you're making her misery all the worse by letting her believe that he's in Jamestown and is responsible for her being held prisoner?"

"What's the difference?" Argall shrugged and signaled to his bosun for his gig. "She'll find out the truth sooner or later. And I don't intend to stand here all day and listen to a harangue from you about the feelings of a savage. I'm leaving to see the governor right now, and if you're coming, you'd better collect your gear."

"I dare say I won't be missed at the governor's," John said in the quiet drawl that appeared only when he was deeply aroused. "You and your friends can claim full credit for your brilliant achievement. When you think of it, you can send your gig back here for me."

He moved away without waiting to hear Argall's reply and, after hesitating briefly, walked back into the corridor. The door to the master's cabin was still open, and he could see that Pocahontas had not stirred since he and Argall had left. He went to her, but she gave no indication that she was even aware of his presence, and he felt awkward. Anything he might say to her in English would be a fresh affront, he thought, so he decided to address her in her own language.

"I am sorry," he said slowly, searching for the right words, "for the grief that has been visited upon the daughter of Powhatan."

Pocahontas's surface composure was unshaken, and to John's astonishment she smiled faintly as she raised her eyes to his. "Not many of the foreigners-from-across-the-sea have troubled to learn the speech of the Chickahominy, which has been the speech of their fathers before them."

"The speech of the Chickahominy was old in the world when that of my people was new," he told her, realizing the compliment was vague and inept but hoping it would comfort her.

She glanced at the grave young man, recognized his sincerity, and had the strange feeling that her strength was greater than his, that he needed sympathy for his sense of shame as much as she needed it for her sorrow. "The ways of Christians are odd," she said, reverting to English. "I try to understand them, but I can't."

"Christians?" He laughed harshly.

"I have thought much about these things."

"So have I." It was weird, he reflected, that at this moment of crisis in her life they should be discussing theology. "And I long ago came to the conclusion that any gods in whom people believe are good, if they lead those people to live good lives."

"No." Pocahontas shook her head and let her arms fall to her sides. "I have worshiped the gods of my ancestors, and they are false gods. They are the gods of those who know no better. My people worship the thunder, and they pray to the medicine man so he will make it come. But when he cannot, they burn him to death. That is stupid, because no medicine man can make thunder."

John remembered the ghastly burning of a woman accused of witchcraft in Cornwall. "All people have their superstitions," he said.

"Superstitions. That is the word I could not remember. Superstitions." Suddenly her eyes became angry, and her face looked as though it had been carved out of stone. "But the Christians should know better. They worship the one true God."

"Do you accept our God?" His astonishment was so great that for a moment he forgot her problem and the reason he had returned to her.

"When one has learned about Him, one must accept Him. There is no choice," Pocahontas said flatly. "But those who call themselves Christians do not believe in Him. They worship Him with their mouths, but they do not accept Him in their hearts."

Under the circumstances he could scarcely blame her for the sweeping nature of her scathing rebuke, but he felt he could not let the accusation go unchallenged. "Not all who call themselves Christians are as unscrupulous as Samuel Argall and his friends. Nor are all of them as weak in living up to their convictions as I am."

She thought he was showing great moral courage by offering her an apology but didn't feel this was the appropriate moment to discuss his valor. He was, after all, a stranger who was trying in a clumsy way to offer her solace.

"It's wrong," John continued, "to judge the many by the few. I'm sure you'll find that virtually the whole town will be shocked and indignant at the news of your abduction."

"Is that a way of telling me that my capture wasn't the official policy of your Council?" Pocahontas asked, a trace of bitterness creeping into her voice for the first time.

He shook his head and ran his fingers through his hair. "Certainly not. It was Captain Argall's scheme, and he enlisted the help of the rest of us. Abduction is against the law and could be severely punished."

"Then I'll be set free again before the day is over, in spite of the threats of that dreadful man with the red beard." She spoke confidently, obviously believing the matter was settled.

John took a deep breath and wondered how to explain that she had leaped to a false conclusion. In spite of her ability to speak English, she was not really a civilized person: her logic was too simple and direct, and she failed to realize that those who enjoyed the benefits of breeding and education held contradictory and misleading concepts. She would not become truly cultivated until she learned to be a sophist, and he was sorry he had to act as her instructor.

"I'm inclined to doubt that you'll be given your freedom," he said carefully. "You see, ma'am, the Council is made up of men whose realism is greater than their sense of principle. Had they known of the plan to kidnap you, their duty would have required them to halt the attempt at all costs. If necessary they would have thrown Argall and the rest of us into prison in order to prevent what the basic law of England defines, without qualification, as a crime."

"Is it not a crime now that I have been brought here?" She was thoroughly bewildered and searched his face to see if he was amusing himself at her expense. But Rolfe appeared to be the most honest man she had ever known, and she did not believe he would hurt her deliberately. Recalling her first meeting with him and Argall in the Potomac hut, she remembered his curious reticence and understood it for the first time.

"What you don't take into account, ma'am, is that the gentlemen of the Council are very practical. The deed has been done, and it would serve no useful purpose to put us in jail now. Besides, they're sure to see the benefits of your presence here. They've all heard that your father holds you in high regard, and they won't be able to resist the temptation to use you as a weapon to force him to make peace with us for all time."

Pocahontas gave up her attempt to hide her feelings, and her reserve vanished. "That will not happen. The governor of Jamestown is above the law, just as my father stands above the law of Chickahominy. Smith has told me so himself many times, and he will not allow the little men of his Council to hold me prisoner." She smiled contemptuously, and her voice was loud and firm. "You forget he has been my husband and will not permit this disgrace."

John had tried repeatedly to lead the conversation gently and circuitously to the news that would be the most crushing blow of all, but each time he created an opening he had shrunk from it. Now, however, the subject could no longer be avoided. "I'm not well acquainted with his lordship, as he is even newer to the colony than I am, but I feel reasonably certain he'll be in complete agreement with the members of his Council." He didn't want to look at Pocahontas but could not take his eyes from her.

"His lordship?" Her defenses began to crumble.

"Lord Delaware is our new governor," John said slowly. "He has just arrived here after a four-month voyage from London. He holds his seal of office from the King, of course." He was babbling, he told himself, and stopped talking.

Pocahontas knew what he was trying to say to her, but a perverse feminine streak in her nature demanded that she hear the worst in so many words. "It is not easy to imagine that Smith would allow any other man to become governor when he is in the same place. At first he was called president of the Council, but it's the same position, isn't it?"

"Yes, it's the same."

She stared at the miserable young man in silence and wished she didn't have to punish him by exposing the deepest roots of her sorrow. Yet she could not stop now. "How does it happen, then, that he allows some lord who is strange to the New World to take his place?" Somewhat to her own surprise, her voice did not waver.

"Smith is no longer a member of the London Company," John said. "The directors accepted his resignation a long time ago. Shortly before I myself left England, I believe it was."

The raw, ugly truth was exposed at last, but Pocahontas discovered that her pain was no greater than it had been a few days ago. She had lived so many months with the knowledge that Smith wanted no more to do with her that nothing was really changed. The few short hours during which her hope of being reunited with him had flared anew were in the past now, and she could not remember how she had felt during that brief time. The familiar bleak loneliness of despair settled over her again, and she recognized it at once, for she had learned to live with emptiness. "He is in London, then?"

"To the best of my knowledge." John discovered that his throat was raw and that his tongue felt like dry leather.

"He's taken up his old life there." This was insane, she thought; Smith's present and future were not her concern.

"Not exactly. King James granted him a patent for a new company, and I believe he's raising funds for an expedition. But," John added hastily, "it's my understanding that Captain Smith intends to explore a new area far to the north and has no intention of returning to Virginia."

The last wispy thread of illusion was gone, and Pocahontas realized she could no longer console herself with even the remote dream that Smith might someday return for her. At times, when her resistance to grief had been low, she had indulged herself in the childish game of giving her imagination free rein, and in these uncontrolled moments she had almost convinced herself that their separation was due to a misunderstanding that would be rectified in the not too distant future. But now, if she was to recapture her balance and create a new and useful life for herself, she would have to put him out of her mind for all time.

She walked slowly to the window, leaned her elbows on the frame, and stared out at Jamestown. She had thought of the colony so incessantly during the dreary period of her visit to the Potomac that it was something of a shock to realize that the town had changed. It was much larger than it had been when she had first come here, and she had difficulty in finding and identifying the few buildings she had known. The blockhouse at the end of the peninsula was still standing and looked precisely as it had when she had first gone there with Smith, but she could not bear to see it and closed her eyes.

It was senseless to think of making a new life when she was a prisoner of the English and was likely to be held here as a hostage for months, perhaps even years. And she had no idea how to create something fresh out of a hollow, flabby shell, nor did she have any desire to build on ruins. She realized that other women had suffered equally tragic experiences and had recovered, but the knowledge was no comfort to her and she was too listless, too lethargic to wonder how they had found new interests and new happiness.

She heard Rolfe stir behind her; for a moment she had forgotten his presence. It was wrong for one who was a foreigner and a man, even if he was tactful and sympathetic, to witness the sorrow of the daughter of the Chief of Chiefs, and she told herself sternly that she must constantly remember she was a Chickahominy. The traditions of her nation were all that were left to her, and no matter how she felt, she could not disgrace her father and her people.

Turning slowly, she faced him and called on the last

vestiges of her self-control. "Will you do something for me, Master Rolfe?"

"Anything, ma'am." Her eyes, he thought, were lifeless.

"I will be beholden to you if you will bring me a quill, a jar of ink, and a sheet of parchment."

He nodded, looking at her curiously.

"I have deceived myself too long and I must write a letter of farewell to Captain Smith. Would you do me the further favor of sending it to England for me?"

"Of course." John bowed and left the cabin. When he reached the open deck he halted abruptly and blinked in the bright June sunlight. Never before had he seen such hopeless lassitude, and he was desperately afraid he had made an appalling mistake when he had given her his knife.

Lord and Lady Cobham were reputedly one of the wealthiest couples in England, but John Smith, their dinner guest, thought that perhaps the stories he had heard about them were exaggerated. In that event he was wasting his time, and he regretted the long journey that had brought him to York. Granted that many members of the nobility who spent their lives in the country were less ostentatious than those who made their headquarters in London, he could not remember having visited a gloomier home than the Cobham castle.

The great hall had been virtually unchanged since the reign of Henry IV, and although the month was June, the high-ceilinged chamber was so damp and chilly that a fire was burning in the hearth at the far side of the room. But, as Smith had noted instantly, the Cobhams conserved on fuel and were burning coal rather than wood, after the fashion of poor tenant farmers in these parts. The tapestries that covered the stone walls were threadbare, and Smith told himself irritably that the newest of them must be at least one hundred years old. Most shocking of all was the presence of rushes on the floor; these days even merchants of no more than moderate means spread rugs over the tiles of the most important rooms in their houses.

And certainly no self-respecting aristocrat ever ate his meals in his great hall, as such an arrangement was tantamount to an admission that he could not afford to hire enough servants to wait on him and his family in a separate dining room. Equally discouraging, the plates here were of pewter, the cloth was a coarse linen rather than lace, and the fare that was spread on the table looked meager to Smith's experienced eye. There was a boar's head, a baked swan, two or three platters of cold mutton, cheese, and ham, and the main dish was a disappointing roast of an inferior cut of beef. Most members of the nobility served no less than fifteen or twenty varieties of meat and fowl, and Smith could not help but feel that his hosts were niggardly.

Lady Cobham, who sat at the foot of the table, might have been mistaken for a shopkeeper had she appeared on the Strand, and Smith was disheartened when he saw she was wearing a plain gown of dark gray frieze, a fuzzy wool so cheap that even the wives of poor artisans dressed in it. Her husband, who was mumbling a long prayer at the head of the table, wore an old-fashioned doublet of black wool and a tiny ruff of the sort that had gone out of fashion some years before the death of the late Queen. It was possible, even probable, that there was nothing to be gained in this household by a man who was seeking funds for his new venture.

His lordship finished his prayer, helped himself to a slice of ham, and directed his attention to his guest, drawing his bushy gray brows together. "I believe in discussing business first and relaxing over the rest of the meal afterward," he said. "Here, try some of the wine, Captain."

Smith tasted the pink liquid in his cup and was not surprised to find it was watery and tasteless.

"Your letter fascinated us, Captain." Lady Cobham picked at a few scraps on her plate.

Although the chances were slight that Smith would leave this place with a contribution of any significance in his purse, he smiled blandly and spoke as though he was addressing the profligate Duke and Duchess of Buckingham. "You've been very kind to receive me," he said, "and I'm pleased that I'm in a position to return your courtesy. It ain't often in these times, when the cost of living and taxes are so high, that an opportunity like this presents itself."

"Opportunity?" Lord Cobham was carefully carving the swan.

"Quite so, milord. Investments in the Plymouth Company won't be subject to taxation, nor will the returns. I have that in my charter in black and white."

His lordship looked unimpressed, and Lady Cobham's face was lowered, so her expression was hidden. Neither of them deigned to reply.

Smith decided to try again. "The returns are what count, of course. The London Company, whose colony I had the honor to head, is beginning to show a small profit after only four years, which is rather remarkable. But I can practically give you a guarantee that the colonies the Plymouth Company intends to establish will be self-sustaining after the first year and will repay our investors at a rate of three gold angels to one by the end of the second year." It was annoying to discover that he was perspiring.

Lord Cobham continued to carve placidly. "Some people," he observed, "will do anything for profit."

"I spoke only of the initial return," Smith said desperately. "After five years, every member of the Plymouth Company will pocket at least twenty angels for each one he's invested. And," he added, "we don't require large sums."

"What do you call large?" her ladyship asked.

He was on the right track at last, Smith thought; the Cobhams were only moderately wealthy, it seemed, so he decided to reduce the size of the request he had had in mind. It would be far better to come away from this ancient castle with something than with nothing. "We're accepting investments as small as one thousand guineas," he said.

Lord Cobham cut a bit of fat from the fowl on his plate. "One thousand guineas can be an enormous sum."

"On the other hand," his wife declared, "ten thousand guineas can be paltry. It all depends on the purpose for which the money is used."

"Oh, that's true." Smith sounded as though he agreed heartily, but privately thought they were both mad. If they were really in a position to spend ten thousand guineas, there was no wealthier couple in the realm.

"We have no wish to bother with profits and losses, Captain," his lordship said sententiously. "Those days are behind us, and we concern ourselves with a far more urgent matter now."

The unctuous piety of his tone gave the visitor his first real clue to the bewildering situation.

"It's the natives of the New World who interest us," Lady Cobham said, color in her voice at last. "There must be thousands of them, all of them heathen. We would like nothing better than to see them accept our faith, and we're afraid the Spaniards will reach them first."

"There's no danger of that," Smith assured her. "And you're absolutely right, of course. The primary purpose of the Plymouth Company is to advance the cause of Protestant Christianity." He was uncertain whether there was any mention of religion in his charter; certainly he had never bothered to examine the document closely for such data. But details were irrelevant. He had found the key to the Cobhams and would have no difficulty in extracting a handsome contribution from them.

"We wish we could be sure of that." His lordship lost his appetite for food and shoved his plate away. "What haunts us is the fear that the Naturals are so deeply rooted in their pagan beliefs that they'll reject the truth about God and man."

"That's an unwarranted fear. I know it from my own experience." Smith had sworn he would never mention Pocahontas to anyone again, but circumstances swiftly altered his resolution. "I dare say you've heard rumors of one sort or another, coupling my name with that of an Indian girl, a native princess, to be specific."

"Frankly, we have." Lady Cobham looked troubled. "And that's another reason we've hesitated to become members of the Plymouth Company, Captain."

Smith laughed expansively. "Some of the stories I myself have heard since I've come home have shocked me. Let me tell you what really happened, as I'm sure you'll find it most illuminating. I made my first trip into the interior from Jamestown for the purpose of converting the Naturals to Christianity, and the girl seemed to be the most receptive member of her tribe. So I stayed with them for a time, living with some of the older members of her family, of course, and taught her enough English so she could understand the rudiments of the Bible. When I left I gave her my own Bible, which had once belonged to my great-grandfather."

Lord Cobham's lean face became animated. "Do you mean to sit there and tell us that a pagan out of the forests accepted our faith?"

"I don't ask you to accept my word for it," Smith replied with dignity. "Others who have spent time at Jamestown are currently in England. They can tell you about her too."

"I congratulate you, Captain," her ladyship said. "But what of the other members of her tribe?"

"They've followed her example, milady." Smith's smile was as devout as his tone was reverential. "One of these days His Majesty will need to appoint a bishop for the natives of Virginia. If I do say so myself, I feel that if I've made any contribution in my lifetime, I can claim credit for introducing Christianity to the Naturals. And I look back with great pride and affection on the girl called Pocahontas, who was my first convert."

August, 1611

Eggs were scarce in Jamestown and were served only on rare occasions by the wealthy or the lucky. Plans to import large numbers of live chickens from England had not yet materialized, as the birds shipped for the purpose were invariably consumed by new settlers during the course of their long and tedious voyage to the New World. Rumors had reached the colony that several Indian tribes living to the south of Virginia raised chickens, and complex negotiations with these natives were in the process of being initiated. In the meantime the town had to depend on its own hunters or on occasional barter deals with nearby nations like the Rappahannock and the Chesapeake, with whom trade relations had just been restored. But the supply was still erratic even though the Naturals, having learned their neighbors prized eggs, were now conducting systematic searches for the nests of wild fowl.

Lord Delaware, who had been miserable during his weeks

in America because he firmly believed it was uncivilized to start the day with a meal consisting of anything other than cold meats, ale, and eggs, sat down at the breakfast table, nodded to his wife, and girded himself for the usual morning ordeal. He did not bother to glance up when the serving maid, a recent immigrant who had already found herself a husband and would soon be leaving the governor's employ, set his plate in front of him. Then a fragrant aroma struck his nostrils. He looked sharply at his plate and then stared at Lady Delaware, who was smiling serenely.

"Enjoy your omelet, Thomas," she said. "I bought a dozen wild duck eggs from an Indian squaw yesterday and had them all cooked for you. I had to pay an exorbitant price for them, as the squaw had been told we'd give her more than anyone else in town. I must say these savages learn quickly. This one was as shrewd as my greengrocer in London."

"If you were generous, she'll be back." His lordship thought that even the cold roast venison looked appetizing today.

"Oh, I was very generous." His wife, concealing her distaste for a dish of smoked fish, ate quickly and daintily. She was a tiny woman, and all her movements were birdlike. "I had to give her two jars of wine."

"Not the good claret we brought with us from England?"

"No, dear, certainly not. The confiscated Spanish wine that Sir Thomas Dale had accumulated."

Relieved, the governor began to eat, savoring each mouthful. "That's all right, then. But I advise you to be careful and say nothing about the price to any of your friends."

"They won't be jealous, Thomas. They know we can afford to pay more than they can."

"It isn't the extravagance, Mary." Lord Delaware frowned and hesitated for a moment before continuing. "Ever since we forced Chief Powhatan to re-establish peaceful relations with us, I've been very strict in enforcing my edict that no firearms and alcoholic liquors are to be sold to the natives.

And if it became general knowledge that we paid two jars of wine for my omelet, people might not understand."

Lady Delaware had been married to him for twenty-four years. "Of course, dear," she said.

Her husband ate in silence for a time. "Are you sure you don't want some of these eggs?" he asked at last, his tone as well as his words indicating that he had been urging her to share the delicacy with him ever since it had been served to him.

She waved aside the offer with a smile, patted her lace-edged cap, and looked demurely at her plate.

His lordship should have been warned that something was on her mind, but the omelet was only the second one he had eaten in the New World. "You look very attractive this morning," he said expansively.

"Thank you, Thomas." She had dressed with care in a blue-and-black-striped taffeta gown, with the front of the bodice heavily stiffened, and a "ruff below the waist," or pleated peplum, standing out above her sidehooped skirt. A stiffened lace collar matched the cuffs of her padded sleeves, her pendant brooch of jet at the modest neckline and a strand of pearls around her throat were inconspicuously elegant, and she could almost imagine herself back at her comfortable town house in London. But she was in the raw wilderness world of America, she reminded herself, and she said nothing more until her husband finished his eggs, drained his cup of ale, and lighted his pipe. This was the moment for which she had been waiting, and she struck swiftly but with care.

"Thomas," she said, "something must be done about that dreadful situation."

"What situation?" He glanced out of the window at the midsummer foliage and wondered whether delegations of settlers and members of the Council would keep him tied to his desk all morning.

"That girl on the *Swallow*. It's positively disgraceful."

"Now, Mary." The governor sighed comfortably and puffed on his pipe. "We've discussed that matter before, you'll remember. The day we release her and she goes back to the interior, her father will break his treaty with us, and we'll be at war with the Naturals again. If we want peace—and more omelets—we've got to hold her as a hostage indefinitely. I simply can't allow your sense of what's ethical and right to interfere with the policy of state."

Her smile did not waver, and the tiny wrinkles at the corners of her eyes seemed to merge with the creases in her face. "You've explained all that to me, dear, and I accept your wisdom. I certainly have no objection to your holding a dull-witted savage as a prisoner. But I do wish you had captured one of Powhatan's sons rather than his daughter."

"I didn't capture anyone," he reminded her. "Captain Argall brought her here, and a brilliant stroke it was too. I'm repaying him as best I can by renting his bark from him to use as a prison."

"That's what I'm talking about."

"Some people are waiting for me at my office."

"One moment, Thomas." She did not raise her voice, but he resumed his seat; after twenty-four years of marriage a man learned that surface compliance was frequently the best defense. "Your militiamen and their officers are guarding the girl."

"Of course. They're the only troops I have, as you well know." Lord Delaware sounded aggrieved.

"Indeed I do. And all I ask is that you issue some new instructions to them. According to some of the stories I've heard, the things that happen on board the *Swallow* are scandalous. And that's precisely no more and no less than one can expect when a heathen girl is surrounded by men. Not that I blame them. They can't be expected to behave in any other way when temptation is offered them."

"Just exactly what have you heard, and from whom?" he demanded irritably.

"Elizabeth," she replied, referring to her sister-in-law, Francis West's wife, "says there are orgies on board the *Swallow* every night of the week."

"I don't believe you and Elizabeth would have the vaguest notion of what takes place in an orgy," his lordship retorted.

"Nor would we want to know," she declared primly. "But I am concerned about the morals of our young men."

"I'm not. I'm the governor of Jamestown, but I'm neither the guardian nor the pastor of my militiamen."

Lady Delaware was not one to give in without a spirited struggle. "Do you yourself know what's happening on that prison ship? Have you ever taken the trouble to visit it and see how the girl disports herself?"

"Hardly. I'm not likely to forget the dignity of my office by paying a visit to a pagan wench, even if she is the daughter of the most important native in Virginia."

"Then you should, Thomas. And after you've seen what's happening there, you can take steps to change the situation."

The governor pushed back his chair and stood, shaking his head. "I'm sorry, Mary, but I have too much that's important on my mind. If you're so interested in the prisoner, why don't you talk to John Rolfe about her? He annoys me several days a week by urging me to do one thing or another for her, and I believe he goes out to see her quite regularly. So you and he will have much in common."

Lady Delaware remained at the table until he left and she heard him enter his office down the corridor from the dining room. Then, her face set in grim lines, she walked with brisk determination to the nearby house of John Rolfe. His lordship thought he had disposed of the matter, but he would soon discover he was mistaken, and she intended to force him to protect his men from the predatory wiles of a pagan wanton who did not care how many honorable young Englishmen she corrupted. Although her husband did not realize it, she reflected, he had helped her immeasurably by revealing that John Rolfe was working toward the same goal she was trying to achieve. The knowledge pleased her, and she thought it was typical of Rolfe to labor quietly, earnestly, and alone for a principle. He was one of the few gentlemen in the colony of whom her ladyship approved, and she made a mental note to send some letters to various friends in England regarding him. He was too young to remain a widower for the rest of his life, and with the proper discretion it should be possible to arrange for a girl of background and breeding to visit Jamestown. There were several young ladies in Sussex and Kent whose parents would be amenable to sending their daughters to the New World in the hope that a marriage could be arranged with such an eligible man, and Lady Delaware wondered why she had waited so long to settle his future.

When she arrived at his house, a modest but substantial two-story structure of whitewashed shingles, she saw his six-year-old child playing in the front yard, and her newly formed conviction hardened. The little girl needed a mother, and the functions that Rolfe's elderly, half-educated housekeeper performed were inadequate. Pausing inside the gate, Lady Delaware watched the brown-haired child dance around the base of an oak tree, unaware of the presence of anyone else, and it was obvious to a woman who had raised three sons and two daughters that the little girl was lonely.

"Good morning, Celia," she said.

Rolfe's daughter halted, recognized the visitor, and curtsied deeply. Her display of good manners was flattering, and Lady Delaware rewarded her with a smile. "Good day, milady," Celia said gravely. "Do you know what I was doing? I was playing. I was pretending I was an Indian princess. I never met one really. But my father knows one. And he tells me many things about her."

The revelation was mildly distasteful, but her ladyship had no desire to waste time rebuking and correcting someone else's child. "Is your father at home?" she asked.

Celia nodded and dashed into the house, shouting, "Papa! Papa!"

A few moments later John appeared at the front door, and although the hour was early, he was shaved and correctly attired in a doublet, breeches, and ruff. He bowed, took his child's hand, and pushed the door wide open. "This is an unexpected honor, milady," he said.

Lady Delaware preceded him into the small, sparsely furnished drawing room, and as she sat and accepted his offer of a cup of tea, she told herself the house badly needed a feminine touch. But she forgot such secondary concerns when the child was sent off to play again, and proceeded to concentrate on the business at hand. "Master Rolfe," she said crisply, "I've been told that you pay regular visits to a certain person on board the *Swallow*."

John was too polite to show his surprise. "That's true, milady," he replied quietly.

"There's no need for me to tell you then that the situation on board the bark is deplorable."

"I'd call it shocking." Anger darkened his face, but he held himself in check.

"I've come here in the hope that you and I can do something about it together." Lady Delaware poured steaming tea into her saucer in the approved manner and drank it rapidly.

John's face relaxed a trifle, and he looked somewhat less gaunt. "I had just about given up hope of anyone improving things out there, milady."

"My husband isn't yet on our side," she warned him. "At times he can be incredibly headstrong, but I've never known him to remain unreasonable after I've shown him the truth. He still doesn't see that what he's permitted to happen on board the *Swallow* is so immoral that even dissolute and lewd people like the Spanish and French would be upset if they learned about it. And he'll take whatever steps are necessary, I'm sure, as soon as I point out to him that all Europe will soon hear of what's taking place under his very nose. But what I need are facts to substantiate my argument. You've been out to the bark often, so you're plainly in a position to tell me precisely what's happening."

"What would you like to know, milady?" The sun was streaming in through the windows, but John felt chilly and slowly rubbed his hands together.

Lady Delaware leaned forward in her hard, unpainted chair. "Don't hesitate to speak freely, Master Rolfe. How wanton is her behavior?"

He seemed stunned and had some difficulty in replying. "You're referring to Pocahontas," he said at last.

"Of course. Does she wander around the ship unclothed, does she entice the militiamen into her quarters one at a time, or does she entertain them with some hideous pagan rituals? Any and every detail you can tell me will be of enormous help to me when I go back to my husband."

John coughed behind his hand, and for an instant Lady Delaware thought he was laughing at her. But his eyes were solemn, and when he spoke again there was no hint of humor in his voice. "It seems to me that you will learn all you need to know if you go out to the *Swallow* and make your own appraisal, milady," he said.

"Do you suppose I dare?" The idea frightened her, but it was exciting too.

"No militia officer who values his position will try to halt the first lady of Jamestown. If you wish, I'll escort you. It so happens I was planning to go out this very morning."

Lady Delaware caught her breath, and as she stood she discovered her heart was pounding. "I'll do it!" she said. "And if you don't mind, Master Rolfe, I'll ask my sister-in-law to come too. She's as anxious to learn the truth and to rid the colony of this loathsome disease as I am."

Pocahontas sat quietly near the window of the master's cabin, reading a stanza of Edmund Spenser's *Faerie Queene* that always comforted her:

Is not short paine well borne, that brings long ease,
And layes the soule to sleepe in quiet grave?

Sleepe after toyle, port after stormie seas,
Ease after warre, death after life does greatly please.

Someone tapped lightly on the door and, marking her place in the leather-bound volume, she raised her head. Her visitor was probably John Rolfe, she thought, as he had said he would come here again today and he never failed to keep his word. His kindness was soothing, and his company was certainly a welcome break in the dreary monotony of her captivity, but Pocahontas told herself the time had come to put a stop to his daily calls. She was sure he was neglecting his work for her sake, and it disturbed her that he should come here regularly for the sole purpose of offering solace to her, never asking anything in return and acting as though he were taking full responsibility for the injustice which the entire colony should have shared.

"Come in," she called.

The door opened, and to her surprise two women entered, pushing and tugging their hooped skirts through the narrow frame. The elder, who came first, was petite, elegantly dressed in blue-and-black-striped taffeta, and although she was middle-aged, her refined features looked youthful. The other, many years her junior, was red-faced and heavy, and her black silk gown with a green-embroidered front panel and a falling ruff of soft lace should have been worn only by someone slender.

They stared so long and hard at Pocahontas that she felt self-conscious about her modest ankle-length dress of gray wool, and without quite realizing what she was doing she began to fidget with a small red pincushion and a pair of scissors which hung from the ends of her black ribbon belt. She raised her free hand to the thick braids of hair that were wound in a coil at the crown of her head, and only after assuring herself that she looked presentable did she find her voice. Even then she was uncertain what to say, as this was the first time she had ever come face to face with adult Englishwomen.

"You wish to see me." She knew the statement was a trifle inane, but her surface calm was unruffled.

"I am Lady Delaware," the older woman declared in a strained voice, forgetting to introduce her sister-in-law.

"I'm honored, milady." Pocahontas curtsied and gestured toward the bed. "I'm afraid I can offer you no comfortable chairs. My jailers don't believe in granting me unnecessary luxuries."

Her ladyship continued to stand just inside the door and, completely forgetting her breeding, could not stop gaping. "You speak English."

"I'm learning, milady." Pocahontas shrugged to cover her embarrassment at the compliment.

The heat in the little cabin seemed insufferable, and the first lady of Jamestown thought she would faint. John Rolfe had given her no hint of Pocahontas's appearance, so she couldn't be blamed if her conduct was rude. "Where," she asked, fingering the girl's sleeve, "did you get that dress?"

"I made it." Pocahontas decided it was necessary to add that she had enjoyed too little practice to have become an accomplished needlewoman. The facts, unfortunately, spoke for themselves.

Lady Delaware sat down abruptly on the edge of the bed. "Where did you get the material?" she demanded in a strangled voice.

"Master Rolfe brought it for me." Pocahontas's face softened, and she smiled. "I didn't like the way the soldiers looked at me when I wore the clothes of the Chickahominy. It was not the fault of the young men, of course," she added hastily, seeing the eyes of her guests grow large. "Warriors of every land are alike. All are men. And it is a woman's duty to discourage them by her modesty."

Elizabeth West decided to sit too. "That was very wise of you," she said feebly, speaking for the first time.

There was a protracted, barren silence, and Pocahontas, having no idea why her visitors had called on her, waited for

them to give her some clue. They, however, were too confused at the moment to think clearly, and both sat rigidly,
occasionally exchanging covert glances. Neither could quite
believe the Indian girl was what she seemed, yet it was
virtually impossible for her to be putting up a false front for
their benefit. And as John Rolfe had not left Lady Delaware's
side since she had first arrived at his house, there had been no
opportunity for him to warn Pocahontas they were coming.

Her ladyship had formed such a sharp mental picture of
the conditions she would find on board the *Swallow* that she
was unable to accept evidence to the contrary, but as she
looked around the neat cabin she could see nothing that even
hinted at the possibility that orgies ever took place here.
"What do you do with yourself all day?" she asked sternly.

Something in her expression reminded Pocahontas of
Ru-Sa. "What would you do if you were in my position,
milady? I pass my time as best I can." She reached down and
opened the sea chest that was the property of Captain Argall.

Mistress West half stood to peer into it, expecting to see
jars of brandy. But she sank back onto the foot of the bed
again, her eyes dazed. "Books," she murmured.

Lady Delaware, who prided herself on being a patroness of
the arts, picked up several volumes and examined them
briefly. "Did you enjoy Sir Philip Sidney?"

Perhaps it was wrong for someone just beginning to become educated to speak frankly, but Pocahontas told herself
that her opinion had been sought, so she saw no reason to
speak other than truthfully. "It seems to me that words did
not come to him easily. He labored over what he wrote,
much as I would labor. But the thoughts he expressed were
very noble, and I can understand why so many others have
written that all England mourned him when he died. There
was once a great warrior of the Chickahominy, Deliceco,
who must have been much like Sir Philip Sidney. He was
young, he was very handsome, he won great battles, but he
was always kind to the enemies he defeated. When he sud-

denly became sick and died the same day, my people put
ashes on their faces for a whole moon in his memory. Now
other warriors pretend they are like Deliceco, but they are
not. In the same way, I imagine, many English warriors want
to think they are like Sir Philip Sidney, but they do not have
his soul or his great spirit."

The girl was astonishingly astute, and Lady Delaware, not
knowing what to reply, took refuge in studying a thick book
that showed signs of heavy use. "You've read the Bible too, I
see."

"I read it every day," Pocahontas said. "The prayers written by the warrior-chief called David are like songs, and they
have been a great help to me in my affliction. I have tried to
learn all of the teachings of Jesus, too, although the men who
hold me captive do not seem to bother following the rules He
gave them. But even if they do not, I believe those rules are
right."

Elizabeth West's jaw hung slack, but her ladyship, who
had spent years at the court of the late Queen, was better able
to cope with the unexpected. "You're fortunate that you
could bring so many of your books with you."

"None of them are mine." A shadow crossed Pocahontas's
face, and she looked out of the window at the water, not
wanting the women to see how she felt. "I left the land of the
Potomac very suddenly and brought none of my own belongings with me."

"I heard how you were tricked!" Lady Delaware was a trifle
surprised to hear the indignation in her own voice. "I think
the men treated you disgracefully and I haven't hesitated to
let my husband know it!"

"You have come to help me then." Pocahontas folded her
hands across her breasts and bowed her head in gratitude.
"You will persuade the governor to set me free."

Even Elizabeth West's best friends had never claimed that
she was endowed with tact. "We've come here to learn for
ourselves just what's going on. We've heard a great many

stories and we want to know how many of them are true."
She ignored the glares of her sister-in-law, who was trying to
silence her, and thought that something Francis had said
recently was quite accurate: Mary was becoming senile, and
so was her lordly husband. "Perhaps you'll tell us where you
got all these books."

Pocahontas instantly recognized the belligerence of this
woman, whose name she did not know, but thought there
was nothing to be gained by behaving antagonistically in
return. "Master Rolfe has loaned them to me," she said
quietly. "Most of them belong to him, and a few he has
borrowed from people in the town."

Mistress West remembered that Rolfe paid daily visits to
the *Swallow*. "It would seem," she declared with low relish,
"that Master John Rolfe has become a special friend of
yours."

"I'm not sure I know what you mean." There was a ring in
Pocahontas's voice, and her meekness vanished.

"I think you do," the red-faced woman persisted, obviously enjoying herself.

"Master Rolfe is a gentleman." Pocahontas's incredulity
was as great as her indignation.

Righteous anger was impossible to simulate, Lady Delaware thought, and her respect for the Indian girl increased.
"But surely not every man in Jamestown has behaved like a
gentleman?"

"No, not every one." Pocahontas remembered the incident that had occurred two days after the *Swallow* had anchored in the river and Captain Argall had tried to press his
attentions on her. John Rolfe's arrival had prevented an
embarrassing scene, and she would never forget how John
had quietly promised to horsewhip Argall if he molested her
again. The captain looked burly enough to tear John apart
with his bare hands, but he had obviously taken the threat
seriously and had not returned to the bark since that time.

"We're not prying, of course," her ladyship said. "But I

can't help wondering how you can protect yourself when your position is so vulnerable."

Pocahontas did not reply in words but reached into the voluminous pocket in her skirt and drew out the knife John had given her. As she grasped it by the handle the thin veneer of civilization she had acquired seemed to fall away, and in spite of her English dress she looked like a ruthless savage who would not hesitate to plunge the blade into the body of any man who dared to annoy her.

Elizabeth West gasped and wiped a film of perspiration from her upper lip. "Have you ever had need to use that ugly weapon?" she asked greedily.

"My prayers have been answered, and I have only had to use it once. Last week a young gentleman who had drunk too much came to see me, and I had to cut him twice on the arm to cool his ardor."

Mistress West began to tremble violently; it was last week that Francis had come home, reeking of sack, with two deep gashes on his arm, mumbling that he had tripped in a bramble patch while hunting in the forest. "It's stifling in here, Mary. I'll wait for you on the deck." She jumped to her feet, gathered her skirts, and fled ignominiously from the cabin.

Lady Delaware's thin eyelids drooped as she watched her sister-in-law's hasty departure. If what she suspected was correct, it merely confirmed her opinion of Francis. As she so often told Thomas, his treatment of his brother was far too lenient. Nodding in grim satisfaction, she turned back to Pocahontas, who was staring at the door in bewilderment, unable to understand why her visitor had become so upset.

"I'm very glad I've come to see you, my dear," her ladyship announced warmly. "You've been used outrageously, but all that will end. Immediately. I give you my personal word that my husband will have you moved to a lovely little house of your own before the sun sets today."

January, 1612

Men who sought to amass great wealth were short-sighted, John Smith thought as he looked contentedly around the living room of his comfortable lodgings behind St. Paul's Church. When a man was famous he acquired everything the wealthy could buy, he had none of the worries that money caused, and the rewards he won were more permanent by far than the paltry advantages gold could purchase. This charming suite of rooms had been rented for him by admirers, furniture and clothing had been showered on him by friends, and his mere presence at a social function guaranteed its success. And not even King James himself kept more exalted company, Smith told himself as he gazed appreciatively at his guest, the Countess of Hartford, whose background was impeccable and who was probably the sauciest baggage in England.

It gave him a feeling of power and pleasure to glance at the low-cut neckline of her rose-colored satin gown, and he knew the cloth in her quilted yellow sleeves and ruby velvet bodice front was the finest that could be bought. He admired the thick row of pearls that edged her high, stiffened collar of yellow lawn, and he had rarely seen a gem as large as the ruby that nestled in her upswept blond hair. Virtually every man in the kingdom would be flattered if Margaret of Hartford crooked a dainty finger at him, yet she was merely one of many who connived to win Smith's favors.

She sat on a divan before the fire, idly leafing through the pages of his recently published *History of Virginia,* and he made no attempt to interrupt her but sat quietly, drinking in the scene. Finally she looked up and smiled at him, her blue eyes sleepy. "This looks very impressive," she said in the husky voice that sounded intimate even when she discussed impersonal matters.

Smith shrugged modestly.

"I shall have my husband's secretary read it to me as soon as they return from Holland." The Earl of Hartford stupidly spent most of his time traveling around Europe on diplomatic missions for the Crown, leaving his wife to create her own diversions for herself in London.

"They won't be home for another month or two, I think you said?" Smith filled his pipe with tobacco and looked on the table beside him for a spill to light it.

"At least two months." The countess yawned and stretched voluptuously.

"That's a long time to wait, when everyone in town is talking about the book," he replied, hiding his faint irritation behind an ingratiating grin.

"Oh, I don't need to read it in order to talk about it." Margaret of Hartford's vapidly sensuous face did not change expression. "You seem to forget that I've never learned to read myself."

"There's no reason why you should." Smith wondered whether it would be to his advantage to offer to read it to her but rejected the idea. If he indulged in such generosity she would be sure to brag to her confidantes, and before he knew it he would be deluged with similar requests from a dozen other women who sought his favors.

"Besides, you can tell me what you've said in it." She paused and then continued brightly, "Would you like to take me with you on your next voyage of exploration? How the whole court would envy me!"

"There's nothing I'd like more," Smith declared, shuddering inwardly, and added hastily, "I won't be leaving for several years, you understand. It takes a long time to raise the necessary funds, build my ships, and recruit my company."

"I'll wait." Margaret stretched out on the divan and let the book slide to the floor.

He jumped to his feet, snatched up the volume, and brushed it off carefully with a lace handkerchief he took from his sleeve. It was unwise to let a woman see he was annoyed with her just before he made love to her, and he knew he couldn't hide his anger at her carelessness. So he deliberately turned his back to her, stood the book in a prominent position at the rear of the table, propped against the wall, and made a pretense of rummaging around in a mass of papers for something with which to light his pipe.

The countess, unaware of what was going through his mind, fished in a little chased silver bowl of sweets, tossing aside several ordinary perfumed kissing-comfits and finally selecting an eryngo, the candied root of sea holly. The exotic tidbit actually tasted rather bitter and caused her to pucker her mouth, but she didn't mind and chewed it slowly, knowing she looked extremely attractive.

Smith's sense of resentment began to dissipate, and he was about to say something to her when a few lines at the bottom of a letter written in an unformed, childish hand caught his eye. It was a strange little note he had received in the late autumn from Pocahontas, and it had amused him to keep it as a souvenir. Removing it from the pile of correspondence, he glanced at it briefly and could not resist chuckling. Women all over the world were the same, regardless of whether they were barbarians or great ladies, although very few of the latter had ever taken the trouble to learn to write. And there was no reason they should, of course, as letters were a man's province.

What entertained him most in the short communication from Pocahontas was its inconsistency. She first bade him a solemn, permanent farewell and assured him she would never love any other man as she had loved him, a natural conclusion which was easy for him to accept. Then, in the next breath, she expressed the hope that when he returned to the New World he would visit Virginia again, and she gave him her promise that if and when he did come back she would make certain that her father greeted him as a friend and ally. Apparently she was incapable of understanding that she completely contradicted herself and obviously she could not see that her frank invitation to visit the land of the Chickahominy again made her renunciation of him ludicrous rather than pathetic.

Until this moment it hadn't occurred to him that Pocahontas's behavior was identical with that of two or three women who had been his mistresses during the past year. Without exception they were grasping, conniving, and secretly hoped to ensnare him permanently. He was glad he had enough sense to see through their shallow maneuvers and that he always remembered the primary reason any female existed was to please and serve the male. Some men clouded their thinking with false sentiment, and by attributing qualities that did not exist to members of the opposite sex, they were asking for trouble. But he was never guilty of that error.

Chuckling again, Smith twisted Pocahontas's letter into a spill and started toward the hearth with it, his pipe between his teeth. Margaret of Hartford, whose presence in the room he had been taking for granted, suddenly sat upright and pouted prettily. "You might share the jest with me," she said. "Or are you planning to spend the rest of the day reading?"

Plainly this was not the moment to light a pipe, so Smith put it aside. "I was thinking how remarkable it is that most of your sex resemble peas in a pod. In many ways it's hard to tell ladies at the court from the savages of America. Of course you're the exception, Meg. You're unique."

· Crumpling Pocahontas's letter into a ball, he threw it into the fire and walked slowly toward the blond baggage who was waiting for him on the divan.

Many of the settlers claimed that the winters in Jamestown were unbearable, that they were always cold, and that the ever-present dampness ate into their bones. But Pocahontas had never known such luxury and comfort, and in a curious way she was content with her new life. By living only in the present, refusing to dwell on the mistakes and misery of the past or speculate on the uncertainties of the future, she was able to achieve a precarious but nevertheless momentarily stable balance. It was not difficult to accept each day as it came, to concentrate on the petty details of routine existence, and to hope that by refusing to permit herself to feel deeply about anyone or anything, she would gradually lose the capacity to love or hate intensely.

Her house, which consisted of a drawing room, bedchamber, and tiny dining hall with a kitchen and servants' annex attached, was a solid structure that had been built to withstand the elements, and at times she surprised herself by thinking of it as a permanent home. It had been easy to adopt many of the customs and habits of the English, and she continued to cling to no more than a handful of her old ways. No woman could possibly prefer the hard, bough couches of the Chickahominy to the soft, feather-filled mattresses of the settlers, but on her very first night in the house Pocahontas had torn down the thick silk curtains around her bed. They stifled her, she said, and although many of the ladies of the colony who had become her friends told her she was courting death, she insisted on sleeping in a bed that was open to the cold night air.

She discovered, too, that many of the dishes served by the English were scarcely edible and she thought they were probably the worst cooks on earth, although she carefully refrained from expressing her views. When she had moved into the house, Lady Delaware had hired a woman from Northumberland as a cook and housemaid for her, and for several weeks Pocahontas had lost weight steadily on the meals that were served to her. Through tact, patience and skill she had taught Nancy to use the native herbs and spices that were to be found in such abundance in the forests, and as a result the gentry of Jamestown knew that when they were invited to Pocahontas's house for dinner or supper they would be offered delectable dishes that could not be duplicated elsewhere in the colony.

During the first weeks of this new phase of her captivity Pocahontas had not been allowed to venture outside the town walls. But after her friendship with the governor and his lady had ripened and she had become acquainted with the members of the Council and their wives, too, the rules restricting her activities were relaxed and she was permitted to wander in the nearby forests if she wished, provided she was accompanied by several responsible citizens. She rarely took advantage of her opportunity, however, as she felt homesick for the land of the Chickahominy whenever she stood beneath the towering white oaks, elms, and poplar trees of the wilderness.

Twice, when she had gone out into the forest and had stood very still, listening to the wind rustling through the branches, watching the dead leaves swirl and the laurel bushes tremble, she had been almost overcome by a yearning to return to her own people. When she had heard a deer timidly make its way around the party that accompanied her and had realized that none of the people knew of the animal's proximity, she had felt once again the strong sensation that they were alien intruders, and for a few moments she had hated all of them. They were destroying the wilderness with their axes, driving the wild animals farther inland, and each time a fleet of barks arrived from England with a new group of colonists, she knew with increasing certainty that these ambitious, hard-working foreigners were gradually transforming her America, the world her ancestors had known for countless generations, into something vastly different.

Yet, as she herself saw, the forest left its imprint on the settlers, too, and changed them, just as she herself was changing. Flabby, pale men and toilworn, fearful women stood erect after they had been in the New World for a time, and they accepted the habits of the Indians as readily as the natives copied their ways. The mutual enthusiasm and eagerness to learn on the part of the newcomers and those whose fathers had been in this land for thousands of years never failed to impress Pocahontas, and when she saw yeomen from Kent and Cornwall and Sussex trading and joking with warriors of the Rappahannock, Chesapeake, and Potomac, she was inclined to believe that perhaps the sacrifice of her own freedom was a small price to pay for such friendship. It was possible that she would be held prisoner for the rest of her life, but she resolutely shut her mind to thoughts of tomorrow and instead watched the alchemy of the forests and rivers and hills shape the colonists into a new breed.

It was far more difficult to recognize the upheaval that was taking place inside herself, although she occasionally caught a glimpse of the fact that she was steadily becoming as much the English gentlewoman as she was already the daughter of the Chickahominy Chief of Chiefs. This strange new ambivalence in her nature did not disturb her, however, and she accepted her ability to look in two directions at once as natural and inevitable. That was the reason, she often thought, why the only trips into the countryside beyond Jamestown that she enjoyed were her visits to John Rolfe's growing tobacco plantations.

His cultivation of a native crop by careful, planned methods that had been developed on his own land was

symbolic to her of all that was good in the new pattern of life
that was emerging in America, where old and new were
blended into one. There would always be a few unscrupulous
adventurers like Samuel Argall among the colonists, of
course, just as some chiefs, like Tacomo, were greedy, but
these weaklings on both sides were in the minority. And
Pocahontas knew without question that they were indeed
weak.

Rolfe, on the other hand, was as strong as his industry was
unflagging, and Pocahontas always shared his pride when
she stood with him and looked out at the acres of tobacco he
and the men he hired were growing. He was wise, too, and
proved it by the system he invented: each of his assistants
worked a part of the time for the colony and part for Rolfe,
but each was permitted to keep a portion of what he grew and
do what he pleased with his earnings. As a result the majority
of every shipload of newcomers clamored for the right to
work for John Rolfe, and several other gentlemen were has-
tening to copy his technique. It was freely predicted that his
method and the superior grade of tobacco he was cultivating
would make all Jamestown wealthy, and Pocahontas, who
had come to think of herself as his friend, was pleased at the
universal respect in which he was held.

It was through John, too, that she developed her most
absorbing interest, which made her forget herself for hours at
a time. John's little daughter had accompanied him on a visit
to Pocahontas's house late in the summer. The lonely young
woman and equally lonely child had been drawn to each
other from the start, and Celia now spent a portion of each
day with Pocahontas. Little girls received a sketchy education
at best, for Jamestown's two schoolmasters devoted most of
their attention to the boys, so Pocahontas undertook to help
Celia and in the process filled the the gaps in her own
learning. They read, wrote, and did sums together, and with
occasional advice from lady Delaware, who thought of
Pocahontas as her protégée, they sewed, groped their way

through the maze of rules that guided the conduct of ladies, and sang together to the accompaniment of the lute they were both learning to play.

Pocahontas did not confine her efforts to the requirements of English schooling, however, and dipped freely into her own background to give the little girl a unique understanding of Indian customs. The other children of Jamestown came to envy Celia's ability to catch fish in the James River with her bare hands, to converse fluently and fearlessly in local dialects with the natives who came to the settlement, and to sit cross-legged, erect, and motionless for long periods without growing tired.

The relationship with Celia gave Pocahontas the feeling she was performing a useful function, and even in those moments late at night when despair suddenly welled up in her and she wondered whether she would ever be anything other than a pawn in the transactions between the colonists and the Chickahominy, she knew that Celia depended on her. Thirstily accepting the child's trust and affection, she poured out her own love in return, and the afternoons, which they usually spent together, were always the brightest part of her day.

Early one evening in late January they sat together on the floor of Pocahontas's drawing room, taking turns experimentally picking out the tune of a madrigal by John Bull on the strings of a lute and compensating for their mistakes by singing merrily whenever they struck the wrong note. They were so absorbed in what they were doing that they failed to hear John tap at the front door; he heard their voices and, entering unbidden, stood in the doorframe and watched them.

Pocahontas's ability to achieve the unexpected never failed to startle him, and he was sometimes awed, sometimes amused by her seemingly unlimited capacity for accepting what pleased her in English culture while retaining some of her Indian habits. Her simple dress of soft green wool was correct attire for a lady, and her hair, drawn back in a soft bun at the nape of her neck, was in the style favored by young matrons. Yet she sat cross-legged and was completely comfortable; what amazed him was that in spite of her voluminous, floor-length skirt she managed to look graceful. Incongruously she wore a wide, cuff-shaped deerskin bracelet on each wrist, and a cluster of wild red snowberries was tucked, Indian-style, into the belt of her dress too. To John she represented all that was best in both the New World and the Old, and having come here today for a specific purpose, he felt the palms of his hands become moist and clammy.

Celia, whose long, pale blue dress was brightened by a white, lace-edged collar and apron, seemed to be conscious of a bunch of snowberries in her hair, for she repeatedly touched them with her fingertips as she sang, and her father realized from their neat, firm arrangement that Pocahontas had adorned her with them so they would look alike. They were, he thought, as intimate as a mother and daughter; to his annoyance a lump formed in his throat, and he coughed.

Pocahontas stopped playing, smiled, and rose effortlessly from the floor in a single graceful movement. Celia remained seated, however, and, folding her hands across her chest, she gazed solemnly at the man in the entrance. "The daughter of John Rolfe," she said in the language of the Chickahominy, "greets her father." Her accent and intonation were faultless.

"I'm afraid," Pocahontas said with a laugh, "that we neglected our grammar lesson today."

"When I grow up," the child declared excitedly, scrambling to her feet, "I'm going to be a Chickahominy princess, just like Pocahontas."

"There's nothing that would make me happier," her father told her, kissing her and then bending over Pocahontas's hand. "I hope," he added over Celia's head, "that she didn't wear out her welcome this afternoon."

"That would be impossible," Pocahontas told him firmly. "Besides, we had almost no time to ourselves today."

"The Reverend Buck was here," Celia added. "And do you know what he said? He said that Pocahontas is the best Christian he knows."

Pocahontas was embarrassed and looked down at the floor. "The Reverend Buck and I have been discussing the possibility of my joining the church," she murmured.

John gazed at her steadily, flushed, and turned to his daughter. "Celia, put on your coat and go out to play. There's ice on the pond, and as I came here I saw several of the children skating on it."

There were times when the child did not accept his authority as final. "May I?" she asked Pocahontas, and darted off only when she received an approving nod.

The adults sat down sedately in chairs of polished oak but did not speak to each other until the little girl's bearskin coat had been fastened and she had left the house. Then John, trying not to drum on the arm of his car, peered intently at his hostess. "It's none of my business, of course, but are you seriously thinking of joining the church?"

"I have no choice. I've accepted God, I've come to believe in Him, so my membership in the English church is just a formality. And it is your business, John, because you're partly responsible for my conviction. Until I came to know you I didn't think any man really tried to live according to the Ten Commandments and the Golden Rule."

"You make me sound like a much better person than I am." If she thought so highly of him, he told himself, there was a good chance she would accept him.

Pocahontas saw he was ill at ease and, not understanding the reason, assumed her frankness had made him feel shy. "The Reverend Buck," she said hurriedly, changing the subject, "advised me to take a new name when I'm baptized. I've given it a great deal of thought and I've decided to call myself Rebecca. I've often thought it was wonderful how the first Rebecca kept her faith in God at the time her sons were fighting against each other and a lesser woman would have wavered. I came to have faith while the Chickahominy and the English were at war. I love both of them, so it seems to me the name has meaning."

John did not reply for a long moment; her sincerity was obvious and touching, but he wondered if she realized the full extent of her commitment. "I'm not trying to dissuade you, but have you thought of all it will mean if you join the church?"

"I don't think I understand."

"Someday your captivity will end. As you've heard, your father is constantly putting pressure on the governor and the Council to set you free." He took a deep breath and discovered he was perspiring. "When that time comes, and it will, you'll probably want to return to the Chickahominy. Their way of life is built on a belief in many gods, whom you now propose to reject. If you should go back someday, would you be happy as the only Christian among heathen?"

She smiled wistfully, but without self-pity. "I no longer think in terms of happiness."

Apparently she was unaware of her vitality and beauty, and John had to struggle to keep his seat. But it was important that the issues that confronted her be made clear to her, and it would be unfair to inject a personal element in the situation until both of them knew the principles on which she stood. "Would it be possible for you to live among the Chickahominy again? And would they accept you?"

Her uncertainty was reflected in her eyes, but his questions did not surprise her. She had devoted countless hours to just this puzzle and she didn't know the answers. "I often feel that I'm lost between two worlds and that I belong to neither," she said. "Some mornings when I awaken I'm so confused that I can't remember whether I'm here or in my father's town. English luxuries have made me soft, but I suppose I could go back to my own hut. Yet I couldn't do it unless I took some books with me, many books. And after I'd finished them, I'd want to read others."

"What you're saying, in effect, is that you couldn't go back." He tried to hide his sudden exuberance.

"No, you exaggerate." Pocahontas corrected him gently without losing patience. "I must admit it would be difficult to become the meek daughter of the Chickahominy once more and to hide my thoughts from the elders and great warriors who do not believe it is right for a woman to hold opinions of her own. But your people do not accept me either, you know. Often when I walk through the streets of the town I see them stare at me and hear them whisper. I am an outsider, and they will never forget it, just as the Chickahominy won't forgive me for adopting so many of the customs of the settlers."

The colonists stared at her and talked about her, John reflected, because she was lovely, and for no other reason. "There is a way," he said, his mouth and throat dry, "to make certain that Jamestown will accept you without reservation."

Ordinarily Pocahontas would have understood the hint at once, but her usual sensitivity was dulled by her concentration on her attempt to explain a complex situation. "I don't worry any more over the warmth of my welcome, either here or in my father's land. If I am to be denied happiness, I know I have found peace through my faith in God. And that is why I have accepted the Reverend Buck's invitation to join the church. It would please me very much if Celia could attend my baptism. You, too, naturally. I told the Reverend Buck that I want no public ceremony, so the only other people who will be there will be Lord and Lady Delaware."

"We'll come. And thank you. I suppose you've heard that the governor has been summoned to London to report in person to the King on the colony's progress?"

"So Lady Delaware has told me. She says they'll be gone for at least a year. That's one reason I'm anxious to have the rites performed soon, before they sail."

John realized he had missed several opportunities to bring up the matter that was foremost on his mind and, angrily calling himself a coward, he resolved not to procrastinate any longer. "There's another ceremony that might be performed before they leave too."

Pocahontas looked at him blankly.

He stood before her. "I want you to become my wife," he said, his voice sounding strained and tinny in his own ears. "Looking back, I'm sure it's all I've wanted since the first time I saw you in the village of the Potomac."

A wave of sympathy for him washed over Pocahontas. Some men could find contentment as bachelors, but John needed a wife, just as Celia needed a mother. "You have paid me the greatest compliment I've ever received," she said.

"You've demonstrated your feeling for my daughter so often that I could appeal to you and ask you to marry me for her sake, but that would be unfair to all of us. A marriage can succeed only on a basis of love. And I love you."

Pocahontas hesitated, not because she was undecided, but in order to spare him unnecessary pain if she could. "That's why I can't accept, John. I don't love you. I've never known any man with your qualities and I'm sure I'll never find another. But long before I met you, I gave my heart to someone else."

"Your romance with Smith is dead," he declared bluntly, "and can't come to life again."

"You may be right," she replied evenly. "But that doesn't change my feeling. I wish I'd known you first. I'm sure I would have loved you. But I didn't, and wishing won't change what is in the past."

She would be shocked, he thought, if he told her she was being as stubbornly fatalistic as the most ignorant savage in the wilderness. "I can't and won't accept either that point of view or your decision."

"You must." She hadn't allowed herself to think of Smith for many months and she was surprised that she could discuss him so calmly. "I don't imagine I'll ever see him again. But I'll always love him, and that's why I can't marry anyone else, ever, not even you."

July, 1612

A bumper tobacco harvest assured Jamestown of unprecedented prosperity, and the colony rejoiced when, after the precious leaves were cured, the crop was packed in the holds of a large fleet of merchant vessels sent to Virginia for the express purpose of transporting the cargo to England. John Rolfe, who was primarily responsible for the success, was the hero of the town, and even the military men, who usually showed open contempt for planters, merchants, and other ordinary mortals whom they believed less virile than themselves, congratulated him warmly. He accepted his unaccustomed role gracefully, but his pleasure seemed strictly limited, and many of his fellow settlers expressed the opinion that he appeared to be preoccupied.

They were right: something urgent was on his mind. He had pressed his suit for Pocahontas's hand vigorously and without interruption through the winter, spring, and early summer, and although she insisted she would not change her mind and marry him, he thought he detected signs that she was weakening. Lady Delaware, who had guessed his intentions, had become his ally, and just before leaving for London had told him not to lose heart no matter how discouraged he might become. As Pocahontas was a woman, her ladyship had said, no decision she might make was necessarily irrevocable.

A turning point had been reached early in June, John knew, and he was sure Pocahontas had realized it too. A crisis had occurred when he had been spending virtually all of his time in the tobacco fields and had been too busy to leave his crops. Celia had fallen ill of the swamp fever that so often swept through the colony and in her delirium had called for Pocahontas, who had gone to the child and, ignoring the risks to her own health, had remained in the same room with the little patient for eleven days and nights. Only after Celia recovered had she moved back to her own house, and the little girl, of course, had begged to be allowed to accompany her and was heartbroken when her request had been refused by her father. The experience had shaken Pocahontas, and since that time her refusal of John's repeated proposals had become less certain.

He felt sure he was wearing down her resistance when she unexpectedly invited him to supper one evening in late July, during a period when he was busily engaged in supervising the storing of the tobacco in the barks and conferring with the ships' captains. Pocahontas had taken pains to tell him she simply wanted to see that he ate properly, for she knew he was working so hard that food meant nothing to him, but he thought there was some justification for believing that this excuse was merely a typical feminine rationalization and that perhaps she didn't really know her own mind.

When he arrived at her house his hopes surged, for he saw he was her only guest, and he had to control an impulse to shout for joy as he followed her into the drawing room. Pocahontas offered him a cup of sack before supper and, drinking it gratefully, he complimented her on her simple, lilac-colored dress. Other women dressed extravagantly in dazzling clothes, yet, as he so frequently told himself, none of them could match her beauty.

She was aware of his admiration and enjoyed it, but she knew that if she failed to introduce a safe topic of conversation quickly, he would embarrass her by proposing to her again. "I hope you won't mind, but I've done something without asking your approval first," she said. "I've promised to take Celia on a picnic in the forest tomorrow."

"Anything you decide regarding Celia is in her best interest and doesn't need my approval."

The warmth in his voice and the expression in his eyes made her uncomfortable, so she pretended to be obtuse. "I thought you might be afraid she wouldn't be safe in the forest."

John laughed and shook his head. "She's safe anywhere, provided she's with you. As a matter of fact, I'm planning to build a new house right on the edge of the wilderness. I want to be closer to my plantation, and it's inconvenient to come all the way back into town every night. So Celia will be living in the forest."

"And I was concerned about a picnic!" Pocahontas thought he was taking unnecessary risks for his daughter and himself and could not help but feel concerned. "Suppose there should be a new war with the Chickahominy. A home beyond the town walls would be very vulnerable."

He looked secretly amused. "There will be no war," he said flatly, smiling in a superior masculine way.

Pocahontas was unable to share his humor and felt irritated. "Do you understand the mind of the Chickahominy better than I do?" She spoke more sharply than she had intended.

"Certainly not," John retorted, "but I can't imagine that Powhatan would attack his son-in-law's house under any circumstances. Nor is it conceivable that he'd declare war against his daughter's adopted nation."

"That isn't fair. You're trying to maneuver me into agreeing to marry you so there will be permanent peace."

"Fair or not," he said, looking at her steadily, "I intend to use every argument at my disposal."

"You make it very difficult for me to refuse, John."

"So much the better. I love you and I won't rest until you become my wife."

Pocahontas sighed and gazed out the window at the delicate branches of a young evergreen. John's gentle, unremitting pressure was far more effective than bluster or force would have been in influencing her, and she felt strongly tempted to give in to him. At no time had he touched her, much less tried to make love to her, so she had no legitimate cause for resentment against him and was almost sorry he hadn't resorted to some physical demonstrations of his affection so she could dislike him. His quiet, persistent tactics robbed her of her natural, feminine weapons and left her helpless, and as he made it so clear to her that he expected her to accept him sooner or later, she had found it increasingly difficult to resist his pleas.

In one sense, she told herself, it would be a relief to become Mistress Rolfe, as she would never again feel uncertainty over the future. And she had to concede that she had learned to love Celia as dearly as though the little girl were her own child. But she could not bring herself to love John himself, and her lack of response to him was a serious obstacle to marriage. Again and again she had reminded herself that there was no valid reason for her failure to develop a romantic regard for him; she admired and respected him, she trusted him implicitly, and she realized, too, that he was unusually attractive in an unobtrusively masculine way.

So her inability to love him was illogical, even stupid, and had it been possible she would have created a desire for him. But she kept remembering the sense of physical excitement that had enveloped her when she had fallen in love with

Smith. She had become aroused every time she had looked at him or heard his voice, and although she knew she had been immature and inexperienced, their relationship had been unique. She and Smith might be separated, but she continued to cherish the memory of what they had once shared.

Of course she was a woman now, not a girl, and she tried to convince herself that she was wrong to insist she would not marry again unless the man who would become her husband made her feel giddy and reckless, indifferent to everything on earth but his nearness to her. She had shared a rare ecstasy with Smith and she knew it was too much to expect that someone else could lift her to the same heights of passion. According to all she had read in the works of such poets as Donne and Fletcher, few women were privileged to love a man as she had loved Smith; whether he had loved her in the same way was irrelevant and confusing.

Her duty now was to weigh the possibility of remarriage, and she was convinced that if she became the wife of someone else she would be dishonest. Difficult though it was to admit to herself, Smith's hold over her was undiminished in spite of his crude rejection of her. Love wasn't reasonable she had discovered, and if some miracle were to occur at this very moment, bringing her face to face with Smith, she was certain she would succumb again to his magnetic appeal. It was shameful to feel so deeply about a brutal man who deserved no sympathy, and she supposed she was confessing that she was a weak woman, but it was far better to face the truth than to hurt someone else too.

John was saying something, and Pocahontas smiled apologetically. "I'm sorry," she said, "but I'm afraid my mind has been wandering."

The vanity of a less perceptive man would have been wounded, but John seemed to understand. "It wasn't important," he replied cheerfully, and finished his sack.

"When are you going to build your new house?" she asked

contritely, simulating an interest to make amends for her inattention.

"I'll start before we leave, and the work will be finished by the time we return."

Pocahontas had no idea what he meant and looked at him blankly.

"As I was saying just now, it will be necessary for me to make a voyage to London early next year. The tobacco crop next summer should be at least three times the size of the current yield, so I want to arrange new terms with the Company's directors. Too large a share of the profit is going to the investors in England, and too little is being kept by the men who are doing the actual work here."

She thought of all a trip to England could mean, and a vein in the side of her neck began to throb. "I see." The remark was meaningless, but she couldn't trust herself to say more.

John, concentrating for the moment on business, had no idea what was going through her mind. "A conflict with the investors has been inevitable and it will become still greater as our production increases, but I'm prepared to give the directors a real battle."

"I'm sure you are." Pocahontas's mouth was dry and she swallowed painfully. "Do I gather that you intend to take Celia to England with you?"

"Of course. And I want to take my bride too." He placed his mug on the table, rose, and stood directly in front of her. He was smiling, but his eyes were solemn and challenging, and he seemed to be demanding a final decision immediately.

"There are some things I think you should know," Pocahontas forced herself to say.

"I already know all that's necessary," John replied firmly. "I know I love you. I also know that you don't yet love me. You've made that plain enough to me, and I understand your reasons. But there's no need to bring the shadow of someone else between us, now or ever. I'll grant you that I may be overconfident, but I'm sure I can help you to forget him."

He was wrong, she thought fiercely, and she was being dishonest by remaining silent, but it would be cruel to disillusion him. He raised her to her feet, and as he gripped her arms she began to tremble violently. "All right, John," she said in a barely audible voice, "I'll marry you."

He bent his head to kiss her, and Pocahontas closed her eyes, realizing as she did that this moment, which should have been significant, meant nothing to her. She knew John was embracing her, of course, but in spite of her desperate efforts to respond to him she remained cold in his arms. Reality was not here but in London, where she would meet Smith again.

Holidays were rare in Jamestown, and the settlers, struggling to establish a foothold on a new continent, usually took time to observe only Christmas, the birthday of King James, and the Festival of July 29, the anniversary of the final defeat of the Spanish Armada by Queen Elizabeth's sea captains in 1588. So the spontaneous celebration that followed the wedding of Pocahontas of the Chickahominy to John Rolfe was as unusual as it was joyous. So many people clamored for admission to the little church that the Reverend Richard Buck, who was trying to be fair to all, ruled that no one but Council members and their wives could witness the ceremony. Stretching his authority to the limit at the last minute, he made an exception and granted admission to the bride's brother, Opachisco, and a delegation of senior Chickahominy warriors, even though heathens were usually barred from the church edifice. Few people realized that the wedding created serious problems for the clergyman, who had searched his soul for a long time before consenting to officiate and had agreed at last on the grounds that, although Pocahontas had been married previously and consequently was not entitled to participate in a church ceremony, her

union with Smith had been pagan, not Christian, and therefore did not count.

The service, at the request of both the bride and groom,
was short and simple, which disappointed those who enjoyed
the usual complicated ritual that ordinarily lasted for more
than two hours. The Reverend Buck's sermon was brief, too,
and in it he stressed the theme that those who deserved
happiness always received their just reward. He tactfully
refrained from mentioning the obvious fact that the marriage
was a blessing to the whole colony because it virtually eliminated all possibility of a future war between the Naturals and
the English.

The bride's only attendant was her little stepdaughter, and
they were dressed in almost identical gowns of pale pink silk,
with white lace collars that lay open at their throats. Celia
enjoyed every moment of the excitement but stared in wonder at the wives of the Council members, who found their
pleasure in their own way by weeping copiously. Pocahontas, at her own request, was married under the name of
Rebecca and seemed to be the most composed person in the
church, making her responses to the minister in a soft but
clear voice. John looked pale beneath his tan, but he spoke
firmly, and his hand was steady when he placed a plain gold
band on his bride's finger.

Virtually the entire population of the settlement was
gathered outside the church, and when the wedding party
adjourned to the parade ground for a Chickahominy ceremony following the Church of England service, all Jamestown followed to watch the unusual heathen ritual. Chief
Powhatan had sent word that he would recognize the marriage only if the ancient customs of his people were observed,
and although Pocahontas had wanted to refuse on the
grounds that she was now a Christian, the Council had
prevailed upon her to give in to her father's desires. According to Chickahominy tradition, she was a widow rather than
a divorced woman, so she gave herself to John in the brief

rites; meanwhile her brother, who stood near to make sure
the proper forms were observed, intoned a song of propitia-
tion to Ek, Ris and Ti-Ba.

Pocahontas and John then disappeared for a moment into
a tent of skins the warriors had erected in the center of the
parade ground, and when they emerged Celia ran to them,
destroying the solemnity of the occasion. This was the signal
for the start of the celebration, and everyone cheered when
kegs of ale were rolled onto the field. Toasts were drunk, and
those who wanted something stronger tapped pipes of wine,
leaving the more sober element to build fires for the roasting
of venison, boar, and wild turkey. The children were drawn
to the tent, in which they played happily, the ale kegs proved
to be an equally strong magnet for the adults, English and
Chickahominy alike, and everyone settled down for a long,
festive evening. Powhatan's warriors, who had kept their
distance from the colonists, now mingled freely with their
hosts, and countless cups were raised to the new era of lasting
peace.

The bride and groom were surrounded by people who
thrust ale and wine at them, but Pocahontas, who did not like
the taste of spirits, begged to be excused and at the first
opportunity she slipped away from the throng. She had not
exchanged any words in private with her brother since his
arrival the previous day and she searched for him now,
finding him at last near the tent, where he stood drinking
with three boisterous members of the Council. Opachisco,
who had always been sensitive to her moods, glanced at her
and broke away from the English abruptly.

Pocahontas did not speak until they walked to the far side
of the parade ground, away from the crowds, and faced each
other. Something was troubling her, and she made no attempt to hide her concern. "Why," she asked, "did the Chief
of Chiefs send his son in his place? Why does he stay in his
own lodge?"

Opachisco reached out and touched her white lawn cap,

which curved away from a deep, heart-shaped point in the center of her forehead. Then he stared at her hair, which was drawn to the back of her head and hung in long curls. "The mighty Powhatan grieves because his daughter is his daughter no more. If the squaw of Rolfe will look at herself in the water, she will see she has become like one of the foreigners-from-across-the-sea."

She was not surprised and drew Opachisco's attention to two white ribbons sewn down the length of her unpadded sleeves. The strips were embroidered with pink rosebuds and green leaves, the Chickahominy symbols for the beginning of a new life. Had the marriage taken place in Powhatan's home, the bride would have worn a headband of live rosebuds and leaves. "The daughter of Powhatan," Pocahontas said, "is his daughter still. She does not forget her father or her people."

In a meeting of tribal elders Opachisco could look impassive in the approved fashion, even when he was disturbed. But he was unable to cope with a woman whose arguments he could not answer, and he wiped his brow. "The daughter of Powhatan," he said ponderously, "brought great sadness to herself and her people when she married Smith. Then she was made free again, and many chiefs wanted her. If she had become the squaw of a chief, there would have been friendship between his nation and the Chickahominy. It is not good when the daughter of Powhatan forgets her duty."

Pocahontas, who had become accustomed to expressing herself freely, could not control her irritation. "I have not forgotten my duty!" she declared emphatically. "The English are a large tribe, much larger than all the nations that hail Powhatan as the Chief of Chiefs."

Opachisco couldn't quite accept such a sweeping claim, but even if she wasn't exaggerating, she had missed the point. "It may be that what the sister of Opachisco says is true," he declared politely. "But Rolfe is not the chief of the English." He gazed at her sternly.

In spite of her anxiety to make him understand her position and her motives, she had to smile. "That does not
matter. There will be peace now between the Chickahominy
and the English."

"That is so," Opachisco conceded grudgingly, fingering
the hilt of his knife, which protruded from the top of his
loincloth. "But if the daughter of Powhatan had not married
Rolfe, the warriors of the Chickahominy would have stolen
into this town in the night and would have carried her to the
lodge of her father. Then the warriors would have driven all
the English into the sea."

"But now," Pocahontas replied patiently, "the Chickahominy will be given many fire-sticks and much cloth that
the English wear." She ran her hand down her skirt to
emphasize the glossy texture of the material.

Opachisco had to admit there were obvious advantages in
the present arrangements, but more was involved in his
sister's marriage than a mere trade treaty. A discussion of
personal matters always embarrassed him, but she was being
so stubborn that he was forced to speak bluntly. "The warriors of the English are not like the warriors of the Chickahominy."

"That is so." She eyed him warily, then inclined her head,
and her curls bobbed up and down.

"The squaws of a Chickahominy live in his lodge until he
joins his ancestors. But the English are different. They take
only one squaw at a time. That is why an English warrior
grows tired of a squaw very quickly and wants another."

Pocahontas knew he was leading up to a point and that it
was inexcusably rude for a woman to interrupt when a man
was speaking, but she felt compelled to protest. "Oh no!" He
looked shocked, but she insisted on saying what was on her
mind. "English warriors stay married to their squaws until
both go to join their ancestors."

He glared at her contemptuously and held up his hand to
silence her. "Smith was married to the daughter of Powhatan. But he quickly grew tired of her and left her."

Unable to meet his eyes, she studied the ground and nodded almost imperceptibly.

"Soon Rolfe will become tired of her too. Then what will happen to her? The Chief of Chiefs weeps in his heart because she will be sent back to the Chickahominy. And no other warrior will want a squaw who has made the love rites with two braves."

"I will not be sent back to the lodge of my father," Pocahontas said quietly.

"When Rolfe sends you away from his lodge you will become the squaw of still another English warrior?" Horrified, Opachisco gaped at her.

"Rolfe will not send me away from his lodge," she replied, knowing she spoke the truth. "Rolfe is not like Smith."

Although Opachisco had taken only two squaws and a Chocktaw concubine and therefore was relatively inexperienced, he realized a woman always thought her man was superior to all others and deliberately closed her mind to his shortcomings. That left him only one argument if he hoped to persuade her to return to the land of the Chickahominy with him now, before the marriage was consummated. As long as there was a chance that she might rectify her error while she could, it was his duty to use every weapon at his disposal. "Then," he said slowly, "the day will come when the daughter of Powhatan will bear a child, who will be the child of Rolfe too."

Pocahontas had been unwilling to face such a possibility in her own mind, and although many Indian women who did not love their husbands raised families, she had absorbed enough of the English viewpoint to accept the belief that in a marriage of that sort it was wrong to bring a baby into the world. Her feeling for John and the problems she would face as his wife were her own, however, and she had no intention of sharing them. Certainly she could not bring herself to reveal her innermost doubts to her brother, who might be sympathetic but whose first loyalty was to his father and to the

nation he would someday lead. So she hid her fears and her
discomfort behind a stiff mask, and if her expression did not
match her charmingly frivolous gown and cap, she was
unaware of it.

"Warriors," she said calmly, "bring meat to their lodges.
Squaws cook it and feed it to their children."

Opachisco, who had always been proud of her agile mind,
knew she was being intentionally obtuse. "Will the children
of Rolfe and Pocahontas be English or Chickahominy?" he
demanded, raising his voice angrily. "Will they walk with
their heads high, like those who are descended from Ek, the
all-powerful, or will their shoulders droop like those of the
braves and squaws of Jamestown?"

He plainly thought he had scored, but Pocahontas gave
him no opportunity to enjoy his triumph. "Wait for me," she
said, and lifting her skirts, a gesture that was distressingly
alien to him, she ran across the parade ground.

Celia was playing with several other little girls outside the
tent, but she darted away from her friends when she heard
Pocahontas call to her, and they walked back to Opachisco
together, hand in hand. The child drank in every detail of the
tall, painted warrior's appearance, and although he scowled
at her, unable to understand why she had been brought
before him, she showed no fear.

Pocahontas was careful to address her stepdaughter in the
language of the Chickahominy. "Opachisco," she said, "is
the son of the great Chief of Chiefs, Powhatan. When
Powhatan joins his ancestor, Ek, Opachisco will become the
Chief of Chiefs."

Celia nodded her blond head, and her blue eyes were
bright; she knew what was expected of her and was eager to
show off her knowledge. Folding her hands across her narrow
chest, she sat without the need to steady herself, ending in a
cross-legged position, and touched her forehead to the
ground. "Celia, the daughter of Pocahontas, greets her
mighty uncle," she said in a high, thin voice. "She begs him

to speak to her so she may remember the honor all of her days."

Opachisco was so startled he replied mechanically, without thinking. "Opachisco, who has won fifteen feathers in battle against the enemies of his people, greets the daughter of Pocahontas and orders her to rise so he may see the face of a squaw-child on whom Ek has smiled by day and Ris has smiled by night."

Celia, who had played countless similar games with Pocahontas, jumped to her feet and embraced him. Opachisco fondled her silently for a moment and tousled her hair affectionately, then he cleared his throat, and although he spoke to the child, he looked straight at the young woman who was watching them. "The son of Powhatan will tell the Chief of Chiefs he has met Celia," he said, the tense lines disappearing from the corners of his eyes. "Powhatan will thank the gods and will offer them fat corn and goats. The warriors and squaws of the Chickahominy will sing the praises of Celia, and their children and children's children after them will remember the words. The whole nation will be happy because Pocahontas is a true daughter of the Chickahominy, and Celia is the daughter of Pocahontas."

Gently disentangling himself from the little girl's grasp, he turned away brusquely and walked off, stiff-legged, to rejoin the gentlemen of the Council for another mug of ale. Pocahontas, taking Celia's hand again, strolled slowly across the field and told herself she had won her first victory as Mistress Rolfe. Opachisco had given his approval of the marriage, and when he reported to his father, Powhatan would send his blessings too. It was good to know that the Chief of Chiefs would realize that his daughter had not renounced her people, abandoned her heritage, or rejected the ideals that made Chickahominy life worth living. Someday, Pocahontas thought, she would return to her childhood home for a visit, taking Celia with her, and Powhatan would surely welcome her with all the love he felt for her, even though she had acquired the surface manners and appearance of the foreigners.

A more immediate test awaited the bride, however, and could not be postponed. Shortly after sundown the children were taken off to their homes and put to bed while the adults ate; then, when the feast was finished, the storehouses were opened and men fought for the privilege of carrying fresh barrels of ale and thick pipes of wine to the parade ground. Everyone seemed to be talking and laughing simultaneously, and John, who had seen little of his bride during the festivities, pushed his way to her side through the rowdy crowd. They made an attempt to leave without calling attention to themselves but were unsuccessful, and a group of thirty or forty celebrants escorted them to John's house, lustily singing songs that were traditional on such occasions. Some had been composed in the time of Henry VII and a few were even older, but regardless of their age their meaning was graphically clear even to an embarrassed young woman who did not understand the slang of a bygone age.

The serenaders did not leave until John had obeyed the custom of kissing his bride and carrying her into the house. Then John closed the door, the crowd dispersed, and Pocahontas was alone with her husband. She tried to smile at him, and as they walked together up the stairs, she could hear the sounds of undiminished revelry through the open windows. Jamestown, truly secure for the first time in its short history, could now look forward to an uninterrupted, prosperous future, and the party would continue all night. But Pocahontas, suddenly chilly in spite of the warm, humid summer air drifting in through the thin cotton curtains, was conscious only of the man who had followed her into the master bedchamber on the second floor. They had known each other for many months, they had spent countless hours together, but at this moment John Rolfe was a complete stranger to her.

He had anticipated her distress and, recognizing it at once,

tried to put her at her ease by chatting about inconsequen-
tials. But she was tongue-tied and, totally unable to make
small talk, sat in a straight-backed chair near the window and
stared at a small formal tapestry of a pastoral scene on the
whitewashed wall opposite her. The first thing she had
noticed when she entered the room was the absence of heavy
curtains around the bed. She knew John always slept behind
such folds, for they had once discussed the subject on the
grounds of what was healthy and what was not. So she knew
he had removed the thick drapes out of consideration for her
habits and she wanted to thank him for his kindness. But the
enforced intimacy gave a new meaning to the simplest
thoughts, and she gave up the effort, unable to express her
gratitude.

John showed extraordinary patience, and after his futile
conversational sallies had fallen on barren ground he offered
her something to eat and drink, even though they had come
away from the feast only an hour earlier and he knew she
disliked spirits. Pocahontas declined with stiff nods and,
realizing she was being unfair to him and increasing his
burden, she wished the earth would open and that she could
disappear into it. She had never felt reluctance when Smith
had made love to her, and while she knew this was no time to
think of him, she could not help but recall that their union
had always been spontaneous and natural.

She could not give herself to John without reservation, and
as a flush of panic swept over her she wondered whether she
could keep him at a distance for a few days, perhaps a few
weeks, until she became accustomed to his nearness. The
idea was absurd, of course, yet she could not help consider-
ing it for a moment. Then, gaining self-control, she told
herself sternly that she was behaving like a foolish girl; she
had known from the instant she had accepted John's proposal
that the hour would come when he would claim his
privileges as a husband. She had accepted the obligations of
marriage freely and she had no right to refuse him.

Nevertheless, it would have been so much easier to tolerate his advances if Opachisco had not mentioned the possibility that she would someday become the mother of John's baby. Perhaps she should have weighed the consequences of marriage long before now, but until today she had not permitted herself to dwell on the subject. And worst of all, she had to admit to herself that she had no desire to bear his child; it seemed wrong to carry an infant that was not Smith's.

Her relationship with Celia was a thing apart, of course, for Celia was a person in her own right, and it would be criminal to deny her the guidance and companionship she needed. Loving Celia was no problem, but Pocahontas told herself it would be a mockery of all she and Smith had ever meant to each other to give John a baby. Shivering slightly, she stood and moved to the window, rubbing her arms. Her fingers touched the embroidery on her sleeves that symbolized a fertile future, and she had to struggle to hold back the tears that welled up in her eyes.

John, who had been watching her with quiet patience, came up behind her, put his hands on her shoulders, and turned her around. "Do you remember something you were reading just the other day in the King's new version of the Bible?" he asked her gently. "It was in Ecclesiastes, I believe."

Pocahontas knew the chapter to which he referred and nodded. "Yes, it was Ecclesiastes: *To every thing there is a season, and a time to every purpose under the heaven . . .*"

He took a handkerchief from his sleeve and handed it to her so she could dab her damp eyes. "If I remember correctly, it says there is: *A time to weep, and a time to laugh; a time to mourn, and a time to dance . . .*"

Soothed, she managed to smile faintly as she returned the handkerchief to him. "You're very patient, John. I don't deserve such a considerate husband."

He stood close to her, and although he did not raise his voice, his tone was firm. "Ecclesiastes mentions the right

time for many things. You'll recall that among others he tells
us there's *A time to love.*"

They looked at each other, and as Pocahontas met her
husband's gaze she knew she could procrastinate no longer.
She realized, too, that in her confusion she had been mistaken: she had no real desire to deny him. On the contrary,
she wanted to make him happy. He had found little contentment in life, but it was in her power to give him satisfaction and inner peace. That was her function as his wife, and
she had accepted the role in the full knowledge of all that
would be required of her. Strangely, her recognition of what
she had been unwilling to see, that his future depended on
her, gave her a new sense of completion too. He needed her,
and she would not fail him.

She unpinned her cap, reached around to the back of her
dress, and struggled briefly with the intricate arrangement of
buttons and hooks. Letting the gown slide to the floor, she
continued to undress slowly and with dignity, never taking
her eyes from John's face. When he embraced her she slid
her arms around his neck and returned his kiss with a tender-
ness and compassion that came from the depth of her being.
Her moment of weakness was gone, and she did not shrink
from his caresses when he carried her to the bed; she was his
wife and she rejoiced that she had rediscovered the core of
her strength.

Later she dropped off to sleep, and John, lying quietly at
her side, thought she looked like a child, trusting and defenseless. He knew it had been difficult for her to accept him
as a lover, but eventually she had responded to his ardor, and
he was convinced that in time she would learn to love him as
he loved her. As he watched her she stirred and muttered
something in her sleep, and he leaned closer to her.

"John," she said.

It occurred to him that Captain Smith's Christian name
was John, too, and for the first time his self-confidence
wavered.

May, 1613

Pocahontas stood on the deck of the bark *Seraph* near
the prow, staring dreamily at the green-gray sea. The steady
breeze that filled the six sails of the vessel cut through the
wool of her billowing cloak, and she absently drew the folds
of the cape more closely around her. Spring was in the air,
but a trace of winter lingered in the wind, a reminder of the
far-off world of Virginia. The one-hundred-and-fifty-ton
ship had been Pocahontas's home for almost four months,
and all through the long voyage she had felt suspended in
space, unable to shake off the sensation that the trip to
England was unreal and that she was actually somewhere
else.

The departure from Jamestown, strangely, had left her
unmoved, in part because she had been busy unpacking
Celia's belongings and tending to her stepdaughter's needs in
the tiny cabin the Rolfe family shared. But even more important, she had suffered no sense of loss while she could still
look out at the familiar terrain of the land in which she had

been born. The trees, stretching out on both sides of the
James River, were part of her heritage and held no secrets
from her; she knew the hills and the placid waters of the river
and the bay, and wherever she might go in America she
would be recognized and accepted.

Then, when the *Seraph* had reached the open sea and the
American shore line had slowly faded and merged with the
horizon, the realization had dawned on her that she, whose
position in Jamestown was as secure as her place in the land
of the Chickahominy, would soon be an alien in a remote
foreign country. In spite of all she had read, she could not
draw a clear picture of England in her mind, and it had not
helped to know that she would be the first Indian ever to set
foot on the soil of James I's kingdom.

The elements had conspired against her, too, and a storm
that had broken on the fourth day of the voyage had made her
violently ill. Never in her landlocked life had she imagined
that waves crashing down on a tiny ship could be so terrify-
ing, and she had spent a week in bed, ashamed that John had
been forced to wait on her and that Celia had been unaffected
by the pitching and rolling of the bark. But in spite of her
efforts to rouse herself, she had remained helpless until the
sea had grown calm again. Then suddenly she had felt
revitalized, and when she had come out on the deck for the
first time in days, the thought that this voyage was a dream
had been born in her. Subsequent storms had not upset her,
nor had wind and weather frightened her, and as days and
nights had blended together she had felt numb, as though
nothing could touch her.

It was easy enough but profitless to look back on the past,
and she was unable to see into the future, so she discovered it
was preferable to live only in the timeless present, where her
most pressing problems were keeping Celia's clothes clean
and trying to make the heavily salted meat and fish palatable
for John and herself. Fortunately she never grew tired of
watching the *Seraph* cut through the water, and she loved to

see the froth on the waves bubble up, seethe for a moment, and then disappear, only to start the whole process again. She was so absorbed in the game now that she failed to hear John come up behind her and became aware of his presence only when he joined her at the rail and slipped an arm around her shoulders.

"Are you warm enough?" he asked.

"I am now." Pocahontas leaned against him, grateful for his quiet strength, and wished, as she did daily, that she could love him. "I thought Celia was with you. Where is she?"

"On the quarter-deck." John grinned and shook his head. "The helmsman is giving her another lesson. If we were to spend another month at sea, I swear the crew would turn her into a sailor."

"But we won't be at sea nearly that long."

"Oh, you've heard the news?" He looked disappointed.

"I saw the captain after our breakfast this morning, and he told me we passed a fishing boat shortly after dawn. He says we should reach England very soon."

"That's right." John studied her closely and thought she had never looked lovelier than she did at this moment, with her long black hair flying loose in the breeze. "If this wind holds, we should sight land by sundown tonight, and at this time tomorrow we'll be sailing up the Thames. By the following morning, at the latest, we'll arrive in London."

"It's strange," Pocahontas mused, "but you always refer to 'London' and 'England.' You never say 'home,' the way all the other settlers do."

"That's because England isn't my home. I live in Virginia and I'm simply paying a visit to England." He continued to watch her. "I'm glad we built our new house before we left. It's good to think of it and remember how it looks while we're in London."

"Yes." Pocahontas knew how he felt, but she couldn't share his joy, so she didn't elaborate.

"You'll like buying furniture for it in England. Chairs and tables and rugs and crockery. Dozens of things."

"Only the other day the mate was telling me about prices in London," she said, taking refuge in a practical subject. "And I don't think we'll be able to afford too much."

"We'll be able to afford anything you want to buy," John replied firmly. "The Company wants my tobacco, so the directors will have to pay for it. Don't give a thought to expense."

"Thank you, dear." Pocahontas leaned her elbows on the rail and looked out at the waves again.

"Are you excited at the prospect of seeing London?" He was a coward, he thought, but couldn't mention Smith's name, even though he knew it would clear the air to bring the issue into the open.

She didn't bother to raise her head. "Not excited, really."

"How do you feel then?" he persisted.

"Curious, of course. I've read so much about the city, but I have no idea how it will feel to walk on cobbled streets or ride in a carriage. We will ride in one someday, won't we?"

John didn't intend to laugh quite so loudly. "There's no other way for a lady to travel, unless you try a sedan chair, which is terribly uncomfortable."

"I want to try everything." Pocahontas was lost in thought for a moment. "Do you suppose we'll see anyone we know while we're there?"

His heart pounded, and he gripped the rail. "Naturally," he said in the calmest tone he could achieve. "Lady Delaware's letter was extremely cordial."

"I'm looking forward to seeing her too." She raised her face and her eyes were without guile. "But I didn't really mean people we know. I was wondering whether we'll see the King and some of the great nobles."

John was so relieved that his head ached. "I dare say we'll catch a glimpse of His Majesty in St. James's Park someday. The official period of mourning for Prince Henry's death is ended, now that Charles has been given the title of Prince of

Wales, so the Queen is undoubtedly appearing in public again too." A relaxation of tension always made him garrulous, he reflected, but in spite of his anger at himself he could not stop talking. "And if you wish I can arrange to have us meet Sir Walter Raleigh as soon as he's released from the Tower."

"I'd like that." Something stirred inside her, and her lethargy began to disappear. But she didn't dare let herself think about the reasons she felt stimulated. It was enough, for the present, to know that warmth and life were flowing through her body again. "I'll enjoy everything, I'm sure."

Never in all the time he had known her had Pocahontas looked so radiant, John thought miserably, and wondered if he was making the greatest mistake of his life by taking her to England.

There was no immediate answer to his question, of course, and the last stage of the voyage dragged interminably for him as he wrestled with the insoluble problem. He would have to wait and trust in his own ability to handle whatever crisis might arise.

Then London itself added to the confusion: neither John nor his wife was even partly prepared for the reception that awaited them on their arrival. The *Seraph* docked at midnight near the Southwark shore, too late for the passengers to disembark, but several representatives of the Company came on board to inspect the cargo and took word back with them that an Indian princess had arrived in the city. Londoners, like the inhabitants of all large towns, were insatiably curious, and when John came on deck the following morning he saw scores of boats paddling around in the Thames in the vicinity of the bark and realized that hundreds of spectators lined the far bank of the river.

He arranged for transportation ashore in a small shallop manned by two oarsmen, and while he was supervising the stowing of the family gear in the boat, Pocahontas emerged from the cabin, leading Celia. Someone in one of the small

craft shouted, word was passed quickly from boat to boat, and
the spectators started to cheer. John was startled but had to
admit his wife's appearance was worth all the excitement.
Certainly London had never seen anyone quite like her.

She was hatless and wore her hair in a thick braid twisted
high over the crown of her head and low around the nape of
her neck. And she seemed to take proud cognizance of her
alien status by emphasizing rather than ignoring or belittling
it. Her simple fawn-colored dress was orthodox enough by
English standards, but the border of the skirt, which she had
embroidered to help pass the time on board the ship, was a
Chickahominy design sewn on a wide band of wool.

Her slippers of soft natural colored deerskin were unusual,
too, for the shoes of English ladies were dyed in bright
shades, and the lower classes wore only black. A finishing
touch convinced her husband that she was indulging in a
brave gesture to hide her uneasiness, for her throat and
shoulders were bare above a short, flamboyant Chickahominy cape of bright orange feathers. He could not blame
London for staring at her, and he felt a surge of great pride in
her as he gave her his arm and helped her into the shallop.

She looked in astonishment at the three- and four-story
houses crowded together in the slums of Southwark, then
transferred her gaze to the London shore, blinking at a
mammoth merchantman, a fifteen-hundred-ton carrack anchored in the river. St. Paul's Church, the solid bulk of the
Tower, and the graceful columns of Whitehall were plainly
visible in the watery morning sunlight, but Pocahontas
caught no more than a glimpse of these marvels as she looked
at the capering figures on the shore. Then the shallop drew
up in front of a flight of worn stone steps, and before she knew
what was happening she was plunged into the center of a
howling mob. Men and women raced forward, screaming
inarticulately, ogling her, jostling her, and trying to snatch
the feathers from her cape. John was forced to draw his sword
and beat at the crowd with the flat of his blade to clear a

passage for Pocahontas and Celia, but he was successful only
when the boatmen and three officers of the watch armed with
thick staves came to his aid.

Pocahontas stumbled as John half pushed, half lifted her
into a carriage and then handed Celia in to her. The woman
and the child shrank back into the center of the spacious,
cushioned seat as faces appeared at the windows and grimy,
thin fingers were pointed at them, but they were safe now, as
John had slammed the door while he arranged for the storage
of their luggage on the carriage roof. At last he joined them;
the driver urged his teams of bays forward, scattering pedestrians, and a trembling Pocahontas turned to her husband.

"I've never seen such barbarians!" she exclaimed, half in
wonder, half in indignation.

She had not yet seen the worst of London, but she observed more than enough during the quarter of an hour that
the carriage bounced through ill-paved, garbage-littered
streets. Most of the people, who stopped whatever they were
doing and stared rudely at Pocahontas, were dressed in thin,
filthy woolen suits and dresses that were little better than rags,
and the houses that lined the narrow, twisting streets were
ancient and decrepit, with incredibly few windows placed in
their sagging walls. Guards armed with pikes stood outside a
high iron fence around a brewhouse to prevent raids on the
establishment, heavily painted females who could have been
no more than thirteen or fourteen years old gestured coarsely
to John and called crude taunts to Pocahontas, and youths
old enough to know better threw stones and rotten vegetables
at the carriage for no apparent reason other than to vent their
ire on people in more comfortable circumstances.

Street venders were everywhere, carrying trays, pushing
carts, riding on small wagons pulled by feeble horses, and the
variety of merchandise they were selling was remarkable.
Some offered thick, irregularly shaped loaves of barley or rye
bread for a penny, others sold rancid-looking butter at five-
pence per pound, and some were seeking customers for beef

at twopence per pound. Venders were offering clothing and candy and weapons, amulets to ward off disease, and love philters, bric-a-brac, and even furniture. Many of the items, John explained calmly, had been stolen, and it was not unusual for someone whose house had been robbed to go out into the streets the following day and buy back his own property.

At one point a street barricade had been erected by a large, rowdy group of young men in stocking caps which identified them as inhabitants of Whitefriars, the most depraved part of the city, where even the most vicious criminals were traditionally granted the right of sanctuary. The toughs were demanding tribute from all who hoped to pass, and while John sorted through his money, Pocahontas, revolted by the savagery, reached hastily into the purse at her waist and drew out several coins. She was about to throw them out of the window her husband had just opened, but he caught hold of her wrist.

"No," he said sharply, "don't give them too much." He threw a handful of tiny copper farthing bits to the men and hastily raised the window again. The barricade was removed temporarily, the coachman's whip sang out, and the carriage rolled forward once more.

Pocahontas, who had never known John to be less than generous, looked at him in some bewilderment. "If men are so desperate for money that they stop travelers in daylight," she said, "surely we should have given them a more substantial sum."

"We'd soon be paupers ourselves if we tried to feed every beggar in the town. Besides, it would have been dangerous to treat those bullies too liberally."

"Dangerous?"

John took the gold coins she still clutched and held them in the open palm of his hand. "A London ruffian will gladly commit murder for a gold angel. The sight of a pair of angels would have convinced our friends back there that enormously wealthy fools were riding in this carriage, and they would have torn the door from its hinges to get the rest of our money. And if they had happened to smash our heads while they were robbing us, it would have served us right."

"Why is such lawlessness permitted?"

"Living in a civilized community is difficult to organize. The watch and the Crown bailiffs do their best, but there are never enough of them, and every time another fifty are appointed, five hundred new rogues spring up from nowhere to plague them."

Pocahontas took the coins from him, fingered them, and smiled wistfully. "What a shame these gold pieces are called angels. When you think of the trouble they cause, they couldn't have been given a less appropriate name." Sighing, she slipped them into her purse and looked out again at the contradictory passing scene.

The carriage squeezed through a foul-smelling alleyway, and then, without warning, London took on the appearance of a different city. The streets were broad and lined with trees, the cobblestones were in comparatively good repair, and smartly uniformed members of the watch patrolled the area in pairs. The buildings, which John said were the homes of the more prominent nobles and a few wealthy merchants, were the largest and most imposing Pocahontas had ever seen. Few were less than four stories high, almost all were built of substantial stone or brick, and many featured glass in row after row of windows. Stately, formal gardens surrounded the houses, which were protected by high stone walls; burly porters armed with clubs stood guard at the entrances, and through an occasional open window Pocahontas caught glimpses of rich draperies, high-ceilinged rooms, and elegant, gold-framed mirrors.

The carriage traveled down Northumberland Road and Northampton Lane, across Agar Street and up the Strand, and traffic in the district was exceptionally heavy. At times four or five coaches were lined up, one behind another, but no two vehicles were alike. Some were painted silver, others were gilded, and all were ornately carved. The only pedestrians were servants in silk livery, walking in twos or fours and balancing the long poles of bulky sedan chairs on their shoulders. It was astonishing to Pocahontas that the occupants of most of the carriages and chairs seemed to know each other and shouted semi-intelligible greetings back and forth as their coaches passed. And what surprised her most was that the ladies wore their hair in ornate styles that had obviously required hours to arrange, all had daubed their faces with heavy coatings of cosmetics, and men and women alike were overdressed in silks and velvets and laces. It was only mid-morning, but fashionable Londoners without exception looked as though they were riding to the grandest of balls, assemblies, and fetes.

Some of the buildings had been constructed with connecting balconies or open walks encircling their upper stories, and these, John explained, were the inns and taverns. He pointed out that each suite or single room could be reached directly from the street by flights of stairs conveniently set along the outer walls of the hostels at short distances, thus allowing guests to come and go as they pleased without being forced to walk through dining halls and public rooms. Even the meanest and smallest of the inns were far more spacious than the biggest buildings in Jamestown, and Pocahontas understood now why John would be required to pay the exorbitant fee of five shillings per week for a small suite of three rooms at the inn with whose proprietor he had been in correspondence.

At last the carriage pulled into the inner courtyard of the place, the Cricket and Rooster, on Fleet Street, and the passengers alighted. They were conducted to their rooms by the owner, while the staff gathered on balconies and gaped at Pocahontas. Attendants bustled in and out with luggage, a pitcher of chilled Canary-and-water, and a platter of heavily perfumed sweetmeats for Celia. When the hubbub subsided,

Pocahontas wandered from one chamber to another, looking in wonder at the rich furnishings, timidly touching inlaid tables, satin bedspreads, and thick, intricately patterned Persian rugs. Not even the house of the governor in Jamestown could boast a fraction of such splendor, and had she not known otherwise she would have imagined she was in the palace of royalty rather than a quiet suite in a modest inn.

She felt dazed but occupied herself with routine tasks, first unpacking several of Celia's dolls and toys so the child could amuse herself. Then she started putting her clothes and John's in chests of drawers, cupboards, and closets so numerous and large that the wardrobes of a dozen people could have been fitted into them with ease. While she was busy John sat at a small desk and wrote several letters to various directors of the Company, placing himself at their disposal. Celia was off in another room, tucking one of her dolls into a bed, and it was quiet, so quiet that Pocahontas suddenly realized that a bird was singing in one of the elms in the courtyard. It was the first familiar sound she had heard since her arrival, and the sense of depression she had felt since she had first come out onto the deck of the *Seraph* this morning lifted.

She laughed, and John looked up at her inquiringly, but before she could explain there was a sharp tap at the door. Pocahontas started toward it, but John waved her away, and after carefully making sure that a heavy chain was in its right place, extending from the latch to the adjoining wall, he opened the door a few inches and peered out cautiously. Then he grinned and quickly removed the chain; Lady Delaware burst into the room, embraced both of them, and spoke so rapidly they could scarcely make out what she was saying.

After the first flurry of greetings had been exchanged and her ladyship sat down, Pocahontas stood and stared at her until the guest became aware of her concentration. "Is something the matter, Rebecca?" Lady Delaware asked.

"Oh no. I'm just so happy to see you, that's all." Pocahon-

tas was relieved to hear the peevish tone she knew so well;
she couldn't bring herself to say in so many words that her
friend gave the impression of being a different person in
London. Lady Delaware looked even smaller here than she
had in Jamestown, and her age was accentuated by a heavy
coating of rice powder on her face, a black patch on her left
cheek, and thick streaks of rouge on her lips. Her hair was
twisted around wires and stood high at the sides of her head,
and she looked uncomfortable in a full hooped skirt of gray
taffeta and a cumbersome padded jacket.

Mollified, her ladyship sipped a glass of Canary-and-water
that John poured for her and fanned herself vigorously.
"You'll dine with us tonight," she announced, "and I warn
you to eat something before you come. We'll expect you at
seven, but supper won't be served until after eleven. It's the
new fashion. I'm sending you one of my own maids to look
after Celia," she added, not pausing for breath. "You'll
find she's very competent. She raised two of my grandchil-
dren."

Pocahontas knew it was futile to argue with Lady Delaware, but she felt compelled to protest. "I intend to take care
of Celia myself."

The ivory fan snapped shut and then flew open again. "My
dear Rebecca, you don't know what you're saying. Mistress
Kendall has been calling on me daily to find out whether
you've arrived yet. She happened to be at my house this
morning when Thomas brought me the news that the *Seraph*
had arrived last night, and she's giving a dinner for you
tomorrow."

"A dinner?" Pocahontas felt gauche and could not hide
her dismay.

"Nothing elaborate," Lady Delaware replied briskly. "The
Kendalls rarely entertain more than twenty or thirty. Be there
promptly at noon, John. Their house is on Ludgate Circus."
She turned back to Pocahontas and beat a tattoo on the arm
of her chair with the fan. "You have no idea how busy you're
going to be, Rebecca. I would have been here half an hour

ago, but first the Duchess of Westminster stopped me on the Strand. She saw you as you drove here in your carriage—she happened to be passing in her sedan chair and recognized you—and she thought you were utterly enchanting. She's dying to meet you."

After an exhausting struggle that had kept her awake most of the previous night, Pocahontas had decided that the best way to avoid temptation in London was to devote her full time and attention to Celia while John was busy on business affairs. In that way, she had concluded, she would not become involved in a meeting which she lacked the strength and ability to handle, and her conscience would be clear when she and her husband returned to Virginia. "That's very kind of Her Grace," she murmured, "but I doubt if we have much in common."

As Lord Delaware often noted, his wife was frequently and conveniently deaf. "Then, right outside in Fleet Street, just as I was coming in, Sir Anthony Howley accosted me and begged to be presented to you. He happened to be in the taproom here drinking his morning small beer when you arrived, and if you had heard the things he said about you, your ears would have burned."

John, who had been listening politely, lost his tolerant smile. "If I remember Howley correctly," he said, his eyes narrowing, "he's a notorious old rake."

"The town is full of rakes, young and old alike," her ladyship declared roguishly. "You'll simply have to learn how to control your jealousy, that's all. You can hardly expect an exotic creature like Rebecca to remain unnoticed in a place that hasn't enjoyed a fresh sensation in years. You have no idea how dull it was while the court was mourning the death of Prince Henry. Only a few people like John Smith have been creating any excitement at all."

Pocahontas and John carefully refrained from looking at each other.

"Someone who knew you in Jamestown," Lady Delaware

continued, "has plans to take both of you to the theater on either Thursday or Friday. A new play is going to be given, something by that naughty Master Jonson. Isn't that frightful of me? I can't remember who spoke to me about it. But no matter. I'll think of it sooner or later, and they're sure to be in touch with you as soon as word spreads among those who have been in Virginia that you've finally arrived."

It would do no damage, Pocahontas thought uneasily, to find out what she could about the one subject that weighed so heavily on her mind. Mere information was harmless and certainly didn't mean she was allowing herself to abandon her new resolutions. "As you can imagine, Mary," she said, trying to sound casually bright but succeeding only in speaking in a high, thin voice, "I've wondered what friends and acquaintances I might see here. It's a peculiar feeling to be a stranger in such a huge city."

"You won't be a stranger for more than a few days, I can promise you that!" Lady Delaware finished her Canary-and-water, and when John, who was preoccupied, failed to refill her glass immediately, she waved it at him until he rose and came to her with the pitcher. "Not too much, now. I'm none too partial to spirits, particularly at this time of day." She watched until he filled the glass to the brim. "Let me see. There are the Martins, of course, and that stupid nephew of the Earl of Pembroke whose name I can never remember. And dear Edward Wingfield's widow. Young Master Wingfield and his wife are the people who intend to take you to the theater, I believe. All of them have been waiting and waiting for you."

"They're very flattering." Pocahontas had more or less expected to hear from everyone Lady Delaware had mentioned, and she made a valiant effort to hide her disappointment over the omission of the one name that mattered. Her guest had referred to him once and might do so again. "Is there anyone else in town I might know?" She averted her face by walking to the door and looking into the adjoining room to make sure Celia wanted and needed no attention.

Long ago John had observed that whenever his wife was under great strain she had a tendency to fold her arms and hug her elbows. She indulged in the gesture now as she resumed her seat, became conscious of it, and deliberately let her arms fall to her sides.

Lady Delaware was still blithely impervious to undercurrents. "There's no one else who means anything, really, except those who spent time in the colony before you moved there. But if I'm any judge, they'll call on you too."

"You forget, Mary dear, that I've known Jamestown from the start." Pocahontas was a trifle surprised at her own ability to simulate bland innocence. "I first visited the colony with my father shortly after it was founded. There wasn't even a governor then, and Captain Smith was president of the Council." She had been afraid she would stumble over his name but spoke the sentence as smoothly as though she had been practicing it for weeks.

"True, I had forgotten." The old scandal stirred vaguely in her ladyship's memory, but she prided herself on her knowledge of character and therefore banished the ugly thoughts that occurred to her. "Thomas would know more about those people than I do, as he's still in touch with some of them in his capacity as a director of the Company."

"Of course."

"Smith himself is here, naturally, as you've gathered."

John jammed his hands behind his back so the women wouldn't see his clenched fists.

And Pocahontas nodded with seemingly magnificent indifference.

"We almost never see him, of course, unless we happen to meet him by accident at court or in St. James's Park. Thomas doesn't think very highly of him, you know."

"I hadn't known, but I can understand the way he feels," John said.

"Thomas believes Captain Smith behaved rather unethically by capitalizing on the reputation he made with our Company to form the Plymouth Company, which is something of a rival, after all." Having expressed a succinct and biting opinion, Lady Delaware proceeded to take the sting out of it. "Of course I know nothing whatsoever about business," she added with a smile. "And in spite of what Thomas thinks I was tempted to call on Captain Smith after I read his book, but I didn't dare."

"Didn't dare?" Pocahontas echoed.

"My dear, he's notorious! And even at my age a woman can't be too careful." Her ladyship simpered and leaned forward in her chair. "Some of the stories I've heard about that clubhouse of his!"

Pocahontas hoped her sharp intake of breath wasn't audible. "He doesn't live in his own home, then, with his family?"

"He has no family and he isn't the type to own a home. He shares a house with several other equally disreputable bachelors. I'll point it out to you someday when we're in the neighborhood of St. Paul's."

Pocahontas shrugged, indicating that she didn't care, but John was not deceived. His heart sank and he knew that by bringing her to London he had exposed their marriage to a risk that could end the relationship that meant more to him than anything else on earth. He had tried repeatedly to tell himself that Pocahontas surely realized Smith was an unscrupulous scoundrel and that she would therefore resist any temptation to have anything more to do with the man. What he had failed to take into consideration was that many women stubbornly refused to allow their intellectual judgments to influence their romantic feelings. And Pocahontas seemed to be one of them.

As a husband, John knew, he could assert his rights and forbid her to see Smith or even to speak to him if they encountered him somewhere. But an uncompromisingly rigid attitude would contribute nothing to lasting marital harmony, and he would rob her of her fiercely independent self-respect, one of the basic qualities that made her dear to him. So, he concluded, he had no alternative: he had to take a chance that his marriage would soon disintegrate, and in the meantime would have to cling to the slim hope that Pocahontas's common sense would assert itself and save her from the infatuation she had formed when she had been too young and inexperienced to know better.

June, 1613

Pocahontas made a far greater impression on London than London made on Pocahontas. She was irritated by the city's noise and bustle, the dirt disgusted her, and the social customs of the people convinced her the English either did not know or had forgotten the essential dignity of the human race. The aristocracy devoted itself almost exclusively to the pursuit of pleasure, but remained restless, bored, and dissatisfied, no matter how many parties it gave and attended. The middle class worked hard to accumulate enough money to copy the pastimes of the nobility and seemed to have no other goal. And the poor, condemned to living out their lives in poverty, with almost no hope of escaping from squalor, cheerfully accepted their lot and apparently expected nothing better.

"The slaves of the Chickahominy," Pocahontas said, "live happier lives in greater freedom than the common people of London." Her observation was repeated everywhere and was enjoyed most by the poor themselves; refusing to take the comment seriously, they regarded her with affection and cheered her whenever she appeared in public.

She won the esteem of the clergy, too, after attending Sunday services at St. Paul's. Scores of carriages were lined up outside, but the church itself was almost empty; the fashionable ladies and gentlemen preferred to spend their time strolling up and down the flower-lined promenade, flirting and gossiping. Pocahontas's simple question, "Have they come to St. Paul's for courting or to humble themselves before God?" was quoted everywhere, and two bishops sent letters of thanks to her.

Her reaction to the theater was unfavorable, too, and although she enjoyed the plays and the players, she thought the manners of the audience were intolerable. The gentry sat at the sides of the stage, conversed incessantly in loud voices, and paid no attention to the proceedings, while the crowds in the pit jeered the actors roundly when they were displeased and threatened to riot whenever they disagreed with sentiments being expressed. The interludes between plays seemed to be utilized, in the main, for the arrangement of assignations, and Pocahontas, watching the spectacle in amazement, was heard to remark that it was impossible to tell the difference between a duchess and a trollop, as they dressed, painted their faces, and behaved alike.

The furor she created during her first week in London meant nothing to her, and even though she and John received far more invitations than it was physically possible to accept, she was indifferent to her success. Whenever she attended a dinner party or rode in a carriage down the Strand, she kept hoping she would see Captain Smith, but he did not appear, and her disappointment became almost unbearable. She did not permit herself to lose sight of the fact that she was now a married woman and that Smith had no place in her future, but she felt that for the sake of all that had happened in the past she had a right to know why he had left her so abruptly.

If she had said or done something to create a misunderstanding, she wanted an opportunity to explain; the relationship with Smith had meant more to her than any other she had ever known, and she wanted him to remember her with at least some degree of the love she still felt for him. It bothered her conscience that she should care what he thought of her, but she told herself she was concerned only because she didn't want him to hold a bad opinion of her.

Finally, on the ninth afternoon of her visit to London, Pocahontas unexpectedly had free time on her hands. Celia had gone out with the nursemaid whom Lady Delaware had engaged, John had been summoned to a conference of some of Jamestown's major shareholders, and the reception at which Pocahontas had planned to spend several hours was canceled. She needed an afternoon to perform a number of chores that had accumulated but decided that none of her duties was urgent. What she had in mind was logical, she decided, and could harm no one, so she changed her clothes quickly. She had been saving her favorite gown for a special occasion, and while she knew it looked out of place in London, she had received numerous compliments on it in Jamestown, so Smith would be certain to appreciate it.

When she had completed her toilet, she looked at herself in the pier glass that stood in a corner of her bedchamber and was satisfied. There was nothing unusual about the white linen apron and cuffs that ornamented the dress of natural, unbleached wool, as such accessories had become essential in Virginia. But the border of fringed, red-dyed leather trimming her wide, square neckline and the hem of her apron were her own additions, and she was proud of them. Her braids were looped to form two large circles which hung behind her ears, and the excited sparkle in her eyes added much to the over-all effect she created. In brief, she thought, she had never looked more attractive.

The little carriage that Lord and Lady Delaware had placed at Pocahontas's disposal was waiting for her in the courtyard of the Cricket and Rooster, and as usual a large

crowd of Londoners was on hand in hopes of catching a
glimpse of her. Apparently the people of the city had nothing
better to do than to loiter in the streets, and Pocahontas, who
had become accustomed to the sight, had made it her business to smile affably and to speak a few words to her admirers.
Today, however, too many things were on her mind, and
when the crowd cheered she merely waved absently as she
climbed into the carriage.

She paid no attention to the now familiar street scenes as
the coachman headed in the direction of St. Paul's, and she
was so immersed in her thoughts that she scarcely remembered to return the greetings of two acquaintances in a
carriage traveling in the opposite direction. The day was
warm, and in similar weather in Jamestown, Pocahontas was
frequently uncomfortable in woolen clothes, but today she
actually felt chilly, and when she rubbed her hands together
they were slightly numb. It was difficult to believe that in a
few minutes she would see Smith again.

A row of solid houses lined the narrow street behind St.
Paul's, and the carriage pulled to a halt in front of a white
four-story structure of wood. The porter, a retired seaman
who had been a gunner on Drake's flagship in '88, hobbled to
the curb, helped Pocahontas to the street, and then conducted her into the cool dark entrance hall of the house. As
all six residents of the place were bachelors, it was no novelty
to receive a woman calling on one of them, but the porter
could not recall a more unusual visitor. In his youth he had
once sailed to far-off Bombay and Ceylon, and his dim
memories led him to believe the lady came from that part of
the world. So he was surprised when she spoke in perfect
English.

"I'd like to see Captain Smith," Pocahontas said, annoyed
to discover she was short of breath. "Captain John Smith."

"Cap'n Smith it is, ma'am." The porter thought that the
most beautiful and distinctive women always called on the
captain. "Who do I tell him is here, ma'am?"

"Mistress Rebecca Rolfe." Pocahontas felt a twinge of guilt

as she spoke her husband's surname but told herself she was being overly sensitive.

"Wait here, please." The porter shuffled off and slowly climbed a flight of stairs.

Although it was infinitely cooler in the reception hall than it had been on the street or in the carriage, Pocahontas thought the heat was unbearable and was afraid she would faint. She leaned against the bottom of the carved banister for support, and by the time she began to feel better, the porter returned.

"Cap'n Smith, he don't know any Mistress Rolfe, but after I swore to him you wasn't the countess, he said he'd see you."

"The countess?" Pocahontas looked blank.

The gentlemen who live in the house frequently complained that the porter was garrulous, but he could not resist sharing a joke. "There's a lady the cap'n don't want to see no more, so sometimes when she comes here she sends up a name that ain't her own. Pays me good for it, too. But the cap'n swears he'll have me throwed out if I help to trick him again, so I had to promise him you ain't her. 'It's a foreign lady,' I told him, 'and I ain't seen prettier in sixty years.' So he got curious right off and told me to bring you up, just like I knowed he would."

The man paused outside a door on the second floor and boldly held out his right hand. Pocahontas, who was quickly learning the requirements of the city, gave him a silver sixpence, far more than custom decreed. The porter, who had hoped to get a halfpenny and would have been satisfied with a farthing, tugged his forelock respectfully and then rapped on the door for her before discreetly disappearing from sight down the corridor.

"Come in!" The heavy oak door muffled Smith's voice, which sounded unfamiliar.

Pocahontas took a deep breath and opened the door with a trembling hand. Sunlight streamed in through bay windows at the far side of the room, so for a moment she could not see the man who sat at a desk in front of the windows, writing. Then her eyes became accustomed to the light, and a sensation of panic came over her as the thought flashed through her mind that she had come to the wrong place. But common sense asserted itself as she studied him while he continued to write or at least pretended to be busy.

There was no doubt that she was in the same room with Captain John Smith, but he did not look at all as she had remembered him. His deep tan had disappeared, and his skin was as pale as that of other Londoners; he had gained at least ten pounds, and it was a shock to see that he looked flabby and middle-aged. His informal shirt of white lawn was probably expensive but it was ordinary, and although he was a tall man, he was shorter and stockier than the picture of him that Pocahontas had carried in her mind.

He glanced up casually, as though just becoming aware of someone else's presence, and for an instant his face was blank. Pocahontas was mortified, certain he did not recognize her, and then a look came into his eyes that sent a chill up and down her spine. She had seen that expression so often, and although she had no idea what it meant, she realized he knew her and she felt rooted to the floor as he stood slowly and wiped the palms of his hands on the sides of his breeches.

"I'll be damned," he said softly, more to himself than to her.

She had rehearsed this scene scores of times but suddenly could not speak.

Smith was so amazed he started to laugh. "You're the last person on earth I expected to see here. What are you doing in London?"

Pocahontas found her voice at last but seemed to have lost control of herself. "You've been avoiding me!" She wished she hadn't sounded so accusing but realized his laughter had angered her.

The Countess of Bedford and a redheaded lady in waiting

who was in the employ of Queen Anne made his life miserable with similar accusations, but he was still too startled to
make his usual stock denial. "When did you come to London?"

"More than a week ago. And you seem to be the only
person in the city who doesn't know it." Pocahontas wanted
to bite off her tongue; she knew better than to imagine that
she was sophisticated, but she certainly had learned that men
always reacted violently when placed on the defensive.

"As any of my friends could have told you, I've just
recovered from a case of the ague. I've spent the past fortnight
in a sickbed and have seen virtually no one."

"Oh, I'm sorry." The hard core of Pocahontas's bitterness
suddenly melted, and she looked at him in concern. "No
wonder you're so pale."

Smith involuntarily glanced at himself in a small mirror
on the wall. "I think I've recovered my color admirably," he
murmured. Then he remembered that the grave-faced girl
who stood across the room was no ordinary guest. "What was
the name you gave our porter?" he asked, looking at her
curiously.

"I am Mistress Rebecca Rolfe," she told him, holding
herself erect.

Smith grinned at her broadly. "You could have done
better. I've never been partial to the name of Rebecca."

"I like it. I chose it for myself when I was baptized."
Pocahontas was ashamed to discover he still had the power to
infuriate her.

"Baptized. Well." The information was useful and would
help to win the support of several devout Scotsmen. Lord
Cobham, too, might increase his investment in the
Plymouth Company. "Did you take the surname for yourself
too?"

This was a moment she had long anticipated, but she felt
no sense of triumph as she said quietly, "No, I've remarried."
She searched his face carefully and was hurt when he showed
neither disappointment nor regret.

Smith nodded vaguely and lost interest in the subject. He had never heard of anyone called Rolfe and wondered why Pocahontas had called on him. He decided to let her tell him in her own good time; it was always preferable to let a woman take the lead in conversations of this sort, for she frequently revealed more than she intended.

"You received my letter telling you that my father invoked the ancient law of the Chickahominy and ended my marriage to you?"

"Yes, I think I recall something of the sort." He shrugged and then added with a smile, "Of course you and I were never truly married. You understand that now, I'm sure."

"You were my husband and I was your wife." Pocahontas was shocked at his callousness, but her voice was firm.

"If it makes you happier to think we were divorced, by all means believe what you please. At least we're agreed that we aren't married to each other now." He had forgotten that Pocahontas was so tenacious and, needing a drink, he came out from behind the desk and walked to a decanter on a table.

Pocahontas, seeing him approach, was alarmed and then felt a sense of frustration when she saw he wasn't coming near her. "I thought it would interest you to know I've married again."

"Oh, to be sure." He poured some sack into a glass and drained it, but offered no refreshments to his guest. "You say you're living here in England now?"

"No, we're merely visiting. We make our home in Jamestown." She paused to give him an opportunity to comment, but he said nothing, so she felt impelled to continue. "My husband owns the largest plantation in Virginia." She knew she was boasting and that she sounded like the stupid squaws of the Potomac, who spent their lives praising themselves, but she could not resist letting him know that her husband was a man of consequence.

For the first time since she had come into the room Smith was impressed. He had been wrong when he had thought the name Rolfe meant nothing to him; it so happened that he had spent an evening with a ship's captain some months previously and had been told much about the man who was making Jamestown self-sufficient by growing vast quantities of tobacco there. "He's that Rolfe? I congratulate you. I must make it my business to meet him while he's here. He shows more ingenuity and intelligence than any other settler in Virginia."

Pocahontas was uncertain whether he intended the remark as a compliment, but she chose to interpret it as one. "Thank you," she said demurely.

Something in either her tone or manner caused Smith to glance at her sharply. Always acutely conscious of nuances in feminine behavior, he was certain she was subtly inviting him to make advances to her. But remembering how difficult it had been to rid himself of her after he had first made love to her years ago, he hesitated. Two thirds of the money he needed to launch the Plymouth Company was already raised, but a fresh scandal involving an Indian girl could do great harm, particularly as most potential investors were extraordinarily strait-laced and seemed to think that men who went off on trips of exploration indulged in frequent debauches. He couldn't afford to justify their fears.

Yet Pocahontas was undeniably appealing, and even though her clothes were so outlandish that he wouldn't want to be seen in public with her, he had to admit to himself that she was charming. She had matured since he had last seen her but was even lovelier than she had been in Jamestown and the forests of the American interior. So he weighed the temptation, and quickly decided there were several factors in favor of indiscretion. Pocahontas had come to him uninvited, of her own free will, and apparently had no purpose in mind other than to see him again. As she had remarried and was obviously proud of her husband, she could not afford to allow her reputation to become tarnished. She was therefore vulnerable to outside opinion just as he was, so it was in her best interests to say nothing to anyone regarding what took place in this room.

Brightening, Smith turned back to the decanter. "Let me offer you a glass of sack. I've been less than hospitable and can only blame my recent illness for clouding my mind."

Pocahontas was instantly aware of the change in his mood, and the oily insincerity she heard in his voice disturbed her. Possibly that same false note had always crept into his tone whenever he had paid court to her in the past, but she had been too inexperienced to recognize it. She felt a sense of shame and wished she could scrub herself with willow twigs in the James River, but she hid her self-revulsion behind a polite mask. "Thank you, but I don't care for spirits." She smiled faintly. "I shall always be a benighted heathen, I'm afraid. Drink doesn't agree with me."

Smith chuckled heartily, reacting as though her mildly humorous comment had been an extraordinarily witty remark. Raising his own glass, he toasted her, wiped his mouth on his sleeve, and then waved her toward the divan. "You will sit down, though, so we can talk. I'm sure much has happened to you since we last saw each other and I'm anxious to hear everything."

Her glance darted from Smith to the divan and back, and his eagerness sickened her. So many men had lusted for her, and all of them, from Samuel Argall to a yound chief of the Cayuga whose name she could not remember, looked alike when they did. Smith was no better than the others, and what dismayed her the most was the suspicion that his intentions had been just as obvious on the day, so long ago, when she had first given herself to him in the Jamestown blockhouse. "I'm afraid I can't stay," she said, and her fingers, plucking at her decorative apron, betrayed her nervousness. "My carriage is waiting for me, and I have a number of errands to do this afternoon."

"Let them wait," he told her, and, maneuvering into a position between her and the door, he started toward her.

"No!" A fresh wave of panic swept over Pocahontas, and she didn't know what else to say, but raised her hands blindly to fend him off.

Smith ignored her protest, swept her into his arms, and kissed her with practiced ease. For a moment she struggled violently, trying to escape, but his grip tightened, and she was helpless, unable to move. Suddenly her terror vanished, and she became passive, astonished to discover that this crucial moment meant nothing to her. Either Smith had changed or else she was seeing him through different eyes now; then it occurred to her that perhaps she, not he, had learned new standards. She thought of John, who trusted and needed her, and of Celia, who depended on her. Remaining very still in Smith's passionate embrace, she rejoiced in the knowledge that he had lost his power over her.

Finally he became aware of her unresponsiveness and released her abruptly. Looking at him, she saw him for the first time as a bold and greedy sensualist; his face was red, he was breathing heavily, and the brutal, wanton desire for her that she read in his eyes made her ill. Smith fought for self-control, deliberately turned and walked back to his desk; he waited until he was sure he would not make a fool of himself and then he confronted her. "Why did you come here?" he demanded.

"I don't know." That wasn't true, and Pocahontas knew it, but she couldn't force herself to admit even to herself that she might have sacrificed her honor and her marriage for the sake of an hour with this selfish man who had never really cared for her. "No matter what my reasons, I was wrong." Her distress was so great she didn't realize that she was folding her hands over her breasts, as she had been taught in her childhood. "Accept my apologies, please. I won't trouble you again."

Smith didn't bother to accompany her to the door.

Pocahontas walked slowly down the stairs and, taking a handkerchief from the pocket of her dress, she scrubbed her lips until they were raw. The strong sunlight hurt her eyes when she stepped out onto the street, and the odors of London assailed her nostrils. The pedestrians who stared at her, invading her privacy when she was in pain, annoyed her so much she wanted to strike out at them, and she hated the city with all her heart. The old porter opened the carriage door for her, she sank back against the seat wearily, and the coachman started back to the Cricket and Rooster. In the dark privacy of the carriage she grew calmer and knew she was being childish to take out her spite on London, which was not to blame because she despised Smith and loathed herself.

In a sense she should be happy, she thought, for she had scored something of a victory over Smith. She had been under his spell for years, unable to see him as vain and weak, grasping and cruel, but she had proved to herself that he no longer exercised power over her. On the other hand, she had demonstrated that she could arouse him, but she knew that was why she grieved: his feeling for her, today and in the dim past, had always been the same, and his supposed love for her had been just an illusion she had created and nourished in her own mind. Certainly it had never existed in reality.

Unmindful of the passing carriages and sedan chairs, Pocahontas wept quietly and stopped only when she realized that she was not crying for Smith but over herself. She had wasted so much of her youth, she had behaved so stupidly, but she could not recall the past and live those years again. It was too late to erase her errors, too late to rid herself of the burning shame that would, she felt sure, remain with her for the rest of her days. It was strange to know she no longer loved Smith, yet she could not enjoy her new freedom; she had worshiped a false god for so long that its destruction left her with a sense of irreparable loss.

She continued to sit numbly after the carriage drew to a halt in the courtyard of the Cricket and Rooster, and only when the coachman told her they had arrived did she compose herself as best she could and walk up the stairs to the Rolfe suite. She knew that Celia and the nursemaid were still out and she looked forward to spending the rest of the afternoon alone, so she was startled when she saw John in the living room. He was pacing up and down anxiously, and even before she caught a glimpse of his face she realized he had been worried about her.

"You're early," she said, trying unsuccessfully to inject a note of gaiety into her voice.

"I knew you'd be alone, so I excused myself from the meeting," he replied, and seemed to stare hard at her.

"That was very sweet of you." Pocahontas felt like squirming.

"Not at all."

John saw that she was deeply disturbed, that she was suffering as he had never before known her to suffer. She was unable to meet his eyes, and he guessed that she had seen Smith; his blood sang in his ears and he felt dizzy, but he did not show his feelings. What had happened wasn't really important; all that mattered was that she was in pain. "Why don't you rest for a time?" he suggested. "You aren't accustomed to the heat of London. It's more concentrated than the summer weather in Virginia, and you look tired."

"Thank you," Pocahontas said gratefully, and started toward the bedchamber, but stopped abruptly at the threshold and turned back, although the effort was almost too great for her. "John, there's something I want you to know."

"There's no need to tell me anything you don't wish to say," he replied quietly.

Pocahontas swallowed with difficulty. "I've never dishonored our marriage or disgraced your name. And I never will."

He forced himself to smile. "It hasn't crossed my mind that you have or that you might," he said firmly.

She closed the door behind her, and after throwing herself onto the bed, she wept again, this time for John. He deserved a real wife, who would love him, gladly bear his children and be worthy of him.

August, 1613

Queen Anne's return to London from Bath, where she had spent part of the summer, signaled the start of a new social season in late July, although King James, who had an aversion to hot weather, decided to remain in residence at Hampton Court for a few more weeks. The restraint that had characterized the first tentative festivities to be held after the end of the official mourning period for the late Prince of Wales vanished, and the capital inaugurated a series of the gayest and most hectic affairs it had known since James had ascended the throne. At least three or four important dinners, receptions, and assemblies were held daily, foreign envoys were entertained lavishly, and the wealthier nobles of the realm competed with each other to see who could present the most expensive masque. The prosperous, growing middle class gave its own parties and filled the taverns of the town; the poor, enjoying an era of almost unprecedented universal employment, in which almost every man could find work, created its own pleasures by holding nightly carnivals in the streets and rioting whenever life threatened to become dull.

Pocahontas, to her own surprise, was caught up in the whirl, and her many new friends and admirers insisted that her presence in England was a major contribution to what was rapidly becoming a unique festive season. Her shyness and reticence disappeared under a barrage of invitations, although she maintained her personal dignity, and no function was considered a success unless she attended it. Fortunately for the peace of mind of most hosts and hostesses, her energy seemed to be inexhaustible, and she made an appearance at virtually every affair to which she was asked.

She discovered that by drifting with the tide, accepting surface pleasures and seeking nothing more, she was able to achieve a state of mind in which she felt nothing and thought nothing, and for the moment it was enough to be relieved of sorrow and pain. In the first weeks after her disillusionment with Captain Smith she had gone to the other extreme, had refused to appear in public, and had spent most of her time alone, weeping and brooding morosely. At last John, concerned over her health but unable to spend as much time at her side as he wished because of the pressure of his business affairs, had offered to send her back to Jamestown on the first ship available. But Pocahontas had no desire to be separated from Celia and she knew, too, that if she left she would be derelict in her duty to her husband.

So she made a determined effort to embark on a new life, and John, heeding Lady Delaware's secret advice, invested generous amounts of the profits he had made from the year's tobacco crop in a dazzling wardrobe for her. She was unique, her personality was piquant, and her reactions to any fresh situation were unpredictable, so she quickly became society's favorite. London, never having known anyone quite like her, was stunned by her.

But Pocahontas managed to retain some degree of perspective. No matter what hour of early morning she and John came home in their carriage, she never failed to rise in time for breakfast with Celia, and under no circumstances would she accept invitations in the forenoon, as she devoted that portion of each day exclusively to her stepdaughter. Then, but only then, she gave herself to the pleasures of the town for the rest of the day. She learned to exchange witticisms with courtiers and to turn aside overly warm compliments with a snap of her fan, she danced the lively *galliard* and the animated *coranto* with tireless grace, and she found it was easy to play three or four eager swains against each other when they crowded around her. But as a number of gallants learned to their dismay, her smile was intended as a friendly gesture, nothing more, and any man who tried to become familiar with her did so at his peril.

Ladies had recently adopted the habit of carrying bodkins, tiny daggers no longer than their thumbs, concealed beneath their gowns, and as more than one gentleman discovered, Mistress Rolfe did not hesitate to use her knife when a beau's attentions became too ardent. In spite of her attempt to live only in the present, she was still Pocahontas of the Chickahominy, and her mind was not clouded by too many civilized layers. When a man, knowing she was married, tried to make advances to her, she wanted to punish him for his temerity swiftly and directly, as she believed he should be punished.

Her background and training helped her in other ways, too, even though she was not aware of it. When she was in the presence of her elders or those whom she recognized as wise, she made no attempt to converse with them as an equal but was content to sit silently, her face grave, and to listen to whatever they wished to say, even when she was bored and restless. As a result the older people, deeply flattered, agreed that she was charming, and an aged philosopher who taught at Oxford University was heard to express the view that she possessed a profound intellect.

Her faith in the Bible also stood her in good stead, and

whenever there were clergymen present at a function, they were certain to seek her company. The dean of St. Paul's created something of a sensation by delivering a sermon in praise of her clear, simple concept of Christianity, and the Bishop of Exeter, not to be outdone, promptly dedicated a treatise to her. As a consequence literary circles were stirred, Thomas Ravenscroft wrote a poem in her honor, and John Ford announced that before the season ended he would produce a play he was currently writing, entitled *Princess of the West*.

It was inevitable that Pocahontas and Smith should occasionally attend the same affair, but these infrequent meetings were anticlimactic. They stood at opposite sides of a large hall at a reception given by the envoy of the French King, but seemed unaware of each other's presence, and a few weeks later, when they came face to face at an assembly being given by the Earl of Pembroke, Pocahontas nodded distantly and Smith favored her with a remote bow. They met a third time at the home of the Bishop of London, where Smith sought out John, who was polite but cool to him; Pocahontas, however, exchanged no words with him.

After each of these incidents she examined her reactions with infinite care to find out precisely how she had felt, and was neither pleased nor upset to conclude that she had been devoid of all emotion. The Smith who swaggered around London and planned to lead an expedition to an unexplored part of America that he was pleased to call New England meant nothing to her. He was a self-opinionated, rather overbearing stranger, and she could no longer recall the intimacies they had shared, details that she previously had believed to be indelibly stamped in her memory.

She knew that John observed her carefully each time they saw Smith, but he took infinite care not to mention the captain's name to her. Her greatest regret was that she had not been able to give her husband the fresh, unspoiled love she had thrown at the feet of a man who took the adulation of

women for granted. But it was too late, and she could only try
to repay the devotion John showed her. Someday, when she
could speak freely of such things, she would tell him how
much she appreciated his loyalty during this trying period.

Apparently John did not resent the demands that their
social life made on his energies, but his negotiations with the
directors of the London Company, which he said were pro-
gressing favorably, continued to take up a large part of his
time, so he could not escort his wife to every party she
attended. When his business took him elsewhere, Lady Delaware, who was proud to act as Pocahontas's sponsor, served
as her chaperone and, basking in reflected glory, the older
woman made it her business to call at the Cricket and Rooster
each day shortly after noon, when Celia had gone to bed for
her nap.

Late in August word was received that two barks from
Jamestown, their holds bulging with tobacco, had just anchored in the Thames, and John canceled all social engage-
ments for himself so he could supervise the unloading of the
precious cargo. He insisted, however, that Pocahontas attend
whatever functions were marked on their calendar for the
next few days, and shortly after he departed for the docks,
Lady Delaware arrived at the suite, somewhat more flustered
than usual. The thickly padded sleeves of her brown taffeta
gown and the boned bodice that forced her torso in the
currently fashionable long, narrow shape looked thoroughly
uncomfortable, and so did her wired, upstanding collar,
which made it impossible for her to turn her head more than
an inch or two to each side. So Pocahontas could not blame
her for being out of sorts and smiled when her friend scolded
her.

"Rebecca, you can't go out looking like that. I'm surprised
at you! After all this time you certainly know better."

The demands of fashion seemed absurd to Pocahontas,
and when her new wardrobe had been made she had insisted
that her own convenience and comfort take precedence over

the dictates of style. She glanced at herself in the pier glass, saw nothing wrong with her yellow silk gown, and was satisfied.

"Stop smirking, Rebecca!" Her ladyship glared at the reflection in the mirror. "You've let all the compliments you've received go to your head. There are certain things you simply can't do, and wearing a soft lace collar is one of them. There are limits to unorthodoxy, you know!"

Pocahontas touched the double collar that fell away from her neck in a deep, wide point, deliberately turned her head from one side to the other, and laughed.

Lady Delaware couldn't admit even to herself that she was jealous of the younger woman, whose daring innovations were being copied by scores of ladies. "It's positively indecent to wear a dress that isn't cane-stiffened through the middle. People can actually see the movements of your body when you walk! What's more, women don't wear belts."

"I made this belt myself." Pocahontas was pleased with the broad band of leather, but it was useless to argue, so she sat down at her dressing table and adjusted the strip of lace that was closely bound around her head at the hairline, beneath her hair, which was piled high.

Her ladyship remembered the retiring creature she had first known in Jamestown and felt a renewed surge of envy. "There are times when you must conform," she said severely. "Will you insist on setting your own styles when you're presented to Their Majesties at court?"

"The King and Queen certainly have no reason to want to meet me." It was obvious that Pocahontas had not lost her innate sense of modesty, in spite of the furor she had created.

Lady Delaware, ashamed of her own feelings, softened at once. "I'm only thinking of you, child. This is one day you'll want to look your best."

One day was like any other, and Pocahontas shrugged. "We're only going to Lord Hallowell's for dinner."

"Our plans are changed," the older woman said triumphantly. "When the King returned to town from Hampton Court, his first act was to release Sir Walter Raleigh from the Tower. They've made some sort of agreement, though no one has learned the details. Sir Lewis and Lady Stukly are giving a reception in Sir Walter's honor, and he specifically asked if you're going to be there. Naturally the Hallowells have postponed their dinner."

Pocahontas stood and smoothed the long panels of yellow silk, lined with green satin, that fell from her shoulders behind her narrow sleeves. The thick, quilted sleeves that Queen Anne had made popular were ugly and uncomfortable, and Pocahontas preferred the more graceful cape sleeves, which were now considered old-fashioned.

"Didn't you hear me, Rebecca? Sir Walter wants to meet you!"

"I look forward to meeting him too." Real humor rarely appeared in Pocahontas's eyes these days, but her face brightened. "If it weren't for his discoveries and explorations I wouldn't be here, would I?"

"Exactly. And you still refuse to change into something more appropriate?"

"I can assure you, Mary," Pocahontas said earnestly, "that when Sir Walter first landed on the shores of the New World, the squaws of the Roanoke and Aquascagoc who helped to welcome him were dressed far more inappropriately than I am today!"

That ended the subject, and Lady Delaware, her perspective restored, subsided and enjoyed a laugh at her own expense as they descended to the carriage that waited for them below. Sir Lewis Stukly, a director of the London Company and one of the wealthiest men in England, had recently built a home in the new residential district that was being established in the vicinity of the ancient haymarket, and by the time Pocahontas and her chaperone arrived at the mansion its public rooms and garden were filled with diplomats and courtiers, soldiers and men of business, sea

captains and landowners who had come to honor Sir Walter.
During the reign of Elizabeth, Raleigh's enemies had outnumbered his friends, but now that she was gone he was a
reminder of the glories of the old regime, and his unjust
imprisonment had elevated him to a new crest of popularity.
As a result everyone of consequence was present, and only
members of the royal family had remained at home.

Pocahontas's entrance created the usual stir; those who
were acquainted with her hailed her loudly, gentlemen jostled each other aside in a polite but grim competition for the
privilege of kissing her hand, and the ladies craned their
wired-collar-encased necks to see what she was wearing. Sir
Lewis and Lady Stukly, who had stationed themselves just
inside the front door, first conducted her to Lady Raleigh, a
pleasantly attractive woman, whom Pocahontas had met
previously on two or three occasions, and they exchanged a
few words.

Sir Walter was holding court in the main reception hall of
the house, and Sir Lewis led Pocahontas there, while Lady
Delaware, who was determined not to miss the historic
moment, followed at their heels. A resonant voice dominated the conversation in the hall, and Pocahontas caught a
glimpse of the guest of honor through the crowd. Tall and
smiling, his beard trimmed and his hair oiled, he accepted
the adulation of the throng as his due, and Pocahontas
thought she had never seen a man who wore his clothes with
such an air. His black velvet doublet and breeches fitted his
muscular frame to perfection, and the gold embroidery set
with small rubies that ornamented the wide rolls at his
shoulders seemed appropriate for a man of his standing. His
thigh-length boots of soft Russian leather, with gold designs
on the wide cuffs, were the finest Pocahontas had ever seen,
and the white ostrich plumes on his black hat were enormous.

The guests, aware of Pocahontas's presence, moved aside,
and a hush came over the assemblage. Sir Walter stood with

his hand resting lightly on the hilt of his jeweled sword, and as Pocahontas approached with their host he smiled, but she felt his piercing eyes studying her and thought that never in her life had she been subjected to such a close scrutiny. Sir Lewis, savoring the moment, halted and bowed. "Admiral," he said, "I am honored to present Mistress Rebecca Rolfe."

Pocahontas was about to curtsy, but to her astonishment Sir Walter addressed her in the dialect of the Rappahannock. "Raleigh, who was the first to see the land which he gave the name of Virginia, greets the daughter of that distant place." His accent was abominable.

It was obvious to Pocahontas that he was putting on an exhibition for the benefit of the crowd, but she did not object and could not help but feel slightly awed by the man who had forged the first link between England and the land of her birth. So she stood erect, solemn-faced, and, folding her hands over her breasts in the approved Indian manner, she bowed her head. If the gesture was incongruous when made by a woman dressed in silks and lace, it was also exceptionally pretty, and she knew it. "Pocahontas, squaw of Rolfe and daughter of the Chief of Chiefs, greets the mighty Raleigh," she replied in the language of the Chickahominy.

Sir Walter had difficulty making out her words, but the delight of the guests was sufficient compensation for him. Thanks to the co-operation of this accommodating young woman, the drama of his return to society was being heightened and would be a principal topic of discussion in the town for a long time. He bestowed his most ingratiating smile on her to show her his gratitude. "I'm told you speak English?" he asked in his own tongue.

"I do, Sir Walter, to the best of my ability," she replied smoothly, and wished he did not remind her of the actor she had seen recently, portraying the role of a character named Hotspur in a play about King Henry IV.

The crowd roared, and Raleigh waited until the laughter died away before speaking again. Then, his face grave, he removed his hat with a magnificent flourish that many men had tried unsuccessfully to copy. Sweeping the floor with the ostrich plumes, he snatched Pocahontas's hand and kissed it more fervently than the occasion required. "Madam," he declared sonorously, "you are the personification of my dearest wish. You are my lifelong dream suddenly come to life."

In a sense his flattery was outrageous, but Pocahontas sensed that he was serious, even though he behaved as though they stood together on the stage of a theater. His flamboyance, his flair for the unusual were natural to him, so she merely smiled up into his penetrating eyes and waited for him to continue.

"When I claimed possession of the New World in the name of the greatest monarch England has ever known," Sir Walter said, blithely ignoring the unwritten law that references to King James's illustrious predecessor were to be avoided, "I predicted that the day would come when the people of this realm and those of America would become one. There were some who called me mad when I prophesied that we would speak the same language, observe the same customs, and worship the same God." His eyes searched the crowd. "I see the faces of two or three of my former detractors, but I won't remind them of their short-sighted lack of faith and vision. Because you, dear lady, have proved that I was right. England and the New World have become united for all time."

The guests applauded heartily, as Raleigh seemed to know they would, and before the hubbub subsided he offered Pocahontas his arm. Slightly bewildered, she took it unthinkingly, and before she quite realized what was happening, Sir Walter whisked her out into the gardens, timing his exit from the reception hall with consummate skill. His eyes glistened, his brow was damp, and Pocahontas, holding his arm, could feel that he was trembling. He had meant what he had said, even though every exaggerated word and every theatrical move had been deliberately conceived.

He led Pocahontas to an arbor covered with rambler roses and, halting there, smiled at her broadly, confident of the power of his magnetic personality. "I'll tell you a secret that no one else knows as yet," he said, "for I believe it proper that you should be the first to hear it. I've concluded a pact with the little King who sits on Gloriana's throne and I've agreed to lead an expedition to the land known as Guiana at the far side of the West Indian Sea for him. I'm sure there's gold to be found there and I shall bring back enough of it to give greedy James his fill."

"I'm honored by your trust," Pocahontas murmured. "I hope for your sake as well as His Majesty's that you find enough gold to make both of you very wealthy."

Sir Walter laughed and waved his hand so his jeweled rings caught the reflection of the sunlight. "Gold means nothing to me. I'll be satisfied if future generations remember me as a giant among giants. Drake and Hawkins and Gilbert have won their places in history, and I have found my niche too. That's enough for me."

He was posturing, of course, which was not unusual when a man is given an opportunity to brag to an attractive woman, but Pocahontas could see that he was absolutely sincere too. Then suddenly his expression changed, and she realized that in spite of his reputation for devotion to his wife, he was not the sort who would allow his scruples to prevent him from appreciating another's charms. "I'm certain there's much you could tell me—in private—that would be helpful to me in planning my expedition," he said.

Pocahontas was relieved that he was too polished to force her to threaten him with her bodkin. "My husband and I," she said with subtle emphasis, "would be pleased to call on you at your convenience, Sir Walter."

The hint was sufficient, and he escorted her back to the house at once, chatting inconsequentially without openly recognizing the rebuff. Pocahontas engaged in no further conversation with him, and after the guests had eaten she excused herself at the first opportunity. Her mind was whirling; she knew she was upset and, realizing that the encounter with Sir Walter had been significant, she wanted time to think about it.

Sitting alone in her bedchamber at the Cricket and Rooster, she analyzed her feelings and understood she had been shocked by Raleigh's attitude in general rather than his attempt to make advances to her. According to every standard the civilized world could apply, he was indeed a great man, and even his own vanity could not cause him to exaggerate his importance to his age. Yet at the same time he was a dissolute, empty shell, and regardless of his accomplishments, he was never satisfied, never happy. He would always set new, impossible goals for himself, and until the day he died he would continue to live for the thrill of public acclaim.

Sir Walter meant nothing to Pocahontas, of course, but behind him she could see the shadow of a somewhat lesser man cast in the same mold, and at last she knew why she was disturbed. Raleigh was a more heroic version of Captain John Smith. Both of them made good their incredible boasts, but their restless search for something new to conquer and their insatiable appetite for applause reduced their stature. No man who was selfish and ruthless, Pocahontas told herself, was truly heroic.

She was still lost in thought when her husband returned from the docks, and one look at his tired face was enough to make her forget everything but the present. John smiled at her through the coat of London dust that had accumulated on his skin, and in spite of his weariness he spoke cheerfully. "Some of the Company people were at today's reception and told me about your latest triumph," he said. "Raleigh, no less!"

Pocahontas didn't care if she never heard Sir Walter's name mentioned again, and brushed aside the topic. "Have you eaten since breakfast, John?"

He frowned, trying to remember. "I had a bite of cheese on board one of the barks. I had to spend most of the day down in the holds," he added apologetically. "London workmen know very little about handling tobacco, and I didn't want any of the cargo ruined."

"Sit down this instant!" Pocahontas's tone was so unusually firm that he stared at her. Leaving him for a moment, she hurried to the cool-storage pantry in the living room and returned with a platter of cold meat, a loaf of heavy barley bread, and a small jug of Canary-and-water. "If you'd like some beer, I'll go down to the taproom for it."

"No, this is more than enough," John protested. "I wouldn't want you to bother."

"Bother, indeed." She spread the food out on a small table and then sat down opposite him. "Tonight," she said, "we'll go to no party. You'll need a hot meal, so we'll go to some tavern by ourselves."

He speared a chunk of beef with his knife and laughed. "This is already more than enough food for me until tomorrow."

"It is not," she replied tartly, suddenly annoyed. "You've been losing weight ever since we've come to England. You need a real meal and you're going to have it."

He was too fatigued to argue, and ate in silence for a time, while Pocahontas, her chin cupped in her hands, watched him. It was remarkable, she thought, that the England that produced men like Raleigh and Smith had also produced John. In his quiet way he was doing as much, if not more, than they to create a colonial empire and make it secure, but he sought no credit for his efforts and would actually be embarrassed if his accomplishments received public notice. No matter how hard he worked he rarely lost his patience or his temper, and he certainly felt no need to indulge in grand gestures in order to call attention to his masculinity.

Perhaps that was one of the most important facets of his character, and it occurred forcibly to Pocahontas that he was actually more of a man than the swaggering lions.

Her unblinking scrutiny made John uncomfortable. "What are you thinking?" he asked.

Pocahontas hesitated for a long moment but could not quite bring herself to tell him that for the first time she was gaining a measure of true appreciation of his worth. "Nothing at all, really," she said.

September, 1613

In the days following her meeting with Sir Walter Raleigh, Pocahontas became increasingly dissatisfied with the life she was leading in London. Aristocratic matrons were expected to be decorative additions to the social scene, but little else was required of them, and Pocahontas, completely cured at last of her infatuation for Captain Smith, realized that her present existence was as meaningless as it was vapid. But it was not easy to change the patterns of thinking and feeling that had been so much a part of her since the day she had first met Smith, and in a world where pleasure for pleasure's sake was the universal goal it was almost impossible for her to see where she was drifting or decide what she really wanted.

She knew, of course, that other women envied the reputation she had acquired as a gracious beauty, and the knowledge gave her no satisfaction. The admiration of the Chickahominy had been part of her heritage, so the stir she had created in England was neither surprising nor significant to

her. Her experience with Smith had taught her that other
people's standards had no value and that only what she
herself created and built and protected had real worth. But
she was convinced that nothing substantial could be grown in
the artificial atmosphere of London and she began to long for
the quiet simplicity of Jamestown.

She said nothing to John about her increasing desire to
return to Virginia, however. His business in London was not
yet complete, and Pocahontas felt it would be unfair to him
and to all the people in Jamestown who were depending on
him to ask him to break off his negotiations just at a time
when it seemed likely that the colonists would be granted a
fair share of the profits from the tobacco they raised. There
was another and more important reason she could not con-
fide in John: she knew a change was taking place in her
relationship with him, but as yet she could neither clearly
define nor understand the subtle difference. So she was
self-conscious in his presence and as a result was reluctant to
discuss anything more important than minor day-to-day
problems with him. And John, feeling her tension, had
difficulty in communicating with her too.

Misunderstandings were bound to arise, and although
there were no open quarrels, Pocahontas became more irri-
table, and John, his patience growing thin, was inclined to
bicker. The strain became even greater when a message was
received from Whitehall requesting the presence of "Lady"
Rebecca Rolfe and her husband at the palace in four days'
time, when they would be granted an audience by Their
Majesties.

Lady Delaware took charge of preparations for the event,
and the little suite at the Cricket and Rooster was invaded by a
corps of seamstresses and ladies' maids as well as hordes of
noblewomen anxious to offer advice. Pocahontas objected to
the upheaval, and John, who hastily retreated to the offices of
the London Company, complained that the atmosphere was
similar to that of Bethlehem Hospital, or Bedlam, where the

mad were confined. But Lady Delaware, determined that her protégée give a good account of herself, ruthlessly brushed aside all opposition. Locking out all well-meaning friends, she drilled Pocahontas in the deportment that was expected in the presence of royalty and, driving the sewing women to distraction, she supervised the making of every item of clothing that "Lady" Rebecca would wear.

At last the day of the audience arrived. The Rolfe family ate an early breakfast, and John, who was already dressed for the occasion in a dark doublet and breeches, needed only to glance across the table at his wife to see that she was exasperated. The reasons for her annoyance began to become apparent to him when Lady Delaware, accompanied by a seamstress and four ladies' maids, arrived, but he had no idea how extraordinarily complicated the procedure would be until he stood at the threshold of the master bedchamber and watched the women unpack hampers of clothing.

They laid out long silk underdrawers with ribbons and frills at the knees, and beside them placed a hoop, a wide, drumlike cylinder made of heavy canvas and stiffened with bands of steel. Over this uncomfortable device Pocahontas would wear a padded roll called a bolster, which would be tied around her hips, and John gaped as one of the maids unfolded three elaborately ruffled and embroidered petticoats in contrasting colors, which would be hooked around his wife's waist.

The corset, or stomacher, which was unpacked next, made John think of the tortures inflicted on victims of the Inquisition in Spain. It was a bodice of thick linen, over which was placed a perforated steel case, hinged on one side and clamped together with large steel hooks on the other, and as he looked at it he began to understand why Pocahontas was disturbed. But other hampers were being opened, and it was evident that Lady Delaware and her helpers had just started to unpack. Over the steel bodice Pocahontas would wear a heavily embroidered covering of soft blue velvet, and bands of fine white lawn with deep lace ruffles would finish the wrists and neck of the bodice, while a wired, starched, and pleated lace collar would stand up like a fan at the back of her head.

These items were placed side by side, and John looked in bewilderment at Pocahontas, who sat morosely at her dressing table. "I thought your clothes were ready," he said, "but they're all in separate parts."

"They're ready," she assured him bitterly. "Everything will be held together with long steel pins. Sharp pins."

She pointed out a variety of other pieces that would be attached to each other with pins too. There was a mantle or long cloak of a sheer, sky-blue material, with wired, wing-shaped pieces standing above the shoulders, that would be affixed to padded rolls over her bodice, and the close-fitting ivory satin sleeves also would be pinned in place. Knitted, bright orange stockings, embroidered with a flower design, would be held up by ribboned garters tied over the frills of the underdrawers, but for safety's sake, Pocahontas said, pins would be slipped through the rosettes of the garters too. And, she pointed out, she was sure she would trip and fall, for the ivory satin slippers, which were laced and tied with ribbons, were ornamented with rosettes and gold tassels tied to still more ribbons, which trailed to the floor.

By this time the women were unfolding her full, pale satin outerskirt, and when John asked if it, too, would be pinned, she nodded glumly. Lady Delaware opened a box containing the more decorative accessories, and John started to chuckle when he saw a gold chain that would hang from Pocahontas's waist, and on which would dangle a lace-edged handkerchief, and a muff of black fox fur. There was a long rope of Lady Delaware's best pearls, too, which would be clasped around Pocahontas's throat, and pendant pearl earrings, which looked almost long enough to touch her shoulders.

His amusement nettled Lady Delaware, and she turned to him sharply. "The steel pins," she said, "come from France.

They're made nowhere else on earth." She saw that, like all men, he was not impressed, and decided his presence was unnecessary. "Be good enough to retire, Master Rolfe," she told him severely.

John retreated to the living room of the suite and smoked a pipe to calm himself. It was no wonder, he thought, that most ladies of fashion rarely appeared until the afternoon, and he could understand why Pocahontas, who ordinarily dressed herself quickly, had no relish for the outlandish ritual she was being forced to undergo. He could hear the excited, high-pitched sound of feminine voices through the closed door of the bedchamber, and as the morning passed he glanced again and again at the hourglass that stood on the mantel over the hearth. The courier from Whitehall had said that the audience was to begin promptly at noon, and although Lady Delaware had arrived early, the better part of the morning was already gone.

Rising, John began to pace up and down the room. It would be unpardonable to arrive late for a royal audience, and he was on the verge of risking her ladyship's wrath by going to the bedchamber when the door opened and Pocahontas, fully dressed at last, stood in the frame. Her hair had been waved, a long curl hung over one shoulder and a tiny heart-shaped cap of stiff lace was set on her head. Deep blue ointment had been applied to her eyelids, black paint emphasized her brows, and rouge accented her mouth. And as a finishing touch, a small diamond-shaped patch made of black taffeta was pasted high on her left cheekbone.

She held herself erect, her bearing naturally regal; somehow, out of the confusion, she had been transformed into an English patrician fit to consort with the King and Queen. She looked no lovelier to John than she had when he had first seen her in the mud village of the Potomac, but her feminine adaptability startled him. She wore the clothes of the court with an air that made them her own, and when she walked into the room she moved with effortless grace, as though she had been accustomed to cumbersome hoops and steel bodices all her life.

Pocahontas halted and spoiled the effect she had created by giggling. "I feel," she said, "like a porcupine."

Lady Delaware, who was behind her, did not join in the laugh. "Remember what I've told you, Rebecca. No sudden gestures. Don't jerk and don't be in a hurry. Don't forget your dignity or you'll fall apart."

Her words sobered Pocahontas, who walked with stately tread down to the courtyard. Lady Delaware, who was to present her protégée to the King and Queen, hurried off in her own coach, and John handed his wife into their carriage, a feat they managed to accomplish together with considerable difficulty, then squeezed in beside her. The carriage rumbled into Fleet Street, and he reached out to touch her hand. "I don't know whether all the work was worth it or not, but at least you have the consolation of knowing you look beautiful."

"Thank you, John." The carriage bounced over a loose cobblestone, and a pin jabbed Pocahontas in the middle of her back. "In my opinion the whole business is absurd."

By the time they arrived at Whitehall her neck ached, and she couldn't turn her head to see the plume-helmeted Guards who raised their muskets in salute as the carriage drove through the main gates. An assistant to the Lord Chamberlain was waiting for them at the visitors' entrance to the palace and conducted them through a seemingly endless maze of damp corridors and badly lighted anterooms. Apparently it was almost noon, for the official tried to urge them to walk rapidly, but Pocahontas, remembering Lady Delaware's advice, refused to be rushed. When they mounted the broad marble steps that led to the rear hall on the second floor she looked completely at ease, and no one could have guessed that she held her breath as she tried to handle her skirts.

The double doors of the great hall were guarded by two

sentries in full uniform, and just off the chamber was a sitting room in which an adolescent boy was reclining on a divan placed so he could see all who came and left. He was pretending to read a leather-bound book, but when he saw Pocahontas he stared at her boldly, then leered at her. She was shocked, and John stiffened, but to their surprise the assistant to the Lord Chamberlain bowed low. "Your Royal Highness," he murmured.

They had just seen the next King of England, Pocahontas realized, and understood why the people had mourned so deeply when Prince Henry had died and his brother Charles had become heir to the throne. But she forgot the boy as the doors of the great hall swung open and she heard Lady Delaware's familiar voice. "Your Majesties, Lady Rebecca Rolfe. And Master Rolfe."

Pocahontas advanced into the hall, with John a step behind her and to her right. She saw a huge room, lined with tapestries, in which thirty or forty elaborately dressed ladies and gentlemen were standing, and it amused her to note that the women, who jostled each other in an attempt to see her better, became tangled in each other's exceptionally wide hoops. King James and Queen Anne sat in high-backed chairs at the far end of the hall, and on either side of them were several smaller chairs. Only one of these was occupied, and Pocahontas knew that the handsome, sardonic man who slouched beside the King was the Duke of Buckingham.

It was difficult to glean a clear impression of Their Majesties on the long, slow walk across the hall, with the sound of her own footsteps echoing in her ears as her heels clattered on the hard, polished wood of the floor. But Pocahontas saw that James's wide, many-layered ruff was made of expensive gold lace that almost hid his face. Anne was a pretty woman, and her eyes were unexpectedly intelligent; Pocahontas took an immediate liking to her and envied her because the Queen's cloth-of-silver gown had a natural, uncorseted waistline. Halting the prescribed seven paces from the chairs,

Pocahontas sank to the floor in a deep curtsy and was infinitely relieved that all of the pins holding her costume together remained in place.

James had not expected to see such an attractive young woman, and, as always, the sight of beauty put him in a petulant mood. "Lady Rebecca," he said without preamble, "how does it happen that a commoner has presumed to marry the daughter of a king? It's a tendency that has become all too frequent of late, and we deplore it."

Pocahontas became so indignant she forgot all of Lady Delaware's careful coaching. She realized suddenly that she and John were being received here today only because she was the daughter of Powhatan, and the King's inability to understand the worth of her husband's contribution to the stability and prosperity of Jamestown infuriated her. If she was being made welcome as the Chief of Chiefs' daughter, she would behave like a true Chickahominy, and she stood before she was granted permission to rise.

Ignoring the surprised murmurs of the courtiers, she faced the King boldly. "As you know, sir," she said clearly, "royalty may do as it pleases. And it pleased me to marry the best of all possible men, not some weakling who happened to inherit his title as chief of his nation."

Her spirit delighted the Queen, who smiled warmly. "Well said," Anne declared.

Buckingham, who liked nothing better than a show of aggressive defiance, came to Pocahontas's rescue immediately and turned to the embarrassed John. "Master Rolfe," he said, "I've heard on all sides that you know more about tobacco than anyone else in the world."

John grinned and shook his head. "The report has been exaggerated, Your Grace."

"I doubt it. And as I've been thinking of investing in some plantations, you can certainly advise me." The duke rose, sauntered over to John, and, taking his arm, led him to a far corner of the hall, where they became engaged in an earnest, low-pitched conversation.

Pocahontas stood alone, facing the King and Queen. James, who was recovering from the bluntness of her attack, stared at her; so few people had ever dared to speak their minds to him that he was disconcerted. "We, too, have heard reports concerning you and we haven't known quite what to expect." He laughed a trifle uncertainly. "In fact, we wondered whether you would appear before us in your native dress."

Still angry, Pocahontas forgot all caution. "If I had, I'd be wearing less paint on my face than has been daubed on me now," she said. "And I assure you that far less of me would be exposed, although I see that nakedness seems to be a virtue at this civilized court." She looked at the ladies in waiting, who, until this moment, had been proud of the low cut of their gowns.

Queen Anne, the most modestly attired lady in the room, laughed and held out her hand. "Come and sit beside me, Cousin."

Everyone present realized at once that she had recognized Pocahontas as an equal, and the courtiers gasped. The King shifted in his chair and glared first at his wife, then at Pocahontas. "How large is your father's realm?" he demanded.

"The land of the Chickahominy is roughly the size of the British Isles, France, and Spain." Pocahontas was beginning to enjoy herself, and for the first time found a release from the frustrations that had plagued her for weeks.

A grizzled man in the uniform of a general stepped forward from the front ranks of the courtiers. "If Your Majesty will pardon my intrusion, I'd like to ask Lady Rebecca a question."

The King nodded.

"Size alone doesn't make a nation great or powerful. How strong are your father's people?"

"Strong enough so the combined armies of England, France, and Spain could not defeat them," Pocahontas answered incisively, paused and then added, "On the other hand, the Chickahominy are not powerful enough to beat those armies either. But in my mind they're stronger, for it would never occur to them to cross the seas and attack people who have done them no harm."

The general's confident smile faded, and a cleric in the rich robes of a bishop applauded softly. Anne could not resist reaching out and patting Pocahontas's arm affectionately, and James, obviously confused, blinked at the visitor. "We have been led to believe that the tribes of America are barbarians," he said querulously.

Pocahontas faced him without fear. "That depends on your definition of a barbarian, sir. Even the poorest Chickahominy is never in want. I have not seen one beggar in our towns, but I have seen many in London."

"We do what we can to eliminate poverty and relieve the distress of our people," James muttered defensively.

"As my father has so often said, that is one of the first duties of a king." Pocahontas glanced briefly at the enormous carved ruby, set in gold, that sparkled on the index finger of James's left hand.

A few independently wealthy and powerful gentlemen smiled when their sovereign hastily withdrew his hand and hid it in the folds of his robe. The sycophants exchanged covert looks, and even the Duke of Buckingham interrupted his conversation with John long enough to raise his eyebrows quizzically and then smother a grin. Not since the days of Elizabeth had talk at the court been either witty or pungent, and James, who had been responsible for the lethargy because of his insistence on absolute agreement with every word he uttered, was nonplussed. He knew how to deal with anyone who dared to dispute him but had no idea how to handle a young woman whose observations were as devastating as her manner was respectful. She reminded him of his mother, Mary of Scotland, and for the first time in his life he felt a twinge of pity for the Earl of Bothwell, his stepfather, whom he had always hated.

"The economy of an advanced nation," he declared sonorously, "is very complex. Some of our most learned men devote their entire lives to the problems of how to distribute money equitably, but no one has yet found the right solution."

"Until then," Pocahontas said with an innocent smile, "the poor would undoubtedly benefit by migrating to some less civilized land."

The Queen was delighted but did not glance in her husband's direction. "I agree," she murmured. "My native country, Denmark, is considered backward in certain circles here. But poverty has been virtually eliminated there."

"Denmark," James said far more loudly than was necessary to make himself heard, "is very small."

"Precisely so, my dear." Anne inclined her head toward him graciously, then turned back to her guest, who was sitting stiffly erect. The posture was anything but natural, as every woman knew from experience, and the Queen leaned forward; some subjects could not be discussed in the hearing of men, so she lowered her voice to a whisper. "You don't find our clothes very comfortable."

Pocahontas saw no reason to hide her opinion of the steel cage that hampered her breathing and pressed against her spine. "I certainly don't!"

"I had been told you ignored our styles. That's why I dressed informally myself." Anne sighed. "In Denmark we were always sensible. Perhaps you and I, between us, can persuade the women of England that the reign of Elizabeth is over and that we don't need to bind ourselves in steel wires. You wouldn't believe how stubborn people are in this country, how opposed they are to any sort of change."

The sympathy and charm of the older woman made Pocahontas forget that she was speaking to the Queen of England, and she giggled. "All I want to know is how it's possible to stand without being jabbed."

"It isn't."

The courtiers, unable to hear more than an occasional word, were pretending to look disinterested, but James was under no compunction to simulate politeness. "What are you saying to each other?" he demanded.

The Queen's expression was bland as she raised her head. "I was apologizing to Lady Rebecca for my inquisitiveness, because there's something I'd like to know. I was once a foreigner in England too," she added apologetically to her visitor, "so my curiosity isn't callous or unthinking, I assure you. I simply wonder why it is that the daughter of a great ruler has chosen to live apart from her own people."

There was a silence, and John, who had been saying something to Buckingham, paused to hear his wife's reply.

"My reasons," Pocahontas said clearly, "are the same as those that cause you to live in London. Your husband is here. My husband makes his home in Jamestown, so where would I live?"

Her response struck a responsive chord in Anne, who made no attempt to conceal her pleasure. "When the audience hour is finished, you and Master Rolfe must dine with me in my apartments."

No one could remember when a guest had made such a complete conquest of the Queen in so short a time, and the ladies and gentlemen of the court muttered to each other in low tones. Many of the nobles present had met Pocahontas at one social function or another, as it had become fashionable in recent weeks for anyone who claimed to be a sophisticate to be on speaking terms with her. But if the Queen was going out of her way to become friendly with her, Lady Rebecca would become a power in society and would need to be treated accordingly. The courtiers began to drift closer to her chair, until King James, who was always upset when he was not the center of attention, glared at them.

"There's a question I'd like to ask too," he said acidly. "When will the pagans of the New World become Christians, Lady Rebecca?" He smiled contemptuously and leaned back in his padded chair.

Pocahontas met his gaze and spoke without hesitation. "As soon as enough of them learn sufficient English to understand your new Bible."

"You've heard of my Bible?"

The courtiers lost interest in the conversation; they had been forced to listen to endless discussions about the King's Bible, and had been in attendance at countless meetings James had held with the translators of the Bible, scholars whose learned arguments over the meaning of a Hebrew or Greek word had been unendurably boring.

But Pocahontas did not share their feeling. She finally had found a topic of mutual interest, and her eyes were bright as she looked at James. "Heard of it? I own the first copy that arrived in Virginia last year and I've been reading it ever since."

The King smiled skeptically; so many of his followers had praised the new edition of the Bible lavishly, hoping to win his approval, but had revealed by their ignorance that they had not even leafed through the thick volume. Lady Rebecca, it appeared, was just a servile flatterer like all the rest. "What's your opinion of the work?" he asked, deliberately prodding her.

"It will be read for many generations, I'm sure. It's infinitely superior to the Bishops' Bible. It has dignity and elegance."

"Could you give me an example of what you mean?" Those who knew him realized he was playing with her, leading her on.

But Pocahontas was unaware of his ulterior motive. "There are so many examples it's hard to know where to begin." She was so absorbed she failed to hear the half-suppressed laughter of the ladies and gentlemen. "The Twenty-third Psalm comes to my mind immediately, as I suppose it does to everyone. *The Lord is my shepherd* is so much stronger than *God leads me.* And the First Commandment, in the Book of Exodus, seems to me to express what Moses really must have heard on Mount Sinai. *I am the*

Lord thy God says so much more than *I am your Lord.*"

James stared at her incredulously and promptly forgot his assumption that she had been shamming. "Some of our clerics," he said, "have objected to the rather poetic cadences of the new translation. There's a citation from Isaiah, for instance, that was prosaic in the Bishops' Bible. *Let them who thirst come to the waters.* Our Hebrew scholars have translated it as, *Ho, every one that thirsteth, come ye to the waters.* As we are something of an author ourself, we prefer the flavor."

Pocahontas nodded. "Prophets like Isaiah were inspired men, and the new version gives the reader the feeling of their fervor and exaltation."

This was the first woman with whom James had been able to discuss his Bible intelligently, and he turned suddenly to his wife. "It has been many weeks since you last invited us to dine in your apartments," he said accusingly.

"You need no invitation, my dear," Anne replied sweetly. "You know you're always welcome."

"Good. I'm hungry for food and even hungrier for talk." The King stood, offered his arm to Pocahontas, and led her out of the chamber.

John and Buckingham hurried to the Queen and escorted her through the door at the rear too; no one else moved, but when they had gone everyone started talking simultaneously. No two courtiers could agree on precisely what had been said, but one fact was obvious to the entire court: Pocahontas's conquest of Their Majesties had been complete.

September, 1613

Pocahontas's triumph at court was the talk of London, and the clamor became even louder in the week that followed her initial appearance at Whitehall. She and John were twice more invited to dine privately with Their Majesties, John received a royal patent which granted his plantations to him and his heirs in perpetuity, and the Queen and Pocahontas became close companions. They attended services at St. Paul's together, the following day they went to the theater, and when the Duke of Buckingham gave a masque in Anne's honor, she and Pocahontas sat apart from the rest of the company. Foreign envoys, the highest nobles and everyone else who was searching for the shortest road to royal favor showered Lady Rebecca and her husband with many more invitations than it was possible for them to accept, and crowds were gathered day and night outside the Cricket and Rooster.

Pocahontas was mildly pleased at the surge in her popularity and was gratified that she had won the friendship of Anne and James, but she felt no deep elation over the stir she had created. What gave her the greatest satisfaction was the knowledge that she had been instrumental in helping John win the concessions he had been seeking from the directors of the London Company. Thanks to her influence at court, the shareholders, all of whom had numerous interests in addition to the colony of Jamestown, were anxious to win her favor and granted the settlers most of the rights for which John had been fighting ever since they had come to England. His business would soon be completed, he told her, and she would not be sorry to leave. The feverish life she was leading in London distorted her sense of values, warped her judgment, and created false perspectives. It was almost impossible for her to think about her marriage and her future in such an atmosphere, and she looked forward to the day when they would return to Virginia.

London, she told herself privately, did not agree with her. She had come here looking for happiness but had not found it, and instead had been forced to accept the meaningless pleasure-seeking standards of the nobility as a substitute. The tensions were too great for her, the strain of maintaining a façade for its own sake began to tell on her, and she found even the weather, which was increasingly raw and damp, was disagreeable. It did not surprise her when she began to feel ill every morning, but she felt sure she would shake off her malaise as soon as she returned to the New World, so she mentioned her discomfort to no one. She saw no need to worry John, so she pretended to eat breakfast with him each morning, although she had no desire for food. And as her strength seemed to increase by noon, she did not curtail her social life; John had told her they would leave on the next ship that sailed for Virginia, sometime within the next month or two, so she tried to ignore her vague ailment. And most of all she tried to conquer the feeling that the visit to England had left her unfulfilled and unsatisfied.

It was easiest to forget herself when something occupied

her mind, and one day, after a particularly listless morning, she looked forward to a reception being given by the Countess of Somerset. The countess, a patroness of poets and dramatists, was entertaining a small group, and Pocahontas, who had been a guest at Somerset House only once previously, knew the occasion would not be dull. She was just finishing her toilet when the nursemaid, who was about to go out for a walk with Celia, tapped on the door of her bedchamber, entered, and curtsied.

"There's a gentleman here to see you, ma'am."

Pocahontas gave a final twist to the curl at her left temple and patted the ringlet that fell over her right shoulder. "Master Rolfe mentioned no callers before he left this morning." She slid her feet into high-tongued, red silk slippers and stood.

"He didn't say he was here to see Master Rolfe, ma'am. He just said to tell you he was here." The woman laughed nervously and wiped her hands on her apron.

"I'm expecting no visitor either."

"He give me ninepence for my trouble, so I figured he wasn't expected, ma'am. He just said to tell you Captain Smith is here. And he seemed sure you'd see him, even though I told him you have an appointment in a little while."

Pocahontas stiffened as though she had been struck, but spoke calmly. "Very well, I'll see him. But don't go out," she added hastily. "I'd like you and Celia to stay nearby in the other bedchamber as long as he's here."

"Yes, ma'am." The nursemaid bobbed her head knowingly and withdrew.

A sense of panic assailed Pocahontas as the door closed, and when she caught hold of her dressing table to steady herself, her hand was trembling. She closed her eyes, fought a wave of nausea that swept over her, and had to resist the temptation to flee. It would be so easy to run down the stairs that led from the bedroom to the courtyard, where her coach was waiting for her, and she had to remind herself sharply

that she had no reason to avoid Smith. He meant nothing to
her any more, she had no cause to be afraid of him or of her
own reactions in his presence, and it would be cowardly to
avoid him.

Having reassured herself that he could do her no harm,
she grew calmer and was about to open the door when she
heard his deep voice and Celia's shrill laughter. She shrank
from the idea of seeing him in the child's presence and waited
until the nursemaid took Celia off into the other bedchamber. Then, when all was quiet again in the living room,
she raised the latch and stepped quickly over the threshold.

"Good day, Captain Smith," she said coolly, noting at
once that he had dressed with care for the occasion. He wore
the new stiff lace collar in place of a multilayered neck ruff,
his legs were encased in blue silk stockings embroidered with
gold clocks, and a red velvet money pouch hung from his
belt. Whatever his reasons for seeking this interview, they
were important to him.

"Lady Rebecca," he declared solemnly, and advanced to
kiss her hand. But Pocahontas pretended to be unaware of his
intention and continued to hold her arm at her side, so he
had to content himself with a deep bow.

He straightened, studying every detail of her appearance
with frank admiration, and it occurred to Pocahontas, who
became increasingly uncomfortable under his scrutiny, that
he was bolder than any other gallant in London. She knew
that she looked attractive in her plum-colored taffeta gown
with cuffs of fine lace and a deep collar of black fox fur, which
swept down to her waist in the front, showing her low-cut
lace bodice. But Smith was staring so hard at her neckline
that she felt ashamed of her gown and, controlling an impulse to draw the fur strips together, she wished she had worn
one of the stiffened front panels that she hated.

Smith's crudeness, in and of itself, did not bother her, and
she was indifferent to the lack of good taste he displayed too.
But what did upset her was her realization that she had once

been flattered by his coarse interest in her and had been grateful for the few favors he had shown her. It was difficult for her to believe that she had ever been so naïve, and she tried not to conceal her mortification by pretending to be unaware of his attention. "Your visit," she said bluntly, "is a surprise."

"It's long overdue," he replied, smiling. "I hope I haven't come at an inopportune time."

"I have an engagement at one o'clock," she admitted, and wished she hadn't been so truthful, for he looked relieved and sat down in the nearest chair.

"Then we have plenty of time to talk," Smith said, making himself comfortable.

"I didn't know you and I had anything in common." Pocahontas hadn't intended to sound so bitter.

There was no change in his expression. "We'll always have something in common as long as I'm capable of appreciating beauty. I must say," he continued, looking her up and down slowly, "that the reputation you've acquired here is deserved. Everyone is saying that you're even lovelier than Lady Benton. And having seen her many times, I must agree that she can't compare with you."

It was difficult to turn aside an elaborate compliment, so Pocahontas said nothing and inclined her head a fraction of an inch, informing him that she had heard him but that she was unimpressed.

"You have no idea," he added smoothly, "how many of my friends have been offering me congratulations recently."

She raised an eyebrow in polite, cautious inquiry but remained silent.

"Ordinarily praise means nothing to me." Smith waved his hand airily, as though thrusting aside unwanted honors. "In this instance, however, I'm pleased to accept recognition." He paused and glanced around the room. "There's no need for us to stand on ceremony with each other, is there? I'm uncommonly thirsty."

Her pride prevented her from waiting on him, and she merely nodded toward a jar of sack and some glasses on a sideboard. His manner, she knew, was too casual, and as he poured himself a drink she tried to understand the meaning behind his words but could not. "You talk in riddles, Captain Smith."

He raised his glass to her. "After all, it was I who found you in the wilderness of the New World, and I'm willing to take whatever crumbs of credit are thrown to me."

Pocahontas knew she should not lose her temper but was unable to restrain herself. "Perhaps," she retorted, "it was I who found you. Whatever name you've acquired is a direct result of your visits to the land of the Chickahominy. No one in London remembers Gabriel Archer or the others who served with you in the early days of Jamestown. But you achieved a certain renown because of the treaty you made with my father. And if it hadn't been for me, there would have been no agreement." She knew she was behaving childishly, but the opportunity to express some of the thoughts she had buried within herself for so long made her light-headed.

To her surprise Smith made no attempt to dispute her argument, and although his eyes narrowed, he merely shrugged. "We're really saying the same thing. You and I have contributed a great deal to each other's fame."

His carefully modulated, reasonable tone was too much for her. "Fame means nothing to me," she retorted.

"Then it's all the more remarkable that your name is known throughout Europe." Smith paused for an instant, and Pocahontas could see that he was going through some sort of inner struggle. As she had suspected, his calm was only assumed. "Is it true," he asked, unable to keep an edge of envy from his voice, "that you've received an invitation to visit the French King at the Louvre?"

Pocahontas had thought that Smith was incapable of arousing any emotion in her, bus she discovered she was reveling in the knowledge that he was jealous of her success. "Milord d'Anjou has mentioned something of the sort, I believe," she said carelessly.

Smith looked at her solemnly. "Be careful, then. Louis XIII is a bachelor and is very young and susceptible. But there's no need to be concerned really. His mother and Cardinal Richelieu keep a close watch over him."

Obviously he was trying to lead the conversation into channels connected with his purpose in having come here, and Pocahontas was irritated by his deviousness. "I need neither the Queen Mother nor the Lord Cardinal of France to protect me," she said crisply. "My husband performs that function and never fails to look out for my interests."

Smith nodded gravely, sighed, and finished his sack. "Your husband." He seemed lost in thought for a long moment. "The little girl in there is Rolfe's child, I suppose?"

"Celia is our daughter, John's and mine," Pocahontas replied firmly.

He raised his eyebrows, then frowned. "You were married to him in Jamestown."

"I fail to see how the details of my private life are any of your concern, sir!" She warned herself that she was speaking too loudly; unless she lowered her voice, Celia would rush into the room to find out what had happened.

"I have a deep regard for you," he assured her, "and whatever touches you is of major importance to me."

Pocahontas had no idea what he wanted, but it was pointless to prolong this discussion. "Your attitude has changed since I've been accepted at court then. Your lack of interest in me when I first arrived in London was rather marked, if you'll recall."

Smith stood and shook his head sorrowfully. "Your memory is at fault, not mine. I distinctly remember that I tried to show you how I felt toward you."

Her eyes became hard. "That's a polite way of saying that you made an unsuccessful attempt to assault my virtue."

"How you will persist in misunderstanding me. I was trying to demonstrate my affection for you." He towered over her, smiling.

Pocahontas hastily moved away from him and put a table between them. "It's clear that you don't know the difference between affection and seduction, Captain Smith. However, I have no desire to debate the matter with you, so I'll bid you good day."

"One moment." Somewhat to her surprise he made no attempt to follow her. "I've been trying to find a gentle way to break my news to you, but I see you're hostile to me, for reasons I can't even pretend to understand. So you give me no choice. I must tell you in my own way and simply ask you to forgive me if I sound rather brutal and direct."

It was typical of him, Pocahontas thought contemptuously, to try to frighten her with vague threats, but even though she recognized his motive she found she was unsteady, and put her hands on the top of the table. "Well?"

"It hasn't been easy for me to keep my distance from you in all these months we've been in the same city," Smith said blandly. "But I owed it to both of us until I made my investigation. It's finished now, so there's no reason for me to stay away any longer."

"Your investigation?"

"At great expense I've hired the services of several of the most able lawyers in England, men who have influence with Sir Edward Coke, the Lord Chief Justice. They've examined the legal archives exhaustively and they've concluded that under the law your marriage to me is still valid."

Pocahontas was too stunned to reply.

"In other words, you're still my wife. You've committed bigamy by marrying Rolfe, too, but it would be senseless for me to press charges against either of you. I certainly bear no malice toward anyone and I'll be satisfied if both of you sign a few simple documents I've had prepared. The legal complications are only technicalities, and the sooner we dispense with them, the sooner this unsavory matter will be concluded. Then you and I can resume life as man and wife."

"You want a marriage to me?" she asked incredulously.

"Of course. It's all I want."

Suddenly Pocahontas started to laugh and could not stop until her sides ached and tears rolled down her cheeks. "How fantastically transparent you are!" she cried, controlling herself at last. "You've been having difficulty raising the money for your new company of exploration and settlement in the New World. Don't bother to deny it, because several people have mentioned it to me. You think that a resumption of marriage to me will smooth away all your difficulties. You think that through my influence at court you'll be able to persuade wealthy men like the Duke of Buckingham and the Earl of Pembroke to invest in your company."

Gasping for breath, she took a handkerchief from her bosom and wiped her eyes.

"I wouldn't dignify your charges by denying them," Smith replied in an injured voice. "Naturally your new friends at court might be helpful to me in completing the plans for my expedition. It won't surprise me if the King himself wants to make a substantial investment after he's heard the full details of what I have in mind. But all that is irrelevant. Of course husbands and wives work together for their mutual good and mutual advantage. What matters is marriage itself."

Pocahontas felt as though her flesh was crawling and she made no attempt to hide her disgust. "I am not your wife," she said in a low, intense voice. "And when I look back on the past, I realize that I was never your wife. For a very brief time, may the Lord have pity on me, I was your mistress." She did not look at him, and holding her head high, walked to the front door of the suite. "I must ask you to leave, Captain Smith."

"I hoped you'd be sensible, Pocahontas." It was the first time he had addressed her by her Chickahominy name since he had come into the room. "I have no desire to create a scandal, but if you insist on opposing me, I'll be forced to take the entire matter to the courts."

"Do what you please." She raised the latch and opened the door. "Good-by, Captain Smith."

He stalked out, and she heard his boots clattering on the stairs as he descended to the courtyard below.

The unpleasant incident did not worry Pocahontas unduly during the rest of the day, and it slipped from her mind for long periods at the Countess of Somerset's reception. As she had told Smith, she had seen through his flimsy maneuver immediately; his sly attempt to turn her popularity to his own advantage was repugnant to her, but she knew him well enough to believe that his threat was an empty gesture. And although she admittedly was ignorant of the intricacies of the law, it was inconceivable to her that any judge would treat Smith's complaint seriously, so she dismissed the entire distasteful subject.

But it was brought back to her mind when she met John after the reception and, along with several of the countess's other guests, attended a performance of a play, *Volpone*, that had lost none of its popularity in the eight years since it had first been presented. The hero was a knave and a scoundrel, and some of his tactics reminded Pocahontas so much of Smith that she could not enjoy herself. She watched the actors in silence, rarely joining in the laughter, and John, aware that something was troubling her, made their excuses to the others when they left the theater and took her home.

Pocahontas undressed quickly and then, attired in her dressing gown and white boudoir cap, joined John in the living room, where he was drinking a mug of ale. He tried not to show his concern and smiled at her as she sat down opposite him. "I'm sorry I didn't feel in a festive mood tonight," she said lightly.

"That's perfectly all right. You aren't ill?"

"Oh no. I'm fine." She hesitated, then added, "There is something I must tell you though." Taking a deep breath, she plunged into the story of Smith's visit at noon.

John listened in silence, but long before she came to the end of her recital he jumped to his feet and paced restlessly up and down the room, halting occasionally to smash his right fist into the open palm of his left hand. When Pocahontas was finished she looked up at him and realized that never since she had known him had he been so angry and upset; his eyes were glowing, and a thin, white line showed around his mouth. "You don't for a moment take his threat seriously, John?" she asked, afraid for the first time.

"Hardly." He continued to roam around the room.

"There couldn't be any truth to his claim, then?"

"It's false, from beginning to end." John halted in front of her chair and put a hand on her shoulder. "I studied the law during my second year at Cambridge, and there's no validity to Smith's charges. In the first place, the English courts probably wouldn't even recognize your Chickahominy marriage to him. But even if they did, you have proof that your father granted you an annulment and that you were later married to me in Indian rites as well as in a church ceremony. You're my wife under English law, as well as according to Chickahominy custom."

Pocahontas felt so relieved that not until now did she realize she actually had been worried all day. "If you can be that certain, the lawyers Smith hired must have told him the same thing."

"Lawyers?" John laughed unpleasantly. "No lawyer who values his reputation would take such a shoddy case. I'm willing to wager the new patent the King granted to me that Smith hasn't seen a lawyer, much less obtained a legal opinion. The whole scheme is the product of his imagination, and for some reason he thinks you and I are so naïve and gullible that we'll let him frighten us into accepting a permanent separation."

Pocahontas felt queasy again but paid no attention to her physical condition; far more important considerations were weighing on her mind. "There was a time," she said painfully, "when I was as naïve as Smith believes me to be now. I accepted everything he said to me without question. So I really can't blame him for thinking I haven't changed. He's the kind of man who accepts one impression of a person and then always conceives of that person in the same terms. Please, John, aren't you going to sit down?"

"Not just now."

"You aren't sleepy?"

"No." His grip on her shoulder tightened. "I think you'd better go to bed, though. You look tired, and it's no wonder." He lifted her to her feet when she would have protested. "But before you go, I want to tell you I'm very grateful to you."

Perhaps exhaustion was clouding her mind, but she couldn't understand his meaning. "Grateful?"

"You minced no words with Smith."

A wave of indignation swept over her, arousing her. "I certainly didn't!"

"By making your position clear to him, you've made it clear to me too." He slipped an arm around her shoulder and led her toward the bedchamber. "The circumstances of our marriage were unusual. Smith came between us, and his shadow has separated us until today."

"He hasn't come between us for a long time."

John knew she was too weary to continue the conversation. "In any case, there were still doubts in my mind, but they've been dispelled now, and that's why I'm grateful to you." The white line appeared around his lips again. "I suppose I should be thankful to him for clearing the air too. However, that's another matter, and there's no need for you to give it any thought."

He was helping her into bed now, and Pocahontas's fears subsided as her head touched the pillow. John had been so enraged that she had thought he might do something drastic, but, she told herself, she should have realized that she was married to the most civilized and self-disciplined of all men. Other husbands might have felt jealous of her social success in London and her triumph at court. But John had been proud of her achievements, and at no time had it disturbed him to remain in the background while she basked in the admiration of the whole city. He had been pleased to acknowledge her inadvertent contribution to the victory he had won in his battle for greater concessions from the directors of the London Company, and although a lesser man might have resented her influence over the King and Queen, he had been quietly appreciative when James, as a gesture to her, had given him the new patent for his plantations.

She smiled at him tremulously as he arranged the blankets over her, and then she closed her eyes. John was opening and shutting cupboard doors, and she turned over, luxuriating in the soft warmth. He always sat down on his side of the bed to remove his shoes, and Pocahontas expected to feel the mattress sag under his weight; when it did not, she opened her eyes.

"Aren't you coming to bed?"

"Eventually."

She saw he had taken his hat and cloak from the cupboard and that he was buckling on his sword. Sitting upright, she clutched the blankets and stared at him. "Where are you going?" she asked, terror thickening her voice.

"I've got to go out on a brief errand." He could not look at her.

"John!"

He turned and faced Pocahontas, smiled reassuringly, and tried to speak calmly. "All right, then. If you must know, I'm going to see Smith."

"Must you?" She felt hot, then started to shiver.

"Yes. He's assumed too much."

Pocahontas's heart pounded in her ears, and she felt faint. "He's a professional soldier, John. He has no conscience and he's as strong as an animal."

He kissed her lightly, silencing her protests. "There are some things in this world that are more important to me than ordinary reason or common sense. Your honor is one of them." He walked quickly to the door and was gone.

September, 1613

They eyed each other narrowly, standing with their feet planted wide apart and their hands on their hips near the weapons that hung from their belts. They were sober, mature men, and both of them had made significant contributions to their country and their age, but at the moment they looked like two wary male animals ready to spring at each other. Their hatred, deep and intense, swirled around them, but they were civilized, so neither leaped at his enemy's throat; they were gentlemen, too, and therefore spoke quietly, in conversational tones, as though they were friends who enjoyed spending an evening together. Had they been French or Italian they would have dropped their polite façade and reached for their knives, and had they been subjects of one of the German principalities they would have fought with their bare fists, but English tradition demanded that they hide their emotions.

John concealed his cold rage behind a courteous mask,

and when he spoke his voice was civil, though icy. "I hope I haven't inconvenienced you by calling on you unexpectedly at this late hour, Captain."

Smith smiled pleasantly as he balanced himself on the balls of his feet, and although he was prepared for sudden violence, he managed to give the impression that he was completely relaxed. "I'm honored by your visit, Master Rolfe."

"Thank you." John continued to look steadily at the burly man who faced him.

"Will you join me in a cup of wine? I have a cask of excellent Malaga that happened to find its way into the country after a Spanish galleon suffered a rather unfortunate accident on the high seas recently." Smith moved to a littered table and gestured graciously toward a thick bottle. In the process he deftly scooped up an earring he had just seen beside a mug and pocketed it; at the moment he couldn't remember to whom it belonged, but that wasn't important. It was wise not to flaunt his conquests before Rolfe, who was certain to make trouble in every way he could.

"You're very kind, but I make it a practice not to drink after I've eaten my supper." John saw the earring disappear, but his expression did not change.

"I wish you'd make an exception." It would be cowardly, Smith thought, to pretend he was ignorant of the reason for Rolfe's visit or to appear reluctant to bring the subject into the open. "It's only fair to tell you that I enjoyed a glass of your sack earlier today. In fact, I liked it very much."

"I regret," John replied slowly, "that I wasn't there to offer it to you myself."

His challenge was too direct to be ignored, and Smith's smile faded. "We're both generous men living in an inhospitable world, Master Rolfe. It so happens that my business wasn't with you this morning, however."

"Any business that concerns my wife concerns me," John said flatly, stating a fact rather than making an accusation.

Smith met his gaze without flinching. "I had been in hopes that I could settle a vexing and unfortunate matter with Pocahontas and that it would be unnecessary to see you until the problem was solved."

"Any dealings with Mistress Rolfe," John declared, stressing his wife's name, "must be arranged through me."

"A man organizes his household according to whatever rules he pleases to make," Smith replied with an indifferent shrug. "And I certainly wouldn't presume to deny you that right. For however long Pocahontas remains under your protection."

"Mistress Rolfe is under my permanent protection." John's poise and surface calm did not desert him.

"You and I seem to hold different opinions, Master Rolfe."

Verbal sparring settled nothing and wasted time, John thought. "I wasn't expressing an opinion, Captain. Society recognizes a husband's responsibilities, and although you're apparently unaware of them, our law courts and our churches are sensitive to them."

"Permit me to assure you, Master Rolfe, that I require no instruction from you or anyone else on the obligations and rights of a husband."

"Then, Captain, you'll be anxious to show me the legal substantiation of your claim that Mistress Rolfe is your wife rather than mine."

Smith looked regretful. "Unfortunately, I don't have the papers at hand."

It was John's turn to smile. "Then I'll have to be content to examine the other documents."

"Other documents?"

"You told Mistress Rolfe when you saw her today that you and your legal advisers had prepared a number of papers, some for her signature and some for mine, which state that our marriage is not valid and that she is your wife."

Smith realized his adversary was a man of quiet strength,

but he had never yet been defeated in a battle of wits, and his confidence in his own cleverness was undiminished. "Had I known you were coming here this evening, I would have had everything in readiness for you. Those particular documents are in the safekeeping of my attorneys, and at the moment are resting in their strongboxes."

"Until such time as I am offered direct proof to the contrary, I shall believe, as I believe right now, that those papers exist only in your own mind, Captain."

A dangerous light shone in Smith's eyes. "Are you calling me a liar, Master Rolfe?"

"One name is as good as another." It occurred to John that he was enjoying himself, that he had been jealous of Smith for a long time, and that this encounter was satisfying a need he had felt ever since he had first fallen in love with Pocahontas. "I know precisely what you were trying to do today. Shall I go on?"

"If you please. I'm entertained, although I must warn you that I'm not amused."

"You came to Mistress Rolfe today with an intricate little scheme in mind. You hoped to frighten her into believing she was still your wife and was guilty of bigamy. If you had succeeded in fooling her, you would have gone to a lawyer and ordered him to draw up a declaration of guilt, which you then would have taken to her to sign. There is no such paper right now, for the simple reason that you weren't going to spend the money on it until you felt reasonably sure she would accept your story. Had your plan worked, you then would have prepared such a document, and once Mistress Rolfe had signed it, you would have come to me. I would have been placed in an untenable position."

"Ingenious," Smith murmured.

"Diabolical is a more accurate description," John retorted. "You would have faced me with my wife's confession that she had married me under false pretenses. You were hoping that I'd then give her up rather than see her hurt. But had I refused, the possession of such a confession still would have enabled you to create a scandal, and you expected to benefit from the notoriety."

Smith hadn't been prepared for such a shrewd and penetrating analysis of his intentions. It wasn't often that he underestimated a foe, and for a moment he was shaken. But he reminded himself that he had emerged unscathed from far more delicate situations and, throwing back his head, he laughed loudly. "Do you expect me to deny this preposterous fabrication?"

"I expect nothing and I wouldn't accept a denial. Men like you have lost touch with the times, Captain. A generation ago your standards would have been admired, and no one would have frowned at your methods, provided they succeeded. But we've acquired a new sense of responsibility and morality since men like Hawkins and Drake became wealthy by preying on the merchantmen of other nations while justifying their acts by claiming they were patriots. You were born at the wrong time, Captain. Piracy is no longer respectable, and just as you can't rob a ship, you can't steal someone else's wife."

The fellow's pious sermonizing was irritating rubbish, Smith thought; human nature never changed. "Spare me your sentiments," he said curtly.

"Certainly." John bowed to him. "I'm simply serving notice on you that you will not molest Mistress Rolfe again."

"Molest, sir? I resent your choice of words."

"And I resent your unwanted attentions to my wife. You will not have an opportunity to repeat them." John carefully removed his right glove and hurled it into the bigger man's face.

Smith was so astonished he could only stare, unable to believe in his good fortune. Had Rolfe left after exposing his plan to capitalize on Pocahontas's fame, there would have been nothing more he could have done to further the scheme. But by challenging him to a duel, Rolfe was playing directly into his hands. He could insist now that Pocahontas was truly his wife, and some people would accept his story. Whether they did or not was almost irrelevant, however. Thanks to Rolfe's impulsive anger, their duel would be the talk of the town, and he would be in a position afterward to reap the full benefit of the renown that Pocahontas had acquired.

Concealing his elation, he stooped and picked up the glove. "I prefer rapiers to pistols, I believe," he drawled.

"As you wish." John knew he had behaved rashly but could not recall a time when he had felt such fierce pleasure.

"Are you familiar with Catherine Parr's Wood, on the road to Windsor?"

"I am." John had not fought a duel since his student days at Cambridge, but he felt no fear. He was in the right and he would win.

Smith wanted a chance to tell some of his friends about the duel so they could prepare to spread the word of his victory, and although it was customary for gentlemen to meet as soon as possible after a challenge had been issued, he needed a day of preparation. And, he thought, after he killed Rolfe, Pocahontas really would be free to marry him. He felt certain he could persuade her to become his wife as soon as he made her a widow, for she would no longer be torn by the divided loyalties that were now confusing her half-civilized mind. Then every door in London, including the gilded gates of Whitehall itself, would be open to him, Smith told himself as he contemplated the promising future, and it seemed right and fitting to him that Pocahontas, who had caused so much difficulty for him in the past, should offer him compensation. It wouldn't be pleasant, of course, to give up his cherished status as a bachelor, but as a farsighted man he realized that the sacrifice of his freedom was a small price to pay for his rightful place in history. Through Pocahontas he would obtain all the financing he needed for the Plymouth Company, and then he would win undying glory as the undisputed leader of the colony he would establish in the region that Bartholomew Gosnold had named Cape Cod. After a time a wife would become something of a hindrance to him, of course, so he would leave Pocahontas behind, and she could continue to enjoy herself as the pet of London society.

"Master Rolfe," he said triumphantly, "I'll meet you at the Wood the day after tomorrow."

"Agreed." John nodded curtly and started for the door, but paused at the threshold and smiled. "I'm glad the air is going to be cleared."

Smith stared at him quizzically and then chuckled. "The pleasure," he said, "is mine."

John did not bother to reply, and as he returned to the Cricket and Rooster he was amused at the thought that it was typical of Smith to have insisted on speaking the last word. When he reached his suite he forgot his flamboyant opponent, for Pocahontas was wide awake and hurried to the door to greet him. She listened in silence as he told her about the impending duel, and although he had expected her to protest, she surprised him by saying nothing. Her eyes were veiled and her face was devoid of all expression as she bowed her head submissively, so he concluded that she was accepting his solution to the problem that had caused such trouble for both of them. John was so relieved that he made no objection when she told him she wasn't sleepy and stayed in the living room as he went off to bed; he couldn't blame her for wanting time to digest the news.

He dropped off almost immediately, happy in the knowledge that he would repay Smith for the humiliating frustrations he had suffered for so long, and he did not know that Pocahontas remained in the living room until the first smudges of dawn appeared in the London sky. Then she crept into bed, and when John awoke she appeared to be sleeping soundly, so he did not disturb her. After dressing quietly, he ate breakfast with Celia and, following his usual routine, departed for the offices of the London Company.

Pocahontas arose as soon as he was gone, sent the nurse-maid off for her carriage, and dressed quickly. She forced herself to drink a mug of scalding tea, and after telling the nursemaid she would return shortly, she left the suite as the sun was climbing above St. Paul's. She was not tired, in spite of her lack of rest, and her step was brisk as she descended to her carriage, where the coachman, who was astonished that a lady would go out at such an early hour, was waiting for her. The courtyard was empty, as her usual throng of admirers had not yet put in an appearance, and although a number of horsemen were abroad, there were no other carriages in the streets. Fashionable London would not begin its day for at least another three hours.

When Pocahontas arrived at her destination she glanced at the upper floors of the building and saw that the blinds inside most of the windows were still drawn. The porter who usually stood at the entrance had not yet reported for work, and she stood indecisively for a moment while her coachman watched her curiously. She told herself that she could not turn back now and, discarding the last shreds of her pride, she opened the door and stepped inside. The air was stale and musty, and she coughed as she put her right hand on the banister; she realized that she was trembling, and she felt queasy, so she waited until the spasm subsided and then quickly mounted the stairs to the rooms of Captain John Smith.

She tapped on the door, and when there was no response a wave of panic engulfed her. It occurred to her that Smith might be entertaining a woman, and she wanted to flee, but she knew that if she left now she would be abandoning all hope for the future, so she rapped more loudly, using her wedding ring as a knocker, and the sound was magnified by the quiet. Her wait seemed interminable, and she finally decided that Smith had gone out. Swallowing her sharp disappointment, she was about to turn away when she heard an inner door open and close. Footsteps approached, and she smoothed her hair, opened her cloak, and tried to smile. Her lips felt frozen and stiff, and for an instant she thought she would faint. Then, as the door opened, she reminded herself that her situation was desperate, and the realization that she had to depend on her own efforts calmed her.

Smith's eyes were heavy with sleep, his face was puffy, and his hands fumbled with the sash of an old wool dressing gown. When he saw his visitor, however, his fingers tightened around the cord, and sleep was forgotten. He did not try to hide his astonishment and he peered over her shoulder to see if she had been accompanied by an escort. He was bewildered but reacted instinctively, and after standing aside to let her precede him into the suite he closed the door and carefully bolted it.

"Pocahontas, the daughter of Powhatan, greets Smith," she said in the language of the Chickahominy, and although she spoke quietly, her voice sounded high and strained in her own ears.

He studied her closely, saw that she was experiencing difficulty in controlling herself, and grinned. He had no idea why she had come to him, but no matter what her reason, he was confident that he could handle her.

She knew precisely what he was thinking, and her resolve hardened; he still thought she was a stupid woman, and she had no intention of disillusioning him.

"I'm not sure I'm awake yet," Smith said lightly. "I was dreaming about you all night and I may be dreaming now."

Pocahontas returned his gaze steadily. "No, I'm here." He approached her, and having anticipated his move, she evaded him deftly by drifting to the far side of the room. Then, smiling to show him that she took no offense, she turned and faced him. "Look at me, please," she said quietly.

Other women were more experienced in the art of flirtation, but she was improving, and the mere fact that she was trying to entice him pleased Smith. He looked her up and down boldly and started toward her again, but her next words were so unexpected that he halted.

"Do you recognize what I'm wearing?"

Her bodice of unbleached wool and skirt of bright blue satin looked vaguely familiar to him, but he shrugged.

"My lace ruff and cuffs are new. But this is the dress I made with the materials you brought to me on your first visit to the land of my father. I wore it when you left me to return to Jamestown."

Smith was always annoyed when a woman actively sought a compliment and robbed him of the initiative that was his masculine prerogative, but this was not the moment to show his irritation. "Very attractive," he murmured.

"I wore it to remind you of the past." She had spent the better part of the night deciding what she would say to him, and she felt like an actor on a stage, but it was too late now to change her tactics.

"I need no reminders, so that was unnecessary."

"I hope you're right."

She was upset, he thought, and decided it would be wise to give her a chance to compose herself. Probably she had not found it easy to renounce Rolfe and was feeling a twinge of remorse, which was responsible for her cool, almost harsh tone and enigmatic statements. Bu she was here and, having won his victory, Smith was prepared to be generous, even gentle. "We'll have a long time to talk. Right now I suggest you join me in some breakfast."

"No, thank you," Pocahontas replied courteously, "but don't let my lack of appetite stop you." It was difficult not to apologize for calling on him so early in the day, but she couldn't afford to take a defensive position for fear he would exploit it.

He went to a chest made of hollow bricks filled with cold water, removed a platter of beef, and cut himself several thick slices of meat. Then he took a loaf of barley bread from the top of the cabinet, poured himself a cup of dark ale from a

jug, and sat down at a table opposite Pocahontas. If she chose
to dramatize her decision to leave Rolfe by remaining hungry, that was her privilege.

Pocahontas sat quietly, watching Smith eat, and did not
speak until he finished his meal and wiped his mouth on his
sleeve. A man was always more inclined to be amenable after
he had eaten. "Have you wondered why I spoke to you in the
tongue of the Chickahominy when I came into this room?"
she asked.

"It was a pretty whim, and I enjoyed it." He smiled and
stretched his legs.

She looked at him soberly. "It was no whim. I must be sure
you have not forgotten the weeks you spent in the land of my
father."

It occurred to Smith for the first time that she might have
some reason other than the obvious one for having come to
him. His inability to judge her correctly in the past had
caused him great inconvenience and hardship, so he decided
to proceed cautiously. "Why is it so important that I remember these things?" he demanded.

She clenched her fists and felt her jaw tighten, but forced
herself to relax. If Smith even guessed that she was afraid, her
visit would end in failure. "I've learned," she said slowly,
"that John came to you last night and foolishly challenged
you to a duel."

He stood and glared down at her. "He's sent you to me. He
wants to call off the fight and he's hiding behind your skirts."

"You're mistaken. He doesn't know I'm here and he'd be
very angry if he learned of my visit. I'm putting my trust in
your discretion."

Smith's vanity had been hurt and, hooking his thumbs in
his belt, he moved toward her until he stood directly in front
of her. "You hope to persuade me not to fight, then," he said
contemptuously. "Like all women, you think your honor is
more precious than a man's and you've come here to bargain
with me. You'll offer yourself to me if I'll agree not to cross
swords with Rolfe."

·"I must admit that the idea crossed my mind during the night," Pocahontas said. "And if I thought it would prevent a senseless fight that will settle nothing, I wouldn't hesitate to make such a bargain with you. But I know better. I know the value men place on their honor."

"You presume to know a great deal."

"Gentlemen in England who like to think they're civilized are very much like the warriors of the Chickahominy, whom you call savages." She stood and discovered that her fear had vanished. "The duel will take place, I know. John will insist on fighting, and so will you. According to the code of men, you would be called a coward if you failed to appear tomorrow."

She was right, of course, and Smith stared at her, unable to fathom her reason for coming to him.

"You, of all men on earth, are no coward. I have seen you endure terrible punishment without complaint, so I know you have courage, even greater courage than the braves of wilderness tribes who are taught from birth to be strong." Pocahontas looked straight into his eyes. "I also know you will kill John tomorrow, for you are a better swordsman."

"You certainly won't be surprised or shocked, then."

"I have come to you," she continued quietly, ignoring his ironic interruption, "to ask you to spare his life. I beg you not to harm him and not to let him suspect that you are being generous. He must never know, as it would be cruel to let him live but to destroy his manhood by crushing his pride. You are the cleverest of men, so you could spare him without his knowledge."

Smith was stunned, unable to believe that anyone could be so naïve.

"Let me remind you again of the time you spent in the land of the Chickahominy," Pocahontas went on, undeterred by his incredulous expression. "I have never upbraided you for the way you treated me, nor have I complained because you took advantage of me. You are a man and I am a woman, and no one is to blame for what happened between

us. And in the years when I wanted your love, I didn't try to
buy your loyalty by reminding you that when you were my
father's prisoner I saved your life."

"I mentioned the incident in my book, you know," he
said, a defensive note creeping into his voice.

"I know. I read that part of your book." She continued to
speak quietly, without rancor. "You gave yourself great credit. But you neglected to mention that I risked my life for you
and that my father spared both of our lives only because he
was generous to me. When I was lonely and hurt, I was often
tempted to make demands on you, but I could ask nothing of
you for myself. Now I am not ashamed to request payment in
return for John's sake. You owe your life to me, so give me
his."

Smith had no ready answer and realized that she had
maneuvered him into an extraordinarily uncomfortable position. If he let Rolfe live, he would be acting against his own
best interest, but if he refused Pocahontas, he would be
admitting to her that he was not a gentleman; even more
important, he would irrevocably spoil his chance of persuading her to marry him after she became a widow. She had
developed a strength and depth of character she hadn't
possessed when he had known her in the New World, and
her growth disturbed him.

"I could ask King James to halt the duel," she said, "and I
know he would send troops to stop it, as he doesn't approve of
sword fights. But if I did, I would lose my husband's love, as
he'd be sure I had no respect for him. You men don't
understand what causes a woman to admire you. All of you
think you must show off your physical strength. You forget
that we wear the skins of the bear and the buffalo, which have
been caught for us by the men who have qualities other than
those of animals. It is those qualities that women esteem."
Pocahontas felt exhausted and moved to the door. "When
tomorrow comes, John Smith will do what he thinks is right.
I can say no more."

She unbolted the door, folded her arms and inclined her head in Indian fashion, and left quickly.

Smith made no attempt to follow her but continued to stand in the middle of the room, his lips twisting in a wry smile. It was mad to consider Pocahontas's request seriously, yet he found he was weighing it, trying to find some satisfactory escape from the dilemma she had created for him. Strangely, none of her arguments influenced him, but what did impress him was the moral courage she had demonstrated in coming to him and the devotion she had shown for Rolfe. There had been a time, he thought, when she had loved him fiercely and without reservation, too, when she had offered him more than any other woman had ever given him.

He tried to tell himself that he was shaken because she had startled him and had employed all of her feminine cunning in presenting her appeal to him. But at the same time he could not rid himself of a sense of lingering regret, and he knew that if he had not rejected her, she would still love him. His smile fading, Smith walked to the window and watched Pocahontas ride off in her carriage.

September, 1613

Pocahontas made a desperate effort to conceal her terror when John came into their bedchamber an hour before dawn to say good-by to her. She knew she should not distract him, as he needed to concentrate his full attention on the dangerous task he had set for himself. It was almost impossible to hide her fears, but she tried: she closed her eyes for an instant, then opened them again and saw him standing just inside the door, dressed in somber black, with the flickering lights of a pair of candles playing on his face and casting long, thin shadows across the room. She came to him quickly, clutching her dressing gown at the throat, and he twisted his sword belt to the side before he embraced her.

As he took her in his arms, Pocahontas, fascinated but repelled by the blade, touched the cold metal of the hilt. She shuddered, and John's arms tightened around her.

"This isn't the sword I'll use. The seconds will provide the rapiers," he said.

"Seconds?"

"Yes. As I told you, Lord Delaware is coming with me. He'll look after my interests. And I understand that Smith's second will be Sir Walter Raleigh."

Pocahontas buried her face in his shoulder. "I'm not in the least surprised that he chose Sir Walter."

"I really don't care one way or the other." John glanced out of the window at the sky. "It's time for me to meet Lord Delaware, and we have a long ride ahead."

She returned his kiss fervently, and when he released her she continued to cling to him. She told herself she must not weep, and made an unsuccessful attempt to smile as she looked up at him. She wanted to shout that he was jeopardizing their joint happiness needlessly, that if he lost his life she would be condemned to spend the rest of her days in an existence that would have no meaning for her. It was difficult, too, to refrain from telling him that she would not regard him more highly if he achieved a victory. The danger sharpened her consciousness of what he meant to her, and perhaps because this intimate moment might be the last they would ever share, she realized she had learned to love him with a tender warmth she had never felt for anyone else. It occurred to her that her love was not new and that it had been the most important factor in her life since the time, long ago in Jamestown, when she had gradually come to recognize the qualities in him that made John so different from other men. She had responded to his kindness and compassion from the first, and little by little it had dawned on her that his integrity was as precious as it was unusual, yet not until now, when she had to face the possibility of losing him, had she been able to understand the full significance of all that he meant to her.

The discovery of the truth about herself did not shock Pocahontas, as it had been a part of her for so long, and she accepted it quietly. She felt an overpowering urge to share the knowledge with John, to tell him how she felt before it was too late, but her intuition forced her to remain silent.

John would not be able to accept her declaration of love and would think she was telling him what he wanted most to hear only in order to persuade him to call off the duel. He believed she admired Smith and was taking a man's way of destroying what, in his mind, was the obstacle that stood between him and his wife. He might be the most reasonable of human beings, but he had been goaded beyond endurance, and she knew she would confuse him and cause him to falter if she undermined his conviction that he would win her love by killing his rival for her affections.

So she said nothing, and he left for his rendezvous, his gait assured and virile, his expression eager and confident. When he was gone Pocahontas had no chance to wonder whether she had been right or wrong, and although she felt queasy, she could not take the time to sit down. She had prepared secretly and carefully for the moment when she would be alone, and she could still hear John's rapidly retreating footsteps as she removed her robe and donned a dress of black-and-white-striped satin which she had planned to wear because she could put it on quickly. Her fingers trembled as she fastened the jet buttons down the front of her bodice, and when she picked up her full, black velvet cloak it slipped from her hand. But the mishaps caused no appreciable delay, and by the time he reached the cobblestones she was ready.

She forced herself to wait until she heard John's horse move out of the courtyard, and while she stood she nervously patted the big soft bun of hair at the back of her head, staring at herself in the pier glass with unseeing eyes. Then, when she was certain John had gone, she left the suite and descended to the ground, her face muffled in the huge collar of her cloak. The pre-dawn quiet of London was strange, almost menacing, and she shivered in the damp, penetrating cold. For a few moments she was afraid her plan had misfired, but the rumble of an approaching carriage reassured her, and she knew her coachman had followed her instructions. She had ordered him to wait in a small alleyway leading off Fleet Street until he saw John ride off, and then to come for her immediately, and his broad grin as he climbed down from the box to open the door for her told her that John had not seen him.

"Drive me to Catherine Parr's Wood on the Windsor road," she said, and, leaning back in her seat, closed her eyes. She was breaking all precedent by attending the duel, she knew, and it was possible that John would be outraged by her unorthodox conduct, but she had to risk his wrath. She was aware of her limitations and realized she lacked the patience to wait at the Cricket and Rooster until he either returned or someone else brought word to her that he had been killed.

The ride through the streets of the deserted city seemed interminable, and Pocahontas dug her fingers into the upholstered armrests of her seat until her hands ached. She was afraid she would become hysterical if she allowed her imagination to dwell on the drama that was about to be enacted, so she deliberately occupied her mind by thinking of her newly discovered love for John. At first she berated herself for not having recognized the state of her own affections, but her irritation vanished when it occurred to her that she was no longer reluctant to bear his children. Apparently her aversion to the idea had dissipated gradually, without her knowledge, and she was filled with a buoyant sense of wonder at the realization that at last she was prepared to enjoy as well as to fulfill every responsibility of marriage to John.

Suddenly she smiled, then she started to laugh, and the coachman, hearing the sound, applied the whip to the horses. Some of his friends envied him because he was in the employ of the most celebrated woman in London, but at this moment he gladly would have exchanged places with them. In his private opinion she was mad, and the more loudly she laughed the more uneasy he became. Obviously no woman in her right mind would ask to be driven off alone to a deserted place in the open country before dawn, and cer-

tainly only someone who was daft would behave as though
the carriage were filled with a group of friends who were
entertaining her.

Dawn broke as the carriage sped along the hard dirt road,
and by the time the stately elms of Catherine Parr's Wood
loomed ahead in the distance, the sun was climbing high,
appearing occasionally, then passing out of sight again behind banks of heavy gray clouds. The road through the Wood
was narrow and rutted, so the coachman had to slow his team
to a walk, and Pocahontas, fretting at the delay, sat erect and
stared anxiously out of the window. She saw no sign of the
men who were to have met here, and for a panic-stricken
moment she wondered whether the site of the engagement
had been changed. Then somewhere up ahead a horse
whinnied softly, so she leaned forward, opened the little trap
door in the ceiling, and asked the coachman to proceed with
care.

A large clearing stood in the center of the Wood, with elms
on two sides and a thick tangle of barberry bushes forming a
natural boundary on the third, while the road, which curved
around a portion of the arena, made the fourth. Pocahontas
saw several horses tethered at the side of the clearing and
immediately ordered the coachman to halt. The carriage
bounced to a stop, and as the window was too small for
Pocahontas to see the whole field, she opened the door and
looked out.

The first person she saw was a short, heavy-set man with
gray hair whose black suit, studded with a double row of
ornamental pewter buttons, identified him as a surgeon-
barber. Beyond him were Lord Delaware and Sir Walter
Raleigh, who stood side by side, holding long pikes with steel
shafts in their right hands, and although Pocahontas knew
nothing of the code by which gentlemen fought, she realized
at once that the pikes would be used to separate the contes-
tants if either of them broke the rules. But she was not
interested in such matters, and her gaze swept past Sir Walter
and Lord Delaware.

John and Smith were in the center of the clearing, and she saw that the duel had already begun.

Both men had stripped off their doublets and had turned up their lace shirt cuffs, but they wore their hats, and their plumes bobbed up and down as they circled the clearing slowly, light but deadly rapiers in their right hands, knives with broad iron hilts in their left. They were breathing easily and neither was perspiring, so Pocahontas guessed that the fight had just started and she watched in horror as her husband and the man who had once meant so much to her eyed each other warily, occasionally striking out with their blades to test each other's speed and strength. Their agile footwork reminded her of the complicated steps of a dance, but the atmosphere was heavy, and she thought of the one time she had been taken to a bearbaiting exhibition and had become so sick she had been forced to leave.

The surgeon-barber was the first to become aware of the arrival of the carriage, and his shout of alarm brought the duel to a momentary halt. Lord Delaware and Sir Walter, who were startled, looked at Pocahontas in disapproval and held a hurried, whispered conversation, apparently trying to decide whether to stop the fight until she could be escorted elsewhere. But neither of the principals gave any sign that her presence would deter them. They separated briefly, and John did not seem in the least surprised as he smiled at his wife. Pocahontas, shrinking back against the seat and wrapping herself in the folds of her cloak, was amazed at his calm, and when their eyes met she knew he was assuring her that all would be well, precisely as he had done before leaving their rooms an hour earlier. And if he was disturbed by the knowledge that her arrival would cause tongues in London to wag all the harder after the duel, he gave no indication of it.

Smith, on the other hand, was openly elated that the woman who was the object of the fight had chosen to be present, and he raised his sword in a flamboyant salute to her. Then he turned back to John and said something that Pocahontas could not understand, but she saw his mocking grin and could not mistake his taunting tone. He seemed to be unable to resist playing up to his feminine audience and lunged forward with such speed and ferocity that his rapier sang as it whipped through the air. John, barely escaping serious injury, caught the blow on his knife, and Smith's blade slid harmlessly past him, but before he could recover, his foe came at him again, and he was forced to retreat.

Pocahontas, not wanting to watch but afraid to look away, was dismayed, and it occurred to her that perhaps she had made a terrible error by coming to the Wood. She should have known that Smith would be unable to resist the temptation to show off before her, and because she had lacked the strength to wait at home, she was afraid she had made John's task more difficult. Smith's skill was bewildering, and his rapier seemed to have become a part of him as he wove in and out, feinting and lunging, striking first at his opponent's face, then at his body, and making his violent exertions appear as effortless as they were graceful.

John backed slowly around the field, and Pocahontas, giving in completely to her fears, was certain she would see him struck down at any moment. But his foe's blade did not touch him, and finally Pocahontas realized that he was far more adept than she had imagined. His footwork was sure, his eye was sharp, and whenever Smith lunged at him, either his sword or his knife appeared at the right spot to deflect the blow and send the point of his opponent's blade over his shoulder or past his body. Curiously, he seemed content to remain on the defensive, and Pocahontas finally began to understand that he was deliberately allowing Smith to carry the full weight of the attack. John was using his intelligence to offset his enemy's greater physical strength and was methodically wearing Smith down.

Pocahontas's fear abated somewhat when she realized that her husband was able to take care of himself, and she was ashamed of her surreptitious effort to aid him, for he plainly needed no help. He had always treated her so gently that she had not dreamed he was an accomplished swordsman, and he always behaved so reasonably in his dealings with others, as well as with her, that she had not imagined him capable of being aroused to a pitch of violent anger. But now, recognizing his shortcomings, she loved him all the more deeply, and she knew that if he survived this ordeal her greater understanding of him would help them build a far more solid marital relationship.

As nearly as she could judge, Smith had chosen to forget her visit to him yesterday; he gave every indication that he was fighting to win and continued to press his attack vigorously. But if he had thought he would achieve victory easily, he had learned better now, and he showed considerable respect for his opponent's blade. John seemed to anticipate each of his maneuvers, deftly turned aside his energetic thrusts, and could not be caught off balance. A quick glance at Lord Delaware and Sir Walter indicated that they were impressed by John's prowess, too, and even though every aspect of dueling was repugnant to Pocahontas, she felt a sudden surge of pride.

No man could maintain the furious pace that Smith had established, and after a quarter of an hour his thrusts, although still powerful, became less frequent. Both men were tiring, their shirts were soaked, and Pocahontas could see that they moved more slowly around the clearing. Then, unexpectedly, John called on his reserves of energy and, lashing out in a series of bold thrusts, he wrested the offensive from Smith. His rapier danced in and out so rapidly that she could scarcely follow his movements, and the harsh, grating clash of steel striking against steel sounded in her ears as loudly as the wild pounding of her heart.

It was clear that John was making his supreme bid for victory, and only a man of extraordinary stamina and skill could have stood up against his powerful lunges. His countless hours of labor in the tobacco fields had made him far stronger than the gentlemen with whom Smith had crossed swords previously, and the captain, suddenly finding himself on the defensive, seemed to realize that he was fighting an

exceptionally dangerous opponent. The smile he had worn
ever since Pocahontas had appeared at the clearing faded
from his lips, and his expression was grim as he parried thrust
after thrust.

John searched relentlessly for an opening, and Pocahontas
soon realized that he was trying to find a weakness in Smith's
defense. But there was none, and although Pocahontas had
become infected with the fever of combat and wanted to see
Smith vanquished, she had to admire his brilliant style.
However, John was not discouraged, and when he could discover no flaws he tried to create his own opportunities and
pressed all the harder. He drove at his foe mercilessly, and
Pocahontas was afraid he was so determined to push his
attack that he was leaving himself unprotected, but the force
of his drive was so great that Smith had no chance to resume
his own offensive.

They moved back and forth across the clearing until
Pocahontas thought both of them would drop, but there was
no change in John's expression. His eyes were hard and
black, and his face was like a mask, reflecting no emotion as
he continued to thrust again and again at the man he intended to kill. At this moment he was a stranger to Pocahontas, and she realized that although she had believed she knew
his character completely, some facets of his nature were still
alien to her.

Then she glanced at Smith and was surprised to see that his
feelings were clear to her. Thanks to his cleverness and her
own inexperience, she long had believed that he was invinci-
ble, indestructible, but the myth was shattered for all time as
she saw the look of apprehensive concern in his eyes. At that
instant she felt a stab of pity for him, and as she realized that
he was as frail as other human beings, she could no longer
hate him. But he was still more resilient than other men, and
the reservoirs of his courage seemed to be inexhaustible, for
as she watched, a wild but calculated frenzy took possession
of him.

Halting his retreat, he stood firm, beat off John's thrusts, and rallied from the depths of almost certain defeat. Pocahontas might know that he was as weak as other men, but he still believed he was unique and, being unaware of his vulnerability, he struck recklessly at John. He lunged forward, and before Pocahontas quite realized what had happened, she saw her husband's rapier fly through the air and land in a clump of barberry bushes. John was defenseless and stood very still, his hands at his sides.

Smith shouted hoarsely in triumph and lunged again, but his right foot slipped, he slid to his knee, and the point of his rapier plunged into the ground. There was a sharp, cracking sound, similar to a small explosion, and his sword broke, leaving him with the hilt and a few inches of the useless blade in his hand. The seconds ran out into the clearing, their pikes extended, and separated the principals before they could come to grips again with their knives. The duel was over, and Pocahontas wept quietly as she leaned back against the carriage seat.

Lord Delaware insisted that, as honor had been satisfied on both sides, Master Rolfe and Captain Smith must reconcile their differences. They shook hands reluctantly, and as they mumbled a few amenities to each other, Sir Walter walked rapidly to the coach and helped Pocahontas to the ground. Gallantly pretending he didn't know she was badly shaken, he ignored the tearstains on her cheeks and bent low over her hand. "When I first met you," he said, "I found myself regretting that you had not been born thirty years earlier. Now I'm sorry I wasn't born thirty years later, so I might be a member of your generation." He released her hand, and after rewarding him with a fleeting, polite smile, she raced off to embrace her husband. Sir Walter looked after her, his eyes wistful, and then turned away. "On second thought," he said to no one in particular, "it's probably far better this way, at least for you, my dear."

Pocahontas was conscious only of John's strong arms and

the ardor of his kiss. They were together, they would never be separated again, and nothing else mattered to her. Then she heard Lord Delaware chiding her for having defied custom by attending the duel, and after John relinquished his hold on her, she saw Smith, standing alone. He seemed to be unaware of the presence of anyone and was apparently absorbed in an inspection of his broken rapier, but Pocahontas knew from the way he held his head that he was watching every gesture she made.

"I must speak to Captain Smith," she said, and walked away before John could stop her.

Smith turned and looked at her as she approached. There was a white line of fatigue around his mouth, and deep smudges under his eyes made him appear old, but his carriage was that of a young man, and when she drew near to him his deep bow was courtly.

"I'm very grateful to you," Pocahontas said quietly, giving him no chance to speak first.

"Grateful?" Smith looked puzzled.

"You have repaid me in full, and neither of us owes the other anything."

He laughed harshly and shook his head. "You think I broke my sword purposely after I disarmed him?"

"Of course," she replied in bewilderment. "I was afraid you wouldn't heed my plea, but at the very last you did."

"You women are all alike," Smith said contemptuously. "You forget, madam, that I have a reputation to maintain. It would do my name no good if it ever became known that an amateur swordsman more than held his own against me, and that at the very last, when I could have skewered him, my own clumsiness betrayed me. In the memory of whatever may have been between us, I must beg you to say nothing of this encounter to anyone."

Pocahontas stared hard at him, unable to decide whether he sincerely meant what he said or whether he was being truly chivalrous to her at last. In this their final meeting,

Smith had become an enigma to her once again, and she realized that she would never know whether the end of the duel had been accidental or whether, having lost her, he was being unexpectedly generous to her and to John.

"Good-by, John Smith," she said. "Until today I wanted to forget you. Now I will remember you always."

Smith watched her as she moved off and joined her husband, and he remained motionless until they entered the carriage together and drove off. A sense of abiding loneliness stole over him, and he knew he would never again meet anyone like her. She was the only woman with whom he would have been willing to share his name and his life, but he had discovered the true state of his feelings too late. Some men were fated to remain bachelors all of their days, and obviously he was one of them.

Throwing away the broken sword, he adjusted his hat at a rakish angle and walked briskly toward Sir Walter and Lord Delaware, who were waiting to ride back to London with him. As he had so often told himself, a man who failed to profit from his experiences was a fool. His hope of enlisting Pocahontas's support and influence for the Plymouth Company was dead, and he certainly would not rely on any woman again. However, that would not deter him from the achievement of his goal, and one way or another he would obtain all the money he needed to secure ships and supplies and men for his next expedition to the New World.

As future generations would learn, he was unique. No setback could discourage him, and no obstacle could prevent him from fulfilling his destiny.

"Gentlemen," he said, smiling jauntily as he mounted his horse, "I've had a busy morning and I've developed an enormous thirst. I hope you'll join me in a jar of sack at the first inn we reach. As my guests, naturally." He refrained from adding that by breaking their ride they would not overtake Pocahontas and Rolfe, and he could not admit even to himself that his one glimpse of them sitting together in

their carriage had been more than sufficient to last him for
the rest of his days.

By this time Pocahontas had put him out of her mind and
was concentrating on her husband as their coach bounced
and swayed on the dirt road that led to London. She had
expected that the last barrier separating her from John would
disappear as soon as they were alone, but it had not, and his
steady, silent scrutiny made her uncomfortable. Her cloak
stifled her and, throwing it back, she smoothed the modest
collar of her dress, touched her hands to her hair, and then
pretended to rearrange her skirt.

"What's become of your horse?" she asked, glancing obliquely at John. "You left him back there at the Wood."

"So I did. Lord Delaware offered to lead him back to the
Cricket and Rooster so I might ride with you."

"I'm glad," she replied, relieved.

"Are you?"

His cold, hard tone disturbed her. "Of course, dear."

John continued to study her intently. "I want to know," he
said, "why you wished to speak to Smith and what you said to
him."

As he gazed at her, waiting for her reply, it occurred to her
that his whole attitude toward her had changed. He was no
longer the humble supplicant for her favors, but her husband, who had earned the right to be told the truth about her
affections. He had risked his life for her, and by fighting the
duel he had achieved his correct and merited status as her
protector. Pocahontas smiled and suddenly felt shy.

"Men fight with swords," she said, "but a woman uses her
own weapons. I wanted him to know that I love my husband
as I have never loved any other man."

John was stunned, and it seemed like a very long time
before he grasped the full significance of her words. Then he
took her into his arms, and Pocahontas, glorying in his gentle
strength, lifted her face to his and was content. There was so
much she wanted to say to him, but words could wait. Later,

after they reched the inn, she would tell him about the vague illness that had been disturbing her and her sudden realization that she was carrying their baby. Later, too, there would be unlimited time to discuss the future that awaited them and their children in Virginia.

But now, as John held her close, it was enough for Pocahontas to love and be loved.

Don't Miss these Ace Romance Bestsellers!

_____ **#75157 SAVAGE SURRENDER** $1.95
The million-copy bestseller by Natasha Peters,
author of Dangerous Obsession.

_____ **#29802 GOLD MOUNTAIN** $1.95

_____ **#88965 WILD VALLEY** $1.95
Two vivid and exciting novels by
Phoenix Island author, Charlotte Paul.

_____ **#80040 TENDER TORMENT** $1.95
A sweeping romantic saga in the
Dangerous Obsession tradition.

Available wherever paperbacks are sold or use this coupon.

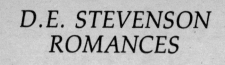

D.E. STEVENSON
ROMANCES

"Finding a re-issued novel by D. E. Stevenson is like coming upon a Tiffany lamp in Woolworth's. It is not 'nostalgia'; it is the real thing."

—THE NEW YORK TIMES
BOOK REVIEW

ENTER THE WORLD OF D. E. STEVENSON IN THESE DELIGHTFUL ROMANTIC NOVELS:

AMBERWELL
THE BAKER'S DAUGHTER
BEL LAMINGTON
THE BLUE SAPPHIRE
CELIA'S HOUSE
THE ENCHANTED ISLE
FLETCHERS END
GERALD AND ELIZABETH
GREEN MONEY
THE HOUSE ON THE CLIFF
KATE HARDY
LISTENING VALLEY
THE MUSGRAVES
SPRING MAGIC
SUMMERHILLS
THE TALL STRANGER

ROMANTIC SUSPENSE

Discover ACE's exciting new line of exotic romantic suspense novels by award-winning author Anne Worboys:

THE LION OF DELOS

RENDEZVOUS WITH FEAR

THE WAY OF THE TAMARISK

THE BARRANCOURT DESTINY

Coming soon:

HIGH HOSTAGE